Gambu's End

BOOK THREE OF
THE DIVINE GAMBIT TRILOGY

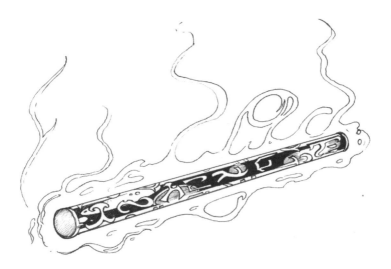

CHAD CORRIE

An Aspirations Media Publication

An Aspirations Media™ Publication
www.aspirationsmediainc.com

Copyright © 2007 by Chad Corrie
Interior Illustrations by Ed Waysek
Cover by Carrie Hall
Layout by Jennifer Rowell
Design: Jennifer Rowell and Chad Corrie

LIBRARY OF CONGRESS CONTROL NUMBER: 2006910485

IBSN: 978-0-9776043-5-7

MANUFACTURED IN THE UNITED STATES

First Printing March 2007

Other books in **The World of Tralodren™**

The Divine Gambit Trilogy

The Seer's Quest
Path of Power
Gambit's End

Tales of Tralodren: The Beginning*

Forthcoming Works:

The Adventures of Corwyn

A Graphic Novel

Thanks to:

My Holy Ghost writer.

Ed, Carrie, Jeremy,
Jennifer, Nancy and
Patti and Ed-- this whole
series wouldn't be possible without all of you.

Mom, Dad it's finally done.

The whole divine economy is pervaded by Providence. Even the vagaries of chance have their place in Nature's scheme; that is, in the intricate tapestries of the ordinances of Providence. Providence is the source from which all things flow; and allied with it is Necessity, and the welfare of the universe. You yourself are part of that universe; and for any one of nature's parts, that which is assigned to it by the World-Nature or helps to keep it in being is good. Moreover, what keeps the whole world going is Change; not merely change of the basic elements, but also change of the larger formations they compose. On these thoughts rest content, and ever hold them as principles. Forget your thirst for books; so that when your end comes you may not murmur, but meet it with a good grace and unfeigned gratitude in your heart to the gods.

Marcus Aurelius
"Meditations" Book 2 paragraph 3.

The Lord has made everything to accommodate itself and contribute to its own end and His own purpose- even the wicked are fitted for their role for the day of calamity and evil.

Proverbs 16:4 Amplified Bible

A man's mind plans his way, but the Lord directs his steps and makes them sure.

Proverbs 16:9 Amplified Bible

Chapter 1

Thangaria was a quiet, dead place.

Once the home to a huge, fertile world that served as the center of an ever expanding divine empire, it now was a fragmentary rocky expanse. All the planetary debris that remained was little more than an asteroid field, holding nothing but bits of decayed ruins at best as it hovered amid a silent, cold expanse. Only on one chunk of rock, still called Thangaria, was there an exception to the rest of the floating rubble.

The piece of the ancient world was engrossed in a tattered cloak of gray tinted atmosphere. Like a ghost haunting the place of its death the phantom sky blocked out all stars and light and illumination of any kind, allowing for only a perpetual dim grayness to permeate the horizon. The only thing that yet stood in one piece on this gray cloaked chunk of a long dead planet was the Hall of Vkar.

To say the Hall of Vkar was breathtaking would be a gross understatement. Tall towers, broad walls and shapely minaret after minaret comprised the structure into a surreal image of unimaginable beauty. Even the gods who came to the place were still slightly awed upon catching sight of the structure. The hall itself was at once smooth and simple as well as regal and assertive in its design. One could look at it and feel both awe and fear, compassion and dominance. Truly it made a fitting home for the first god who once ruled from behind its walls.

The Hall of Vkar rested in the center of the empty asteroid, climbing heavenward into the tattered atmosphere. Ten stories tall it was built of marble, gold, silver, gems and granite with a white

1

marble, iron spiked crowned, jewel encrusted curtain wall as thick as the widest roads outlining the structure. This curtain wall went a mile left and right, forming a perfect square in which rested the hall. A set of colossal doors crafted with pure silver to resemble a great monstrous face rested between the sturdy walls, allowing access to the courtyard around the great hall.

This courtyard was paved of granite; polished to allow a shine of an unearthly hue. Once its pools and fountains had been filled with crystal clean water and its groves of trees thrived and blossomed, but that had been a long time ago. Longer than the world of Tralodren was old, and now only the specter of time haunted the open space with all the echoes of such past memories dancing amid petrified trunks and resting in cracked, bone dry pools.

The Hall of Vkar had become a memorial or a shrine, a sacred place where all the gods of the Tralodroen Pantheon could meet on neutral ground. If ever it could be said that gods could have shrines or temples to things they revered, then the Hall of Vkar served this purpose for the Pantheon.

For it was in this place the gods of Tralodren set up a council to help govern disputes and decide matters which affected all of them or Tralodren itself. The council had been established to help maintain a discourse between the divine family and provide each with equal voice for matters brought to its table from any god who had a dispute, or to deal with any threat of a violent manner that came against the Pantheon and their interests. Outside of the council each of them were free to rule their own realm and manage their own affairs as they saw fit.

They barred each other from bearing arms, having a personal guard, or even coming in their true form – taking on a mortal guise for the entirety of their meeting. In this way the peace of the gods had been maintained over many divine councils, allowing disputes and conversation to be just that – a warring of words and positions, and not a place to vent disagreements in a physically violent matter.

Though effective, it wasn't always perfect at stopping the flow of violent dispute from taking place outside the hall. Thankfully these few times were the exception to the rule.

Inside the Hall of Vkar, the gods silently assembled around a long, wide stone table, taking their assigned places. At the head of the table, granite steps rose up to a granite dais covered with green silk on which rested three thrones, two lower than the third which rose betwixt them. All three seats were crafted of pure gold and shone with a soft amber incandescence. On these thrones sat Dradin, Gurthghol and Ganatar, who claimed the highest throne.

Ganatar sat calm and composed. His tan, clean shaven flesh and square cut white mane of hair complimented his powder blue eyes which looked over the other gods gathered with a studious gaze.

"Are we ready to begin?" Ganatar turned to his older brother beside him; golden tunic billowing over his strong body.

Gurthghol, who was seated at Ganatar's left, turned to his brother with a sneer. "You know I hate formalities."

He appeared as a gnome, a creature similar to dwarves in stature but more nimble and finer boned so as to appear more like human children or adolescences.

"Between you and Dradin, it's a wonder we get anything accomplished with all these blasted traditions and orders." His dull red eyes glowed from his pale skin. Absentmindedly he picked at his rich purple cloak – covering an outfit the same color as his black hair; the long strands of which had been pulled into a ponytail.

"The rules are in place for the benefit of all," green robed and cloaked Dradin spoke dryly. "You yourself agreed to them with the rest of us."

Ganatar focused his attention then to his bookish brother on his right. The god of light was fascinated by Dradin's possession for a moment before he regained his composure. All in the Pantheon shared that fascination with the slender, yet elegant six-foot wooden staff resting at Dradin's side. Even though this was

3

a replica of the original staff always in the true form of Dradin's hand, it was a sight. The present staff that was before them was a reflection of the original worn smooth with age. Both the orginal and this copy had never left the god's side since crafting it when he rose to become the greatest scholar of all the Pantheon. None of the other gods knew just what it did or could do. It remained to them an enigma, a constant symbol of what the god knew that they did not.

At the staff's top was a foot and a half long stylized, mystic rune covered, angular curve of gold that allowed for a rather sharp point at the tip and a large concave opening in the middle. In the center of this curve, floated a pure lead crystal globe no more than six inches in diameter. The golden light from the crystal continually hummed outward in a soft murmur, adding a strange glimmer in Dradin's bright green eyes, as if the whispers of a thousands secrets hovered around the staff like a cloud of flies.

"Yeah, well I can change my mind," Gurthghol huffed.

"Something you do much of, brother," Dradin smirked dryly causing his short cropped white beard to widen on his face.

"Some of us can't just sit and think all day," Gurthghol flung his brother a verbal jab.

"Peace," Ganatar mediated between them. "Stop this. We have much to discuss.

"Let the council now commence," Ganatar's voice dominated the room.

On the opposite end of the table, from where the three enthroned gods sat, resided the last gods to be allowed into the Tralodroen Pantheon: Panthor, Aerotription, and Drued. They were called race gods by some theologians. So named as each represented three of the more numerous and civilized races of Tralodren, having ascended from the rank and file of mortality during the Shadow Years. These mortals had shown great courage, leadership and dedication to their races during those dark years— so much so, they were granted godhood by the Pantheon.

Once ascended, each was given the charge to lead their people and guide them to better things and developments for the war-torn world at that time was in need of being rebuilt. So, since the ending of the Imperial Wars, they had resided with the gods as a deity in their own right, and were worshipped by many of their former kin.

The race gods appeared mostly as they did in their mortal lives, save for minor deific modifications. Aerotription, god of the elves, but only worshipped by the Elyellium, looked like a fine specimen of a middle aged Elyellium himself; elegant purple cape falling from his shoulders over a matching toga which almost hid a gold-trimmed white tunic underneath.

Next to him was Drued, Lord of the Dwarves. He seemed like a normal dwarf, hearty of frame; not as ornate as the other race gods. He looked more mortal than the rest, more like a common dwarf than their god. Deep blue eyes highlighted his chest length, iron gray beard, showcasing twelve braids, alongside long white hair flowing out like a soft river from his head to cascade to his shoulders.

Beside Drued was Panthor, goddess of humanity: a brown eyed human female, built like a warrior of average height, but with a mixed complexion and facial shape along side chestnut hair so she seemed to take in all the various traits of the humans who populated Tralodren. She wore a panther skin cape, a medium length leather dress of savage design and tall, fur-lined boots laced with leather strands which made a subtle compliment to her athletic build.

Left from the head of the table resided the first generation of gods, brothers and sisters to the council's leaders, the children of Vkar and Xora. These were: Asora, Asorlok, Olthon, Khuthon and Saredhel.

"So we gather together in fear of *one* mortal man?" Khuthon's disdain was extremely mocking in tone. "Why not just kill him and get it over with then?" The god of war's soft brown eyes sparkled with wicked blood lust at the thought.

"Not everything can be resolved by killing everyone," Olthon, the sister and opposing deity to the policies of Khuthon, addressed her brother.

"It's the simplest of strategies in this situation," Khuthon sat back in his chair, arms crossed over his open leather jerkin covering his muscular chest. The strongest of all the gods gathered, his basic nature held a tyrannical aura about it – an air of pride tied up with his incredible strength. By contrast, the very image of Olthon was opposite that of her brother.

She appeared as a fair-skinned human, but with angelic dove-like wings folded behind her back. A soft, sleeveless, slender gown of white gauze hung from her shoulders to the floor like vapor.

"War and violence are never as simple as they seem," Olthon's golden eyes shined softly as she addressed the other gods, blonde hair falling in curls about her head and neck.

"They are when *I* do them," Khuthon smirked. His white, wolfish grin adding radiance to his thick curly red hair and scruffy goatee, which jutted out from his chin like a forest of broken, bloodied, spears shafts.

Used to her husband's bravado, Asora sat next to him in silence. She too had favored the guise of a human, but one great with child. Her soft green eyes overflowed with compassion and long reddish brown hair tossed about as she turned to listen to Olthon, causing the silky locks to fall toward her back and outline her sun kissed skin in simple elegance.

Next to Asora sat Asorlok.

"Quite right," the enigmatic god of death responded to Khuthon. "Khuthon vastly adds throngs to my gates in the simplest of ways."

Asorlok rarely traveled from his realm. No god sought to harm him for all knew that in time they would pass into his clutches in The Great End, which Saredhel, the great seer, had spoken to them as happening in ages past. So it was that all treated him well as to keep on his best side when the god of death gave out his judgment as to where the deceased deity would go in their afterlife following this prophesied demise.

"Why not deal death to this mortal and be done with this affair altogether? Diplomacy with a mortal from the likes of divinity is far from becoming in such a situation." The god of death's adopted guise was that of a very tan human in his middle years of life. He had a hawkish nose, hairless head and body which was draped in rich clothing and jewels, mostly of ruby and onyx design; a string of rubies dangling from each ear. His eyes were a piercing blue, darting over everything around him like spear points.

Besides Olthon sat Saredhel, who was barefoot and covered in jewels and gems of all kinds: toe rings, bracelets, necklaces, rings, earrings, anklets and more ran wild on her coffee colored flesh. It was as if this very adornment dripped from her body like a strange perspiration, providing dazzle to the mysterious seer.

She was quiet and still. Seldom did she speak about what she knew, for it would confound and drive all to madness with such things – mysteries beyond mysteries. The opaline woolen cowl covering her head and snaked about her swan-like neck, painted her pure white eyes in some dim shade.

"Obviously you don't understand the forces at work here," Olthon's face grew more serious.

"I don't understand what importance this has to all of us," Aerotription now turned to Olthon. "Another mortal wants to seek godhood. He'll fail, end of story. Why bother ourselves with such a trivial matter?"

At the right side of the tables head sat the grandchildren of Vkar and Xora, the third generation: Causilla, Endarien, Perlosa, Rheminas and Shiril.

"All will be made clear soon enough," said Causilla, the child of Ganatar and Olthon, goddess of love, arts and beauty. "Just give it time."

Her soft, creamy skin, wrapped by a rainbow hued gown, shined with the radiance of youth matching the twinkle in her gentle gray eyes. Her long, silky brown hair was like dark honey pouring from her head and down her tall, lithe frame.

On her right sat Endarien, the son of Dradin and Saredhel, whose adopted form was little more than a thick, gray cloak drawn over a darker gray robe. Underneath the hood his face was not discernible from the shadows, mimicking the clouds in the sky which waver and reform at will.

Beside Endarien rested Rheminas, Khuthon and Asora's son. The Lord of Flame appeared all too human, with deep coppery red skin, bright yellow eyes, fiery red hair and beard that was thick and curled like tongues of flame.

"Oh, the reason for this council will come to light soon enough," Rheminas' manner was predatory, as was his smile which glistened with sharp white teeth the same color as bleached bone. Adorning his wrists were also thick leather and steel studded gauntlets decorated with etchings of flame. His fingers even ended in long black nails that looked to be able to rend anyone who came into disfavor with the god of fire to shreds.

"We suspect you have a part of this current enterprise as well brother, for another whom you have invested with your favor, is now intertwined with this divinity seeking mortal," Perlosa, the sister of Rheminas, sat beside the Flame Lord.

She would have been naked if not for a few scraps of white cloth wrapped around her ample chest and slender lower waist. Her skin was a tranquil bluish-green; eyes a gentle pale blue, hair a shimmering icy white traveling down to the middle of her naked back.

"What?" Rheminas glared back at his sister; eyes blazing hotter than the sun, "That human gladiator? What matter is that to you?" Rheminas was bare chested save for a leather harness he wore as a breastplate of the same tough material making up his pants and boots.

"He seems to us *more* than a passing fancy. More so than your other toys of late." Perlosa's tone was icy, reflecting the feeling of the delicate silver chain with small lead crystal icicles dangling from it like chilled daggers around her neck.

"I would have to agree. And I would know," Aerotription peered into Rheminans' face with his own ponderings.

Rheminas' gaze flared to a terrible wrath before the ascended elf. "You should concern yourself in matters of your own. You wouldn't want to rouse my wrath."

Shiril was the last in line on the right side of the table, the sister to Endarien and most stoic in her expression. She'd chosen for this council a guise which appeared as a human crafted of black marble with ivory nails, teeth and eyes, gold hair, and a backless silver breastplate reflecting the light shimmering from a mid-length lapis lazuli chip skirt.

Being a solitary goddess, few took much stock in her, nor paid her that much respect. Shiril had not been bothered to intrude on others since her birth and preferred her own company to that of the other gods, even refraining from taking servants in her realm like her family. So the others in the Pantheon paid her no heed as well, unless warranted, which pleased the goddess greatly.

"Enough now," Ganatar's tone was level though he was growing frustrated with the petty snaps and snarls about him. "It is time to put this bickering to rest so we can address the matters at hand. What shall we do with this rising challenge?"

"It seems clear that the effort alone is daunting." Asora drew all eyes her way. "Can we be sure that he could even do such a thing?"

"The effort is nothing if he is truly determined, which he seems to be. If such is the case then he will most certainly attain his goal. The question is what do we do if this mortal gains godhood?" Dradin's words were as flat as parchment.

"How are you sure he will attain his goal?" Perlosa mused.

"His patron will make sure his survival will be certain in this endeavor." Saredhel silenced all other questions but one. She was so calm even the silver brassier of intertwining snakes holding aloft the globes of her breasts seemed to not even rise at all for breath.

"Who is this patron?" Panthor turned to Dradin.

"Something we would rather not encounter or speak about ever again." Dradin seemed to reflect the sudden feeling of unease, which filled the room, on his face.

"But the patron's presence is proof enough of the challenge coming once more." Gurthghol looked over to Dradin. "And it might be impossible to stop it this time."

"I don't understand," Panthor looked to each god around her for insight, "Could we not welcome him in as we were welcomed into the Pantheon? Won't that pacify any ill will that might be brewing?"

"You were a special case, Panthor." Ganatar looked directly at the goddess now; his blue eyes like his words: fatherly and kind. "We chose you, Aero, and Drued because you were needed to help your fellow race rebuild after those dark years, and were worthy of the mantle for godhood. After your ascension, we lost the ability to bring mortals into our fold. Besides, this mortal is far from worthy and would cause nothing but death and destruction not only to Tralodren, but this Pantheon – even the cosmos itself because he is driven by a force that has no compassion for mortals or gods or even existence."

"What about Galba, though?" Asora's green eyes sought her husband's face.

"What of her?" Khuthon's voice boomed across the hall. "She won't help. She can't. Remember what happened last time," the god of war's face grew as hard as steel. "She just stood and watched it all happen."

"Don't expect her to lift a finger now either. The battle is in our hands now, as it was then."

"Let's just kill him now, get it over with before it starts." The suggestion was almost a plea or as close to as the god of war had and would ever come to a plea. "Why risk any chance of success?"

"I agree." Endarien's shifting face nodded, allowing for some thin, smoky strands of a beard to flow out of the hood before becoming insubstantial once again.

"What are you talking about?" Drued cocked his head. "Who is this Galba and who is this mortal's patron? Why are you all so frightened by this?"

"You weren't here in the beginning obviously. We tend to forget that at times." Asorlok turned to the dwarven deity. His tone reminded the dwarven god of an older brother speaking to his younger, more foolish sibling."

"Naturally, you would have no understanding of what we are talking about so let me do my best at enlightening you to the situation at hand. Understand this. Before the death of father, the great Vkar and mother, Xora, there was born a godling who was the servant and agent of one of the creating forces Vkar had sought to master on his path toward godhood."

"That force used this godling to slay our mother and father, and nearly succeed in wiping all of us out of existence – slaying almost the whole of this Pantheon and the realms which each god now calls home as well."

"We barely halted it's plans from being carried out then, and now it seems that it wants to return to take out it's revenge against us. This time we will not be able to salvage a recovery from this attack as we did before."

"We don't have any more favor of Vkar to waste."

"What do you mean?" Panthor's face reflected her confusion. She never realized how much was not shared with her upon her ascension. She had to absorb so much when she first arose that she never thought there was still more to learn. It seemed there might be even more to study than she could even begin to fathom. "Vkar left you *power*?"

"Yes," Asorlok continued. "When he and Xora died we were able to use the remaining fragments of their being to turn back the attack, and heal and restore what we could. It took almost all that remained of our parents', but we stopped the first attack, and now a second attack seems to be coming. The remaining power of Vkar was further weakened when we used it to raise you three up to godhood."

"It should come as no surprise then to all gathered here," Asorlok continued, "this is the latest step in the dark entity's plan of ending Tralodren and us. It knows we have grown weaker with age, as all things do, and has returned unchanged in it's own strength to try again."

"Ending Tralodren?" Aerotription's eyes went wide. He, like Panthor was shocked to learn of this 'hidden' knowledge.

"Of course," Asorlok's smile was grim – like the sadistic gleam of a torturer to his victim. "What better way to do it than with a mortal being who rises to godhood. It's just using this mortal as a puppet for its own ends. It wants to destroy all of Tralodren, and then the rest of us along with the realms we rule."

"It *can't* do that." Drued pounded his fist on top the table. "It'd never get to Tralodren, all of us would protect it."

"Don't be so sure." Gurthghol smirked now, though his was birthed of a mocking humor rather than some dark pleasure. "You weren't here when we faced it last. Asorlok's right, we're weaker now, as all things become over time; we've gotten older, and it knows this. And if anyone around us should know anything about this dark entity, it should be Asorlok since he is so intertwined with its nature; dealing in the spoils of dissolution daily."

"Indeed," Asorlok grimly voiced, "but I don't serve it as this mortal unknowingly does. I don't crave the end of the Pantheon or Tralodren."

"That may be true, but we seem to recall something of a relationship that was formed between the dark force and Gurthghol himself." Perlosa coldly blasted the god of chaos. "Perhaps you might have some favors to call upon it…that is if you haven't sired any new offspring from that harem of yours of late…"

"Enough of the past," Ganatar scolded his niece before the matter could bloom into a larger series of exchanges. "We have moved on from there and have to forgive what has transpired between us all, even if we can't forget. That is why this whole council was formed."

"So then, what do we need to do if the mortal is backed by our enemy?" Causilla spoke up, thin lines of worry marring her flawless flesh. "We might not be able to destroy it without taking heavy losses. Could we contain it instead? Why risk a battle to the death if we don't have to?"

"Containment could work, "Olthon nodded in approval, "But there is no guarantee we could keep it contained, and are we sure we could make such a bold plan work in the face of it?"

"Are you sure this mortal's actions are for real?" Shiril's alto timbre drew all to her as she spoke. "Maybe this is just a ruse to get us all distracted from discovering and trying to halt what its true plan is. Perhaps the mortal is moving to his own death as the hand upon him distracts us from what the other hand is doing."

"No," Endarien sharply retorted. "I fought Cadrith a short time ago and while it wasn't in my true form, I did manage to do some harm, but he is far more powerful than I care to admit. He has great mystical abilities augmented beyond his understanding – even if he arrogantly thinks he alone has attained this increase.

"This bid is for real, and has been backed by a serious investment of power and will behind it. Our enemy wants this bid for godhood to succeed."

"You've been silent, my wife," Dradin turned to Saredhel, as did the others assembled, "tell us your thoughts on the matter. Share with us what fate has to tell."

None would dare speak or think another thought until the Seer of the Pantheon had said her peace.

The bald goddess pondered for a moment more, reflective in a deep inner thought, her pure white eyes shining, then finally spoke with a soft, low voice. "If one of us is willing to make a great sacrifice we would gain an advantage over this new threat."

"What type of sacrifice?" Endarien's face swirled beneath his hood.

"Confrontation against the dark patron's agent that would take something dear from the confronter as payment for success." Saredhel's answer was cryptic, but didn't take any of the gods gathered too much unawares. Each knew of her nature to give out just enough of the future in vague bits of insights each god had to wade through in their own mind, as they did now. Sometimes this riddle of sayings was understood and other times each came to their own interpretation. None knew for certain just what was meant until the end, though it played out before their eyes.

Such is the way with all prophecy.

"A sacrifice, huh?" Endarien rubbed his cloudy chin as the gray mists of his face slowed in their swirling as if they too pondered a meaning behind the seer's statement.

"So you're saying we can't go and kill this mortal without sacrificing something?" Khuthon leaned forward, focusing his attention on the white eyed seer, "You're saying we have to give up our own lives to gain victory?"

"I have spoken what I have seen," Saredhel responded flatly.

The god of war knew to keep quiet, stilling his rebuttal to the seer for she was never wrong in what she foretold. It did little to answer his question though, and the god of warfare hated not having all the facts when he made war plans.

"So we'll have to confront Cadrith then?" Rheminas looked over the council, measuring their faces in his eyes. "So that's what we've come down to then if we haven't yet voted on it?"

"That's how I would see it," Khuthon nodded.

"Little surprise in that," Olthon chided her brother. "This can't be the only option though." The goddess of peace pleaded to the other gods. "This can't be the only interruption to Saredhel's words."

"What would you have it mean then?" Gurthghol's red eyes narrowed. "You know as well as I that no interpretation we make is going to be totally certain."

"Do you see another way than Gurthghol?" asked Olthon.

"My thoughts are my own." Gurthghol folded his arms across his chest. "Regardless, this council will still have to vote to take action."

Olthon thought a moment in the silence provided her by the others. She didn't believe that fighting Cadrith was the answer, especially if whoever faced him would have to sacrifice something dear to themselves, such as their life, or spirit or something equally as dear. Perhaps this could be an angle for an argument to be put forth. After all, who among them would risk sacrifice of something as precious as their life on the whim of a prophetic interpretation?

"Who'd want to fight him, and where could they do so since we're forbidden from manifesting our true form on Tralodren." Olthon thought she had them there as each of the gods' gaze sunk to the table...but that soon changed.

"I would." Endarien drew all attention to himself.

"This does not surprise us in the least," Perlosa snorted.

Nor did it truly surprise anyone else present.

"How are you going to get past the barrier hindering us from directly confronting him?" Olthon tried to dissuade him with some logic, but it was like holding onto the tethers of rags. "You couldn't beat him without your true form, you said so already – and to do that you'd have to get past the barrier." She could see she'd lost the argument she was trying to raise.

"Is there anyway we could bypass the barrier holding us back?" Endarien searched around the table for an answer.

"There is nothing I know of which could pierce that veil..." Saredhel remained detached in her answer "...save the first gods."

All fell silent at the statement.

They knew what the other was thinking.

"So *that's* the only way then?" Khuthon peered over to Ganatar, who was unreadable. "If Endarien wishes to fight, I won't stand against him. It is to every warrior to pick his own battles. I will not stand in the way, but must we sacrifice the last remaining substance of our father to do it?"

"Maybe *that* is the sacrifice which needs to be made – the most precious thing to all of us: the last remnant of our father's essence," said Ganatar.

"Can we be sure this will even work?" Asora's face now was lined with a slight etching of concern. She was fearful of losing any life, even that of the remaining essence, if it wasn't needed.

"Might you not want me to fight this battle instead, cousin?" Rheminas turned toward Endarien. "After all, it is about revenge, is it not? You burning hot for the blood of this mage."

"No," Endarien's voice went cold. The swirling cloud-like visage of the god grew dark and stormy for a moment then returned to plump light gray and white hues. "This battle is mine alone to wage."

"I thought you said the essence of the first god was gone. How much yet remains then?" Panthor's brow wrinkled in further confusion.

"There still is a small portion of that power which remains hidden away deep inside the vault of this very hall." Ganatar's voice was low and heavy, as if he felt the weight of the upcoming decision pressing upon his spirit.

"So this remaining essence would be enough to allow Endarien to break through the boundary then?" Drued wondered aloud.

"It should be, but it wouldn't allow unlimited access," Dradin spoke up then. "It would be enough to get one of us down there in our true form and then give them enough time for a battle–"

"And win the battle–" Endarien cut in. "If the council agrees to this course of action I will gladly take on this task."

"If he's ready to do it, then let's just put it to a vote and prepare for the occasion to arise." Gurthghol's smile was reptilian. "A good fight is just what this place needs to get shaken up a bit anyway…and should Endarien die– "

"I won't die, Gurthghol." The cloudy mists beneath the Storm Lord's hood darkened again as he turned to give the god of chaos a glare.

"Well, just in case you do die, we should have a contingency plan for who would get to have your realm, and how your former responsibilities would be divided up amongst us," Gurthghol continued; reptilian nature of his expression only deepening.

"I think not. Hold off on that debate until such a time arrives. Lest you give too much incentive to others here to plot against me in this fight." Endarien's gazed fluttered over to Perlosa.

Feeling the weight of that strange, cloudy visage, Perlosa responded in the most sincere tones she could find, but it still seemed snotty and petty coming out of her mouth. "Cousin, our love of you is far from warm, but our hatred of this mortal mage is greater."

"We shall see, cousin." Endarien stood up and turned to the three head gods of the council. "So what is the vote then? What do you say?"

"Have we decided then that this is the course of action best suited to the words given us by Saredhel?" Ganatar addressed the council with a regal air. The god of light could see nothing but nodding heads, save for Saredhel who remained still. Olthon who still opposed the idea of direct combat, and Gurthghol seemed to support the idea and not support it at the same time.

No matter though, the majority carried the motion.

"If that is your wish then we have no choice but to honor it." Ganatar rose from his throne. "Who here supports such an action?" He continued.

All the gods, save Saredhel and Olthon raised a hand in support.

"Very well, it is agreed then. Endarien shall battle Cadrith should he raise up to godhood and we will use the last remaining power of our father to give him the time and abilities he needs to defeat this threat." Ganatar then turned to Endarien. "Be ready for the signs of his ascension and prepared for the power we will imbue you with for this task should it be needed."

"You shouldn't have any doubt in me. I will destroy this upstart, before the threat can be even raised against us," boasted the wind god.

"Let's hope your boasting proves true cousin," Rheminas muttered beneath his breath.

And so the action of the Tralodroen Pantheon was decided.

Chapter 2

"There, I got them to Arid Land." Brandon Dosone, burst through an intricately designed, sixteen-foot tall, silver shod wooden door into the tranquil chambers of the goddess Saredhel. This was Sooth, the home realm of the goddess, where she busied herself with the perpetual divining of the future.

The goddess herself was undisturbed from the sudden eruption and merely kept to her own thoughts, hovering over a great water filled pool. Unlike her chosen appearance at the council, this was Saredhel's true form. The form she was in the truest sense of her being, and not another guise or semblance as the other gods had brought to the table. Her true form was exactly the same as the one she had taken at the council, only her height had changed. Whereas she had been equal in stature to a normal human woman, here Saredhel stretched to a full fifteen feet.

Her pure white eyes remained closed in meditative focus as she hovered with her back toward the door, near the edge of the great reflecting pool where she had scryed since the beginning of Tralodren. The white skirt about her waist, slit up both sides to her thigh, dangled between her crossed legs, almost touching the smooth water beneath the cloth's reach. The pool was about six feet deep and at least twice that in width with water as smooth and clear as glass reflecting back those gathered around it in contemplation. The calm water also reflected the brilliant torches lined along the top of the chamber where they gave off pure white radiance akin to the brightest of days instead of smoky, flame spawned illumination.

The others in the chamber with her were not so calm during the sudden entrance of the gray haired, stubble faced Telborian. Brandon closed the door behind him with a quick shove. This was a feat most men would have found hard to do with all their strength, for the door was massive, but Brandon did so with merely one hand.

"Must you be so loud, Endarien?" With a dignified air, Asorlok curled his lip slightly at Brandon. Blue eyes, hawkish nose, and clean shaven head making for a perfect image of royal disconnect at the actions of a lesser beneath his station.

Asorlok was of the same size as his floating sister but dressed more somberly. A deep claret cape flowed down Asorlok's back; stopping even with tall black sandals resting beneath a black silk robe overlaid with gold, silver and maroon, gray and parchment thread to make a splendidly rich design shimmering in the light of the room. Asorlok's jewelry was of a more macabre nature; skulls and motifs of death and dying being found all over his person from ruby humanoid skulls dangling from his ears to a satin crimson sash tied about his waist and weighted with two ivory vulture skulls.

"Who's going to hear us here?" Brandon drew closer to the pool and the others beside it.

They were a motley gathering of deities, gathered by a common thread thinner than a strand of hair. Still though, that strand was strong enough to hold them together long enough to be gathered in Sooth. Asorlok, Endarien, and Panthor each were pulled toward the same action as made manifest by Saredhel to her fellow gods – an important duty that each had to perform in the upcoming events on Tralodren. The importance of the calling was too great to be ignored, and so the gods who were strung together came.

They had planned this meeting to take place the same time as the council, as none would then suspect anything was amiss while they communicated with the others via their chosen manifestations. Here they could speak more to each other in their true forms with some relative safety and anonymity from the Pantheon. It wasn't a hard task at all, as this was how the gods could be in more than one place; by using as many manifestations of their presence as they could maintain and as were needed to complete all that they had chosen to do.

Each of the figures who had come to be gathered around Saredhel's scrying pool had been assigned to take a certain collection of mortals and lead them to Arid Land – to Galba. Working together they would have to unite the mercenary force which freed Cadrith in the first place to the stone circle and convince them to fight the lich one last time. Why this was to be, the gods were not told by Saredhel. Instead, they were simply informed that it had to be done. None argued with the goddess, for her words and visions had always proved true in the end. So each simply acted, a bit reluctantly at first, to do their part and so had finally managed to pull the group together again with the addition of two Asorlins for added measure. All seemed to have been progressing rather successfully.

"Words spoken can always be heard." Saredhel spun around in mid-air to address those who stood behind her. This action caused rays of light to strike the various jewels and gems about her person causing them to wink with pulses and twinkles as if they were almost living eyes peering all around the chamber, hungry to take in all they could.

As she faced the others, Saredhel opened her dark lids and let her pure white eyes shimmer outward upon those gathered about the pool. Upon taking stock of those before her, her cross-legged body hovered toward the middle of the pool, then she turned her gaze toward its liquid confines again.

"Yeah, well, it's done anyway, they should be able to get to Galba in no time," Brandon continued as he moved toward the lip of the pool, the shortest figure in the room of giants.

"Rowan and Clara are there now and should be getting inside the circle as we speak." A savage looking panther hide clad Celetoric woman, which was Panthor's true form, spoke to Brandon beside her. She was shorter than the other two gods, being only twelve feet, but was still double Brandon's current size. Tone and strong she had the body of a warrior and dress of the most primitive of cultures: bone and beads worked all over her outfit and thick, rich black hair, knotted into dreadlocks.

"I see them now." Saredhel spoke down into the still pond where rainbows now danced on its surface. "They are with Galba."

"Good, then things are going according to plan." Asorlok was pleased with the report.

"*Whose* plan though?" Brandon lifted a questioning gaze toward Saredhel. "This whole thing is based upon one insight that may or may not be true. An insight she still hasn't come to reveal to us." Brandon jabbed a finger toward Saredhel.

"You doubt Saredhel?" Asorlok turned his visage down toward the mortal guise of Endarien. Ruby earrings swinging from the swift action as hooded eyes darkened his countenance at the question. Asorlok didn't have any time for such foolishness. He wanted to be done with this matter, for there was still the council decision to consider and Cadrith himself...

"I don't *doubt* her, but I question why this is all being done? Why we just can't let me fight off Cadrith myself and be done with it as the council just voted. Instead we have *two* visions here, *two* prophesies. They can't *both* be right." Brandon looked into the face of the Spawn of Dreams, as some called Saredhel. "Why haven't you told us anymore about this vision?

"Are we just supposed to assemble this group of mortals as an advanced charge in the attack?" Endarien continued. "If this is so, then it is a wasted venture because Cadrith will slay them all without working up a sweat."

"What I have seen, I have seen." The Seer of the Pantheon peered into the sockets of the mortal guise of Endarien. There was no anger or rebuke, only the flat brick wall behind those words that said: 'I will go no further in speaking on the matter.'

Brandon huffed, then leveled his gaze toward Asorlok. "I still don't know why you're here and helping either. Aren't you tied to the very force we're fighting against?"

Asorlok's eyes narrowed for a moment, then smoothed open again. "Recall that though I am bound in an oath to the dark force, as my sister is so sworn to the opposing force to which I hold allegiance, I still helped create Tralodren. I molded the globe as did all of you and put into it a piece of myself which I would hate to see die as would all of you who are fighting for it's protection. I also understand that what this mortal puppet intends to do is kill off the Pantheon as well."

"I'd thought you'd like *that* part." Brandon's eyes narrowed when speaking to the god of death, whose own face was six feet above his own.

"Contrary to what you think, I prefer to let things happen naturally, not to accelerate the inevitable." Asorlok's face grew grave in its seriousness.

"I did notice though that when Saredhel spoke to the council about the first word she had you didn't need reassurance. You acted just like the rest of us, believing in the words of my sister who has never spoken false in all her days." Asorlok's face grew cold and sharp. "Why bring this up now only at the end of our actions? Why do this cowardly thing?"

"I don't know if it *is* a cowardly thing," Panthor countered the god of death. "I just don't feel right going against the council like this. We are making a move on our own when we have already agreed to do another by nearly unanimous vote.

"Doesn't that unsettle your resolve a bit?" Panthor scanned the room, hopping from one to another with her gaze. "I don't want to start causing more trouble than what we already have."

"You're young." Asorlok's countenance lightened with a chuckle. "When you've lived a while longer you'll see that all the gods have or will plot and scheme apart for the council. It is just the way of family and unlimited power in the hands of that family.

"Don't be troubled. We aren't planning *sedition* or any *serious* doings, merely acting upon the protection of the Pantheon by taking a few extra *precautions*. I can assure you every other member of the Pantheon is doing some sort of measure to protect his or her own realm even as we speak. If what Saredhel says is true, and I have every reason to believe it is, then we have done the right thing."

"I know, but I still can't get it out of my head that you have two distinct visions, Saredhel." The goddess of humanity fixed her attention to Saredhel. "One to have Endarien fight The Master and then another to have the same mercenaries who let him free gather again to fight him aided by Asorlok's priests.

"How can that be? How can both visions be right?" Frustration edged into Panthor's voice and around her eyes.

"I have seen what I have seen, and what I have seen has and will come to pass. As to the two visions I tell you this: both are tied to the other, and both must happen in order for this threat to be stopped – but how you interpret what has been said…that has fallen to the three of you and you alone." Saredhel's milky eyes cast Panthor's reflection back to her.

"One was shared with the council for it pertained to all, and one was shared with you gathered here for it pertained to you and your followers and interests. I merely have acted to do all that was needed in light of what I have seen." The goddess of fate's words were dry and flat as her gaze returned to the mystical water beneath her; white cowl hiding her shaved head and face as she spoke.

Brandon sighed as he looked over into the water. "So what do you see now if you know they are near the circle?" He couldn't quite see anything beyond some swirls of color. Only Saredhel could make sense of what the pool was revealing and so he'd have to wait on her.

Saredhel was silent for a time as she concentrated on the scintillating shimmers across the water. All gathered joined her in silent wonder as they watched the one of their number who could

24

see into the flow of time and view its twists and turns and was able to bring discernment from such currents as years and freewill.

"I see them gathered around Galba, waiting to unite under a banner of one. That banner, though, shall lead into the next volley to come."

"*My* battle?" Brandon's chest puffed with pride. "So we brought them there to be defeated then? How can I battle Cadrith should he be defeated by these we brought into the circle to aid us in the fight?"

"Indeed." Asorlok raised a lone, well groomed eyebrow in contemplation. Endarien did have a point. Saredhel, however, only raised her head to look at the mortal guise of the Storm Lord with her pupiless eyes. Eyes that had seen the fate of all things to come and only shared what could be understood, and dealt with even by divine minds.

Brandon couldn't help but suppress a shudder.

"All things serve their purpose. The veil in front of the two words I have given must be pulled back by the hearer, not the bearer of the insight. Such is the way of things pertaining to the nature of fate. One makes an assessment from the knowledge they have at hand." Saredhel spoke with a calm, but authoritative tone. "The artist who must give explanation of his work to the viewer is indeed a poor craftsman. It is in the interpretation the piece comes unto its own and gains a place of understanding and appreciation."

"Right," Brandon shook his head as if to clear away cobwebs that had gathered inside his brain. "I'm still going to fight Cadrith if the council has given me their favor to do so."

"*If* Cadrith rises to godhood though," Panthor clarified this point. "He might not succeed – especially if we have gathered these others to stop him."

"I'll fight him soon enough, Panthor, rest assured of that," said Endarien.

"How can you be so sure?" Panthor was troubled by Endarien's apparent glee at getting to battle this mortal – even looking forward to the failure of the others who they had called together to help stop such a conflict from taking place.

Panthor didn't like this at all.

What did he know?

Before she could ask him though, Asorlok began to speak.

"You ready for it then?"

Brandon nodded solemnly then added, "I'm waiting outside Tralodren now, that's why I've come in this aspect. Once I have Vkar's blessing, I'll strike."

"The others will probably want to release the remains of Vkar soon then." Asorlok continued.

"No," Saredhel drew all attention back to her. "They will wish to watch the event first hand only moving to act should Cadrith gain what he seeks."

"But you already know what the result will be, so why not tell us already." Asorlok crossed his arms. "It seems fairly obvious that for Endarien to battle with the Cadrith, those we have assembled will fail."

"Then why did we assemble them in the first place?" Panthor wasn't getting any more sense out this conversation than before – in fact it seemed to be getting even more convoluted by the minute.

"The future is a river moving forever onward, steered by choice and circumstance. What I have seen moves in one manner and as you know, many things can alter a river's flow." Again, the goddess' words were flowery and elusive.

"I thought you already said that Cadrith *would* succeed. Now you're saying he might *not*? Which is it?" Brandon was growing frustrated now. He always hated trying to make sense of what Saredhel had said and had been a common point of contention for him, as well as other gods over the centuries with previous words of knowledge passed on to the Pantheon.

"Yes, you said as much to the council regarding your recent fight with him," added Panthor with a slight echo of the deeper ponderings of matters occupying her mind.

"This is pointless." Asorlok waved his hand like a blade to cut off the words of his fellows. "We all know that Saredhel is never wrong in her declarations. Whatever the fate, we have to be ready to walk into it head on, and I believe these measures, however they were brought to us, will work out in the end for our benefit."

"So *you* say," Brandon curled his stubbly lip.

"So I *believe*," the god of death countered.

"There is nothing you can do now but rest. All have been assembled as I had made known to you should be assembled. Now is the time for the deed to be done and the council to decide the manner in which to follow the events to come." Saredhel's milky eyes glanced over each one gathered about her pool as she spoke with authority behind her words that each could feel inside their own spirits. "Now you must go your own way and await the outcome of these things."

"Agreed," Asorlok snipped. "We've wasted enough time here as it is already and done what we felt lead to do." He peered down at Brandon. "Let's just hope we don't have to use the last of our father to stem this threat."

"Why? You don't have any faith in my ability to crush him?" Brandon was slightly insulted from the god of death's comment.

"I would hate to have to use the last of his remains, that is all." Asorlok tried to smooth over Brandon's feelings, but the god of wind knew it was a false appeasement and resented it more than the insult. He knew what his uncle had really been saying anyway; knew where his real interest in all this lay.

"Hate to use the last of him up before you could figure out what his fate really was you mean." Brandon countered with a smug expression. "You still think he didn't die after all this time?"

"What-" Panthor started but was stopped by Saredhel's words.

"If you are to argue, do it in your own realms, with your own time. I have matters which require my attention."

Asorlok and Brandon looked at each other, then turned toward the door of the chamber. What they had to say to each other was said. There was little point in arguing about anything anymore. They had more important issues to contend with now and turned their focus toward them. Panthor followed behind them not wanting to get between the two lest it came to her detriment. When each had left the chamber, Panthor closed the large silver shod wooden door behind them. With the echoes of the closing door still dancing off the walls, Saredhel closed her eyes and focused her mind toward the pool beneath her once again

"It is done." She spoke in a soft voice. "The ones you have called are in your grasp and the council has made its vote upon the matter as well."

With these words the pool turned a solid white, as if the substance in it was liquid marble instead of water. This whiteness shimmered with a brilliance of daylight itself covering the goddess above it in a seemingly living radiance that made all colors onto which it fell paler than was their nature.

"Do now as you will," spoke the goddess of fate.

"I shall," came a voice from the pool that was both feminine and masculine merged into one even tone.

Chapter 3

Galba appeared to the group gathered inside her circle in a flash of pure white light. They had been plucked up from all over the world to be gathered to this place for one final task before they could return to their lives. One task which no one really wanted to do, but had come to understand they had to do if they wanted to return to the normalcy of their former existence.

So all the mercenaries who had been present at The Master's arrival, sans Cadrissa, had been summoned to Galba to meet the being to whom they had to honor this final obligation.

Joined by two priests of Asorlok and a messenger of Endarien, they stood fast inside the eldritch stone circle named after its inhabitant. A brief reintroduction was all they were afforded before the brilliant pulse of light of Galba's appearing swallowed everything around them. When it subsided each tried to move, but found themselves transfixed with the transcendent person of Galba hovering above them.

A gray, clinging, long sleeved robe outlined her firm, lithe frame, allowing for a small sporting of cleavage, and stopping halfway down her calf where delicate feet of alabaster cast dangled above the ground. Though her dress was rather plain and unadorned, her face more than made up for the simplicity of garb. Smooth and clear as porcelain her skin told of a youthful manner, which seemed almost eternal. Eyes as deep and green as the leaves of a grape vine sang of hidden depths and mysteries residing behind them – a secret collection of insight none living had ever seen or known. These eyes were gems of shimmering light, a radiating effervesce adding richness to her silky red serpentine locks slithering around her head in a wind only she could feel.

"*You're* Galba?" was all that Rowan could say or think when he looked up at the spectacle of the woman before him. Because he was so overwhelmed with her presence he had also spoken in his native, Nordic tongue.

Ruby lips parted into a smile that was at once inviting, comforting and attractive to the youth. "I am." Her tone was gentle like the words of a mother to a son and also in the Nordic language.

"Now that you are all here, we can begin." Galba slowly descended to the grass as she turned her words to Telborous.

The others still couldn't say anything – didn't dare, as to what she meant by a 'beginning'. Instead, they merely looked at each other in silent wonder at what was going on before them. When it was clear that the others shared her same concern as to figuring out just what was going on and they didn't seem to be getting any answers…yet. Clara turned toward Gilban, who stood emotionless and still beside her.

"What's going on here Gilban?"

For a moment the old priest was silent. The dark enigma plaguing him since his wait outside the sanctuary doors on Rexatious had only grown stronger. It now even seemed more physical in nature; a dark claw that gripped his heart attached to a severed arm that plummeted into his stomach where it's bitter root was starting to make him feel sick. His head was still clear though…for the moment. That too had been clouding over as more of the enigma moved into his mind, preventing him from seeing too much by aid of Saredhel. He assumed that in time he would lose all lucidity and still never know why. It was an irksome matter the elder priest tried to take in stride.

"I have seen many things – and not all have come to pass as they were first seen – for the future is always in motion, diverted and directed by actions in the present. However, *this* I did not see." Gilban answered Clara, but continued to stare ahead at Galba as if his sightless eyes could actually see her glorious personage before him. There was something about the mysterious woman he had to know…something important, but also something eluding him…

"I don't like this Gilban." Clara made a scan about the people gathered and saw they shared her sentiment as well on various levels. "We've been led here by things outside of our understanding; visions and strange coincidences that just happen to bring us all together to this one spot. I don't like being led around on a leash." She also didn't like the fact that Gilban *hadn't* seen this event. If *he* was unable to make sense of all this then they stood little chance of making any understating on their own.

"So what is going on here?" Clara's face turned stern as she took in the alabaster visage of Galba. She might as well go to the source if it was all which remained for her to get an answer.

"True, you have all been used to this greater end and though it might anger you, it is for the best of intentions." Galba drew closer to the elven maid.

"I don't care what the intentions were. You used all of us, took our lives as sport for your own amusement and I'm sure the rest of us gathered, would like to know why." Clara caught a glimpse of herself in Galba's green orbs as she spoke. She marveled at how small, almost trivial her reflection seemed in such a massive expanse of green – like a pebble in a sea of grass. In that moment her rage, though it had once seemed important and right, fluttered away from her – ebbing out of her body like dross from silver.

"She has told us some of the reason," Cracius offered Clara. "But I think it best to hear her tell it to you four so we are all informed of what is happening."

"Where is Cadrissa though? I was told she would be here." Rowan finally managed to get his thoughts back together in his head, even speaking Telborous as the rest of those gathered did. "Panthor told me that–"

"Cadrissa is safe and on route as we speak." Galba's pleasent face took in the young Nordican with a serene aura that made the young knight just want to wash away into such a presence if somehow possible and simply be no more…

"But–" The knight shook his head as if awaking from a daydream and tried to get his say in once more, like someone trying to get their head above water before they plunged under again…but to little effect.

"First you must listen. All of you must listen to what is now expected of you and why you are here. Far from being playthings as some of you might think you have been," Galba's gaze swept by Clara for a moment. "you have all been chosen as champions of a great and important cause. All of you have a purpose and a role to play. Some greater than others." Galba peered down before she moved on toward the center of the circle. For a moment, the green gaze of the woman weighed heavily upon Hoodwink. The goblin's yellow eyes grew wide and he swallowed hard at the implications of her words. He didn't like this already. Was his great purpose, the one Gilban had told him he had, really *that* great?

The green creature broke out in a cold sweat.

"All of you have been chosen to hold back The Master from claiming his prize." Galba continued. "He comes here to attempt to gather the laurels of godhood. He must not be successful in doing so."

"Godhood?" Clara was more than a little astonished.

"Yep." Vinder nodded slowly. "Madness I know…and we're all a party to it would seem. I still don't think he can do it, no matter what these priests might think."

"So you think he could succeed then?" Rowan asked Tebow.

"Anything is possible," the older priest responded dryly.

"He comes here with the aid of a patron who he is yet to be made aware of, but will in time. With that aid he is almost certain to succeed unless you stand in his way." Galba stopped her movement to hover at the exact center of the circle; the others now arrayed in a semicircle between her and the outer ring of stones.

"Stop him *how*?" Rowan crossed his arms. This was going to be an interesting explanation he was sure. When they fought him before in the ruins he had easily defeated them, nearly killed them if he hadn't left when he did. How do you fight against *that*, let alone win?

"Now you're getting the picture aren't you?" Dugan smiled at the youth. "It's a fight to the death from what I reckon." There was no mirth in the Telborian's smile, however. It seemed as emotionless as the grave.

"A fight to the *death*? But this isn't even *my* fight." Rowan voiced up. "I came here to save Cadrissa from this Master – and that is what I intend to do, not defend some circle of rocks from a fool trying to claim godhood." His Nordic blood was rising. This went past Clara's previous apprehensions and premonitions about what they now were told was a reality and had moved into something far more serious. He wasn't about to fight to the death for this entity, no matter how much he felt enthralled by her charms.

Clara gripped his arm. "Calm down," She whispered in his ear. "You might want to watch your temper around her. The same power I could feel coming off the stones before we came in here is coming from her as well."

"I don't care who she is." Rowan shook his arm free. "I'm not going to be someone's puppet in a war that isn't even mine in the first place. I may have been duped to get this far, but I'm not about to be used again. I have a duty to my Knighthood first and to Cadrissa second. Nothing comes between these two priorities."

"On the contrary," Galba raised her hands.

Suddenly, the earth beneath them grumbled and moaned as it shook about in wild tantrum. Each did their best to hold fast to their balance, but had a difficult time with it.

"This war is universal and effects you all." The shaking increased as Galba rose up on top a mound of dirt which had begun to jut up from the earth below like an unwatched cauldron boiling over. As the mound rose, it shed its dirt shroud, revealing a ten-foot tall, white marble dais on whose top rested a majestic throne, which looked like it could have seated a giant quite comfortably. This throne was carved of solid white marble as well, but was covered in diamonds, rubies, emeralds, onyx, peridot, lapis lazuli and pearls.

Every inch that could be puckered with these precious stones of various sizes was. Besides the gems, the rest of the throne itself was rather simple looking in design: a tall backed chair with sturdy square armrests. Despite this plain design, it seemed worthy of the most grand of beings – something a seat of the god of the gods would rest upon to rule. Even as they all watched in amazed silence, the pristine jewels shined with a brilliant fire all their own.

On either side of the throne stood two statues, no more than fifteen feet tall. These too were of white marble, but the images they represented were strange to the eye, and at the same time vaguely familiar.

The one on the left was a strong male. His lineage of race seemed mixed as to prohibit speculation on his origins save that they appeared to be human. However, the statue also hinted at something of a supernatural origin as well, an unearthly nature about his frame that all who saw it knew but couldn't explain. In his right hand he held aloft a great mace with a strong arm. This arm matched the incredible muscular nature of the rest of his frame. For his dress he was shown with a kilt made of leather strips, a breastplate, tall sandals, and a flowing cape stopped at the back of his knees. He also possessed a long handlebar mustache, flowing hair and eyes which pierced the soul of anyone who met their cold, lifeless gaze.

The shape of a woman of similar racial lineage stood on the right. She was strong like the male, but just a hair shorter. She carried no weapon, wore no armor. Instead, her long haired figure was draped with a simple gown that fell just below her knees with tall sandals on her feet. Her hands were outstretched in a welcoming gesture, her face and eyes warm and inviting.

It was in the middle of these two statues and before the throne that Galba stood as the last of the dirt and debris poured down the white marble steps as if it were water. The quakes then subsided and each had regained solid footing once more.

"He comes for the Throne of Vkar, which I have protected since the creation of Tralodren. It has remained here since the beginning and though some have sought out its boon, none have succeeded."

All of them were speechless at what they saw. If being near Galba was beyond compare than getting a glimpse of this throne with its flanking statues was to have been taken to Paradise while still alive. The emanation of its importance – its spiritual power was thick in the air.

"And *we're* supposed to stop him?" Rowan asked with wide eyes once more adjusting to a more cognitive state of mind, though it took some struggle.

"What did I tell you kid," Dugan seemed darkly comedic as he spoke, "suicide mission."

Rowan found the Telborian's grim statement more than unnerving.

"Not as such." Gilban's voice caused all eyes to spin his way. In truth, everyone had forgotten him when faced with the splendid scene before them. How could they not?

"I have secured a means by which The Master can be defeated with little effort or bloodshed on anyone's part."

"Have you now?" Vinder was less than cheered. "Isn't that just *convenient* then." He liked all of this as little as the rest of them.

"This scepter will stop The Master should he be able to claim godhood." Gilban held up the object which he had bartered Gorallis' eye for with some amount of pride. He was proud and why not? He had been able to do what few others could – survive a meeting with the dread linnorm and better still, been able to trade with him as well. Though it had been the favor of his goddess that rested upon him to do so, it still had been him doing the actions needed to bring it about and that made him feel good…even if the pesky dark thought rolling around his head made him feel increasingly worse.

"How?" The bird chirped the question everyone else was thinking.

"I will explain what I can in a moment." Gilban's words were calm but all could tell he was restraining his own frustration and perhaps even a little anger at being forced to rush through his thoughts and explanations. Gilban came from a race whose ways were bit a more relaxed and slower in inclination and declaration. Being pressed for rapid fire answers just ruffled his feathers.

"Well, if he should prove to be able, we might need a plan then as to how we are going to deal with The Master if we are to fight him then." Dugan tried to clean up some more of the grease paint from his face with little success.

"Indeed, and you must do so quickly for time is falling fast before he will be here to try and make good on his bold claim," Galba replied.

"You don't have to stay." Clara put her hand on top of Rowan's shoulder – which caught the knight's attention. "You can leave at any time you wish and none would think less of you. You've done more than what you set out to do and if you want to return to Valkoria there is no shame in that."

"I'm here for Cadrissa." His words were resolute but his face was filled with affection for Clara. He didn't work at hiding such sentiment from her now…there was no need.

"Who is in the bondage of The Master." Clara returned.

Rowan drew in a deep breath, held it, then let it go. He knew he didn't have to stay and fight with them. He could take Cadrissa and flee the battle but then would that be right? To leave them alone to fight such a battle? Would it be the right thing to do, and could he live with himself if he did it?

And what if he stayed to fight? He might risk the death of Cadrissa along with himself and everyone else. Could he take the risk? Rowan began to notice the eyes of the others all turned on him, focused on him like the tips of arrows held taut by archers ready to fire at any moment.

"If you value your commitments lad," Vinder's stern glare dug into the youth's heart, "you'll stay and fight. You're a part of this just like we all are and bear a responsibility to finishing up what you started."

Vinder's words hit Rowan hard.

"You had just as much part in setting this wizard free as we did and if you ever want to be a good man, as well as a knight, you need to take responsibilities for your actions," the dwarf dryly concluded with all the elegance of a lecturing father.

Though it was a dwarf who had said the words, they struck true to the knight's heart as he could hear the echo of his own father in them. He also knew in his heart it was the right thing to do. He wouldn't have fulfilled his mission, why he had been sent to the Midlands in the first place, if he didn't take a stand against The Master. That was an obligation that had to be kept. Once the choice had been made, everything else fell into place.

"Okay then," Rowan looked about those gathered. "What's the plan?"

Clara gave him an affectionate smile.

Each then turned to another. Hopeful at least one savior in their band had some brilliant scheme…they discovered none had one.

"No need to be shy now," Vinder's sardonic grumbling soaked into his beard.

"Perhaps we should assess what the other knows." Cracius took a sideways glance at Tebow and then the rest. His face did well at keeping calm though his mind behind it raced for ideas. Both he and Tebow were separated from the voice of their god as long as they remained in the circle. Without this supernatural wisdom, they were as blind to the situation as the others…with the exception of the priest of Saredhel. That was if he wasn't cut off from his goddess inside the circle as well, as both death priest's believed him to be.

"A good idea." Clara made a move toward the center of the group as they slowly closed ranks around her to listen. Behind them, Galba stood serenely as she faded from their sight like dust in the wind. She would return when needed again.

"Well, I don't know anything." The Telborian was rubbing at his cheek now, continuing to try and get the smudges of greasepaint off his face, but only managing to smear them around more.

"And don't go looking to me," Vinder added sourly. "I was done with all of you and this before these vultures got their claws into me." He ended his statement by fingering out the two death priests.

"I don't think I can be of much aid either." Hoodwink meekly offered his words, eyes focused on the ground before him.

"I don't think anyone thought you would." Vinder fired off his barb.

Clara flung darts from her own eyes which aborted the sneer on the dwarf's face in an instant.

"Then where do we start?" The bright plumed bird fluttered to settle upon Tebow's shoulder.

"What?" He squawked as all present turned to give him a puzzled stare. "I'm a part of this too."

"I'll keep that in mind." Dugan nodded dismissively.

"So what now?" Rowan was just as much at a loss of ideas as his companions.

"I suppose we wait to kill this lich then." Dugan shrugged his strong, darkly garbed shoulders.

"We need some sort of plan though." Tebow built upon the gladiator's advice. "If you run into this haphazardly then we'll be picked off easier than gnats."

Dugan's face was the haunting expression of a man who no longer cared if he lived or died; a reckless maniac who had only plans to take as many with him when he went in the end. "Not much of a plan you can have if you're trying to fight off someone powerful enough to be a god."

"Well some of us plan to *survive* this encounter." Clara took charge. Somebody had to or they would get nowhere and waste the precious time they had been afforded to plan. "So let's hear it then. Any and every idea that you've got."

"Perhaps it would be better to hear what each of us knows like Cracius was saying" said Rowan. "After all, we all were brought here under different means; different pretenses. I came here to rescue Cadrissa...and in a sense," the young knight swept the people gathered near him, "I'm still going to do what I came here for, just now with some extra help.

"So what are you here for – what were you told you were needed to come here for?"

Vinder let out a wavering sigh. "Obligation."

"We have only come by request of our god to destroy the lich." Tebow answered for both he and Cracius.

"I'm here to just see one more person off to Mortis before me." Dugan followed the priest.

"Well I'm here because I wanted to help save Cadrissa, but in order to do that it's obvious we'll have to stop this lich as well." Clara felt the frustration rise. Some how she wasn't getting them where they needed to go but she was having a difficult time getting them where she thought they should be since even she didn't know where they needed to be.

Clara spoke out loud with a milder version of the frustration she felt inside. "We're all here now and we have to deal with the coming of this lich and putting an end to him.

"How we do this though is what we should be focused on here." The mantle of leadership she had put on again would never sit right on her shoulders.

"I agree." All turned toward Gilban as he raised the silver scepter before his chest once more for all to see. "And this is the means by which we shall win. This scepter has been given to me to stop The Master after he has come into power. This was the reason why Hoodwink and I have come." Gilban felt comfortable in what he said. While he couldn't completely understand what was going on, it now seemed obvious why he had been called here.

"How is *that* going to help us?" Dugan took a good long gaze at the silver object trying to figure out just what it was and how it would bring them victory. "You going to *pummel* him to death?"

"I got this scepter from Gorallis." The blind priest brought the head of the scepter down into his other hand so that it now rested between both fists at about waist level.

"Gorallis?" Rowan's eyes widened, as did all the others gathered.

"Yeah," Hoodwink spoke up softly, his gaze still at his feet, "Gorallis."

"So what does it do then?" Asked the knight.

"It was designed by the Wizard Kings in their fourth age to defeat a god." Gilban released the scepter to his right hand where he held it tightly at his side.

"Defeat a god?" Vinder was astonished with the revelation. "You mean they could do that back then – mortal men could actually *defeat* a god?"

"Well, this scepter alone wouldn't *slay* a being of such power, no." Gilban moved his line of sight toward the stout warrior. "It was designed to drain the very strength of a god away from it and weaken it so they could face off with it on a more equal level."

"Wizard Kings were able to craft such an item though, huh?" Vinder still was in wonder at what he had heard. "Are we sure we want to save Cadrissa as well? After all, I have my suspicions she wants to be the next Wizard King, well Queen anyway. If they could have stood against gods and even planned to do so then might it just be wiser to stop Cadrissa too? She has been under the influence of this other wizard for a while. She could be corrupted by now."

"What?" Rowan turned sharply to Vinder, blood hot in his veins. He couldn't believe what the dwarf was saying. Abandon a human woman in trouble? "I'm only here because I want to save Cadrissa, not *kill* her. She isn't the threat here. It's her abductor who is, and we have to deal with him. By doing that we will save Cadrissa from any harm and influence that this lich might have over her, which I believe would be minimal to none."

"I'm not saying kill her Rowan," Vinder grew a bit flustered at the rapid resistance to the idea. "I'm just thinking maybe we could stop her from getting any more magic – keep her from rising to places where she doesn't belong."

"I can– " Rowan started into what he thought would be a good retort, but was cut short by Clara's commanding voice. It almost reminded him of Journey Knight Fronel for a moment.

"We have to get on task." The elven maid pulled all eyes back toward herself. "We can't be divided right now on petty issues when we have so much to get done and not that much time in which to do it."

Clara nodded toward Gilban. "Please continue Gilban."

The elder priest bowed his head then spoke.

"The scepter can drain the power of a god or similar figure of substance from beyond our world, with the right incantation. However, it can only be used once against such an opponent in the wielder's lifetime. It has such an incredible effect upon these beings, draining them of their very life force, that it had to be limited in such a matter in order to work. Such is the way with the arcane arts I am told.

"I have also been told the incantation needed to work the scepter and what needs to be done once it has been activated. I would put forth the strategy that you should let me attack The Master if he should prove successful in gaining godhood. The scepter would then drain him of his new found strength and allow the rest of you to attack him on an equal plane."

"*You* attack him?" Dugan grew concerned. "You're not really a warrior Gilban and I don't think what we need is a blind man trying to hit something with such a powerful weapon.

"Why not just tell me the incantation and let me do the deed?"

41

Gilban drew still for a moment. None dared say anything more until the blind elf spoke up again. When he did his voice was calm and small; many having to strain their ears to hear what was said. To Dugan though it sounded louder than it was as it spoke to some part of him deep inside and was amplified there for his own benefit.

"No, you have a work yet to do and this is not it. I have my task and it is to use this scepter as I have already stated."

"Who told you how to use it anyway?" Vinder returned with his skeptical eye pawing the scepter which had not left the priest's hand.

"Gorallis." Gilban's answer chilled the air between all gathered.

"You're going to trust a linnorm?" Vinder was almost beside himself with what he had just heard. "Not just any linnorm mind you, but the oldest and baddest of them all?"

"I have, and shall," came back the elven priest's calm reply.

Silence.

"I trust him." Hoodwink tried to add some weight to Gilban's words – even looking up at the others with his answers, but the dwarf didn't seem to want to hear what he had to say – snorting with disgust at the goblin's comment.

"What if The Master doesn't make it to godhood?" Rowan entered the conversation with this new thread of thought. "What if he failed?"

"Then our task would be far simpler." Tebow reminded everyone of his presence. "However, I doubt we were brought all the way here if it was assured or even assumed that The Master would fail in his attempt. I think it wise to consider that there is a very good likelihood the lich will succeed in his quest."

"So we just sit back and wait for him to become a god and then attack him, assuming that what Gilban says is true and he can land a solid blow and the incantation will work?" Dugan shook his head at the sheer madness of the proposal. Madness he had already experienced and accepted with these two priests before he came inside the strange stone circle. This was the last day he'd be alive, that was for sure. How did you expect anyone to stand against a god, even a weakened one at that?

"Yes," Cracius matter of factly answered the Telborian's question.

"Doesn't that seem a bit idiotic?" Dugan snorted his displeasure.

"Maybe not. Just sit back." Clara could sense the confusion and desperation of what had just been said. And it would only continue to grow about the company if she let it. The only cure she could devise to combat it was action. "We should still have a plan as to how to attack The Master, once he achieves his goal. Probably should have a plan where to place ourselves before he arrives."

Silence again returned and lingered for a while, bringing along its companion: awkwardness. Together, they stayed until Rowan shooed them away with his words.

"Clara, I don't think we will need much of a plan to lead an attack." His face was solemn, but still kind toward the elven woman who he was learning to and allowing himself to love more with each passing hour.

"No," Cracius added. "We'll all allow Gilban his path to strike when the time comes and Galba will take care of the rest."

Vinder scanned the circle with sleight concern. "Hey, where did she go?"

"She'll be back again when the time has come." Tebow started to move away from the others. "I would advise we make use of the short amount of time we have left to see to it we make peace with what we have to do before the battle begins."

"You sound as if you expect all of us to die." Rowan's worries deepened.

"They're death priests," Vinder slapped the knight on his back in passing toward another area of the circle. "What do you expect them to think."

Rowan managed a slight smirk at this modest jest but his spirits still failed to be lifted. He couldn't die now; he was just starting out on his service to his goddess. Panthor wouldn't let him die; had told him he had a great destiny to fulfill and he wouldn't be able to accomplish that if he was dead. The queasiness of his stomach wouldn't leave him no matter how many positive words he tried to flush into it along with his mind and heart.

"A good idea Tebow." Clara formally dismissed the already dispersing gathering. "Let's all prepare as best we can before its time to do what we came here to do."

The others then went to a separate location of the grassy circle to be alone with their thoughts.

Chapter 4

The inside of the stone circle had grown quiet as each person present marinated in their thoughts. It was like the stillness that came before a storm; the eerie quiet laced with tension which was ready to unleash itself at any moment. Each knew the stakes in the back of their mind, but none wanted to deal with them now. It was over – the decision made. Time now to look forward toward the event at hand; the final battle to come.

Rowan sat off from the others, near a portal currently showing a thick woodland scene not unlike from somewhere inside Arid Land. He stood watching the opening between the two stone posts shimmering away for a little while longer and then pulled out the mummified panther paw amulet from under his armor and shirt.

Grasping it in his left hand, he prayed to Panthor for wisdom and strength, courage and protection in the battle ahead. As he did so, Rowan felt a peace wash over him and still his heart and mind. He continued to desire an understanding of just what this amulet was supposed to provide for him – what it was meant to do. He supposed that should he die today it really wouldn't matter anyway.

However, he didn't think he was going to die here. No, his Nordic logic and superstitions told him that he wouldn't be promised a destiny and then left to die before it came to pass. Unless…unless of course he had already served his purpose and this was his final part of his destiny: defeating The Master and saving Cadrissa.

No, that too felt wrong somehow – almost premature in a way. So if he had a larger part to play in some drama, as Clara would have him believe and he was seeing now this was more and more the case, then what role did he play? Everyone gathered around him had been brought together for various reasons for the common purpose of stopping the threat of The Master. This was only one matter though, if Rowan was correct in his assessment of his calling, before he came to the real focus on his destiny. So what was it then that he had to do? Rowan closed his eyes again and prayed to his goddess in humble voice.

"Panthor. I beg of you to show me the larger plan you have for me, reveal your purpose for my life so I can better walk in it and honor you by fulfilling the purpose for which you called me.

"What is this amulet for and what part does it play in my future? Please, reveal this to me before I go to battle so that I might have a hope of a life beyond this day. If it can help me in the battle to come I want to know how so I can survive to serve you for the rest of my allotted days."

The knight then stood silently in meditative thought; eyes still closed and heart and mind cleared and calm to hear what his goddess might say.

He didn't have to wait long.

Open your eyes and see a reflection of your future. Came the familiar voice of Panthor to his mind.

There was nothing more.

Rowan did as bidden and saw the portal before him had changed locations to show the familiar landscape of the Northlands. Where it was he wasn't quite sure nor as to when. Gathered in the picture's center was a collection of armed and armored men who Rowan felt he knew, though from where he stood they all were strangers to him.

They handled themselves like Knights of Valkoria, even had similar arms and armor, but they were different too. Looking harder, Rowan discovered that each had a shield painted with the symbol of Panthor: a stylized panther roaring in profile. He could see some banners too with the same symbol around them. So far these were normal things the Knighthood carried. So where was the difference then? His eyes focused between the group of men at a figure who had caught his eye.

Reddish-brown haired and beard, he seemed to be the leader of the group. He was dressed like and even carried himself like them in stance and actions. However, he wore the same amulet Rowan now held in his hand. He couldn't believe it at first, but saw it rise and fall from his chest with each great bellow released from the silent image's commands.

Peering closer still, the knight could see the face of this strange, charismatic figure more closely. It was his own! The bearded leader of this group of men was him! He'd been thrown at first by the man's age, for he seemed to be at least twenty years older, but it was Rowan. He was also amazed at how much he looked like his father. It seemed the old sayings of his people were true: men do grow up to be their fathers…at least in appearance, for Rowan didn't have the ability to judge the character of nor what was being said by this future version of himself. Still though, the closeness to his father in appearance was quite haunting.

What were these men doing here with him and where was this place that he was seeing? They appeared to be in the midst of some conflict, though Rowan couldn't see their opposition. His thoughts were interrupted by a gentle hand coming to rest on his shoulder.

"Rowan?" Clara's voice came softly from behind him.

The youth shook himself awake as if from a dream and turned around to see the elven maid.

"I didn't want to bother you if you don't want to be disturbed–"

"No," said the knight with loving eyes, "you're not bothering me at all. "How are you?" Even in the midst of his chaotic thoughts the sight of Clara brought a sense of calm to his heart.

"Good." Clara removed her hand from his shoulder and took a step back from the youth. She caught a short glimpse of his dragon crested shield slung over his back. She didn't know what the two dragon heads that faced each other on it meant; only that Rowan had favored it since he discovered it from their treasure vault of the ruins they found in Takta Lu Lama. How long ago had that been now? A year? It seemed longer even to her elven sense of time, which progressed much slower than other races. Logically she knew it had only been a few months but it seemed to be so much more than that...

"What were you thinking about before I came over? You seemed pretty much lost in thought."

"An oddity for a Nordican, huh?" Rowan teased.

"Well, you're not a *typical* Nordican now are you?" She returned with a similar spirit. No, Rowan was someone she had come to learn to love more and more over those passing months. Strange and feared at first she had come now to embrace it only to know that it might end here now today.

Rowan looked back over his shoulder to the portal. The image had changed now to an underwater scene full of swaying seaweed and swimming fish. It appeared to be the bottom of a lake somewhere...

"Nothing really," he spun back around to the elf. "Just trying to make sense of what's been happening these last few weeks." Rowan felt the same way as Clara about their relationship. Well, the development of the relationship itself. He wouldn't go so far as to say he was courting the elven maid, but he couldn't deny the developing feeling he had for her either. Just another thing to lose if he should die today, another thought in the battlefield of his head and heart.

"What's that?" Clara pointed to Rowan's amulet.

"Something very dear to me." He looked down at the shrunken paw still in his grip.

"I've never seen you wearing it before." She drew closer to it with her face, examining it with her sapphire eyes. "Is it a dried out panther's paw?"

"Yes." Suddenly Rowan felt a bit uncomfortable with the situation. He didn't know why but felt like he was naked before Clara.

"Why on earth are you wearing a panther's paw around your neck?" She pulled away from him now and looked him in the face to wait for his answer. "I didn't know you had so many superstitions you still clung to–"

"I received it from Panthor in the first ruins we discovered in Takta Lu Lama. When I ran off inside them that night I was led to discover it and was given it as a gift by her and have worn it ever since."

"I hid it at first to keep it safe because I didn't know what it was for or was supposed to do, if anything. Now though I'm letting the world see it because should I fall today I don't want to be ashamed of what my goddess has given me." The feeling of nakedness had passed but the knight still felt a bit vulnerable for disclosing the amulet to Clara.

"So you don't have much hope for the future then?" Clara's eyes fluttered around the youth, not wanting to look him clear in the face.

"I didn't say that." Rowan felt the heaviness grow in his heart when he thought of being unable to see that beautiful gray tinted face once more. "I'm just being practical to the situation at hand."

"Well try to be a bit more optimistic in that pragmatism." Her eyes finally found his again. There was some joy mixed with each's resolve. "It won't be that much of a victory celebration without you." Both were silent then for a span; awkward silence growing thick between them.

"Rowan, I just wanted to say that in case we do–" The elf's sapphire eyes had become more radiant with the increased wetness welling up within them.

"Any new theories to your idea of us all being pawns?" Rowan swiftly changed the subject.

Clara lowered, her head slightly, sighed and then allowed herself to follow the new thread of conversation. She was confident that each knew how the other felt though they hadn't expressed it verbally and didn't seem like they would before The Master's arrival. She at least could rest in some comfort with that understanding.

"I think we can safely say we both know who is behind this now." The elf moved a few steps back from the young knight to look at the throne in the center of the circle. "I just hope we'll be able to survive what we have to do."

"Gilban said it would work out." Rowan placed his arm around her shoulders. Clara turned to look at the youth with a pleasantly surprised face. Rowan, for his part, did nothing but grin into her sapphire pools.

"You're right, he hasn't been wrong before." Clara let herself continue to stare into the Nordican's dark blue eyes; eyes the same color as the seas, which would soon carry him back to his homeland.

"What are we going to do after this?"

"What do you mean?" Rowan kept his eyes focused on Clara's gentle features.

"I know you have to travel back to Valkoria–"

"And you can still come with me," Rowan interrupted.

Clara blushed slightly as she lowered her head to look down at her boots. "I know, and I really want to, but I have obligations too. I can't just pick up and follow after you even if I really would like to," she sighed. "What I said in Vanhyrm I meant Rowan."

"So did I." He drew her closer still with his arm as it fell to her waist.

She looked back up at him with a smile so wide it almost seemed to touch the base of her ears. "I know."

"So come with me, then it would–"

"I can't…" her smile faded. "You know that, Rowan. I have to report back to my own superiors, my *own* people…"

Rowan nodded in thought. He didn't want to admit it but she was right. They both had tasks once this was all over. Each still had their own lives and obligations that went along with it, both great and small.

"How about we pick a time and place to return to after we have fulfilled our obligations?" Rowan put forth a hopeful solution.

"I don't think that would work too well either." Clara's statement robbed some of the hope from the Nordican's heart.

"Why?"

Clara opened her mouth, but nothing could come out. She tried again and after some prodding with her tongue, some words managed to find their way to Rowan's ears.

"We're going to be too far away to make anything very meaningful as far as a date to meet up again and then when and where. It takes months to get to Rexatious and it's some distance to the Northlands too.

"How would we get a time and place figured out when we don't know what the future will hold. You might be called into another mission right away, I might have some urgent matter that is sprung upon me – or both."

Rowan let his grip around the elf wither with another heavy sigh. "You're right I suppose…"

"Listen," Clara gently slid out from what was left of the Nordican's embrace. "I want to check up on Gilban and see if he needs me for anything. That scepter is what we're anchoring this whole plan on. I want to be sure it will work."

She hated to leave him but she did have other tasks she had to be attending to. It wasn't a time to live for herself. She had come to relay her heart to Rowan should they fall in the upcoming fight and now she had to be off to other matters before The Master arrived. She didn't like it at all, but it was part of being a leader – and if she was going to continue to call herself one, she needed to do what was required of the position.

"I probably should finish getting ready then." The knight's words were weaker than he would have liked at covering up his emotions.

Clara gave him a hurried peck on the cheek and then moved off to Gilban, who was seated a little ways away with Hoodwink at his side. Rowan watched her go for a moment, then picked up the amulet in hand and stared back into the portal as he had done before Clara had interrupted him.

Dugan sat alone. Silent and somber, he rested his back up against one of the stone posts and took in the scene around him with alert eyes. He wanted to have a good look at all the others and see to their plans. He was curious how each would try to prepare themselves against a wizard so strong in arcane mysteries as to seek out godhood with a very high chance of success.

The Telborian thought any preparations worthless and would have none of it. He had his sword, and that was enough. He didn't need any armor; figuring it wouldn't save him from his fate anyway. When last he faced the lich he was fully armored and was nearly killed in one simple brush of an attack. Should he succeed in becoming a god, then it would be pointless to try and armor himself against any of his attacks. No, it was best to just charge into it, face him head on and be done with it.

He didn't have much to live for now anyway, he'd already determined that before he got here. He still carried the scar of his slavery to Colloni. It could still be seen on his left shoulder, under the torn black tunic he wore. And he knew for certian now that no god would hear his plea for release from his pact with Rheminas. With little coin left, if he somehow managed to survive, there wasn't anywhere he could go where he'd be free from the knowledge of his slavery in death. A slavery that would and had haunted his days and nights even though by most accounts he was free.

He was ready to meet Rheminas and begin his service to the god. Why hide from it anymore? Why deny he actually seemed to enjoy the sensation that came over him when he had the opportunity for revenge – to shed blood for his own sense of justice. It was just like Galba had told him when he had first come into the circle: this choice to sell his soul and future to the Vengeful One was his and his alone to make. He made himself his own victim. He alone was to blame.

He supposed Vinder would be proud of his act of personal responsibility, especially after his little speech to Rowan a short while ago. He noticed the stout warrior across from him in on the other side of the circle twisting strands of beard into three strong braids. Dugan didn't even notice the dwarves beard had been unbraided in the first place. He'd just watched Vinder finish sharpening his axe a little while ago and marveled at the dedication the dwarf put into being here. He was dedicated to this enterprise whole heartily, more so than what the Telborian would have thought. Too bad that he too would probably be dead with the rest of them before the battle even began.

Dugan doubted that any of them would be alive once the fighting started, which made him all the more curious as to why they had to fight this lich in the first place when they were all going to die before they even broke a sweat. It was damn foolishness and the former gladiator knew it. He understood what it was like to be used by others for their own ends of either profit or pleasure. This felt little different than what he had undergone in the arena. It was only fitting he supposed, that he would end up dying doing the same thing he ran away from in the beginning.

This was all some great cosmic joke; a grand show for another's amusement. And while such a thought would have previously irked the Telborian into a rage, now he could care less. More a cinder of a man, the fire he had once experienced inside him had long since left to leave him feeling empty and hollow – a husk of who he had been.

Could it even be Rheminas who had planned this all? Did he really want Dugan so badly as to make such a spectacle to fully ensnare him? No, Dugan supposed not. He wasn't so vain as to think himself that important to the dark god. If anything this was a fight just for Galba and her amusement.

Hah. Priests and their gods. He was glad to be done with them. Even as he thought about all the faiths he had to go through in order to be told the same thing: "We can't help you," he caught sight of Cracius and Tebow knelt in prayer to their god, silver hammers at their side. Why they needed to pray to a god they would end up meeting soon enough Dugan hadn't a clue, but he found their actions worthy of staring for just a little while longer. Then he caught Rowan and Clara talking some ways off from him.

He could tell something was going on between them and that *something* between them was pretty easy to see. You'd have to be blind not to. He also saw the tension that was there too. Dugan followed Clara with his eyes as she moved away from the knight after giving him a small peck on the cheek. Had Dugan been in Rowan's shoes he would have demanded something more, then moved on to the blind priest and goblin.

Dugan still couldn't figure out what Hoodwink was doing here anyway. He seemed totally pointless to help at all in the upcoming battle. What would a tiny, cowardly goblin be worth in a fight with a god? More comedic relief to the force who had organized this all? Bah. It was all meaningless anyway.

Seeing how it might be a while until they were needed, he settled back against the stone for a short nap. At least he would be able to enjoy the few moments left to him without fire and brimstone about. A decent rest would do his body good too by allowing him enough strength to deal out the last bit of death the gods would allow. So the Telborian closed his eyes and rested as best he could. The end would come soon enough.

54

Gilban knew Clara was drawing near before she even left Rowan's side. He had been fondling the scepter as he thought about what he needed to do in these last few hours before the final fight. He had the incantation and had firmly burned it into his mind by repetition so no matter what was happening around him he'd be able to recite it flawlessly.

The priest had taken a seat a little ways in from the stone ring, about midway between the large dais in the center and circle of stones. Here it was he thought and listened or tried to listen to the will of his goddess who had yet to come to him since entering the circle. The dark gnawing was still on the corners of his mind but the elf had come to tune it out for a while as it seemed to have mellowed since he had taken his seat. At his feet was Hoodwink.

Hoodwink was looking at the scepter with a silent, hollow stare as his mind raced elsewhere to what he was doing here and the purposes and schemes far beyond him and probably would be forever. He played absentmindedly with a dagger Dugan had given him when he found the goblin was unarmed – spinning the tip of the weapon in the grass. The blond Telborian had told him if he was going to stick around he might as well be useful and so gave him one of his own daggers.

Hoodwink wasn't too keen on the negative attitude that Dugan seemed to voice for most of the others about his presence and was happy to see Clara walk up to meet him. It gave him something to do besides be lost in his thoughts. He wanted a little freedom from pondering the mystery of the things to come. He didn't dare bother Gilban who was so enthralled with the scepter. No, he doubted that would be wise or if he'd get any answers anyway. As least with Clara he could get some conversation – something to pass the time and get his mind from his thoughts.

"Hello." Hoodwink bowed his head in greeting.

"How is everyone over here?" Clara came to a halt next to the goblin.

"All is ready." Gilban looked up toward the elven maid.

"I didn't have any doubts–"

"You did, but you don't need to worry about anything. The incantation is firm in my mind, as is my purpose." The blind elf returned to the scepter.

"Don't you think it wise to share the incantation with me or someone else in case something happens?" Clara squatted down before the priest. "You did say it could only be used once. What if something should happen and it would need to be used twice or more? Battle is pretty chaotic. You might trip and cause injury to yourself and the opportunity would be lost."

Gilban was silent as was Hoodwink who watched the exchange between them with growing wonder at what resolution might come of the conversation. When Gilban finally did speak, his words were low and dry.

"One chance is all we have with it here and now. One chance is what we will need. I have every confidence I will succeed."

"You had a vision then showing our success?" Optimism erupted from within Clara like a geyser. If Gilban had a vision of their success then she could stop worrying about everything then. After hearing that Gilban hadn't foreseen any of what they now were experiencing she wanted to be sure that–

"No." Gilban's answer instantly capped the geyser with a heavy iron lid.

"I haven't seen any vision that spoke of our defeat, however." Somehow this statement did little to cheer Clara's confidence.

"So what does *that* mean then?" Hoodwink asked.

"Exactly what I was wondering." Clara shot the small goblin a glance before looking back to Gilban.

"It means what I have said; I have had no visions about this venture being a failure or meeting with failure." There was a slight strain of irritability in his voice, one Clara hadn't heard before.

It did nothing but increase her concern over the success of his upcoming action. After all, this *was* what they were basing the battle on and should it fail...

"So does that mean we can still fail then?" Clara pressed the priest. Gilban's silence which followed didn't help out either. In fact, it made her grow more anxious then before.

"You can at least tell me the incantation," Clara pressed as hard as she dared with Gilban, "in case of–"

"We shall only have one chance." Gilban's face grew more forceful now; stern and hardened in its disposition as the faint irritation had also grown into full fledged frustration. Before anything else could be said or done, a bright flash burst over the entire interior of the circle, drawing everyone's attention.

"It is time." Galba suddenly appeared in the center of the circle. She simply stood before them in a peaceful manner; her voice rousing them to their duty.

"It is time for you to join me in the center of the circle for they are at the outside now looking to enter."

None said anything more, merely rose from where they were, shuffled off the last of what they had been doing, and joined Galba in the center of the circle, near the base of the throne. Clara lead Gilban; Dugan awoke from his light nap; Cracius, Tebow and their avian companion joined them; Vinder grabbed his axe, placed the necklace of Drued given him in Elandor about his neck, and made his way toward the center. Rowan mechanically joined them. None wanted to say anything, for all were thinking the same; their hearts beating to a frenzied rhythm and foreheads clammy with perspiration.

The battle would soon begin...

Chapter 5

Cadrissa's green eyes were wider than rexiums as she craned her neck to look at the descending multitude of green fletched arrows. Bronze, stone and bone tipped shafts of death cried out for her blood. She could do nothing but remain frozen in her present location, hoping – praying for some miracle to take place. If it didn't she knew she was going to die.

She doubted anyone would come to her aid.

Not here.

Not now.

Endarien had proved himself unable to save her in the past when promised and she didn't think The Master had much more strength to work yet another spell, since he was siphoning all his power now from her just to get to Galba. No, this was her end. A young life cut short before its prime but – the wizardress doubled over as what felt like a strong punch to her stomach overcame her. At the same time she heard the words of The Master beside her growling in heated frustration.

"*Kelrap Oltane Geptari.*" He flung up his right arm over his head in a dramatic gesture along side the words, completing the spell.

Cadrissa heard the words and understood what had happened. She had been used again as a cistern for The Master's spell – a spell of protection of some sort if she wasn't mistaken. The pain which was part of her mystical energies being ripped from her insides had disappeared as quickly as it has come and now she found herself able to stand once again, though a bit dizzy, which she knew would pass momentarily. This shouldn't be the case she knew and the whole matter of her still having something to siphon off was odd too. She should have been bone dry of mystical energy – her well needing to be replenished from rest before The Master could draw out any more. Yet, she was still full of energy – her mystical well more than half full as her experience helped her gauge her strength.

Why?

Pushing back her long, sable hair from her tan forehead she felt the heat of the medallion she had hidden on her person growing warmer. Again with the medallion. The relic she'd found in the ruins of Takta Lu Lama was proving to be quite the interesting find. If only she could have some time now to study it…

She thought all this as she pondered her death flying down from above. The mind is able to run circles around the flow of time at such crucial moments. She could have thought of more – would have but she was being slowed by the gravity of the situation at hand. She was going to die, and there was little she could do about it.

Clara flinched as the arrows struck the shimmering azure hemisphere surrounding both her and The Master with the sounds of birds flying into a glass window. Shattering into tiny remnants of debris, the arrows fell down the slope of the hemisphere to the forest floor below.

"Gnats," The Master's stern lips curled on his cruelly lined face.

Cadrissa then looked at her captor in silent thought. She had learned it wasn't wise to make this dark mage walk into an even fouler mood since he wasn't one to be so forgiving now that his ire was raised. Cadrissa had seen it before on her recent trip with the lich. She thought back to the time she tried to rebuke him for using his magic against helpless sailors and boats before their confrontation with Endarien and how that experience had taught her much about the dark mage, revealing his true nature and temperament in a clear light.

Since then that anger had only risen to higher peaks as they made their way to where they now stood. It was here, amid the virgin pine forests of Arid Land that the lich had his anger elevated to a whole new level. For some reason The Master was unable to use his own magic and had to turn to the wizardress for his arcane needs. Why this was and just what was going on Cadrissa didn't know for sure...and she knew better than to ask too much. She somehow felt that the leniency of The Master (if indeed he had expressed any previously) was at an end. If she got too much into the affairs of the dark mage; got him too riled up with her questions or concerns, then she felt she might indeed be in more danger than she was now.

Besides this revelation of self-preservation, she understood they were seeking what The Master called Galba: a place or thing lying ahead of them. She was happy for the momentary rest they were taking now though. She was sweaty and sore, and her feet burned in her tall leather boots from the effort of constant hiking across the land she had previously been forced to endure. Cadrissa hadn't been used to such exercise before. She was used to short walks and quiet strolls – not forced marches through the wilderness. So even if it is was an unexpected cessation of their march, she took it as a boon as long as she could.

At least there was that good side out of this bad situation she supposed...

"How do you fare?" The Master asked the wizardress.

Cadrissa cleared back a few loose strands of hair with her hand that had fallen forward again; the gold fingerless glove covering her hand glittering in the sun. The dark locks skirted the collar of her white woolen robe and bunched hood of her golden cloak. Was he really asking about her welfare? For what purpose? She doubted it would be purely altruistic. Though would she have told him how she really felt anyway? She supposed not.

"I-I'm okay I guess," she said, cautiously making sure it did not open up any speculation of confrontation or anger which might give rise to The Master's own temper.

"Your endurance is remarkable." There seemed to be a scrap of genuine amazement in The Master's words. The arrows, which had been pelting the azure dome with a steady percussion, now stopped. "Prepare yourself for another spell. We have to be out of here."

"What's going on now?" Cadrissa's eyes darted about the world outside the shimmering blue light and got her answer.

From out of the sprawling pines, a gang of Syvani ran toward Cadrissa and The Master. The horde was smaller than what Cadrissa had first estimated just a short while before when they had hidden amid the tree trunks to obscure their numbers when they had lobbed their volley of arrows. Now the numbers were larger, a staggering fifty persons at least, if not more, but less than the one hundred she calculated; a swarm of reddish-blonde haired danger and death charging toward them with bloody cries of violence.

Once more Cadrissa couldn't move. Fright had seized her joints and she could feel her heart jabbing against her rib cage as if it was desperate to flee from its confines and run to safety. Though she knew the dome would hold back the attackers, it was head knowledge and her emotions were the ones in charge now.

The Master, for his part, didn't move more than a small step to stand before the onslaught of hollering Syvani. He crossed his arms and stared out at them with a face overcast in conceit.

The elves continued to run at the wizards, screaming their shouts of challenge and warfare, in a language Cadrissa didn't understand, and then were suddenly halted. They had run face first into the azure barrier; those behind them ramming into the ones before like a tidal wave crashing against a rocky cliff.

After they had a chance to right themselves the warriors, who the wizardress could see now were all men, swarmed around the hemispheric barrier where they proceeded to attack it with their bronze axes and stone and bone tipped spears.

Now that they were closer, Cadrissa could also see their faces clearer and the savage anger playing about their tanned skin. Wild coppery-red hair, some spiked up all over with a white substance which the mage thought might be lime, dominated the group. Blue face paint had also been applied to some who howled and wailed like fiends as they hammered away at the hemisphere with their axes and in some cases fists. Others were tattooed with dark black swirling designs with knotted loops and other geometric patterns Cadrissa found quite lovely actually. These were found all over their bodies: faces, necks, shoulders, chests, arms and legs.

They wore little more than simple skins and handmade cloths held together with rough sinew cords and large plant fibers. Some wore bone and bronze jewelry pierced in their flesh as earrings, lip rings, nose rings and other places where various objects could be placed in the flesh of a person and stay relatively put. This again drew Cadrissa's fascination.

A heavy thumping noise drew the wizadress' focus up above her where the dome rose to its peak, some three feet above her head, to witness the dirty bare feet of Syvani jumping up and down on the dome in hopes of breaking through. Others had climbed the shoulders of their fellows to pound away with the butt of their spears, even taking to head butting the barrier from time to time for added emphasis. Of course, all their attacks against the dome were fruitless, but they fought on with a tenacity that reminded Cadrissa of wild dogs intent upon their kill.

"Idiots." The Master shook his head.

"It's time to go." He pulled up his white hood then turned the full effect of his cold eyes toward the wizardress. She said nothing, only returned his gaze, waiting for what he would do next. "Galba awaits and these savages are not going to stand in my way."

Cadrissa flinched from a pinch in her chest as The Master's eyes glowed a bright blue. At the same moment the Syvani gathered around the barrier flew off of it with a violent eruption of force scattering them in all directions. Some hit hard against tree trunks, others toppled over on to their fellow warriors behind them, and still others bypassed their comrades and pine trees to land upon the solid earth between them.

Following this, The Master's eyes faded to their normal nature as he started to walk toward the direction they had been moving toward before. This time, the dome followed them as they traveled, molding itself between the spaces where they walked between trees and other obstacles as if it were rubber. Though it altered its shape, it still was as strong as ever and would protect them from any future assaults.

Cadrissa walked behind the dark mage with a determined gait – the brief rest had restored some of her strength. She turned her head back now and again though to take in the scene behind them. The beleaguered elves had risen from the ground and were regrouping. Some had taken to firing arrows at them again while their brothers in arms shook their heads to bring back the pain-free nature of their ringing heads.

"You shouldn't have such concern." The Master spoke but didn't turn around to address the mage. "These are nothing to us – the true nature of magic makes us better than those around us, higher in all things. By right we should treat those under us as inferior, for they haven't nor will they ever claim the great abilities we have and can attain only by favor of birth alone."

Cadrissa remained silent to The Master's speech. His words were aflame with the Path of Power, the path he had chosen to follow a long time ago and had come to dominate him in time to the exclusion of all other thoughts. Instead, she kept turning her head around to see what the elves behind them were doing. She knew that though the dome would protect them, it was still tied to what energy she had in her and it wouldn't last forever…or would it? The whole surreal nature of that abundance of power inside her concerned her.

To her amazement the elves had all stopped and merely stood among the trees. They didn't even fire their bows anymore, merely watched the two wizards depart with a deep anger brewing about their eyes, which even Cadrissa sensed from her growing distance.

When she turned her head back, again after they had gained some more ground, she noticed something new. All the Syvani parted to form a path for a lone figure to walk between them. This figure was also Syvani and wore the garb of a simple traveler: a brown hooded cloak and an oak branch that had been turned into a walking staff. His manner was calm and still, but in that stillness he held access to a source of mystical might. Cadrissa could sense it from her location and knew this power stemmed not from the arcane arts or even the divine, yet it was similar to the divine in many ways...

"Do you sense that?" Cadrissa turned back to The Master who did nothing but soldier on in their tiresome woodland trek.

"Shaman." The Master's response was flat and low.

"A *shaman*? I've never really seen a real life shaman. I thought they were myth."

"Might as well be, for what power they can control." The Master's words were indifferent.

"Don't you think he might-"

"Keep moving. Nothing is able to harm us." The Master's tone was not icy, but cool enough to know that she was risking his anger if she kept pestering him further.

Despite The Master's assurances, the wizardress dared one more look behind them. The shaman had raised his hands in the air and was chanting a weird hymn Cadrissa was unable to decipher, but could hear the faint melody frolic about the wood. The other Syvani around him fell silent in homage. If he was a true shaman, then Cadrissa knew at least he held no connection to the gods of Tralodren, which would explain the nature of the mystical connection she felt.

A shaman followed his faith by honoring nature and the workings of its inhabitants: animals and plants. To a shaman a tree was a sacred shrine and an animal a holy object of delight in a godhead that was at one point visible in the natural world around them and in another esoteric in the inner-connected, invisible workings of the spirit realm. It was a different faith, and none knew much about it. Every shaman and their followers interpreted their faith a bit differently. None also knew really from whence the power of their belief came. It wasn't of a true divine source, that was certain.

Any priest of a Tralodroen god could have told the common observer that. No, their power came from some other place. Many saw it as evil or a waste or misplacement of faith. These people wanted the hard facts and the sense of reality the gods brought them. Beings you could touch and see in their temples – the presence of a power that could be said to truly exist and governed the world in ways they could understand. The shamanic faith, if indeed it was a true faith, was a strange over-spiritualized thing that Cadrissa didn't really understand, along with many others in the world. This had been and was why the practice was almost completely unknown in Tralodren, save for isolated pockets like Arid Land.

However the divine power was collected, the Syvanian shaman managed to bring forth a petition of his own which he flung toward the two wizards with a grunt. A large hawk made of pure green, flaming light then manifested itself as it soared toward the two wizards; a high shrill screech from its beak. The cry made Cadrissa recall their previous encounter with the Roc and she shuddered.

Before she could react, the energy crafted bird struck the azure hemisphere. The source of might behind his hymn shattered the dome into a shimmer of gold dust and silver glass-like shards that fell all around the wizards like a shower of rose petals.

"They broke the dome!" Cadrissa shouted.

"Impressive." The Master, who had now stopped, spoke on stoic lips.

Seeing their success, the Syvani renewed their campaign with a deep rumbling yell as they made their way toward the wizards, weapons drawn and ready to sup blood.

"What are we –you– going to do? They're going to kill us!" The mage ran up to The Master and tried to hide behind him as best she could only to discover he made a terrible shield.

"Get control of yourself! You're a wizard." The Master growled with more than apparent disdain at Cadrissa's antics.

The Master then closed his eyes for a moment to pull forth more energy from Cadrissa to cast another spell. He found he could no longer do so. At first he thought she had finally run dry as the lich knew she had to at some point, but he came to doubt that. He could still sense the energy about her oddly enough.

What was at work here?

Was this mage something greater than she let on?

Was she blocking his attempts at casting?

The Master thought against this too as he knew that she wanted to be free from here as much as he did.

A moment later, the truth of the matter came to him. He now knew he was being hindered from casting his magic from another source. They had grown very near Galba and the aura surrounding the place was blocking his attempts to cast any magic at all.

"What are you waiting for then?" Cadrissa still cowered behind the mage. "Pull what energy from me that you need for your spell."

The Syvani were gaining ground and would soon overtake them. They were perhaps only ten, maybe fifteen yards away. They didn't fire any arrows though, no this time it was more personal. A wild warlust was rising within them – a warlust that wanted nothing more than to get their hands bloody. They wanted to go hand-to-hand, face-to-face with their enemies. Never mind that Cadrissa wasn't their enemy. It was like what the priests of Ganatar said about those found in even innocent interaction with a guilty party: 'guilty by association.' And she supposed that the Syvani thought the same way and with little hopes of telling them otherwise – even if she did know their language, she was doomed.

"I can't," The Master spat out in rage. "Galba is blocking my attempts."

"Then what can we do?" The fear inside Cadrissa now had gone beyond overpowering. "I can't think of any spells to cast on my own–"

"Run!" He said with an incredibly sour sneer.

The two wasted no time in doing so, and bolted from the area as fast as their tired legs, now awash with fresh adrenalin, could carry them. The Syvani wasted no time in closing the gap around them; their own efforts increased by the joy in seeing their prey turn from them in flight.

Fear now settled upon the two mages in thick and heavy outpourings, even upon The Master who had thought he had rid himself of its foul taste centuries ago was made to sup deeply. Cadrissa felt at any moment she would die, in an instant she would be welcomed into Asorlok's arms and all for the foolishness of an adherent to the Path of Power. What a waste of her life when there was still so much more to see and learn and do…and be…

The yells and presence grew closer to her like a maddening swarm of locusts. She trembled in cold sweat at the distance that she knew was now narrowing between them. She didn't dare look behind her in fear of seeing a leering painted face with an out-stretched spear point leveled against her, ready to run her through in an instant. The Master still ran on ahead of her, but he had begun to show signs of fatigue in his mortal body and slowed his panicked run to about half of what it was when they began their dash for their lives.

Even with the added boost of adrenalin, they were still mortal after all, and worn out from previous travel and encounters. She watched him closely as he continued to work a fast jog before he suddenly disappeared in front of her eyes.

One moment he had been running past a section of the forest that seemed to be thickening up with younger trees and some low-lying bushes making for a slightly greater curtain of green before her and then the next moment he was gone from sight!

Had he worked a spell to escape?

No, she would have seen and felt him do so and he already said he couldn't work any more spells…Perhaps the shaman had done something…As she pondered in her run she entered into the very spot where The Master had vanished and suddenly felt the world circumnavigate her head. In that moment, all the noise of the quickly gaining Syvani fled from her, and she knew nothing but a tranquil stillness.

Somehow she had found herself beyond where she was before, a place she knew wasn't in front of her at all. As her eyes became accustomed to the change of scenery the wizardress let out a marveled gasp at something that would resonate in her dreams for years to come and overshadow her life forever. For here, in this strange elsewhere place, she had found the resting spot of Galba.

The Syvani had been on the heels of the two wizards when Cadrissa disappeared into the wood before them. They would have gone on running further too had not the shaman shouted out for them to halt. Instantly they did, stopping before the thickening increase of growth through with the two mages had passed.

A moment later the shaman was amidst them looking at the area with a wary eye. For a moment more he stared beyond the terrain where nothing beyond it showed any sign of the wizards' passing, only endless forest in all directions where parts of growth had clumped together into thicker, younger tangles than elsewhere.

This shaman was wise though and like all his kin had been raised on the oral tales and traditions of the ancient resident who made her home in this land hidden away from all mortalkind and sought after to one's own peril. He felt the air around the area with his body, and he tasted it with his tongue. It was ripe with the tang of the great energies of which the stories spoke. The two strangers were fools if they thought to get something from Galba, as this most feared and respected resident was called by the Syvani. Let them entreat her. They would be dead before the sun fell.

Seeing that nothing remained for them to do, for the shaman would not run his fellow Syvani into the most sacred of places in Arid Land, he told the others to break off their pursuit. Saddened, but accepting of the command, each warrior turned back the way they came and silently marched back into the wood. Dispersing as they went their way they blended in to their surroundings so that after a few yards all of their number had been swallowed by the forest once more, leaving nothing to remain as evidence of their passing.

Chapter 6

C adrissa stopped herself.

It took her mind a moment to overcome the pounding heart that rattled behind her ears to fully understand what was going on before her. One moment she had been running for her life, now she found not only the threat abated, but her world drastically changed as well. The wizardress was inside a simple open glade removed from the forest around it as to form a perfect circle of low cropped grass, with a ring of sturdy stones at the glades center.

Could it be they had finally found Galba?

It was almost like a dream, an ethereal presence about the whole place made her feel lightheaded. Just being near such a place seemed to shoot electrical currents through and around her, charging her with life and eldritch energy. Energy the likes of which she had never known could exist. The longer she stayed on the outskirts of the stone circle, even at some distance still, the more she felt the need to walk into it, to experience the strange monument in all its splendor.

She fought back the urge though, for she knew that it wasn't grounded in the Path of Knowledge, but the Path of Power. She wanted to possess the energy of the place for her very own – and for a moment, she could understand what The Master felt; how he thought and what he craved. She had to admit it was very intoxicating, tempting and addictive. It took all her inner resolve to push the need, the compulsion down and keep it from rising again. It seemed that she may have learned more from The Master then what she may have wanted – a sobering truth to reflect upon later if she survived this venture.

"You feel it too then." The Master observed Cadrissa with a modest degree of visible delight. "The power that is in this place, the power that is Galba. Cadrissa also felt something more as well. This came from the medallion she had hidden away on her person. She was sure of it! The heat – the vibrating twang and…and the wreath of whispering voices rising about her head–

She shook the thoughts from her mind; banishing the voices and feelings along with the urge to pull it out of her pocket and behold it once more. Such urges frightened her.

"Come." The Master's wicked smile added to her fright. You'll get just a taste of what it's like to be a god. Unlimited power at your command – and the ability to wield it at will. This is what Galba is, this is what Galba offers to those who are worthy."

The Master stood still then.

No word escaped his mouth, no action shifted his body. He was still like the very air of the place around them. His eyes focused in on the circle and didn't move. An object of lust long sought after was never more scrutinized then beneath his ancient brows. He could feel something else at work around him as he studied the stones. It was similar to the sensation he felt now from Galba, but completely different at the same time…almost like its opposite. However, it seemed strangely familiar too, as if it was somehow a part of him – had been for some time now. It also seemed to be filling him with another sensation he had been without for a short while now…

"Is it safe to enter?" Cadrissa finally interrupted the lich's thoughts.

The Master slowly raised his hands in a soft gesture in reply. The motion seemed to cause no immediate affect, though Cadrissa buckled over from the pain of the spell ripping it's energy from her own. The spell was a very powerful one indeed and the wizardress was barely able to stand after it. He should have killed her by that forced withdrawl of mystical energy, but yet, she lived…and even seemed to have still more energy upon which to draw…

"I-I thought…you couldn't work…your magic anymore. Even if…you were to draw it…draw it from me." Cadrissa panted and tried to swallow the pain that still flared up in echoes of the pain.

"So did I." The lich's eyes cackled

"It seems I was wrong about that." The sensation that had come over him and granted him the small spark of energy he needed to fuel his spell, granting him access to Cadrissa – at least to fuel his spell – had departed from him once again. "Now hurry. I have made it as safe as it will be." His voice was dry and distant.

The dark mage then stalked his way into the stone circle, the wizardress barely able to keep up behind him. As he got closer, Cadrissa heard a faint crackle of energy, which grew louder as the lich entered into the circle's heart; passing through the seemingly empty portal between the two stone posts.

As he passed through, he motioned behind himself for Cadrissa to join him as one would do to a slave. And so, like a lagging dog, the young Telborian maid followed behind The Master. As she too passed into the heart of the mystical rock ring, she felt as though she was pushing through some sort of gelatinous wall. She had to struggle with all her strength to push through the restraint, an electrical popping and snapping, playing about her person as well, and then she was inside.

Behind the protective barrier of force, a simple landscape, much as she had seen from outside the circle, was displayed before her, save with one major difference: a marble stone throne sat at it's center, flanked by two statues. The scene was beyond intense as the reality of where she was – what she was doing, came fast into her head. She was inside the most sacred spot in the world, a place where the essence that flowed through all creation, through her own veins even, made its residence!

A quick turn of her head allowed the mage the sight of the portals around them. Each had the scene of some stellar image portrayed between the two posts like some fleeting mist, or scrap of frosty breath rippling between them like waves in a calm sea. The images reminded her of the illustrated lecture that The Master had revealed to her before they left on this journey, a foretaste of the cosmos outside the confines of Tralodren and of which she still had much to learn. The Master, however, paid it scant mind. He had something more pressing on his agenda.

"Galba. I am here." The dark mage shouted into the center of the circle. The sound didn't travel, seemingly to be eaten up as soon as it left his mouth. "I've come to claim the right of godhood. I am strong, powerful and more than worthy. I ask that you appear so this gift can be given to me."

All that returned was silence.

Cadrissa quietly watched as The Master marched forward, his face set with a stern countenance. "Galba. I am ready. Show yourself. I–" The Master was cut short from his demands. His body suddenly was unable to move; tongue and mouth forbidding him to speak. He was helpless.

"Who is this mortal that brags of his greatness?" A quiet voice soared above the two wizards. "Answer woman."

"H-he calls himself The Master, but his real name is Cadrith." Cadrissa stammered when she realized the voice was talking to her.

"Does he claim to be worthy of godhood then?"

"Ye-yes he does." Cadrissa had found it easier to communicate with her head down. It somehow felt right, and kept her from viewing anything in front of her where her mind and heart might take great fright, should anything enter her field of vision.

"Do you think he is worthy of such a blessing?" The voice continued.

Cadrissa's heart raced. She felt as though she was going to faint. Was he worthy? She would love to tell her thoughts on that opinion to the voice, but feared for her life. She had seen two manifestations of a god so far in her young years, and none of them filled her with such fearful awe as this powerful being did.

What should she do?

If she would answer against The Master, as she wanted to, she would surely be killed by the maniacal wizard after he was released from the voice's hold, which the young mage now took to be Galba herself. *If* he was released from the voice that was. She had learned much about The Master since her abduction and none of it was that inspiring to say the least. Granted, she did learn something from the mage during her kidnapping, she could honestly not see him being that great of a deity even if he was a former Wizard King. She had seen an inherently evil being in action and had come to understand that perhaps a division of morals and ethics into the camps of good and evil were a very good thing and that evil shouldn't be allowed to roam free if she was given a choice on the matter. This was a different view which she had adopted in her studies and which was shared by the world of books and learning, but a needed change in her own mind.

Maybe if she said no the voice would let him stay that way for good, or even destroy him outright, keeping her safe from his retribution. Maybe though that wouldn't be the case. Maybe she would be in deeper than what she'd been before. Endarien hadn't protected her, so what made her sure that Galba could or would either? What was in it's best interest in protecting the wizardress anyway?

"Answer woman." The voice was strong, but still soft.

What could she say?

What would she say?

"Why are you asking me? Let *him* tell you. This isn't my quest. *He* wants this, *not* me." Upon uttering the words, which Cadrissa thought as being a shout but sounded more like a simple whisper, she fell to her knees and was silent. Fearful to move, look up or do anything, she shook with a terrible fear.

There was a long silence which troubled her more than death. The quiet stillness hovered over her and seemed to even permeate her very being– hushing the biological chorus of her very existence; seeping into every pore it threatened to drive her mad as her mind fought with her heart…

"Arise." A voice, softer and more feminine than before entered the wizardress' ears. "Don't be afraid. I will not harm you." Cadrissa chanced a look up as her curious nature got the better of her for a moment despite what she had and still felt from the presence of Galba.

Above her was the form of a beautiful woman who was of human descent and seemed to radiate a presence beyond breathtaking. Soft green globes of peaceful light played off the subtle curls of her red hair, and gentle ruby lips. The whole face spoke of tranquility. The face of someone that Cadrissa could get lost in for all eternity.

"Galba?" Cadrissa dared.

"Please stand." Galba invited.

"That's right," she gave an approving smile, "there is no harm to you here child. I see now that you are just a tool in this mortal's agenda. You are innocent from anything he wants, though his taint haunts you." Cadrissa didn't think much on this last statement but would in years to come…

"You *are* the great Galba then? Is it true what he said then about you possessing the very power of the cosmos?" Cadrissa blurted out the first thing to come to her mind, the previous fright and uncertainly now swallowed whole in the jaws of her ravenous curiosity.

"Such hunger for knowledge," Galba smiled, "you truly will be great in time should you stay your true course. Yes, this is a conduit for the very powers of creation to converge and be used as I see fit. Here all things are possible and wishes and fears become reality."

"With such power, why have more not sought you out? Cadrissa desire from answers began to take over. "Surely the very circle would be full of people wanting to get into your presence and have their heart's desire granted." Cadrissa walked beside Galba who formed a blue soft cushioned seat out of the ground a little ways ahead of them, then motioned for the young mortal to sit.

She did so.

"Many have, but none were worthy, not until *he* appeared." Galba replied.

Suddenly Cadrissa was brought back to the understanding as to how she had gotten inside the circle in the first place. Her senses returned to her along with some forgotten fear.

She turned to look at the lich. "What are you going to do to him?"

The Master still stood motionless; a statue with no purpose.

"He has proven himself worthy to take on the challenge of his desire by being able to enter my circle and live, but he still needs to claim his worth to the power he so desires in order to possess it." Galba passed her hand across the air and The Master was free from his restrictive condition.

"Galba, I've come for my reward." The Master spoke through clenched teeth. Her hold over his mouth had lifted, allowing him to speak, but he still had to push past her grip over his body. The whole inner circle would be against him now; testing him in every way possible.

"So I hear you constantly proclaiming." Galba drew a few stops closer to the lich. "You think then that you are worthy of what you seek, then prove it. Show me your worth."

"Very well, if you need the convincing, then I will." The Master proceeded to prepare a spell, but found he was still blocked from accessing any. His power wouldn't flow from him, and he couldn't tap the needed energy from Cadrissa. It was as he had half expected, but completely hated none the less.

"Return my magic to me!" He foamed with wrath. "You took it from me before I got here, and tried to render me a mortal man, but yet I prevailed. That test has passed, return to me now what is mine!"

"I didn't take anything from you." Galba's reply was even toned as she continued to watch the dark mage. "What mantle of mystical might you had claimed left of its own free will, not by my decree. Perhaps there is much you still do not understand.

Besides, your arcane mastery does not prove your worth." Galba's face was stoic, though her eyes danced with mirth.

"Return it! I shall not ask again." The cold eyes of the wizard tightened in rage.

"*You* would threaten *me*?" Galba stood still beside Cadrissa. "Truly you are not as wise as you proclaim to be. You have nothing now. The same worth you bring to your claim. You want godhood, but are not worthy of it."

"Not worthy! Not worthy!" The Master's rage was stoked into a blazing fire. "I am the last great Wizard King of the Fourth Age, a power unto these lowly mortals who now dominate this world. I have seen centuries pass before me. I am immortal, and the most skilled when it comes to use of arcane insight. My presence alone should be proof enough of my worth."

"You have proved nothing except that you can brag well. You must show not only me, but the divine investment which you seek that you are worthy. Behold the throne of Vkar." Galba waved her hand toward the throne.

"In days past a handful of men and woman came to me speaking like you, declaring that they were able to wed their spirit with the mantle of godhood. None were able and so perished from reality, their very substance erased from time and space." Galba than took a hard look into the face of The Master.

"Are you still sure it is worth the risk to your very spirit and existence to continue this path, to seek out a goal that so few have sought and none born of mortal stock have achieved on their own since the beginning of time?"

"I am more than ready and willing to sacrifice all to achieve my true destiny and nothing you or anyone else can say or do can dissuade me from it." The fire still burned inside the lich.

"I thought as much." Galba seemed a bit saddened by The Master's unquenched passion for gaining his goal. "You may become a god then if you can sit in the throne of once proud Vkar."

"That's it?" The Master furrowed his brow as he took in the thought – searching it out for any deeper meaning. "Sit in that throne, and I shall be taken up to the ranks of the divine?" What was she doing? *Mocking* him? *Tricking* him? It couldn't be that simple to become a god…could it?

Galba motioned toward the throne. "If you can make it to the throne and withstand its embrace, then you will have proven your worth. Be warned though, to reach your prize, you will be forced to reveal your inner self. It will judge you as all your mortality is eaten away and your spirit is tried in the fires of the divine."

The Master grinned widely as he looked at the bejeweled throne. This seemed much easier than he had thought it to be. Godhood was his for certain.

"I will be found worthy." He approached the steps.

Cadrissa meanwhile watched The Master's advance with Galba from the comfort of her plush seat. She was so absorbed by the actions of the lich and at everything around her that she didn't notice when another came up behind her to speak.

"Cadrissa." Rowan whispered, touching her arm slightly from behind her seat.

Cadrissa jumped, then turned to see the former mercenaries she had teamed up with on her last adventure looking at her in the face.

"What are you all doing here?" They had seemingly come from nowhere as the mage didn't see anyone inside the circle when she had entered. She found herself smiling uncontrollably though when her eyes took in Dugan which deepened when she noticed the grease paint smeared over the lower half of his face. The sight reminded her of a small child who had become too wild in his play outdoors.

"Who are they?" Her smile faded as she pointed to Cracius and Tebow. Her voice was now lower too.

"Allies." Rowan whispered back.

"Allies for what?" Cadrissa's eyes squinted then darted a quick look back to The Master to see if he heard or noticed these new comers. So far he hadn't. He seemed lost in his own world now...or was she in a world all her own now with these others?

More secrets it would seem.

"Don't worry about him hearing us lass," Vinder addressed the mage, "Galba has allowed us a little bit of time to meet and plan our methods here without the knowledge of the old egomaniac over there. We'll be safe for a while yet."

"But–" she stammered.

"We don't have much time to explain," Dugan started, "We're going to kill The Master if this godhood thing doesn't get him first. Which these two priests," he pointed to Cracius and Tebow, "seem to think won't."

"I think it's very important I–"

"Cadrissa." Rowan's voice was stern.

The mage sighed. She wasn't going to get any answers here, not now at least. Best to just wait out this discourse as it came, and hope that all of this made sense here sooner rather than later. Before that happened though, she had to try one last attempt at least to find an answer for one question which plagued her mind.

"Rest easy. Are you hurt in any way?" The knight now studied her body looking for any signs of wounds or abuse. Cadrissa had to admit that in spite of everything she had been through recently she was amazed she was alive at all. Though she was a little bruised and battered, she was still more than able to live through this...she hoped.

She'd have to rest to regain her strength, but if she survived all of what she had felt was about to take place she thought it a small thing about which to worry. Cadrissa was comforted in this line of reasoning by the warm presence of the medallion. She could feel it again beside her; glowing with heat like an ember from a fire from inside one of her hidden pockets in her robe. It felt like a beating heart – a warm beating heart.

Somehow when it beat, the confidence in her own abilities rose, and Cadrissa felt stronger than she had ever felt before. It was a strange, yet peaceful feeling that drove all the previous fears away. How long had it been beating like this anyway? She didn't know and really couldn't focus on it too much more as there were other matters to contend with at the moment.

"How did you all get here though?" She half whispered. "You aren't wizards."

"That is not important now, nor is who we are." Cracius said. "We have all been called together to stop this lich from attaining his goals and we have little time to do it."

"How can you kill him if he passes the test? He'd be a god then," Cadrissa countered.

"Not quite," Gilban stepped forward. His blind eyes reflecting the coming death of the afternoon. "I've been given a powerful artifact that can be used against him and destroy him utterly, regardless if he passes his trial or not."

"How did all this happen?" Cadrissa put a hand to her head. "When did all this happen? I can't keep up with it all. I get kidnapped for a little while and the world gets turned upside down. Does Galba know all of this – of what you're planning to do?"

"Ask her for yourself." Tebow nodded to the red-haired woman.

Galba turned to Cadrissa then, a subtle hint of a smile upon her splendid face. "It was my doing that brought them inside this circle and brought you all together. You have been purposed with the defeat of this arrogant mortal – it is the final test." Her voice, though soft, bore a heavy weight behind it.

"What if he survives then? What then?" Cadrissa became lost in Galba's green eyes.

"Then Cadrith will have earned his godhood." The great Galba frankly replied.

"You will have to strike him swiftly though. He will not be able to understand his new powers at first and will be weak, weaker than he is now, and therefore your chances to overcome him increase greatly.

"Behold he now reaches the top of the dais."

Cadrith had slowly ascended the clean marble steps toward the top of the dais. He didn't know what to expect, especially since the task at hand seemed so easy; to just sit in the seat and claim godhood. He also didn't have the aid of his spells anymore to help discern things before him, and so was completely helpless should anything strike him now. One strike and he was done.

It was time to prove his worth.

He felt something lift off him as well as he approached the throne. It was as if a hand, which had been upon him since before he could recall, suddenly removed itself. Cadrith felt weaker in a way, somehow less of what he had been, even moreso than before with his lack of access to his own mystical energy. This was something different than that, but he couldn't place his finger on exactly what it was. However, he still felt like he could complete the task, after all, he just had to sit on the throne and it would be done. Surely he didn't need anything else to aid him…not now.

Resigning to move forward to his goal despite his feelings, he was relived in a small part when he got to the top without incident. He had made it to the top and not yet suffered. He knew that in his present state he would be unable to defend against – or even survive – an attack leveled against him. But then again he had his back door as well…

Cadrith examined the throne and the two statues near it. All three seemed innocent enough, but the two statues seemed to stare at him, following him with their eyes as if watching his progress with great interest. The Master couldn't quite place the two beings whom the statues immortalized, but he felt they were important for some reason, more important maybe than the throne itself. Again though, without his arcane abilities or a great amount of time with which to study, he was unable to learn more about them.

The throne itself, while large for his frame, was oddly inviting, as if it called him to just rest a moment in its embrace, to sit down and let the weight of the world leave his body completely. Seeing that it looked safe and his goal was so close to his grasp... he moved toward the throne, turned around and sat down.

Nothing happened.

The lich's face furrowed in confusion, then grew volcanic in rage.

"Is this some kind of *trick*?" He shouted back toward Galba. Turning toward her he saw that she was silent, and Cadrissa watched with an emotionless face beside her. He didn't see the others gathered around the wizardress watching him as well, however.

"If you've tricked me—" The lich's black rage boiled out between his lips.

"It is no trick Cadrith, just the beginning of your testing." Galba calmly replied.

Sitting in the oversized throne he felt like a fool, a child in the chair of a grown up. It had to be built for a giant, and he was barely able to get his hands across to each armrest with an exerted strain. The mage didn't notice its size upon his ascendancy. It seemed to grow larger only after he sat in it. He was about ready to get down and take out his revenge upon Galba, demanding she show him the true way to godhood, when the throne began to hum. Then it grew hot to the touch and Cadrith found his body awash with burning cherry flames. The throne lit up with vermilion runes which covered its surface all over; blazing like lava upon the white marble. The statues eyes themselves then shone with a deep crimson light which burst into flickering tongues of flame amid their previously dead stone eyes.

The Master screamed in horrendous agony.

His clothing evaporated in a puff of smoke, his skin seared away like bacon fat in the fire leaving the sinew beneath to melt like wax from his bones; the very gel itself igniting in flame so as to seem like flame pouring out fire. As his eyes peered down at Galba and Cadrissa, he now saw the others from the previous mercenary band standing behind the dark-haired mage before his blue orbs started to liquefy from the heat.

What were they doing here? Attempting to destroy him? The thought was laughable. They couldn't do anything – not now. Still though, he did his best to ponder it as he struggled against the pain, his vision fading for a moment as his eyes fled from his fleshless sockets like raw egg yolks. Within moments, the consuming fire abated to leave behind a blackened and heat – cracked skeleton.

"Is he dead yet?" Vinder questioned Tebow. There was no need to whisper now.

"No, just beginning the change…he yet survives," replied the younger priest.

The Master felt whole still, but lesser than the sum of his parts, as if he was being pulled away from himself; shredded piece by piece, layer by layer. At least his vision had returned to him. He had reverted back to his old lich-like frame – former guise of a mortal man now totally burnt away. No matter, he would have had to shed it anyway once he had ascended. He just wondered what was next for him. He didn't feel divinity seep into him yet and so knew the throne had yet to serve its purposes. Before he could ponder further though, the ancient throne bestowed more of it's nature on Cadrith.

Still emblazed with the glowing red runes, the throne then took on another transformation, this one more macabre. All the gems embedded in its marble flesh slowly transformed into eyes, their multicolored and stylized pupils opening like hideous flowers. The hard, crystalline surfaces folding back like colored eyelids so as to allow the maddening and alluring pupils their sight; bulbous orbs swimming about their stone confines. The Master could feel the eyes, could feel them looking into his very spirit and it chilled his bones to the core.

He felt them scratch and paw around his inner being with their gaze as a dog might paw around an area of interest. He could feel and hear his bones cracking, crumbling to dust around him as pieces of his skeleton fell into ruin like an ancient plaster wall. The sensation increased in short time, creating a domino effect until his entire skeleton sank into a dusty cloud upon the throne's seat. Cadrith screamed as he again felt the sensation of pain which he had been divorced from for so long now magnified a thousand fold.

In moments, the dust cloud cleared to leave a swirling blackness that still held a faint semblance to a human form with veins of blue fire that raced about the appendages and over the rest of the body now sat in The Master's place. The seat itself had become as white hot iron, even shooting off small geysers of flaring metallic sparks from where white marble had once existed as the eyes looked on and vermilion runes continued their irritating neon blaze.

"What's happened now?" Cadrissa softly spoke as her eyes remained fixed to the scene before her. It was too horrible to tear away from.

"His true self, his spirit, has now been revealed." Galba answered. "Now we see if he is worthy enough to take on the final test: the mantle itself."

"What happens then if he isn't worthy?" Cadrissa couldn't help but ask.

"As I said, he will cease to be. The very divine power the throne will grant is too much for mortals to hold onto. If they cannot be about the matter of will and spirit – the very substances of deity, then they cannot share in the powers and blessing such a benefit would bestow, and so must be destroyed." Galba calmly replied.

"You see Galba." The Master's voice tore itself out of the vaguely humanoid cloud. "I still exist!" The dark energy that formed The Master laughed in cascading, decadent glee. He was so close. His dreams and aspirations were only an arm's reach away.

He had succeeded!

He had won!

"There is still time to turn away from your quest." Galba's voice was calm and gentle amid his thoughts.

"Turn away? Now?" The Master spat the words from his spiritual mouth. "Never."

"You do not fully know the mantle into which you are about to step–" Galba continued

"I *don't*? Your tricks might have worked on lesser men over the years, but none who have been so infused with power as I, who have tasted it for so long and coveted since the beginnings of birth and beyond death itself. I am the one who will succeed! I have amassed the spirit and will to do so! I'll pass the final torment of this throne, then raze my enemies to the ground!" The dark spirit cackled once more. It was the jubilant glee of a tyrant finally gaining his victory over everyone and everything that had ever tried to stand before him.

"Does he always brag so much?" The dwarf shook his head.

"You get used to it after a while." Cadrissa shot a sideways comment to the dwarf. She was surprised she could still joke at a time like this. Absently her hand went to rest beside her side to where the secret pocket resided and the warm medallion inside it.

"Actually," the bird started, "He kinda reminds me of Endarien."

Their tepid levity ended, however, when a dark thunderhead boiled overhead, emerging from a clear and empty sky. It overflowed into the heavens, spilling over the horizon and dominating the circle itself, devouring the day with lightning-arcing night.

The Master looked up with his incorporeal semi-formed head at the gathering vaporous brew above him. He knew it was the final test, the final part of his mortal substance being torn form him so as to embrace the divine.

"You've failed Galba!" The Master shouted in delight.

As he was speaking a fat bolt of green lighting struck the throne and the thunderclap which followed shook the earth. Sparks and thinner, electrical strands of the strike shot out to the two statues, where it arced between them then snaked back to the throne as well so that the whole top of the dais were covered in a web of electricity.

"I've done it! You couldn't have stopped me, and now you will all suffer my wrath for daring to stand in my way." What remained of The Master rejoiced over the near maddening pain of the electrical current.

"Now comes the final trial." Galba stood motionless in observation.

"So then he might be killed anyway still, right? That's how I heard it, right? He could still die here." Dugan watched the event before him like a hawk.

"I doubt it. He seems to be more resilient than diamond." Vinder pulled out his axe from its holster, his body was tense. "Best to get ready. We'll be fighting like lunatics soon enough I'm sure. Seem fated to do so of late."

"At least we have a plan though." The colorful bird chirped from besides Tebow's head.

The others joined the dwarf in readying their weapons and minds for combat, while hardly stealing their gaze from the epic vision before them. Even Cadrissa made ready for what she could do. The more she let her hand rest near the medallion, the more at ease and stronger she felt. There were no voices this time, but a strong sensation of inner strength welling up inside her.

"Are you sure that scepter will work, Gilban?" Clara turned to look at the blind elf.

"Worry to your own self and I will occupy myself with the task at hand." The seer was pert.

Clara said nothing at the priest's words, merely pinched her lips shut and then turned and unsheathed her own sword. Gilban didn't notice these actions – his mind was elsewhere. The dark gnawing vision he had been trying to unravel since Doom Maker's island had finally parted, allowing him to see behind the previously restrictive veil. It was then that the old elf learned of his death. This day, this very hour would be his last.

He wasn't given any image of the final moment itself just a simple peaceful assurance his time had come. He smirked at the ironic nature of this insight. Where so many had come to him looking to seek their own time of death he now had advanced warning of his own demise, but what would *he* do with such knowledge? He didn't know what would happen next, save that his life would be forfeit regardless of the outcome. With such knowledge, how could he do anything but look to make the last few moments of his life purposeful and to give the others a fighting chance to get things corrected in his approaching departure.

"Well, for what it's worth, it was nice to see you all again. You too, Dugan." Cadrissa flashed a short smile to the warrior. "Though I liked you better without the greasepaint."

Well, she would have liked to have seen a lot more of him in truth, but she didn't think it mattered now. She doubted she would make it out of this alive and didn't want to hold to fantasies now. No, rather much better to have a sound and focused mind when the time came. Then passing would be at least a little better. Why she felt this way she didn't know for sure, but it helped her mind change gears from dreaming of the muscled, moody gladiator toward the matters at hand. The matters that were *really* the major issues at the moment.

Dugan made a small grin back.

Ah, she did love him though. At least *lusted* after him. Fool for her emotions, Cadrissa allowed herself one final indulgence in her dream life with Dugan before reality stole her away once more.

"Maybe when this is over you can wash it off and we could—" the wizardress said no more.

"A new god is birthed today!" The lich raised his spiritual hands into the air with laughter.

"You have still to prove your spirit can take the the new mantle it has now had placed over it. You are yet unable to boast, Cadrith!" Galba took a few steps closer to the dais.

"I have passed the test! I am a god–" The Master suddenly buckled over in midsentence. The web of dark green lightning that still covered him had intensified. His inconstant, swimming black form suddenly changed to a pure white light that seemed to shine like a star until his whole spiritual body was a mass of radiant snow white illumination.

"Agh. The fire burns through me!" The Master shouted as his body slumped forward, almost folding in upon itself.

"It purifies your being, taking out all vestiges of your once mortal life." Galba explained his fate. "If you are able to survive, all that will remain will be the godhood you crave. If not, then you will be burned away like chaff being sifted from wheat."

In a moment the form which had been The Master had changed. Where once it had been a black fog, pure light as clear and white as the day itself, emanated outward from the nexus of what was once The Master's spiritual body. All was silent. All was calm. For long moments none gathered could say anything. The action was beyond words and beyond all comprehension.

Chapter 7

The net of consuming green lightning had vanished.

The Master didn't say anything – it seemed he couldn't. Indeed, it appeared that the last trial he'd went through might have been his last. Only a soft globe of light remained where he had once sat, the darkness had left entirely and in its place was silent, tranquil light.

"*Now* is he dead?" Dugan asked Cracius.

"I don't know." The Asorlin responded with measured uncertainty. "I've never seen this before, no mortal ever has. I don't know what to make of it."

"Cadrissa?" The Telborian turned his attention to the young wizardress.

She didn't answer. Her whole attention was focused in the globe of light before them. It almost seemed to be speaking to her, like a faint echo she could hear in the back of her mind…and there was a sharp coldness in her joints as well…

"It would seem that Cadrith was not able to withstand the infusion of divine essence and is no more." Galba spoke in a dry, regal tone.

"Don't sound too happy now." Vinder stepped closer to the base of the dais to get a better view; hands tight over his axe hilt.

"I don't like this. Something doesn't seem right." Tebow scratched his chin absent mindedly.

"Gilban?" Clara turned toward the old seer.

"I have no vision of any of this." The old elf clenched his eyes and shook his head solemnly. "No, nothing."

Rowan stepped closer, stopping just shy of the base of the stairs, to peer at the shimmering globe. "So how long is that ball of light going to be there?"

He received no answer.

"Seems to me you priests brought us here to waste our time." Dugan huffed. "So when can we get away from this place?" Though, in truth, the Telborian had no real place he had to be, he was a bit uncomfortable with his present location.

"Be patient." The bird left it's perch on Tebow's shoulder to fly over to the ball of light, trying to circle around in what it judged to be a safe enough distance. "We'll all get home soon enough, if this is indeed the end." The bird sang happily as he hovered over the globe, it's eyes taking in every detail to relay to his master when he returned.

"Be careful." Cracius cautioned. "You don't know what that light is doing or what is going on. None of us do."

"I *am* being careful." It squawked. "I need a closer view through if I want to be sure The Master is gone for good before I return home." The colorful bird sang out.

Instantly, the globe swirled from white to a deep azure as the bird repeated his flight pattern above it and was suddenly shot by a bolt of blue energy from deep inside the globe. The bird gave out a pathetic squawk before it vanished from existence; singed out of the very fabric of reality itself. The bird's last tortured cry was followed by a deep resonate laughter as the globe began to pulsate with a rhythm similar to a heartbeat.

"The Gates of Asorlok!" Tebow shouted as he stepped back wide eyed and stiff legged, "The Master lives!" His hands drew tight around his hammer.

"Quickly, use the scepter!" Cracius motioned to Gilban.

Another bolt of crackling blue fire hit Cadrissa square in the chest accompanied with a scream. The wizardress fell back from the blow with a golden covering of energy enveloping her frame like some sort of transparent cocoon.

"Cadrissa!" Rowan ran to the fallen mage as another bolt rang out, this one directed at Galba. It got as far as ten feet from her person before it evaporated into nothingness.

"Gilban, get that thing working!" Vinder turned to look at the priest who was already chanting over the device with delicate hands.

"You've all failed!" The voice of The Master emanated from the blue light which now had taken on, and was continuing to take on, a slightly more humanoid shape. "I have succeeded! I have stepped over the threshold that no mortal has ever reached in their wildest imaginings!

"I am a god!"

"The time to strike has come." Cracius raised his silver hammer, the weapon shimmering to life.

"Now begins my reign." The Master's tirade continued.

Dugan ran forward from the others, a warrior's scream upon his lips. He raised his long sword in a violent arc, content on slashing into the blue form of light and rending it into oblivion. The Telborian's heart pounded and his vision was tinted red; the warlust was heavy upon him. His final battle had come and he couldn't be happier than to die fighting. He managed to climb the dais with little effort; bounding up the steps to the throne where pulsed the mutating entity. His valiant efforts allowed him to swing into the soft glowing form of The Master.

The sword fell into the azure light, cleaving deep into the essence of godhood. As soon as the blade struck, there was an explosion of illumination and energy like nothing anyone gathered had experience in all their life. Crackling energy followed wind then force, then cold. The blast was enormous and shook the very circle of Galba to its invisible and eternal foundations.

Bright blue streamers flew up and outward from the globe like sparks birthed from a disturbed campfire, scattering into the area around it. Dugan was flung high into the sky by the forceful eruption before falling to connect solidly with a violent impact into a standing stone. The Telborian hit the stone with a crack as his neck nearly seperated from his spine, splitting ribs that cut deep into internal organs. His very brain was ablaze by the crushing blow as he came to be crucified; each hand anchored to a post leaving him to hang midway between heaven and earth. It was in this time of suffering that his blurry, bloody eyes saw Asorlok coming for him.

In the aftermath of the explosion, which had knocked everyone but Galba down, a lone figure stood where once the azure globe had been. No longer seated on the throne, sneering down at those below the dais in contempt.

This figure appeared similar to Cadrith, but was a little taller and more muscular than what the wizard had been in life. He wore a deep blue diamond studded cloak under a robe of fine white ruby and emerald studded silk swayed with the motions of his limbs. His strong waist was tied by a leather, golden skull relief covered, belt which complimented the various rings, and a silver necklace he now wore with similar motifs.

The figure's countenance was radiant, and shined with a soft white light from the tan, healthy skin like the reflected gleam of the sun off calm, clear waters. His very expression seemed etched from stone; a monument to self serving power. Rich black hair fell to his shoulders like fragrant oil to meet his strong and rugged countenance which showed no more than thirty years under time's lash. His lips were like fresh blood, but his eyes were the most dynamic, a piercing blue, like the bright sky itself seeming to absorb all they surveyed. This was The Master as he saw himself, now reflected externally for all to see.

"Behold your new god."

The others stood with their mouths agape, their hearts fluttering and pounding in their ears and chest. Amid them was the carnal chaos of the battling godling in his rise to ascension. He had slain the messenger of Endarien, attacked and subdued Cadrissa, mortally wounded Dugan – all with the slightest of efforts.

What could they do?

How could they respond to such a display?

"Now that I have achieved my goal, you all can suffer the rewards of my success." The Master cackled with an electric burst of power and the air became tinted with a sulfuric aroma that singed the nose hairs of those present like small fires planted inside their nostrils.

It was time for their push.

At least, with a valiant effort, they could put up some form of resistance. If they didn't they would never be able to live with themselves in whatever afterlife was awaiting them. They had to try to at least stop him, delay him from getting any further in his plans...if not for a little while at least.

Together, the survivors rose.

Rowan looked at Clara, and then at Gilban. Both were now in their battle hardened composure. He turned to Vinder and the two priests of Asorlok and then spied the silent and fearful Hoodwink. What could he do? He knew the answer to that. Gilban had to use the scepter on The Master in order to destroy him. How would the elf attack though if he was blind?

Rowan knew that he'd have to help Gilban into position and that if he did, it would be a sacrifice of himself to do so. He knew it and somehow he accepted it as his call, his sacred duty to humanity, to keep it safe from the foul clutches of the newly formed god that would want nothing more than destruction and ruin for the world. He also knew he didn't want Clara or Vinder to do what he saw as his task to complete. No, to suffer for the task it fell to him; his heart and soul confirmed his plan. He just needed to make sure the others didn't stop him; try to take his place or mess up his only means of aiding the blind seer in hitting his mark.

Amid all the chaos Rowan noticed that for some reason the familiar voice that would have mocked the blind elf, would have degraded his worth, was silent. All he heard were his own thoughts, his own conscious and feelings and a peaceful reassurance deep in his gut that he had come to some place of truth as to how he really was at that moment.

Chad Corrie

"Vinder. Clara. We have to rush him so that Gilban can get to him." The others nodded their understanding of the situation.

"I'll help too." Hoodwink appeared from behind the seer's leg; looking up at the young knight. New dagger clutched firmly in his hand, Hoodwink was almost certain now this was his great destiny Gilban had told him about – it had to be.

"Sure," Rowan whispered, then tightened the grip on his shield and sword. He had no time to argue with the goblin. Now was a time of action, just as they had planned. "Ready Gilban?"

"Yes." The old elf spoke in a dry voice, his white knuckled hand gripping the scepter.

The stench of sulfur continued to rise in intensity along with the electrical energy in the air around them. "If you bow to me, I might spare your lives." The Master took a step down toward them. His hands glowed with a navy aura which danced around and between his fingers, which was mimicked in the depths of his cruel eyes.

"Now!" Rowan shouted.

The company rushed forward, Vinder and Rowan on either side of Gilban who was protected by Hoodwink in the front and Clara on the opposite side of Rowan, next to Vinder. Gilban had taken up the scepter and spoke a final prayer to Saredhel, his aim would need to be true for he knew his life was over, only having one attack to make, a final sacrifice for the good of all. The two priests of Asorlok charged up the outlying edges of the dais to try and flank the new god and smite him with their sacred hammers.

In the midst of this assault, The Master could do nothing but entertain a hearty mirth. "You cannot harm me now. I am *immortal*, *all powerful* and *immune* to your *pathetic* attacks."

"We'll see!" Rowan swung his blade. It hit The Master's outer body and stopped short of any penetration, like it had struck solid rock instead of skin.

Vinder's axe as well as Clara's sword met similar resistance. The Master redoubled his laughter as each blow, which should

94

have wounded if not dealt a death blow to any other being, did nothing to the dark god.

"Fools." The Master struck Vinder with a glowing blue fist which caused the dwarf to go flying into the air then land hard upon the ground with a pummeling force some distance from the skirmish. Once grounded he immediately convulsed in agony as electric blue bolts transferred from the strike riddled his frame. A moment later, Clara was struck by the new deity in the chest. She fell to her knees in pain.

"Clara!" Rowan went to the elf's aid.

Clara looked back at the knight through her teary eyes as she coiled up into a fetal position before The Master, her body shaking from wild convulsions.

The dark god screamed as he let loose a fiery bolt at the dais-ascending youth, which Rowan countered with his shield. The flame struck his shield dead on, flicking tongues of fire – trying to seek their way to the youth behind the protective disc. The blast was intense and Rowan fell to one knee on the lower steps of the dais to hold it back, pushing all his weight against the shield, teeth grit in defiance and spirit set to see his every ounce of substance spent in removing this monster from existence.

"Fall! Fall!" The Master chanted in rage as he continued his fiery assault, even taking a step nearer the knight to intensify the searing geyser. "Pathetic excuse for a man. Just give up and die."

"No." Rowan growled, sweat pouring from his forehead from both the effort and heat.

Cracius then charged up the left side of the dais, his hammer blazing like the sun. It struck the dark god with a thunderclap. The Master growled forth his rage as a black ripple pulsed through his body.

"Insect!" The Master shouted as he punched into the chest of the death priest with his free hand, having it exit the other side of his ribcage with a sound that reminded Cracius of celery stalks being torn apart as all other senses quickly fled with his life.

"Go home to your god." Cadrith flung the dead priest off his arm where he burst into flames before he hit the ground beside the dais.

Tebow followed with his own attack from the right side.

"Asorlok curse you." The older priest swung true, hitting Cadrith square in the face.

The hammer hit hard, but The Master didn't apparently suffer from the attack. Instead, he took hold of Hoodwink who had been rushing forward, dagger still in hand, instantly whisking him up from the dais. Hoodwink tried to fend of the gesture but was unable to do so no matter how hard he tried. The Master's grip was like iron, and the action so rapid, the goblin could do little to prevent himself from barreling toward the grassy ground rushing up to meet him. As he fell a burst of orange light shimmered over his whole body – a dazzling light that was beginning to swallow him whole.

And then the goblin was gone.

Again a black ripple swarm across The Master's form. He could feel his newfound strength ebbing from him, being eaten by the devouring spirit of The Gatekeeper. He needed to get free from the area without suffering any more attacks or he might indeed be destroyed. He had yet to learn what he was capable of, and he was beginning to see, that was a dangerous place to be when confronted as he was by a myriad of annoying but determined adversaries.

Cadrith recoiled from the recent blow to snap his focus squarely on Tebow. "For that I will hear you scream."

It was at that moment that Gilban struck.

"Now I save the world from a terrible monster." Gilban shouted as he raised the scepter high for the upcoming downward strike. He only had seconds to make this work. The opening allotted him and the surprise he had would only last for a heartbeat at best.

"Wrong, you've only delayed the inevitable." A swift strike from the Master broke the neck of the old priest which sent him tumbling to the ground, hand holding the scepter falling limp and dropping the silver object in his fall.

"Gilban!" Somewhat recovered from the recent fiery assault upon his own person, Rowan made a mad dash for the new god in his rage.

"I've had enough of you too." The Master made a dismissive gesture toward Rowan. The knight was struck by a blaze of purple light which came to quickly to block with his shield so as to shudder over his whole body before sending him to the ground shaking uncontrollably.

As all this was happening, Tebow had raised his hammer to do one last swing but was stopped by The Master who caught the weapon in its downward arc with his right hand while grasping the throat of the priest in his left.

"I'll be seeing your god soon enough priest…as he begs for his own life at my feet." The Master then threw him from the dais where he landed with a hard thud upon the ground, his body convulsing with thin stripes of ruby lightning, which tore into him fiercer than the lashes of a barbed whip.

Seeing that only Galba remained, he smiled even though he continued to feel his hold over the divine energies within him stabilizing. He was still weak and unskilled in its usage and should be free from here if he wished to gain a better understanding of what he had accomplished. For a moment though, he chose to address Galba once last time.

"You won't stand before me in challenge?" The Master half mocked, half challenged the entity.

Galba remained both calm and seemingly unimpressed with the new god. "You have proven your worth to handle the divine energies now inside you. However, the true test is what you do with this new found identity you hold. How will you wield it, and with what skill?

"I am unable to hinder you from whatever choice you make or path you choose to pursue. You walk the divine road as your own person, free from any restraints that hold mortalkind back in their own existence."

"That is all I needed to hear." A soft laughter ran from the new god's lips like a gentle stream of pleasant rain as he vanished to a place where he knew he'd be safe till he could come to terms with his new nature and plan his next action. In his wake he'd left the horrid evidence of chaos, death and doom – a foretaste of his plans for all. A deep sadness was also present and hovered over all the wounded and dying. It seemed to whisper of things to come and echo the loss of those gathered in Galba's domain, an echo of the world's own coming lament.

It seemed to offer no hope.

Yet, in the midst of the seemingly impregnable gloom, there was still a glimmer of light, an ember of hope which had not yet faded away, but was quickly cooling to ash in a pool of churning pitch.

Chapter 8

In their dwelling place outside time and space the two entities of opposing substance had finished watching all that had transpired in the circle of Galba. The Darkness was quite happy with the result, rolling about the span like jubilant, crashing ebony waves into the shore of Light around it.

"See my triumph? It is all coming to an end now." Its words were joyous and harmonic.

"I see nothing but your pawn moving on to yet another task before your final move is made." The Light's voice was measured and calm, as the obsidian waves crashed against it. "Things are still in play."

"All those who you have called together have failed." Roared the Darkness in sinister mirth. "I have won!"

"True, they might not have stopped your vessel from accomplishing his ends, but there are still more that I have called who yet have to act and those who have failed in this attempt shall yet have more opportunities to hinder your agenda."

"Hold out your hand to whatever vapor of improbable hope you wish. As long as you abide by the rules it is no concern of mine." The Darkness had grown calm again, coming to resemble a vast starless night sky, "Tralodren shall be consumed and my growing desire for its annihilation shall be satiated." "What if *your* vessel fails?" The Light then questioned.

"He can't. He won't." The Darkness was confident in success.

"You choose to focus on one vessel only, placing a great deal of faith in his success to see your own plans met. Already you have come close to breaking our agreement by interfering with him to get your vision met. Should he fail, all your hopes would be lost."

"Close to interfering *directly,* but just close enough to prod him onward. I have done no harm to our agreement."

"He could betray you." The Light glimmered like a condensed sea of stars.

"I am expecting he will." Replied The Darkness. "It is his nature after all and why I chose him in part so long ago to meet out this task."

"So you still believe you'll be able to control him then now that he walks as a godling rather than mortal?" The Light's tone was inquisitive, more so than The Darkness thought it should be, but it put little stock in it since it was already confident in the progress of all that was transpiring on Tralodren.

"If you are hoping he would rebel now, then you are hoping in vain. I am more than capable of reigning him in for the final leg of his purpose.

"Once the servant releases who it is he really serves then rebellion is quelled for a time…he will do as I wish, have no fear."

"I wouldn't expect anything less." The Light repeated the truth to The Darkness. "The rules have to be obeyed after all and each has to call forth what they have known since the beginning."

"Enough of this talking then. Action is about to take place finally and I hunger to watch." The Darkness purred with a wicked delight.

The two then grew silent and turned their attention to Tralodren once more…

Chapter 9

The gods started to act.

Their unanimous vote assigned them to the single action of backing Endarien in his attempt to defeat the now deified Master. In agreement, they set out to use the last remaining shreds of power and substance that had been their great father, the first god of all, to empower Endarien in his battle and help him overcome the barrier that blocked the planet from a direct, divine corporeal presence.

After this vote, they had convened deep beneath the Hall of Vkar, to where the last bit of the first god's essence was stored away. Even though now much of the world that had once been the seat of a divine empire was shattered in a field of rocky debris, this chunk of Thangaria in which they stood still held many mysteries. The cavernous depths under the hall were unsearchable, as were much of the foundations of Thangaria. It's tunnels would trail off into nothingness and into stranger places still that were connected to the old, long-forgotten and disused realms since before Tralodren had been formed.

Like much of the hall above, below the hall felt like an old shrine or museum; a relic of the days that once had been and would never be again. No gods explored the tunnels any more, no one had a reason to. The cosmos had changed with the death of Vkar and Xora, a sudden and irreversible change that forged the current Pantheon from its ashes and brought the order and semblance of the current party who now traveled the ageless tunnels and hallways with silent reverence.

Ganatar had lead the council down the snaking stone spiral steps to the resting place of his father's remaining essence. Behind iron clad doors, twisting tunnels and yet more stairs they traveled. Lit by the radiance of the Lord of Light's presence himself, the tunnels slithered to a cold, empty and silent dead end. It was here, amid the naked and feral rock walls, that a small, plain silver chest sat nestled into a tight niche about waist level to a man.

Gently, Asora pulled the chest free from the niche. The container was no larger than a human heart might be. Her delicate hands gave the touch of warm life to the cold inanimate thing. The other gods were hushed in their response as she took the small box to her chest, walking it back to them who had now formed a circle in the open area of the tunnel.

Asora, goddess of life, found the act that they were about to do troubling. Here she held close to her heart the remains of her father, the last piece of his essence and yet, it had to be sacrificed to save more lives. Though she understood the purpose of the sacrifice and their current need, she still felt the pang of the action that must be done – sacrificing life for life. With this in mind the goddess entered the middle of the circle, which closed behind her as she did so. Taking the center of the circle for her mark, she then looked at Ganatar.

"Let it begin then." Ganatar addressed them in an even voice.

Silently, Asora opened the chest. As she did an aggressive aura of illumination covered the area, even overpowering the luminescent presence of Ganatar. Together the gods dug deep into the contents of the chest, using their own will to draw forth which had been held inside for eons. They had to subdue it, and make it obey their will. Though Vkar had been strongest of the gods, and still held such rank in death, he was not able to stand against the collective will of his prodigy and the race gods even in their adoptive guises.

In a moment the Pantheon had a hold of Vkar's essence, wrenching it free from the chest and changing it into a foot-wide globe of bright red light which silently hovered above them.

"Now we must send it to Endarien," Ganatar continued.

Once more, the gods concentrated their wills upon the action. The globe became hot and flared with a life all its own so much that the room they were in suddenly seemed to become the center of the sun, and then the globe was gone from sight. The council looked at each other in silent agreement with still, stoic faces.

The action was complete.

It was in Endarien's hands now.

Endarien, Lord of the Wind, hovered over the peaceful deep blue orb of Tralodren. Scattered with dark green and brown islands and continents, it seemed too idyllic, too perfect to be home to the dark vices and nature that plagued its inhabitants, but the gods knew better. From high above the world, a world among a handful of others which made up the solar system where Tralodren resided, none would imagine or indeed be able to see a mystical barrier powerful enough to hold back a god's entrance, encompassing the planet.

Indeed, only the gods themselves could see it as it was they themselves who put it in place. The barrier was meant to protect the world from the divine incursions of their fellow gods. When Tralodren was formed, a council vote had agreed that only in the manner of indirect intervention and adopting a guise tied to the world (this being the semblance of mortal flesh) would they be allowed to interact on the world itself. Understanding the dangers that could arise on the newly forged world after the countless wars that had plagued the cosmos before and during the foundation of the current Pantheon, so mortalkind would be free to make up their own minds, live their own lives without direct divine confrontation, only guidance from the Pantheon which mortalkind could accept or decline as they so chose.

The gods would only be able to act chiefly through their followers and then in various natural expressions related to their dominions, along with messengers they could send from time to time. They also agreed to be allowed a form of interaction with the world in a slightly more direct sense, but only with mortal flesh, not divine.

This meant that they created the manifestation of themselves as a mortal creature they called an avatar, a being of mortal flesh with a spark of the divine encased within. Though similar in nature to mortalkind because of their construction, the avatar was a real suit of flesh the gods, and indeed divinities, could use to house their natures. Through these forms they managed to circumvent the barrier and ruling of direct intervention but were still limited when compared to their true selves in terms of interaction. They would have to follow the rules of mortalkind and nature, and so their true self would not be present, but a weakened mortal expression of that self could still walk the world where they so willed.

When the race gods were raised to godhood, during the aftermath of the Imperial Wars, the divine council wisely waited until their spirits had departed the world and then they brought them to godhood by divine consent. Doing so allowed them to be raised to godhood without trapping them on Tralodren, behind the barrier, where they would be able to do incredible harm if they so wished without any divine restraint from the council.

It was just such an action that The Master had done: he attained godhood inside the barrier thus being blocked from leaving Tralodren, but also being protected from divine encounters. Endarien knew this as he hovered over the barrier, and it was the major reason he had to be stopped now before he grew too strong a hold over Tralodren. Only with the last remaining essence of Vkar could he hope to circumvent the barrier for not even a divine decree from the council could undo what had been said without destroying Tralodren in the process.

The god of the air waited with growing impatience in his divine form, the true nature of himself, for he knew what had transpired below. He knew The Master had risen to godhood and that even now he grew in power and understanding of how to use his ever increasing abilities to become a greater threat. This couldn't be allowed to continue for much longer, or it would all be for naught as the dark patron who backed the godling would surely return to him and make him much more challenging an opponent as he was now, even with the essence of Vkar running through Endarien's veins.

While in the council or in his recent meeting with Saredhel in Sooth, Endarien, like the other gods, adopted a form suiting the environment. His real self looked different than his adopted frame that was just a simple avatar. However, it would only be in his true form that he could defeat The Master who would not be on the same playing field as Endarien.

Endarien, in his true form stood fourteen feet tall, his body a massive collection of sinewy tan skin bedecked with a silver breastplate emblazoned with golden eagles with outstretched wings overlaid a pure white toga covering much of the god's upper body. On his feet he wore black leather sandals with silver grieves shaped to appear as the upward arching wings of a great bird; a match to the silver bracers motif on his forearms.

At his back, Endarien was held aloft in the emptiness of space by two majestic cordovan wings, akin to those of a hawk but speckled and sprinkled with gold that shined like the stars. His head was crowned with a bronze helmet shaped like the head of a hawk in mid-screech, the opening between the beak was where the god's face could be seen; his radiant yellow, avian eyes scanning the globe below him in eager anticipation.

The god had come to do bloody battle, and so held in his right hand his famous spear, Heaven's Wrath. This great long spear was crafted of solid light; the searing intensity of lighting itself, and stretched into a twelve foot length. It's crucl head sparked with electrical pulses and arches of life thirsting to be unleashed on those it engaged. His left arm held aloft a large circular, silver shield with the detailed relief of a hawk in flight reflecting back the light of the sun, which blazed behind the god toward the world below. The shield was called Storm's Eye and radiated a gentle golden aura of its own which seemed to be like the beating of a heart.

Donned in armor and armed for war the Storm Lord's patience was waning as he waited for the other gods to act. For though he knew what was happening with his fellow kin, for indeed a portion of himself was in the council under his chosen guise, he still grew impatient over the matter.

Though, as he waited that began to change.

Silently at first, Endarien felt something swim around him. It was subtle but soon grew in intensity. Fixing his keen vision on a distant crimson star he squinted, then smiled. The time had come at last. Within a blink of an eye, the red star had grown closer, flying toward the god at an incredible speed. In a heartbeat it was mere inches from him and then struck him full in the chest, causing the god to double over from the impact.

Vkar's last speck of substance had come upon Endarien.

Neon red lightning sparked and arched about the god's body, riddling him with a spider web of living illumination. It was like liquid fire, flaming oil over his body, mind, and spirit, but instead of consuming him, *Endarien* consumed *it*. The last remnant of the god Vkar came into his very mind, overshadowing various aspects of his being and molding it into a new and grander image of deity than before. With this essence the god instantly came to know the secrets of the cosmos, more so than he would ever find in his existence. Knowledge and insight that went beyond even the grasping of a god flooded the halls of his thoughts as he supped deeply the tide of insight that was his grandfather.

Endarien had to fight against the onslaught of confusion that came from the bombardment of the images and thoughts of his grandfather's mind, having to focus instead on the task at hand. For though he would have loved to take in their rich meaning, he didn't have much time. He needed to find the answer to break down the barrier or all was lost and this last bit of Vkar would be wasted.

Endarien struggled to straighten up his frame then followed with his mind. The essence of Vkar had entered into his spirit now and was enforcing it with its own presence, making him strong enough for the task to come. Body awash with red electrical currents, his eyes flared with magenta fire. With them, he could see the way past the barrier. Stretching forth his left hand he touched the protective surface invisible to all but divine eyes. The very action caused a ripple like that of a pebble in a pond upon its cloudy surface.

The god smiled.

"Your time is over Cadrith."

Taking Heaven's Wrath, he jabbed the sparking spear into the barrier with a shout that sounded like the screech of a thousand birds of prey. Thunder boomed from the impact to echo in the cosmos beyond. In its wake a hole quickly spread over the barrier like an ink blot on white cloth until the opening had grown large enough to allow Endarien to pass. Seeing this, the Lord of the Wind closed his eyes and began to glow white hot, blazing about like a star, then turned himself so that his head faced the opening; wings fluttering about in the airless vacuum to place him into position. Then he disappeared down to Tralodren below as a fast bolt of vengeful lightning.

Even as a great quake of thunder rolled over the world and out into the outer reaches of the cosmos the opening closed in on itself once more, like the healing of a wound with not even a thin scar to mark where the opening had been.

And once more silence reclaimed the solar system.

Chapter 10

The Master materialized near his tower. It rested on an island far from civilized lands in the Yoan Ocean, one of the land masses called The Wizard King Islands. It was from here that his journey, aided by the annoying, yet beneficial Cadrissa, had taken him to his goal of godhood. A goal which he had now attained. He'd fled here in hopes of gaining understanding into his new nature. He needed to prepare for his plans to come and none knew of his residence on the island save Cadrissa, and should she track him down…well, he had placed a safe guard in order to stop that situation from becoming reality.

The dark god appeared on the island from a burst of azure light in the same form he'd adopted upon ascendance in Galba's circle. He thought about his last trip here after he had been freed from the Abyss. It had been many weeks ago now, distance and time were distorted to him in their mortal meaning as he came to understand his newfound godhood. It was but one of many new changes he was noticing. Now he returned in force to take up what few items he still needed or desired for his new existence and then begin to claim rulership over the planet – and then the gods themselves.

He had toyed with the idea of using his tower and the island on which it sat as his home, but decided against it. He needed some-place new that would allow many more to understand his power by seeing it first hand. The Master also knew the gods couldn't come down to the world in their natural form, this being banned from them. He also knew that if he became a god on Tralodren, then he would be trapped on the world unable to leave it, instead, having to use intermediary methods to reach beyond the world, the very opposite law to which the Pantheon was bound.

While it was another type of prison in a way, it also protected him from any deities who might have wanted to do him harm, allowing him to grow in strength and control virtually unopposed until he was strong enough to make his next move, assuring that he could then rule Tralodren as he saw fit. This was the wisdom of his plan and really the other assurance he had to safeguard himself from harm. So far all had seemed to be following it quite nicely.

The Master stood on the grass and looked at his hands as he held them out in front of him. He tried to bring a spell to mind but found that it was blocked in the attempt. Angered, he tried again only to have it rebutted once more. Was Galba still hindering him? No. She had told him she wouldn't hold him back from his plans. As he struggled through in what had once been so normal, indeed second nature to him for centuries, a deep well broke inside him and filled him with immense energy; a flooding of electrical might that surged out his fingertips and toward the sky above him.

The Master laughed at his success.

He had been thinking like a mortal wizard, trying to cast his spells from formulas, corrupted ancient phrases and esoteric training. This was not the way of a god at all. Deities were beings of will and spirit, all he had to do now was think of a desired result and the deed was done, even his own words could bring things into existence.

Putting this new understanding to the test, the dark god thought of hovering above the ground and instantly found himself floating over the grassy hill, his feet no more than a foot above the soil. It was like no spell he had ever experienced before. So fast acting, so potent, and so limitless in scope. Only his will and the strength of his spirit hindered him. He knew that in time, with training, such actions would become second nature to him as his magical mastery had been before.

He realized though that he would have to grow in his mastery of divine nature before he could do much more. It wouldn't come easy to him, but he was prepared to do what it took to see his abilities raised. He would need to think some things through a bit harder now until he got more skilled but was confident he'd meet with great success sooner rather than later. He had always assumed once he raised himself to godhood it would be easy to enact his plans to gather followers, incite worship of himself and build temples in his honor and for his praise, but now, as his mind drifted into the concept of eternity, he felt a tug at his core being.

It told him to let go of his former mortality – the frail fringes of his own inner world to which he still clung and framed his thoughts; to abandon what had once been for the new-to-be reborn entirely. To do so he knew he needed a new form, the one in which he resided now was too limiting, too…mortal. He couldn't place how he understood all this just yet, but he knew what he wanted – what he was, and also understood that it had to be reflected in his outer self as it was in his inner self to make the transformation complete. This yearning thought was birthed from deep inside the core of his spirit where the river of eternal divinity bubbled forth to water his whole being.

An image, a truth of his own nature, then came to his mind as The Master saw his soul, closed his eyes and made the thought manifest itself. When he opened his eyes he discovered his whole appearance now reflected his inner self: his skin had turned an extreme pale white, the color of snow or marble, his eyes glowed a soft blue and his hair was short and black. On his body he now wore pure black, form-fitting robes over which a long, high collared, charcoal gray cape rustled in a gathering breeze. The dark god was overjoyed with the result, and thought the outfit was simple yet elegant and regal enough to house his frame.

Holding out his right hand he conjured up a staff of pure darkness which shimmered like wet tar. Force of will shaped it into the semblance of wood, and on its tip rested a black pearl the size of a man's fist. It was getting easier to control the power of his transformation. It flowed about him and ran over his frame like raging rivers. The whole sensation was beyond gratifying. Even as he marveled at his new found powers, however, he felt a twinge in his being.

Like needles riddling his body, poking him all over, the dark god knew another, more powerful being like him was on the horizon. The thought was troubling in and of itself for who could be his equal on this world if all the other gods were hindered by the protective barrier to Tralodren?

Nevertheless, he knew that another great being was coming. The Master knew there were other weaker forces at work in the world that were beneath deities but greater than mortalkind in their abilities, but didn't believe they would threaten him. No, this was something much greater. The feeling grew in his awareness so that he learned it was another being of substance equal to his own…another god.

Even as he pondered who or what was coming, the sky grew dark and thunder rolled across the heavens. Cumulous collections of dark grays and blacks spread over the once blue canopy like a growing cancer for as far as The Master's eyes could see.

Then came the birds…

The avians burst forth from the dark mass of clouds like rain, splattering and scattering over all that could be seen. They descended upon the grassy field and outlying trees around the open glade with such a massive flutter it sounded like an army on the march, covering every blade of green and leafy branch with a rainbow of feathers and beady eyes which all looked at The Master – beaks squawking some sort of rebuke. Song birds and parrots, ducks, geese, quail, birds of prey and even a collection of rare flightless birds milled about the island, surrounding the dark god.

A great screech then rose over the constant rumble of thunder followed by the sound of massive wings lifting up a gale to flutter about The Master, scattering stray debris and a whirlwind of feathers his way. Looking up, he saw his tower had become a roost for a Roc, the golden beak of the creature giving off a defiant flash

at the newly ascended god below. Indeed, the rest of his tower had been dominated by still more birds. Ravens and kites, doves and hawks perched amid whatever foothold they could find alongside eagles and vultures, condors and falcons and a host of smaller gay hued creatures.

Looking higher, the dark god could see still more circling about the island. Below the clouds they flew in continual circles, their own heckles and cries adding to the unsettling medley of others who had managed to find a roost. Hissing, chirping, cawing and screeching amid sharp musical rebukes Cadrith gritted his teeth in anger. Behind him – all about him, they covered the trees to form their own feathery canopy. Hundreds of beady eyes stared back at the dark god with an unnatural light of malice burning inside them.

Unable to move without stepping on a bird (something he would do without the least amount of concern) he stayed still, for he knew who had come to face him. He knew this was just the prelude – the audience gathering for the gladiatorial game which would soon begin. His challenger would make his appearance very soon…

It was then the wind picked up, becoming a screaming zephyr against The Master. His new frame was battered by the gale, yet it left the birds all around him untouched. Just how or why Endarien had come to Tralodren The Master didn't know…yet. He knew it was a desperate act for the god of the air to risk being trapped here – regardless of the battle's outcome…a foolish and impulsive choice, but that was the Lord of the Wind.

Swifter than an intake of breath, a colossal, white bolt of lightning shot down from heaven like a javelin. Parting the slate clouds above as it exploded into the ground before The Master; birds scattering in all directions. The impact fiercely rattled the earth in unison with the burst of thunder which would have shattered a mortal's head, but left the birds present unaffected. In its wake the bolt created a good sized crater, sending up debris in all directions. The Master had to right himself with his staff to keep from tumbling over from the blast and into the newly formed pit before him as a purple globe of crackling energy protected him from the flying chunks of rock, dirt and sod.

From out of the ten-foot-deep crater the golden helm of Endarien craned up at The Master. His head, tops of his wings and shoulders were free from the wide maw of shattered earth as he stood defiant against his foe. Even with much of his body sheltered by the crater, Endarien was an overwhelming sight. Heaven's Wrath crackled in ravenous hunger which found audio companionship with the spits and snaps of the opaline serpentine bolts that snaked and popped around the god's skin and even leapt off a short ways from his divine person, as an attacking cobra, where they fizzled into nothing with a spark filled snap.

The Master met the gaze of the god's large, yellow eyes. They were strange avian things dipped in the rich oil of bloodlust. Around the island the thunder rolled and the birds continued their cacophony. Winds went wild and danced drunkenly about the place, first from the east, then west, then north – crashing together with great force upon The Master who did nothing but hold onto his staff as he stood his ground.

His own eyes meet back Endarien's anger.

He would give no quarter and not back down.

It would seem their final fight and the dark god's first challenge had come earlier than he expected.

Chapter 11

ollowing their release of Vkar's essence, the Pantheon
had returned to the upper levels of the hall. However,
they didn't return to the former council room. That place's time
had come and left. Now was the moment to see how their decision for action fared on Tralodren. They couldn't discern such an
outcome from the council room, having to travel to yet another
ancient and majestic, nearly forgotten room in the Vkar's former
palace.

This room was massive, seemingly too conceivable to be
placed inside the whole hall. Built as a circle, its fresco- and
mosaic covered stone walls rose some one hundred feet into the
roof where they met overhead in a painted dome. The archaic artwork spoke of times now past when the hall itself was the center of
Thangaria, the world that dominated an empire ruled by Vkar. The
images on the dome were of the first created race, called Titans,
who were locked in battle with one another, scattering blood and
violence all about.

Titans were not alone in such a feverish battle, being joined
here and there with a whole varied host. Angelic beings fought
against demons and dragons, Titans clashed with forces behind
the inkling of mortalkind to fathom; great and awesome creatures
long since forgotten through extinction bloodied the field as well.
The whole image, though old and faded with time, still could be
made out from below the dome in places, especially where the
images of Vkar and Xora dominated the landscape, towering over
all before them as regal reavers of death and destruction.

At the dome's center was a large lead crystal window. Pure and plain, it funneled unadulterated light below it in a fat, continuous ray. This shaft of light fell into the center of the room below where there rested a clean, calm pool amid a brass basin, deeper than a human was tall and four times wider than that. A granite lip perked up around the pool's edge where silver rails were worked in a delicate form of twisting vines amid slender, cylindrical poles that tied it all together as if it were a simple fence hedging all out of its confines – keeping the pool as still and clean as possible.

This great chamber was the domain of Xora, first goddess, wife to Vkar, and first mother of all the gods of the Pantheon save the race gods. The goddess was fond of divination, a trait she passed on to her daughter, Saredhel. While her husband reigned over his great empire, she would aid him in seeing into far off corners of lands and worlds where rebellion might be brewing, gathering intelligence or even seeking the future of events to come.

When she too fell by Vkar's side during the bloody ending of both his age and empire, the pool remained with the hall as the last of Xora's legacy. Since that now distant time the gods had taken to using it well, converging from time to time to watch events when they were so warranted by the Pantheon as they were now. While none had the ability to peer into the future (as did Saredhel) and try to discern fate, each could use the pool to peer into Tralodren and see its present situation.

While not master scryers like Saredhel, each deity also had a manner and method for peering into the various worlds about the cosmos in their own realms, but were unable to gain access to any here save Xora's pool. This pool, also called The Great Eye, was the most powerful scrying device the gods could ever use; for it could see farther and clearer than their own methods – even superseding the impressive abilities of Saredhel should anyone arise with such divination abilities to challenge her.

They would all need to watch together to be ready for a sudden vote that might come up in the process of viewing. Being present was crucial to make sure matters were resolved quickly – as with the current episode that brought them here again. All would watch as Endarien battled The Master for the Pantheon. Each hoped for a swift and relatively easy victory. None knew for certain though what might happen as there were things at play in this event that were beyond their power and abilities to stop. Matters such as the patron of The Master for one thing...

Despite this, some of the gods believed the Storm Lord could best the upstart mortal. Others were not so open to declare their thoughts and still a handful thought the boastful god had finally bitten off more than he could chew, and now would smart for it; perhaps with his very own existence as well as pride...

Regardless of their varying thoughts on the outcome, they still all entered the massive room with a silent reverence. Each filed in from behind the tall, arched oak planked double doors and across the black, white and gray marble checkerboard tiled floor toward the pool. Like dutiful monks, each god found a spot beside the calm water, behind the railing, drew their full attention to it, and was silent.

The pool reflected back their faces, and though they were all different gods, followers of opposing philosophies and natures, in their reflection a unity had been found: serious faces and troubled minds. Only Olthon broke their contemplative silence.

"Are we prepared then to take the actions necessary to insure our survival should Endarien fail?"

The faces grew more grim upon the goddess' remark. Though they didn't want to speak it aloud, they had seen the havoc that had followed the last encounter with the dark patron of Cadrith and knew what would follow should Endarien fail. It was something that caused some gods to even ponder the ancient prophecy of Saredhel which told of them their own demise...others were not so pessimistic as of yet.

"Let's give him the benefit of the doubt first," Panthor spoke up.

"I'm ready to do what it takes should the windbag fail." Khuthon clung on to the silver railing in a death grip. "I just want to see this battle first." His smile was alight with a sinister mirth.

"So then we watch and the deciding factor comes to play in the end. Win or fail, the vote has been made, and this council has ruled." Ganatar swept his hand over the waters.

"Are you all ready to take up arms should Endarien fail?" Olthon repeated her concern searching the gathered gods with her golden eyes for someone else who believed as she did.

"That was what was agreed to," Dradin added dryly.

"I am aware of this, but are we sure that there is no other way?" The goddess of peace returned, obviously saddened by the turn of events and inability to find another of like mind on the matter.

"The time for debate has ended." Ganatar made a strange motion with his hand. The calm surface swirled with a rainbow hue, then congealed into a single scene, conveyed in crystal clarity. All the gods peered down into the forming image . The blotches of color soon merged and cleared to reveal Endarien and The Master coming to blows.

"Olthon-" Khuthon started, but Asora, his wife stilled his tongue by placing her hand on top of his.

"Your husband is right, sister," Asora's soft green eyes soothed the emotions of Olthon, "The time for debate has ended. We are all pledged to follow through on our commitments."

"Even you?" Olthon wanted to push the matter harder with Asora, knowing how much she hated the loss of any life.

Asora remained silent as she adjusted her gaze toward the pool once more where Khuthon was already grinning with glee at what he saw from the pool below him.

"So far it seems just fine." Khuthon's face was feral with excitement. "Endarien seems able to hold his own."

"What if he becomes trapped on Tralodren?" Asora added softly. Her eyes were touched with a bit of fear. "He could become locked behind the barrier regardless of this battle's outcome when the boon we granted him finally fades away. What should he do if that happens?"

Rheminas smiled at the thought. His yellow eyes flickering with some hint of inner glee. "I don't think we need worry about that. Endarien isn't that foolish, and it won't happen to him anyway. Not with the infusion of Vkar inside him now. It will take some time for the last of grandfather to work his way through him."

"Still," Asora continued, "should that fail him and he be victorious, he could be trapped on Tralodren forever."

"Our cousin knew the risks when he took on this task. We have no love lost for such an event occurring, if it should, for we accepted those risks with the rest of you when the idea was presented and brought to vote." Perlosa's cool eyes never leaving the pool as she spoke.

"Would that be such a bad thing though? To have all of Tralodren to yourself..." Drued rubbed his beard in thought.

"But you would be trapped there." Olthon tried to reason her point, "cut off from your own realms and domains as well your followers, you might even lose your vote in council."

"But you would rule Tralodren." Khuthon laughed a hearty mirth at such an idea. "Not the most intelligent of ideas, but you–" the god jabbed his fist up toward the sky. "That's right Endarien! Make him suffer!"

"Enough of this talk." The rebuke of Ganatar silenced all gathered. "Let us watch this battle unfold."

All then turned to the pool once more.

All that is save Gurthghol.

The Shifting One's eyes were elsewhere, his mind working the angles of some great thought brewing in his mind. Somehow this didn't seem right. He was starting to see something of deeper meaning in what Saredhel had said. Now he was starting to plan an action based upon this speculation and desire to follow through on what he felt was left unfinished. He wasn't concerned like Olthon but there was something not totally right about the whole matter, and he was getting a greater insight into what. Something bolder than anything he had done before was bubbling up into his consciousness and it gave the god of chaos delight. Delight because it would be solving all the problems they now faced and allow him a brief change of venue for a while…and of course be tremendously entertaining in the process. If he was correct in his thought process, he'd have a very different venue than before…maybe bringing a change that will shake the very cosmos itself.

Chapter 12

The battle was over.

The Master had won.

Alone and broken Dugan hung from one of the stone portals. Each hand was affixed on opposing posts where they anchored his bruised, battered and bleeding flesh like a butcher's hook. The only thing holding the Telborian to the stone was a twitching bolt of purple energy crackling about his wrists and digging through his hands, pinning him to the rock.

In between and behind the grievously wounded Telborian was a wondrous scape of beauty. A soft sage and heather covered hill meandered up and over a few other mounds of land around it like some drunken turtles trying to play leap frog. Clear skies and tranquil air danced about the venue, but the gladiator who hung in front of the scene could take no part in its delightful presence.

Dugan could barely keep up his struggle for consciousness. He couldn't feel his legs or much of his arms past his elbows. He felt each of his cracked and bruised ribs as they clawed his lungs with each struggle for breath. His head had sunk into his chest; chin digging into his sternum while his neck screamed out in agony. Blood continuously ran into his eyes from the myriad of cuts and gashes in his scalp, blurring his vision with fiery tears.

He had forgotten what had happened before; what led him to this predicament. It was getting hard for him to think – to bring any sort of focus to his mind but with momentary flashes of insight, like heavy cloud cover parting to reveal the sun, he was able to remember some things with rare illumination.

He recalled a violent shove of force from The Master, and then the cracking of his back, the lolling of his head and the searing set of claws assaulting him from within as he felt as though he was being continuously nailed up to the stone posts making up Galba's circle. The Telborian had also been raised a good four feet above the ground where his blood had dripped, yet still trickled and streamed into a dark growing pool beneath him amid the verdant grass.

It was as if he was being crucified.

A grim smile haunted his face for a moment at the thought. His fevered brain told him he was dying. He knew there was nothing he could do to stop it. He was damned, and Rheminas would come for him soon enough. He had made his peace with the god already, was content to die once before and was so resigned in this instance as he hung before the stone portal which had now changed to reveal a barren desert land; dunes of toffee colored sand replacing the lazy, lush green hills. At least he would have these last few moments of freedom in this life before he crossed over to the realm of The Vengeful One. He could at least derive some bitter comfort in that.

It hurt to think about anything else; hurt to try and lift his head or look out further than his blurred vision would allow. What he could see was negligible at best. It seemed he rested in the middle of a battlefield. Bodies lay all about him, some dead, some dying and others gravely wounded.

He had seen such scenes before.

In the arena he had often caused such carnage and lived with it on a daily basis. Now, however, it seemed a faint glimmer of reality, an echo of some former thing; an afterthought at best. He felt his weak vision fading, his concern for the reality around him slipping away. His body felt lighter, much lighter than it should. He even began to wonder if he was still breathing as it seemed he had lost feeling in the rest of his body as well, a strange euphoric rush of deadening nothingness washing over his frame as the stupor of death's embrace overtook him.

Somehow, amidst everything else, it felt now as though he was on a real cross, a wooden one, its splinters digging deep into his back as he struggled for life even as it flowed from him. In his mind's eye he could see the crowds around him witnessing his death...The crowds of the coliseum of Remolos once more shouting and jeering at the Telborian, the gladiator who had suffered his whole life for their amusement now entertained them by his own execution. He had returned to his former home and prison even in death, never being free from it so it would seem. The irony was deeply seated.

As his mind faded more from where he was and fled deeper into delusions of the past and things that never were. Even as he hung on the cross in the arena he saw his life being played out before him. Like ripples on the surface of a clear lake they reflected back his forgotten life before the times of bondage to Colloni.

He saw himself as a child, a fair-haired scrawny youth from a village long since lost to Elyelmic expansion. He watched as his younger self played with a small stick swinging it as if a sword as he fought off imaginary monsters and villains. There was an innocence, a purity about the boy that brought a deep sadness to Dugan. He saw what he had lost, what had been taken from him by the hands of the elves and years of compelled service in bloodletting.

The images grew darker and his mind felt fuzzier than before, a blurring even of these images of his mind and memories occurred and soon all faded into senseless darkness. Only a faint voice echoed to him from some long distant time and place. It was beseeching the god of death, Asorlok, to hear the petition of the speaker. Dugan thought it amusing to hear that as his last words into death. Had he more strength he might have argued against such a petition to the god but he had nothing left with which to make even a feeble stand.

Nothing else mattered anymore...

"Asorlok, hear me I pray," Tebow cried out to his god.

His robes were singed and lacking in some locations, his hair had burned away with much of his scalp and face and a thick black ooze leaked from his ruined flesh that now seemed more like burnt cherry pie than skin and muscle.

The death priest had managed to stand on his wounded legs and move to Dugan where he placed his charred hand upon the limp leg of the Telborian who hung dying between the stones. Even though his hand had suffered much, the priest could still feel the growing coldness congealing in the Telborian's veins. Tebow had barely survived The Master's attack. Cracius, had taken the worst of his fury, having already greeted his god before the older priest. Tebow felt that in these last minutes allotted him he should at least do some good.

Tebow didn't fear death, rather, he welcomed it. In his faith, he believed he would get to serve his god even in the afterlife by ushering souls to their final destination. It was into this place that he knew he was drifting when he felt compelled to arise and do his final tasks for the dead and dying. He needed to perform last rites to those that would soon pass into the great gates of the Sovereign Lord of the Silent Slumber. He especially felt compelled to address and aid Dugan. Though he didn't fully know why when compared to the equal amount of death and destruction about him...he simply did as he felt compelled to do; as the remaining fragments of his god's spirit in him – which he could now feel again near the last moments of his own life – told him to do.

So he raised himself with great pain and moved toward the Telborian with heavy labored breath. He could sense the Telborian's life breath fading away. He knew he had to hurry to perform the last rites for him to ease his passage into the afterlife.

He deserved that much, as did the others who had tried to stop The Master along with him and had failed. For a moment Tebow thought about what his god would think of him for failing in this task. Both he and Cracius had been unable, even with the great anointing of their god, to destroy The Master. What would their fate be as ones who were so favored of his power and then who failed in the divinely appointed task? He pushed the thought from his mind at the moment and turned to the dying Dugan. He figured he would find out the answer to his question soon enough.

"Asorlok, Lord of Death, Master of the Afterlife, I humble myself before you and beseech you for a fair and peaceful transition for Dugan, a man who died in service for a great cause, one that you yourself have issued to myself and Cracius, your fellow servants. Give him the assurance that he needs to pass over without regret, without anger and without fear. Grant him peace."

Dugan moaned for a moment, then opened one lone, blood-shot eye to form a gooey, crimson, slivered almond allowing him to take in the priest.

"W-what are you doing?" The Telborian's voice was dry, cracked and weak.

"Rest Dugan, be at peace." Tebow looked up at him. His own visage was far from the image of calm that he had wanted to display and encourage in the gladiator.

"I'm in the arena again. I-I see them…I have splinters in my back…" Dugan drifted between this world and the next.

"You're going to be with the gods, Dugan, and your ancestors. Be at peace, don't fight it, let go and rest…sleep." As soon as the priest had finished speaking the Telborian's eye closed again as his breathing slowed, then stopped. The great chest fell like a bellows one last time and then Dugan was dead.

"Safe journey brave warrior." Tebow allowed himself a small rueful smile that could not totally be discerned from his ruinous features as he looked on the dead Telborian one last time.

Turning, he went toward the others to see what help he could be before he too died from his grievous wounds. As he moved on

Tebow took a mental inventory of who would need his help, and who was left alive. He knew that Hoodwink was probably dead for he'd seen him vanish in a flash of orange illumination. Cracius was dead, and so now was Dugan. Tebow added Gilban to the list when he noticed his fallen figure amid the grass. The blind priest's neck had been broken; his body already growing cold. He would have offered up rites, but the priest followed a different god and while Asorlok ushered all on to their final destination, Tebow didn't know what rituals were right and proper for a priest of Saredhel, and so thought it wise to let the body lie. His spirit was already with his goddess anyway.

So that left Clara, Rowan, Cadrissa, and Vinder. All of whom had been wounded and might very well be near death themselves. Hobbling over toward where the others layed out in bruised, pain-filled displays, he wondered where Galba was. She had seemingly vanished after The Master's ascension. The death priest supposed it mattered little now. At least to himself. Still though, it would have been nice to have figured out at least in some part where she was – what she was. He supposed he'd find out his answers, if there were any he could gleam, soon enough. He moved closer to Vinder who lay a little ways from his feet.

The dwarf was solemn as he fought to stay conscious and emotionless though savage pain screamed from deep inside him. His body and clothing were pockmarked with black circles from where burnt skin and cloth overlaid his formerly gray skin: the remnant of electrical bolts that had seared through his body mere moments before. His hair was singed, salt and pepper beard was partially burnt from his face, his steel gray eye still blazed though, determined to live. Only the necklace of Drued, given him by his old friend in Elandor remained unscathed.

Tebow looked down at the dwarf.

Vinder looked back.

Much of his armor still remained, but parts of it smoldered blue-gray, greasy plumes where smaller circles of the studded leather had burned away like an ember on parchment. His right hand was still strong though, and gripped his rune-etched axe with a white knuckled grip.

"You promised…" His lips were cracked and bled with his words; a collection of black gel globbing out of his mouth.

"Vinder–" The priest moved to bend down toward the dwarf.

"Don't…you…dare." Vinder's eye blazed defiantly.

"Don't what?" Tebow asked.

"You promised…honor…" More blood flowed over his chin, down his singed beard and chest where it spilled out around and behind his head and neck like a grisly pudding. "Once…once this was done…you told me…I'd have…my honor."

"So you were promised," Tebow stated.

"Don't rob…deny me…not now. I upheld…my duty…did what was…what was right…"

"No Vinder. I shall not back down from a promise I made to you under the eye and enforcement of my god. You shall have the honor you were promised, rest easy in that." Tebow placed his hand upon the battered and bloodied chest of the dwarf then closed his eyes.

"No tricks…" Vinder huffed.

"No tricks." Tebow repeated. "Asorlok, god of death, grant this warrior the honor which he so sought in life in death as he now comes to greet you at your majestic courtyard and throne for judgment. Honor the promise given him by your priests and bring it to past so that you are known as a fair and impartial god – and that you look favorably upon your priests as well as honor your word."

No sooner had Tebow finished his prayer than Vinder looked up at the death priest with a grim smile, then began to fade away before him, taken by the power of a prayer toward his final destiny in death before his great journey in the afterlife began. In the blinking of an eye the dwarf's figure grew dimmer and dimmer until at last it vanished from sight all together. All that remained was the small pool of blood on the grassy field to mark where Vinder's head had been. All else had faded away.

For a moment Tebow stared at the empty spot where the dying dwarf had lain, then stood up on shaky legs. He needed to act quickly. His own time was just about up. He moved on toward where Clara lay; her form sprawled out near the dead Gilban.

Clara had managed to sit up slightly and look at the scene around her, taking stock of what she could. She had been bruised on her chest and stomach and had taken a great beating to her shoulders and back. Moments after the battle, she had managed to station herself up from a lying position from which she fell after a great convulsion threw her to the ground. Using her elbows to prop herself up she spied Gilban who lay crumpled not too far from her.

Gilban's dead body lay on its side, his neck broken – head off kilter from its normal position, his face staring blankly into space. His blind eyes no longer able to hinder him, his inner sight granted by his goddess no longer of any use. Near him was the silver rune-etched scepter which his body half covered from view as his frame was still in the process of rolling over when he died.

She knew he was dead of course, and it was a very painful blow that wounded deeper than anything she had ever known. Gilban had been like a father to her in the past months of this journey and travel around Tralodren. Seeing him dead before her drew forth a great pang that she knew would stay with her for years to come.

Suddenly, Tebow came into her view.

He looked horrible and she knew he too was dying. His body was black and torn away like paper when it is first alight with flame, most of his hair was gone, and the remaining charcoal and crinkled skin on his face was barely able to hold the flesh behind it.

"Are you able to stand?" Tebow asked the elf.

Clara didn't answer. Grief had taken her captive as everything that had happened and the reality of the present situation became clearer; weighing down upon her. All had been for naught, the battle was lost.

"He's dead. We lost." Tears began to form in her eyes.

The burnt priest moved closer to the elven maiden with comforting steps.

"What are we supposed to do now? I-I..." Clara finally surrendered to the grief and wept bitter, soul wrenching sobs. They only seemed to increase when Tebow rested his hand upon her.

"Rest easy, you will survive, I can sense it about you. Asorlok has not called you yet. Take care of the others and help them recover. You're all they have left now to hold to. You have to be strong for them and the times to come..."

"You still-" Tebow was cut short as he fell to the ground with a heavy thud; body falling on its side so that his eyes, still locked in a gaze with the elf, dimmed away the last of their light under her gaze.

This matter was unsettling enough, but Clara was speechless by what happened next. Before her the priest's body melted into nothingness only leaving his ruined clothing behind as proof he had even existed. Struggling to turn to where she had a fair reckoning of where the priest's companion had laid, Clara saw he too had now vanished, only his clothing – what was left if it, remained.

Turning back to the remains of Tebow, her mind couldn't take in what she had seen – she had experienced far too much far too soon and now the old mantle of leadership which she had tried to take up and use with greater ability had grown heavier still upon her shoulders. How could she lead? Who would follow her? Why lead now? What was the purpose? Where would she lead them to when the victory had been taken from them?

After a series of chaotic moments, she managed to slide to her side, pushing herself so she ended up on her right side. She was close to Gilban and the scepter under him. Reaching out with her left hand she seized it and pulled it free.

She then proceeded to use the silver scepter to prop herself up, then rise to her feet in an unstable progression under agonizing effort. She didn't want to lead anymore, didn't want to fight. She felt beaten and tired, alone and afraid. This wasn't what she pictured on those fields when she had been a child watching her father's herds and practicing with her imaginary sword and armor. She didn't see the suffering behind such great efforts, only the end result: the perfect path to completion. She never even would have imagined about what it might be like to truly suffer defeat and have to deal with a weariness that seemed to seep up and through her bones themselves.

She wanted to die.

She struggled against her feet and made it to where Rowan lay unconscious. He too had suffered much under the deadly attacks of The Master. Her heart was relieved a bit when she looked into the face of the young Nordican. A thin line of blood trailed from his lip, though his chest still heaved, showing that he lived…at least for now.

She wondered what she would do now with Rowan too? Where were they going to go now? Would they even go together or move on in their own separate ways? Too many questions to wade through and her heart was weaker than her jostled bones.

The elf then turned her attention to the others around her, and found Cadrissa, who had managed to stand up as Clara had seen to Rowan. The mage's movements were weak and labored, her face lined with worry, fear and exhaustion. She looked to be the least wounded of them all – indeed her body, even her garb itself was unmarred in any manner whatsoever. It had seemed The Master had spared her his onslaught for whatever reason struck his dark humor at the time. Cadrissa's face went cold though when she saw Dugan.

Clara was silent as she also followed the mage's gaze toward the hanging gladiator then hobbled closer to him, using her falchion as a feeble cane. The elf couldn't quite process all of what she was experiencing and it would be a long while till she would be able to do so in the days that followed. For the moment all she understood was that Dugan was dead.

"Dugan!" Cadrissa screamed and ran toward the dead Telborian her feet nearly betraying her a few times on her rapid flight to the site of crucifixion. Her eyes filled with tears when her hand touched his cooling stomach. "Dugan. You're going to be okay – going to be okay." The image behind the Telborian had changed to a snowy wasteland - an arctic tundra of flat meaningless white winds. "We just have to get you down off this stone. We–"

"He's dead, Cadrissa," Clara's hand found the mage's shoulder, "leave him be."

"He's just wounded, he'll be okay." Cadrissa tenderly stroked the gladiator's muscular side.

"He's gone Cadrissa. There's nothing we can do…nothing any of us can do." Clara's eyes misted at the sting of her own words.

The mage could do nothing but weep and sob violently, as she buried her face in the fallen Telborian's lifeless torso. Clara did what she could to minister to the wizardress. She new the wounds of the heart, even if birthed in infatuation, were painful. Helping the mage cope with her grief the back of her mind pondered just how she would deal with the reality of herself and Rowan. She knew deep down that the two of them would have to come to the same confrontation at some point. The elf thanked the gods that Rowan hadn't left her yet there was that positive note in this dark symphony at least. She was so absorbed in her comforting that she failed to notice the scene between the stones change once more. The frozen wasteland was warping into a scene of a desert realm with tall ash-belching volcanic mountains, meandering streams of lava and roving consuming flames, which seemed liked living serpents of fire.

Suddenly, Cadrissa felt a warmth from under her face, where it touched the once cold flesh of Dugan. The warmth grew so rapidly that she had to pull her head back quickly to escape the heat before it would have burned her cheek.

Both women then stood transfixed at what they witnessed next. In a heartbeat, a geyser of flame erupted from the heart of Dugan and spread over his whole body, his entire frame being devoured by famished fire. It consumed him entirely, melting the man's flesh and blackening his bones instantaneously so that only fine dust remained. Dust which fell from the stone to the ground below. Only a thin layer of soot coated the two pillars where the Telborian's hands had once been bound. Then, just as suddenly as the image had changed, the scene in the doorway vanished, becoming simple blackness. Both woman were silent and would say nothing for sometime as the episode made its way through their minds.

Chapter 13

Vinder felt his very spirit become lighter as it tried to seep away from the ruined corporeal prison of physical substance that now held it back from the worlds beyond. He knew he had little time left and that had made Vinder's plea to the death priest all the more urgent.

He would not die without honor.

He'd been promised it by the priests and would hold them to their agreement, even if they themselves were dying with him. They owed him as much. He had done his part and now it was their turn to uphold their obligation.

He didn't really know much of what had followed Tebow's prayer. His mind was fuzzy, like someone was packing it with cotton. His vision grew more and more narrow, so that his view of things became more like he was looking through a tunnel. He didn't really think he could hold on much longer to life for anything and that, in a way, was fine with him.

He knew that Tebow was unable to heal his wounds since his faith forbade such things. In truth though, it would have been nice to come back to his family, his clan and be one again with them – be able to live with regained honor. He understood though that his final acceptance in death was just as important, if not more important to him. If given a choice he would choose death with regained honor, than more years with the ones he loved without it. He had come to peace with the understanding of his demise when he had stood at the mouth of Cael's lair. He knew he would probably die inside, but welcomed it if it would bring him the redemption that he desired.

Strange as it sounded, Vinder had an epiphany, as he lie dying. Only then did he come to know that the most important things in life *were* faith, honor and family. Duty was the byproduct of such ideals; duty to all three – which then became a proud tradition to uphold. Only now in death did it all make sense to him. For what would he leave behind? What would mark his existence on the world? How would he be recalled?

It was clear to Vinder then that life was not so much about being alive, but how one lived – what they left behind, and that was the basis for and strength of the dwarven philosophy, which he had only recently come to reembrace. For without death, life would have no meaning. There would be no measure with which to compare if one stood up to the test of time or produced something worthwhile within their given days of existence. No, here was the purpose and meaning of it all. And it was here, on the precipice of death that he learned what he should have been living for in life.

As he pondered this epiphany, he didn't even realize that the scenery about him had changed. The green grass under him had given way to cool, rocky earth. The blue sky had darkened into a foggy pitch and the stone circle itself had become a womb of rock. There was something familiar about this place. Even in the gauzy haze of his mind he found his subconscious drawing parallels to familiar remembrances.

Vinder struggled to sit up from his prone position. His fading vision scanned the area around him and a smile traced its way across his pale and worn face even as a scarlet liquid cough ripped out of his lungs.

He was in Cael's lair.

He noticed the dead Troll's bones beside him then. Its skin and muscle melted away by the prayers of the death priests to leave the empty bones behind. A hollow, meaningless thing now, the dwarf fixed his narrowing gaze upon it. It would be the last thing he beheld when Drued called him to his ancestors.

As he contorted his upper body to better view the Troll's skeleton, he understood that it wasn't enough. This wasn't going to get him his lost honor. He may have been willing to die before in battle with the Troll, but now his foe was dead. Failing to fall in battle won't win him anything if he died alone on the cold stone ground. Though those who might find his corpse later might assume he died in battle with the creature, he and Drued would know the truth, however. His family may have been comforted in his death by perceived restored honor, but Vinder himself would be unable to rest in any afterlife knowing the truth of the matter. Worse still, if it wasn't believed that Vinder died in battle his death won't do anything for his family and their lost honor. His death would serve no purpose for them and their loss would be two fold. For they not only would have lost a son, but some honor amid the clan as well. No, something had to be done for them and for him.

Suddenly, Vinder's back give out, his head lopped backwards and his body grew cold and slack as he slammed into the rocky ground. A bloody groan escaped the dwarf's mouth after the short impact and it jarred his mind toward action. He had one last thing he could try.

Slowly, he managed to fight against the cold numbness of his flesh to turn his head toward the skull of the Troll beside him; forcing the growing blackness that swallowed his sight long enough to fix his gaze upon the skull's empty sockets. For what seemed like a great span of time he spied the jet pits and jaws which would have rent him limb from limb, split his bones and torn his flesh. Now they were dull, blunted and silent; impotent in death. Then Vinder had an idea to remedy his troublesome thoughts.

In one last burst of will, the dwarf called upon the deepest reserves of life that yet remained free from Asorlok's gates. It would have to fuel him for one last action, an action which he thought could at least restore honor to his family. It was the best he could do for them in life. He would have to face Drued on the merits of his own life, as all dwarves did, and live with the verdict his god decreed. He would leave behind at least some comfort to his family though for all he had done to them by his past selfish actions...

Vinder forced his numb right hand, the hand that held his axe, to tightly grab the weapon. Slowly and laboriously he focused his mind, his will and his faith on the task. Watching the skull of Cael fade further into darkness before it disappeared all together and his heartbeat ceased to resound in his ears, he took a deep, rattling breath that was smoothed in blood. It was slow, painful and labored, but gave him the strength to do what was needed to be done. Vinder let out a powerful yell which helped to fuel the weapons arc toward the neck of the skeleton, severing it with one hit and sending the skull rattling off against the nearby wall like an out of control child's toy top.

With the strike, the last of Vinder's life flooded from him, his spirit was set free and his body became like the clammy lifeless rock around him.

The deed was done.

Silence then returned to devour all inside the lair.

Honor was regained.

Chapter 14

ᕙᕗ

"**Y**ou're breaking your own laws Endarien." The Master shouted over the screaming gales and squawking birds. "I can't believe the council granted you permission to face me. This is a very grave risk you take: breaking your own rules; upsetting your own balance of things."

"They have granted me the joy of bringing about your death by my own hands." Endarien's voice echoed into the horizon like rolling thunder.

"Really?" A sardonic smirk crossed the dark god's lips. "Last time you boasted such a feat you died screaming in agony by *my* hands. Do you think much has changed now? Why not just leave now and live. I'm a god now and we're on equal footing. When you were unable to fight me in your true nature I won. Ascended as I am now, how could this time be any different?"

"You faced only a representation of me before godling. Now you face me in my truest manner and in that there will *always* be a difference." With that Endarien released a silvery aura which rapidly grew brighter than a solar flare. The Master felt it dig into his own divine flesh and tear away at him, dissolving his own essence like vinegar to baking soda. The intense experience was almost unbearable, so much so that the dark god fell to his knees, keeping to his staff for balance lest he fall over completely into a fetal position and give the god of wind even more to gloat over than he already possessed from his attack.

"Ha. You look to do battle and you can't even withstand the mere *presence* of my being." Endarien lessened the radiance of his aura, making it a soft ambient light again as he climbed out from the crater; large strong hands lifting up his gigantic frame from the impact crater. He would enjoy teaching this upstart what it meant to be a god.

As soon as Endarien's aura diminished, The Master willed himself to fly upward and out of range of the god and future efforts of such attacks. "We shall see. If you wish to fight me-" The Master could say no more before twin bolts of hoary energy burst from Endarien's eyes and struck the dark god in mid take off.

They hit him so fast and with such force The Master had no time to react and was flung through the air for miles, before the sea embraced him; it's bottom cushioning his jarring impact. All the while the rays of light were like vipers gnawing his bones; picking away at who he was, what he would be. The Master was unable to process the sensation. It was something he had never known was possible to feel, let along endure. The wounds gods could inflict on each other were truly amazing.

Once The Master knew what was happening he willed himself to stop falling deeper beneath the depths of the sea as the dwindling serpentine rays of light had wished and instead to stand before the rival god. Instantly, he stood before Endarien once more on the avian littered ground of his island. Time and space mattered little to the effort of thought, will and reality in the way of divine understanding of things. The dark god had come to realize it wasn't so much the strength of the body or as he once thought, arcane insight that gave divinity its power, but the muscle of imagination – will and spirit that was key. Back before Endarien The Master's garments weren't wet nor was any part of his body, which he had also willed to heal from the grating recent attack of the Storm Lord.

"Impressive Endarien." The Master's tone was mocking in reverence.

Endarien responded by a swift jab of his spear.

Heaven's Wrath violently dug into the island's crust, where once The Master had stood but a moment before. Reflexes born of willpower had spared Cadrith from the strike. Thunder echoed the movement; the gathered audience of fowls clamoring their own cheers to their god.

"You learn quickly, Cadrith." Endarien's eyes shimmered with an amber glow. "It will not save you, though. You'll be dead in a moment and the cosmos will be rid of you forever."

"We shall see." The Master glared up at the winged god.

Blue jets of flame blazed out of The Master's eyes toward Endarien. Like coiling serpents they entwined his frame, searing his exposed skin. The hawk helmed god was stoic toward the attack. A shrug of his shoulders and wings dislodged the clinging flames; his body and garb unaffected by the blue coils.

"Is that the best you can do *godling*?" The older god threw back his empty spear arm. A glint in his yellow eye was all which proceeded the volley that shook the earth as a bolt of fierce lightning exploded through The Master, continuing its path into the island beneath him. Birds scattered and spun about forming a symmetrical funnel cloud high above the island below the depressed and turbulent clouds as the ground shook as if under the duress of an earthquake.

The Master himself was shoved down to land in a small smoking crater which had instantly formed beneath him. The echoing thunderclap covered over Endarien's laughter and cries of the gulls and Roc.

"That is how gods fight!" Endarien drew closer to the smaller depression where the dark god lie. "I'd thought you'd have mastered some more of your abilities by now. You always claimed to be a great study and the most powerful mortal in the world. Seems to me as if you are the most pathetic god to have yet arisen."

The Master didn't move. Not yet. He needed to wait for the right moment for action. It seemed this fight would be a bit more challenging then he had first envisioned. He smoldered inside the pit which was ripe with the fragrance of ozone. An attack that would have incinerated a normal mortal did little more than give him a slight feeling similar to a bruise. No matter, he could – and still would – win out over Endarien in the end. The crater was just deep enough to pull the dark god down into a five-foot drop, but not enough to swallow him whole. He could get out of it quite easily when he had to…

With will and spirit he would be able to heal himself once again, reforming himself in wholeness as per his newfound understanding of self. It was when the will gave out and the strength of spirit dimmed that gods began to die and lost their hold on existence. Cadrith was far from that reality.

"Come on Cadrith." Endarien walked closer to the lightning wrought crater and peered down upon the seemingly motionless body of his prey "Get up if you can and attack me. You're always declaring your mastery of power, show me your power as a god, show me your worth." A swift move uprooted Heaven's Wrath, and directed the sparking tip toward the dark god's center. This would be far easier than Endarien thought.

A silence fell down upon the scene, the thick clouds stopped their motion, the lightning and thunder ceased. The avians halted their cries, and even the air fell still. All the world seemed to be waiting for the result of this battle, a final sparring that would see the end of The Master, with baited breath.

"You'll never win." The Master thrust his hands into the air as he rose to his feet outside the lip of the crater. The action was very fast and carried the land with it so as to shoot up all around him. Moving toward Endarien like a worm, its rocky maw swallowed down the god in one gulp, piling him high with stone and sward pulling him under, deep into the island. Upon this attack the birds scattered in a flutter of feathers from the grassy glade to roost on the tower and trees and in the slate colored heavens, circling above for any sign of their creator and god.

Arrogant and vain thunder and lightning paraded across the heavens, but The Master remained silent. It was too soon to declare victory, he had to prepare for his next act. He knew it would take far more to defeat Endarien than what he had just unleashed. The dark god quickly jabbed his night colored staff into the earth then worked his hands as if mixing dough to form a ball of pure black energy that crackled with its own malevolent lifeforce.

"Let's end this now." The lich's words were dry and purposeful.

Before The Master could do anything else, however, a column of red fire burst up from the ground beneath him, swallowing him whole. In an instant the unquenchable flame had reduced the dark god to charred bones. The Master's will was unable to stand against such an attack. He couldn't even begin to for it was the will of Vkar that he fought now, not Endarien's. His strength faded from him like sweat from pores. He knew he was dying; knew he'd lose the battle of wills and spirit and fade from existence in moments like a puff of smoke.

"It *is* ended." Endarien's voice echoed back at The Master though he couldn't see him any more, only sense him above, floating high in the gloomy, bird riddled clouds above mocking him.

"You were never meant to wear the laurels of godhood Cadrith, they don't suite you." Upon speaking, Endarien slowly fluttered down from the sky, his great wings parting the charcoal vapors and mist before him. His jubilant expression quickly melted away though when he gained a better vantage of the battlefield below. What was happening was impossible…

The tattered remains of The Master were being reenergized; reformed into the semblance of a whole once more. This was unheard of by the god. None could stand against Vkar. None.

"How is this possible? I destroyed you. How can you still come back from the brink of desolation?" Endarien hovered above transfixed at The Master's condensing image. His charred bones were now rapidly healing themselves; fresh and clean skin folding over his pinkish sinew. "Unless…" the words were a whisper on the wind.

Endarien had forgotten about The Master's patron in the excitement of the battle. He hadn't played this as well as he should have and now would have to deal with the results as best he could.

He'd let his anger of the lich govern him more than he should and failed to see what he should have been prepared for.

"It seems even you cannot destroy me as easily as you once thought. Imagine what will happen when I gain full understanding of all the abilities that I now possess." The Master's voice faded in and out from existence as he began to flutter like a flag in a strong wind.

"You will *die* and stay *dead*!" Endarien finished his descent with a speedy charge, Heaven's Wrath lowered to skewer the impudent godling to the ground. The spear's sparking point got no farther than an inch from The Master before his body was swallowed whole into a nothingness. Endarien, unnerved by what had just happened, had continued his charge. Heaven's Wrath stuck into the island with a jerk which sent the god somersaulting so his face landed in the crater where The Master had once languished.

A violent curse blew out of the god's lips then Endarien struggled to stand. Seeing he was alone now the hawk helmed god lifted up his arms as he voiced his rage to the clouds above where it echoed with the hundreds of birds still circling around the battlefield.

"You won't be able to hide from me forever. You can't leave Tralodren. You're stuck here and there is nowhere on this world where you can be safe from me."

"Nowhere!"

Silent.

It was too silent.

The Master didn't know where he was. His ethereal eyes swam across the pitch scene before him, taking in nothing at all. He was unable to know *what* he was. The lich was blind and confused; a wraith hovering in unfathomable darkness. Recent events rushed by him as a blur. Nothing seemed to make sense.

"This won't help you Endarien." The Master shouted around the pitch black emptiness that threatened to devour him.

Silence.

"You can't win Endarien and you know it…"

Again, the dark god only had empty silence return his comments.

"That was very foolish, Cadrith." A new voice soft as silk slithered all around the misty image of the dark god.

It wasn't Endarien's.

"Who are you?" The Master tried to seek the speaker out.

"You could have faded away before you completed your task." The voice ignored the question.

"Where are you?" Again Cadrith looked about the landscape to discover nothing that would aid him in his quest for answers. "Where is Endarien?" All was a wide expanse of dark emptiness; expanding nothingness. "Where am I?"

"Were it not for the part you play I would have let Endarien kill you." The voice took on a hateful tone. "Now, it is time to be about what is really of import and stop this childish rant for power and your already inflated ego. I have no more time to waste on your idiotic and reckless actions."

The Master didn't know what the voice was talking about but wasn't about to be spoken to in such a manner and was about to unleash some of his new found abilities against such disrespect when he found himself somehow powerless. He was unable to do anything, enact even his will for a desired effect. All he could do was hover in place and listen to the disembodied voice insult him.

For the first time in his unnaturally long life he felt the tinge of fear slide down his spine. For once he wasn't in control and seemed like he wouldn't be able to reclaim it anytime soon. For once, he began to have a glimmer of insight into the presence about him and recognized that it was something even greater than a god. He didn't know how he knew this, but The Master understood that it was something which existed on a level to which he could never ascend. Such a proposition was unsettling to him to say the least and rattled him to the core.

The voice didn't speak for some time, as if it could read the dark god's thoughts and wanted him to come to an understanding about his current position. After some more empty moments, the voice then returned.

"Listen now to my words. Obey them and you yet may survive."

Endarien stood under the dark canopy of clouds gnashing his teeth in rage. He gripped Heaven's Wrath with alabaster knuckles. Anger, thicker than molasses, coursed through his veins and he craved nothing more than to release it full force upon the one who had kindled it: Cadrith. No matter where the dark god hid himself, Endarien would destroy him. Turning with a gust of brooding air, he spied The Master's tower. This would be the perfect spot to begin his search for the cowardly godling.

Letting loose a scream, the god of the air flung his spear toward the demon shaped doors at the tower's base. Changing into lightning, in mid-throw, the spear impacted the barrier with an earthshaking rumble which shook the entire island, shattering the dark wood and its locking mechanism into fiery splinters. This was followed by a mass exodus of the avian life which had previously roosted on the ebony structure. As if one mass, the many-hued feathered frames scattered with caws and cries, screeches and chirps fluttering to the trees and the sky for safety. Even the large Roc who had made its roost the tower's top lifted into the stormy sky.

"Come out and face me godling!" Endarien made his way toward the charred opening. Small puddles of flame were now bubbling up through the grass where bits of debris and small sparks had conjured up the fire. As he neared the doorway, Endarien's size diminished. Each step brought him lower and lower in stature until, by the time he reached the doorway, he resembled a human man in height. Stopping to pick up his weapon, which lay on the flame sprinkled grass around the opening, Heaven's Wrath changed in proportion to match his new height.

He then entered the tower.

Inside it was a wonder of richly decorated art and fine tapestries. In truth it seemed more a museum than the former home to some fiendish mage. Rich rugs sat under exquisite furniture that seemed to have been made only for the use of kings. Entering the interior, he discovered it was larger inside than the outer structure of the tower could allow. More tricks birthed of Cadrith's magic, Endarien assumed. He stopped in the middle of what could have been called a lobby. Here he spotted many odd, horrifying and beautiful objects from all ages and places on Tralodren. Sculptures of elven maids bathing, powerful dragons, great griffins cast in bronze, unspeakably obscene creatures ripping young human females apart and other collections of artistic merit dotted the immediate vicinity. The god was far from impressed though.

"Come out Cadrith," Endarien mocked in cold glee. The god's voice traveled far, but not throughout the whole tower. He knew this just as well as he knew Cadrith wasn't here. So where had he gone?

"At least you won't have your tower to return to," the god of air snarled. Endarien strolled to the first black marble step of the ascending stairs and stopped. He closed his eyes in concentration and within moments, his body had become a living tesla coil. Rings of electrical fire rose and fell off from his body in a crackling rhythm echoing the snaps and pops from the god's spear point. He held these rings to his presence for a short span more until he finally released them in a cascading explosion of lightning which leapt and galloped all over inside the tower.

Hounded by hurricane force winds, the ravenous bolts charged up the stairs and laid waste to everything in their path. Metals melted, precious stones were pulverized into powder and tapestries and other flammable objects caught fire and quickly transmuted into ash. Fanned on by the fierce winds which rallied behind them, these fires cruelly ravished their victims; devouring all they could in their supernaturally accelerated hunger. The destruction continued all the way up the stairs which cracked and exploded from the lightning's heat as it tread up the ascending spiral spreading the wrath of the Storm Lord all around – sowing seeds of destruction everywhere it could.

The bullying winds jogging behind toppled statues, torn down wall coverings, blew in countless doors and scattered other treasures and mysteries of the tower. When it could, the aggressive gusts burst into close chambers housing books and scrolls. In these it toppled the archaic shelves, throwing the volumes to the floor, scattering scrolls to tattered dust. Nothing was left to survive intact.

The destructive edict of Endarien assailed even the outer door of the room which held the green globe that had trapped Embulack long ago. Endarien knew this, as he saw all that was happening in the tower, for his eyes were in the gales and the hot sizzle of the lightning. Embulack had long been a prisoner of The Master and for his freedom he had agreed to bring Cadrissa to Endarien. That had been the first time the Storm Lord had tried to defeat The Master after he had returned to Tralodren.

It did not go as he had planned.

Cadrissa did come and the battle he had wanted with the lich had come to pass, but it didn't go as he had planned either. He hadn't expected to be defeated. In truth, he wasn't. It was the boon of his dark patron who had aided him in the battle even then. Because of this he was unprepared to look after Cadrissa as he had promised.

Somehow she had survived though. Probably due to The Master's ally from what he could gather from Saredhel and the others in their secret cabal on Sooth. It was of little matter now. She had failed along with the others to halt The Master from taking hold of godhood, and now it was down to him to set things to right…and take his revenge. But first, he would honor his promises.

"You've waited long for release Embulack." Endarien's voice came to the green lit room from below. "And I honor my promises. You did your part and now I shall do mine."

The globe behind the now shattered door was struck with lightning, shattering it into a hundred green-tinted fragments. Only a small bottom portion no larger than a jagged lipped bowl remained to churn out green mist like the yolk of a broken egg. Pooling around the dwarven skeletons which had for so long held the globe, this mist seethed and swarmed with a life all its own as it began to take on the semblance of Embulack. No longer wounded as he had first appeared to Cadrissa, he now was whole and pure in shape as he had been in life before his death.

Looking at his hands, which he then placed to his face in disbelief, the spirit smiled. Though still translucent and far from living in the mortal sense, the former Wizard King was free from the trap of The Master and able to finally travel to the afterlife and enjoy the consequences which his mortal life had afforded him.

"Praise Endarien." His words were raspy and weak like the breath of dying man, but his affection and joy was overflowing. Resting his hands at his side, the slain Wizard King rose into the air growing more vaporous and indistinct until he melted away into a green mist, which hit the ceiling of the room to fade away like fog before the dawn.

The ancient door that once held the spare body of The Master was next in Endarien's assault. It couldn't withstand the god's assault either, being split into two charred halves. The wind picked up and scattered the dusty remains of The Master's former body like a small tornado, kicking about the room and toppling, smashing and crushing all that it could.

And so it went. No room was safe from the attack, and nothing withstood the onslaught of lightning and air. Content upon the destruction Endarien left the inside of the tower, taking on his full height as he moved into the open. With a swipe of his wings he was above the tower and looking down upon it with a cold, avian eye. Leveling Heaven's Wrath against the gem encrusted, gold capped rampart he now let loose the most deadly of barrages.

Fat, silver shafts of light slammed into the top of the tower again and again. Black bricks exploded and fell like rain from gaping holes rent into the sinister cylinder. Again and again the bolts punched into the sturdy, dark stone. More holes rocked the tower until it started to teeter then tumble and finally crash in upon itself with a swarthy cloud of smoke and ash. At this all the birds who had been seated around in the outskirts of the glade on trees scattered to the heavens in a fluttering of wings which muffled the echoing thunder roaring about them.

Flame then sprouted up like weeds amid the rubble to lick across the broken stone. Soon they would grow into a strong bonfire and consume what remained; leaving only ash in passing. This cheered the heart of Endarien. Satisfied with this matter, he rose higher into the slate clouds and circling birds and then beyond them. He had spent enough time with this matter. He only had a short while until the blessing of Vkar wore thin and had to deal with The Master before then. He was confident he would find the lich before that time though.

He had his sources after all.

"Fly now and find my enemy." The god addressed the great company of birds circling around him in the turbulent heavens. "Seek him out and bring me to him so I can finally crush him."

The birds, heeding his command, then scattered across the sky. Soon the great multitude had spread itself in a growing net over the whole of Tralodren; thousands of eyes searching the terrain below with feverish dedication. Endarien himself joined them then as he took flight toward the east.

"You have nowhere to hide." Muttered the god.

Chapter 15

Hoodwink awoke to find himself on a stone floor in what he was coming to see was a circular room of some kind – a *large* circular room. *Awaken* was a rather odd word since the last thing he remembered was being flung by The Master and sailing through the air. He'd certainly been awake then but it had seemed…or rather felt like…some time had passed between that event and his current existence, and it also seemed like this passage of time had been spent in sleep.

Hoodwink stood up and began to look around. It was a tall room and circled with some torches that gave off a strange, pure white light which Hoodwink felt uneasy about. In the center of the room was a pool, and hovering about it was a giantess. Her light brown legs were crossed as she hovered over the center of this pool; dressed in silver and white, she kept her back to him. This vision alone was enough to send his head reeling with a whole swarm of thoughts.

Was he dead? Was that what happened? Instinct, birthed from fear, told him to arm himself, but he couldn't see anything to do that with and the dagger Dugan had given him was gone. Perhaps he died in that fight with The Master after all and now this was the afterlife, maybe even one of Asorlok's agents to judge him. That was what had happened hadn't it? The logic behind that thought was too much for the small goblin to ignore. What else could it be? It made sense now, it–

"Welcome Hoodwink." Saredhel kept her back to the goblin. Hoodwink said nothing, nor did he move. He felt petrified with a mixture of awe and fear.

"Be at peace goblin. You're not dead, nor in any foul place." Saredhel continued to stare into the pool beneath her, which only reflected back her white eyed, light brown face from its mirror-like surface. "This is Sooth, my realm, and you are my guest."

Hoodwink fell to his knees when he figured out it was a goddess who was speaking to him, and he was in her very own abode as well! This was just too much for the goblin who had already seen many things in his recent travels. He didn't know what to do and never felt more like some kind of bauble adrift on bobbing waves than now. Cresting and falling, cresting and falling his fate seemed to be like that bauble. Such analogy did little to comfort the small creature.

"I thought-" Hoodwink barely lifted his eyes and started to speak, than he grew frightened at how small and hollow his voice sounded here. Stunned for a heartbeat more he then continued his statement. "I thought The Master had me. Why have you brought me here, may I ask?"

"You have to fulfill your destiny." Saredhel's words pounded again the old drum the goblin had been hearing too much of late.

"My destiny?" Hoodwink felt a cold sweat wash over him. He had grown to fear that concept now for he hadn't come any closer to understanding what it was and how he was so 'special' in having such a 'great calling', as Gilban had told him. He'd pushed the thought totally away from him too when he came to accept his inevitable death from The Master in his most recent attack. Now it raised its head again – cresting and falling, cresting and falling.

"Yes." Saredhel lifted her head from her gazing but still kept her back to the small goblin.

"I thought that was over. I helped fight The Master. *That* was something *great,* right?" Hoodwink's heart raced now. He didn't know what to say or why he had been called to Gilban's goddess and he didn't think he wanted to know either. Why he had this fear tied to the revelation he wasn't sure, but it couldn't be good. Why couldn't he just be dead? It would all be so much simpler if he had just died.

Saredhel spun around slowly; hovering in the air like a serene cloud. "Rise." Her voice was soft, but powerful.

Hoodwink did as he was bidden.

He kept his eyes low though to avoid looking into the face of the deity, whom he had learned from his brief travels with Gilban, knew all things that were to come and other mysteries of the cosmos. He didn't want to peer into her eyes and see such knowledge for he felt it would drive him mad.

"There is much you do not understand, Hoodwink and much more you still need to do." The goddess descended silently before the goblin; bare feet touching the floor like silk on satin. "Time is not an ally for you either, but neither is it an enemy."

Saredhel stooped to one knee and lifted the tiny green head of the goblin with her finger so that it peered into her hooded face. "All are born with great potential, Hoodwink. Some find it, others never do, still more have it forced out of them through challenges and circumstance."

It was then that Hoodwink's eyes found themselves in Saredhel's and he would never be the same. In that moment, which seemed like forever, he saw himself reflected back at him. It wasn't just his reflection though, no, this was something far more compelling then that. Here he saw not only himself as he stood now, but himself as he had been in his youth and as he would be, he supposed, in later years, if he lived to that day. All three of these images he saw at once, each imposed over the other in the goddess' pure white eyes. He couldn't explain it but they were all over lapped and yet he didn't see a blurred image of himself because of it. only himself…

"You were born with a great potential that has to be realized, else we will all suffer a great defeat…perhaps even an eternal defeat." Saredhel's statement did little to comfort or clarify.

"Why *me* though?" Hoodwink heard his words but they were so small, so distant – like the image of the goblin resting in Saredhel's large white eyes.

"It is *your* destiny," came the goddess' strong words, which seemed to snap up his spine, pulling him straight and tall before her.

"What if I don't want it?" His voice was a little stronger now, but still far away. Hoodwink was lost in those milky pools and couldn't free himself from them even if he wanted to.

"If you understood what it is you have been called to do you would be rejoicing over the opportunity to embrace it. For never has one of your race been heralded as great, but you, should you hold true to this purpose, will be the first of your race to be so honored." Saredhel released Hoodwink then from her gaze and rose to her full height once more. Hoodwink, for his part, shook his head to clear it from the past few unending moments then turned his gaze down toward his shoes once more.

"Come here." Saredhel motioned him to stand beside the pool.

Hoodwink hesitated.

"There is nothing here that would harm you save yourself." Her voice and manner softened.

"Now you sound like Gilban." Hoodwink grinned as he made his way forward. He saw little advantage to refraining from the goddess' command. It was foolishness to resist a god – everyone knew that, especially in their very realm. Saredhel motioned with her hand for the goblin to stand at the lip of the pool.

"Look deep into the waters and you will understand all that you need to in order for you to see the importance of your destiny being fulfilled at this hour." She pointed to the pool.

Hoodwink took a deep breath, held it for a moment, and then let it out as Saredhel had instructed. At first he saw nothing but his own reflection staring back at him from the clear waters, and the bottom of the pool where bluish-gray marble tiles encased the bowl of water. That changed though in the blink of an eye when the pool began to swim with an oily mix of colors upon its surface. This rainbow soup spun and blended about in wild dervishes of silent passion as the goblin could do nothing but stare into it helplessly. And then a strange scene appeared before his eyes and the goblin would never be the same again...

Hoodwink wasn't in the chamber he'd been in before. He now stood in the middle of an even grander venue: a throne room that would have made the best of bards try to fumble for words to describe its majestic beauty and opulence which swam in the air between the marble pillars and walls studded with jewels, silk tapestries and splendid sculptures. It was so large it looked to be built by giants for giants. Then Hoodwink spied the throne in the center of the room. It was the same one The Master had used to gain godhood! He was sure of it, save now it sat empty.

Hoodwink didn't like this at all. The room was as empty as the throne that allowed the goblin to wander about the great spaces. His echoing footfalls chased his steps. Where was he and what was going on? Again the ill at ease feeling of dread fluttered up his spine.

"Saredhel?" He tried to keep his voice a whisper but it seemed more like a shout which grew weaker with each echo that reverberated around the chamber.

"I am here." The voice of the goddess gave answer which seemed to come from everywhere.

"Where?" Hoodwink scanned the area to discover nothing.

"Listen and watch." Came the reply.

Suddenly the door to the chamber opened and Hoodwink watched as a giant, who looked exactly like the moustached statue on the dais inside Galba's stone circle, appeared and took residence on the throne. He had only just seated himself when the doors burst open again and allowed a pale looking giantess access.

She was dressed all in black; even her lips were painted black on her porcelain flesh. In her hand she held a sword and was rushing forward toward the seated man who sat before her bloodthirsty advance showing little concern for the whole affair. The man continued to sit still until the dark clad woman came within striking distance and then he rose only to have the giantess' sword sheathed inside his chest.

"Before Tralodren was formed there was Vkar and his wife Xora, both of whom were killed by Sidra, the daughter of Gurthghol." Saredhel's voice now narrated the scene of Vkar dying at Sidra's feet. "She had been used by a dark entity which had existed before the cosmos to bring about this death for it wanted to destroy the gods and the empire of Vkar."

The scene before the goblin grew wavy like a distorting ripple on water, then reformed to show The Master now seated on the throne only this time the throne was inside Galba. In fact it looked just like what he had left just moments ago save there were no others present but the lich upon the great seat. "Now that dark entity has returned and with the same plan as before. Though it has decided to make use of Cadrith instead of Sidra, the desired result is still the same: the death of the Pantheon and now Tralodren."

"So what am *I* supposed to do?" Hoodwink asked as he watched The Master's eyes turn toward him and glow with an azure malice before the scene disappeared entirely. The sheer hatred for the goblin that they emanated shook Hoodwink to his core for a while after their disappearance. Even as he recovered from the occurance the goblin came to swim in empty blackness; hovering over seeming nothingness.

"You must help defeat him." Hoodwink watched Gilban step out of the darkness around him.

"Gilban?" To say the goblin was shocked to see the priest would be a great understatement.

The old elven priest now had eyes where once blind orbs stared out of his head other than this, he looked much as he had in life, though younger – probably no more than middle aged if the goblin had to hazard a guess. He held up a warning hand toward the creature; silencing his questions instantly.

"You are a key figure in this final battle, as are all who have survived The Master's attack." The elf walked over to Hoodwink. He still held his staff, even though he was now no longer blind, and followed the rhythm of its fall with his tread. "The destiny I spoke to you about when I was alive will be coming soon. You must be ready for it and prepare now for when it comes, you won't have time to miss your opportunity."

"I don't understand." Hoodwink watched the elven priest draw near. "I thought we were all facing The Master. Wasn't that the destiny you kept talking about? We were just fighting him and–"

"That battle is long over." Gilban solemnly shook his head. "The new one though, is soon to start. When I first gathered us all together I was led by my goddess in finding the candidates best suited for the mission I was to undertake. I thought it was for one mission and that once completed, the need for them had ended."

"I was wrong."

"What I was to discover was that they had been chosen for more than one mission and for a task grander than what took us to Takta Lu Lama. We all had been chosen as champions to stand against The Master's threat and would be united until that confrontation had been completed; thin threads of fate binding us all."

"So I'm one of these *champions* then?" Hoodwink raised his eyebrows in blooming understanding, though with a healthy degree of skepticism.

"Yes." Replied Gilban.

"So *that's* my great destiny then? To defeat The Master?" Hoodwink thought it didn't sound as great as he would have hoped. He didn't know exactly what he would have hoped it would be – perhaps a fulfillment of dreams he had while in his silent contemplation at Takta Lu Lama...

"Yes and No," Gilban fuzzied up the goblin's thought process with his explanation. "We were all called to stand against The Master. How we do that is our individual destiny."

Hoodwink's brow wrinkled in troublesome thought. "You're *dead* right?"

"I died, yes." It didn't seem to bother the priest in the least to admit this fact.

"Then why are you here doing all this if you don't have to worry about it any more? It sounds like we all failed against The Master. If you're dead, you can't do much more individually anyway. So why are you here telling me all this?"

Gilban smiled that familiar, enigmatic smile which looked much different now that he was both younger and had sight again to direct toward the goblin. "Because it is *my* destiny to do what I am doing now, and what I shall do in the future. Each of us who has been called together for this task – to stand as champions, has an integral part to play and we must play it or else we will lose. And if we lose, then so does Tralodren."

Hoodwink closed his eyes and lowered his head with a sigh. Keeping his head low he asked: "I don't really have a choice in the matter then, do I?"

"There is always a choice." Gilban's face had gone unreadable again.

It was Hoodwink's turn to smirk, though his was sarcastic as he rose his visage to look up at the dead priest once more. "Where have I heard *that* before?"

Gilban said nothing, merely peered down into the green face of the goblin. There was an awkward silence in the black scape until Hoodwink couldn't bear the crushing weight it was adding to his shoulders and back any longer. He knew where this was going anyway. There wasn't any way to fight it – at least as far as he could tell so he just might as well get it over with as soon as he could and get on with his life as best he could afterwards…assuming he still had a life to get back to.

"Fine." He sighed in defeat. "What do I have to do?"

"First we will have to set you in position to be ready for your task when it comes to pass." Gilban answered. "Then we will just have to wait for it to come."

"Sounds like fun." The facetious goblin scowled.

Chapter 16

For a long while there was silence inside the mystical circle of Galba. The horror and stress of it all, the very trauma of the past few weeks which had brought them here and the following short, violent moments, taking hold of all who had survived the bloody aftermath. The details and wear seeped into them, soaking their bones on route to their souls.

Clara and Cadrissa had taken to solitary tasks following Tebow's death and disappearance; continuing to remain in their own thoughts after Rowan had stirred. There was just too much to think about to do anything else. And so Rowan had awakened to a still and crestfallen company. He didn't join them, not right away. Like them, he had some thoughts that needed pondering.

The young knight's head had throbbed like the smith's hammer upon an anvil upon his awakening, but it subsided in time until it was just a dull annoying ache. He didn't really know what to do or where to go now. He'd saved Cadrissa from her fate and so had fulfilled the obligation he felt he owed her, but now The Master had risen to godhood despite his best efforts to stop it.

Was his mission over now?

He couldn't help feel that he was duty bound to stop this new threat as well since he was, in truth, responsible for its creation. Though he was still obligated to report back the success of his first mission for the Knighthood, he kept finding himself under new situations that seemed to call for his action, which in turn, upon completion, called for still more action. If he stayed here long enough, following all the threads through as they were woven into the other, then he would never get back to his homeland.

He knew it was time for a choice, but what to choose. For it wasn't just duty that called him, but now emotions had got their clutches into him as well. What would he do about Clara? What was the best choice with her? Should he stay? Should he go? The questions were tearing him up. More importantly, his feelings toward Clara had increased since he had first met her and that only served to complicate matters all the more. Where as before he had some focus to his purpose in life, a compass to guide him, all now were tainted with the elven woman's presence and his growing attachment, and perhaps even dependency on her presence. This grew worse after their talk in Vanhyrm. There, both told each other exactly where they stood emotionally but that had seemed like years ago now. Could they get back that feeling after what they had gone through and would probably go through in the days ahead? And if they could, did he want it back?

Coupled to this were the words of his goddess telling him that he had some great calling on his life, greater than what he even realized. He even was told that the Knighthood might not be that important to the goddess either, at least it was seeming that way the more the young knight strayed from his report and chewed on the words of the vision back in Vanhyrm and outside Elandor. Then there was the amulet and what it had shown him in the circle...

Still The Master was a threat to the whole world and in so doing he was threatening all of humanity...so there was the possibility of staying with the others, with Clara and helping put an end to the threat; delaying his return to the Knighthood. That was certainly an option...

He knew what Clara would decide to do. She'd fight to try and do what she could to remedy the situation, fighting until death if she had to since she had come so close to it before. She had already lost Gilban and her hope of a rapid return home as well. Her sense of responsibility and her own duty to the others – to what her actions for her nation had brought forth, would compel her to such an action as well.

So if the knight was to be honest, it really then all came down to what *he* wanted, what *he* felt was right in *his* mind, *his* spirit and nothing else. Clara had helped him separate his true self from the unnatural dogma that had been overlaid with his training in the Knighthood and now he had to search out what his true self wanted, and his true self alone. The Knighthood was important, but wasn't saving the lives of millions of humans more important than reporting back to give a report of his last mission? Weren't the words and implications of his goddess more worthy of concentration than the last edicts of a superior knight?

Once more he stared at the shrunken paw and savage adornments around his neck with a thought cluttered mind; trying to make sense of anything and everything. His life had nearly been lost. He was convinced that his goddess had saved him from certain death. It frustrated him though as to what this purpose he had been saved for might be. He didn't like to be kept in the dark and Panthor's silence on the matter thus far was far from encouraging, yet he drew his strength for the moment from Clara. He envied her seemingly steely resolve, which conflicted with her rather delicate appearance. There was a fire that burned so brightly in her, radiating out toward those around her with the same passions, igniting them as well. Indeed she was a fascinating and inspiring woman.

He could see now too why he had fallen in with their lot before. Why he had traveled with them to Takta Lu Lama and beyond and why he felt no shame in having the elven woman beside him on his hope of saving Cadrissa as well though he warred with himself at times over her race. He knew where his heart lie while his head was elsewhere. It was time to come to a decision and stick to it. It was time to become a man, to step out and do what was needed. As he decided, Rowan turned his gaze once more to Clara.

The elven woman had readied what gear she had, preparing to head out as best she could to do what she thought she was able or should be able to do. She had gathered what supplies she could from the others' remains and her own limited stock, piling them at the foot of the dais.

Though she bore a purposeful look, a war between duty and emotion was also being waged in her heart and stomach. She knew it would be right to take Gilban's body home to rest, but also wanted to stop The Master as best she could, though she didn't know how. The options presented her were terrible in their assault. She knew she could only do one of them, forsaking the others…it was just the agony of the choice that ate at her.

In her right hand she held the silver scepter of the Wizard Kings. It felt impossibly heavy in her grip, like the weight of the world itself struggled to be freed from her delicate hand. Gilban had passed on now without being able to share the secrets of the artifact. Poor choice of action for one who was supposed to see the future. Maybe though he didn't see a future with them losing. Could that have been the case? If so, then perhaps they got something wrong; messed something up and the battle was lost because of it.

She hefted the scepter in her hand again to verify the weight was real and not in her mind. It was real. Even though she saw him use it – well thought she saw him in the battle – she couldn't be sure of what truly happened in that short splurge of madness, it didn't seem to work. Had he spoken the incantation he said he received from Gorallis? If he had, did it work? Gilban had said the scepter could only be used once in the wielder's lifetime. Knowing of Gilban's nature and love of enigmatic sayings, she wasn't certain if that meant once for a whole generation or just once for that *particular* wielder.

The question was meaningless of course if she decided to stay far from The Master to go and hide somewhere else, to try and make a new life knowing that a great evil she had helped release currently stalked the world. If she did decide to go after The Master, then she would have to understand how to use it. And she had no idea how to figure that out; short of going back to Gorallis, which she knew wasn't even a possibility.

Since the attack, however, Clara had become convinced that it hadn't been used right or something had gone wrong. She seemed to recall now, though vaguely, that Gilban had never struck The Master with the scepter. So perhaps the scepter could still be used as it never struck the dark god in the first place. This was of little aid though, for the scepter now appeared dead, at least as far as the elf knew, and there wasn't anything she could do about trying to make it work. Clara wasn't skilled in the arcane ways, but, Cadrissa might be of some help. She was a mage after all and they were skilled in arcane things. It was crafted by Wizard Kings after all. If she wanted to pursue The Master then the elf would have very little choice left but to see if the mage could aid her in any way.

Cadrissa showed little if any signs of injury herself. Both Clara and Cadrissa were dumbfounded about this. There were too many mysteries here for her liking. She needed some answers soon, and some sense. Clearing her mind for a moment, Clara got up and moved toward the mage who sat solemnly near two charred stone posts where once the body of Dugan had writhed in torment.

"What do you make of this?" The elf asked.

"Huh?" The mage turned toward Clara, her mind again focusing on where she was, but her red, puffy eyes and lined face telling of her loss.

"This scepter…how do you think it works?" Clara shoved the object in front her face.

Cadrissa had been feeling strange of late, ever since the blow from The Master. She heard constant whispers in her ears now and there was a greater sense of mystical might inside her. Stranger still, she felt the medallion she had placed in her hidden pocket of her robe burning with some sort of intense heat – even hotter than she'd felt before the confrontation with The Master. It was like a miniature sun was beside her frame. She didn't pay it too much mind though for most of her concentration was on Dugan's recent demise.

"I don't know." Cadrissa stood up and walked toward Clara, taking up the silver object and looking it over. "Didn't Gilban tell you anything about it?"

"Nothing really. I don't think he thought he would fail."

"Guess he didn't see that coming." Cadrissa added then wished she hadn't.

Clara bit her lip in sullen silence.

"Sorry." Cadrissa looked up from her observation of the object. "It just slipped out. Gilban was a good man." But there was a faint echo of laugher in Cadrissa's head – a cold mirth dancing between the whispers circling about her head...

"Yes he was." Clara returned on the wings of a sigh, then added "So was Dugan."

Cadrissa peered over her eyebrows at the elf. A weak smile on her lips. "Yes he was."

The mage then returned to the scepter as she turned it in her hands, looking over the minute details of its simple design, searching for anything that might offer some hope of cracking its mystery. Her training in the arcane arts should not have been able to aid her in discovery of the scepter's nature, but that same added energy she now felt and had been feeling since her capture, continued beating through her veins greatly augmented her abilities of understanding and discernment. It was like nothing she had known before and she was quickly growing to like it.

"It seems to be of marvelous craftsmanship. The object resonates with an energy I can't pinpoint, almost like it had built up a charge for release. It might be that Gilban never had a chance to even use the scepter, if its still active...You might be right about it not being used properly then. I couldn't tell you much more without having time to look it over and study it better."

"Do you think if it is still active and was used to strike The Master it would be enough to destroy him?" Clara asked.

As they spoke, Rowan drew near the two females, interested in their conversation.

"It might…" the mage struggled with the whispers now. There were more like flies buzzing louder near her ears and were starting to congest her concentration. "Like I said, there is a lot of energy already in it. How to get it out and use it, however…

"He said he needed to recite an incantation. I thought you might know it since the scepter was crafted by Wizard Kings." Clara continued to watch the mage examine the scepter. "I wasn't able to hear it during the fight."

"I don't know of any incantations, but I know of a place where we might be able to get some answers." The mage looked up at the elf, the pesky whispers persisted in their activity level.

"Well then, that's the best option we have at the moment." Clara made a move to go back to the center of the circle where she had placed her gear. Upon turning though, she ran into Rowan.

For a moment neither spoke, only looked into each other's eyes. They knew what the other was thinking, what the other felt. Now they had to decide.

"You heard what we were talking about then?" Clara moved a few steps back from the knight.

"Most of it, yes. Sounds like a pretty far fetched plan."

"As far fetched as going to find some Ice Wizard you only knew about in legend to help save a human wizadress?" Clara tossed a lock of her silver hair behind her pointed ear.

Rowan granted himself a grim grin. "No, not as far fetched as that."

"You are welcome to come along with me – I mean *us,* Rowan. That is, unless you have somewhere else you have to be." Nervous fingers put the other strand of hair on the opposite side of her head behind her other pointed ear.

"I haven't decided that yet." Rowan lowered his head to watch himself kick the grass with his boot.

"I understand." Clara set her hand on his armored shoulder.

Rowan's dark blue eyes darted up to her gentle face, taking in her sapphire eyes. "A lot has happened here, to me…to us."

Clara blushed.

"Do what you think is best. You have a duty to your knighthood–"

"And a obligation to help you out as well," Rowan countered.

"There's no obligation here Rowan." Clara moved toward the supplies.

"Oh yes there is," he followed the elven maid. "I helped set that thing free."

"You didn't know you were doing it at the time, and you tried to stop him from rising to godhood–" Clara tried to comfort the knight with her words.

"–and failed," Rowan added dismally.

Clara looked up at him then. Her gaze held his mind tightly in a decided course of action and silenced all further words from the knight. She had yet to have her say in trying to comfort Rowan in his current mindset. You did your best Rowan, which is more than most would do. Most won't even try to solve the problems they created.

"What more can you do now?"

"How can you stop this?"

Cadrissa had stopped her examination to peer up at the couple. After some time she found the conversation between the two too hard to ignore, even beyond the hindrance of the scampering voices in her mind, and took to open observation as they spoke. A pleasant joy washed over her face as she delighted in the couple's budding affection for one another as a parent might delight in their child's first love.

"How can *you*?" The knight crossed his arms. "How do you plan to go about stopping a god then, huh?"

Clara stopped for a moment.

Taking a breath she noticed Cadrissa staring at her and Rowan and blushed again. "The scepter is the only way we can hope to beat him now." Clara turned to Cadrissa.

Rowan parroted the action.

"The scepter? I thought you just got done saying you don't know how it works." The knight followed Clara back to the wizardress.

"I didn't say I didn't know how it works," Cadrissa addressed the duo, "just that I'm not able to figure out the incantation unless I am able to study it a bit more in depth."

The voices had silenced a bit from her head now – at least enough so she could hear herself think a bit clearer than before.

"So how long would you need to study it?" asked Clara.

"It's not a matter of time per se as having a place in which to study," the mage returned.

"You can't study it here?" Rowan crossed his arms over his chest.

"No. I need a secure environment where I cast some spells, use some tools, research books for answers. None of that is here. My books were lost when I was abducted by The Master, and I don't know where to begin on trying to figure out this objects workings."

"Okay," Clara moved toward the mage, "do you have any place in mind we could go that would help you then?"

"There is one place that might work." Cadrissa let the scepter fall to her side, her left hand holding it like a club beside her.

"Where?" Clara pressed.

"We go to the Great Library." Replied the mage.

"Great Library?" Rowan's face grew puzzled.

"In Cleithious, the capital of Rexatious, there is a great library that was built and filled with all manner of insight and musings from the foundation of the Republic. It holds the only complete history of Tralodren and many legends and myths, indepth documentation of the various ages that have come before and the rule and reigns of kings and queens from all races and lands.

"If we just need some knowledge, this should be the place where we would receive it. If what we wanted wasn't there, then we could use what we learned to help us get what we need to know as well from other sources."

"Exactly." Cadrissa's eyes sparkled.

"This scepter is too old too have anything of worth in my school or any other academy I can think of. The Great Library is the only place where I'd have a chance of ever figuring this thing out."

"You still don't have to join us Rowan...Rexatious is a very long ways from here." Clara's voice was low and soft, like a touch of silk on a rose.

"Stop it." Rowan lifted her chin with his hand to look at her face with his own. "I already made up my mind. If I leave you, I *will* leave humanity."

For a moment neither spoke. Each was frozen in the span between heartbeats, taken with the deepening affection for one another and the admiration of the other's position on the matter at hand – what they were fighting against and for. The strong truth of the words Rowan had spoken was but merely a reflection of the inner truth both shared. Then the next heartbeat came and the moment was over; raptured from between them.

Cadrissa shifted her weight as she watched the couple. "So... ah, are you both agreeing with me then?"

Both Clara and Rowan turned toward the mage.

"Yeah," Rowan straightened his pose before her, "I'll fight along with you. There won't be much need for a Knighthood should this dark god have his way on Tralodren."

Rowan clenched his jaw tight to grind down the last of the feelings to flee from the circle and be done with this whole situation once and for all. He wasn't sure if he was doing it for his goddess, Clara or Knighthood...might even be doing it for all three really, but it had been resolved with the youth then and there. The time for emotions had departed. Now he needed steady resolve and steadfast duty.

"So how do we get out of here then?" Rowan asked Cadrissa.

"Well...I could try and cast a spell to get us there, but I haven't been there before so I won't be able to anchor us that strongly, and, I don't know how it will work in this circle or if we can even get out of it to begin with."

"You have a spell that strong?" Rowan was slightly amazed at the potential of the possibility. "You're planning on going almost to the other side of the world. Don't wizards have a limit to their spells? Aren't you tired by now?"

Cadrissa ignored the knight. She had to if she didn't want to tell him the truth: that she didn't feel tired at all – in fact she was feeling better than she thought possible…

"I should be able to get us to the library if I have a strong enough connection." Cadrissa looked Clara in the face. "Have you been to the library before?"

"Yes, many times." Clara recalled some of those visits when she had been younger, traveling there with her father when he would go seeking supplies to complete his next piece of art.

"Recently?" The mage's question awoke the elf from her reverie.

"Just before I left with Gilban, why?" Then before Cadrissa could answer Clara spoke out her deduction. "You want me to be an anchor for your spell."

"Yes," Cadrissa was impressed that Clara had known something like that when most outside the circles Cadrissa frequented had no grasp of anything magical.

"Do you think it would be dangerous to try anything while we're inside then?" Clara scanned the stones around them to emphasis her concern.

"I'm not sure…it could work," Cadrissa joined her in surveying the scene as well, "it could just produce nothing or it could do something really bad."

"Like what?" Rowan pondered aloud.

"Like causing our bodies to be scattered over the cosmos." The mage's gaze fell upon Rowan.

"Oh." Was all the youth could say.

"What happened to Galba anyway?" Clara looked about the empty circle once again.

"I don't know." Rowan joined her search, "I didn't see her in the battle either. You don't think she is dead do you?"

"Hardly," said Cadrissa, "It would take a lot to destroy her I'd wager…if she could even be killed, that is. However, I was wondering where she had gone to as well. I thought maybe she would be able to help. I mean she did call us here and all. Though I doubt every being is able to live up to their word." The mage again recalled the broken promise of Endarien.

"Well, it looks like she has deserted us, so it's up to us to get out of this circle." Rowan moved back over to the supplies Clara had heaped up at the base of the dais, and proceeded to load up on what he could.

"I don't know if she left us here on purpose." Cadrissa looked at one of the open stone doorways, this one showing a thick forest. "Maybe she has other things on her mind…there is a new god now in the world…"

"You think you can contact her?" Clara made her way to join Rowan.

"Maybe call her to help?"

"Me?" Cadrissa's eyes widened. "I don't really know much more about Galba other than what The Master told me. I didn't even get us in here the first time, he did."

"Well then, if none of us can leave…" Rowan finished his pack rat scavenging and was drawn back to the mage; Clara still loading herself down with supplies.

"I didn't say that." Cadrissa corrected. "I said that I didn't know how to contact Galba. I might be able to get us out of here… but this place is able to hinder even gods from getting inside so it isn't going to be easy."

"Great." Rowan shook his head softly as he came to stand before the wizardress once more. "So we're stuck here then?"

"I didn't say that *either*." Cadrissa added hastily. The voices had faded even more and the heat at her side was gone now. Good news…she hoped.

"Calm down." Clara interjected as she made her way back into the conversation; with what supplies she could take now on her person. She needed to calm them down as best she could. Like or not, she still held some of the reigns of leadership among them and knew they wouldn't be able to do anything without first being able to reason together without being hostile to each other. She also needed to be the strength the other needed for both were too young in years to be truly wise in all their ways. The eldest of their number, though she appeared little older than her companions, she would have the voice of command once more. Even though she hurt and was tired beyond thought, she had to lead.

"We won't get anywhere by arguing." Said Clara."We need to think."

"Cadrissa," the elf turned to the mage, "can we just walk out of here?"

"I don't think so." The mage thought aloud. "The mystical warding around the stones would be strong enough to hold us back."

Rowan had an idea. "How about asking Galba to let us out like Gilban asked her to let us in?"

Cadrissa contemplated the question for a moment. "It might work."

"All right," Clara had a course of action to follow that seemed successful. "Let's just get together what we can, and then get ready to head out – I think I have a plan if we can get out of here first."

"So do I." The voice was familiar but different, like a well-known tune played on a different instrument. All turned to the sound to behold Galba. She stood a little ways off from them, nearer the throne, and sparkled like diamond dust, her rich green eyes ensnaring them all with her comforting and inviting gaze.

"Galba." Cadrissa's voice was only a whisper.

"I will not hinder any one of you from leaving." Said Galba.

"So you just let The Master get his wish then, huh?" Rowan bit back the anger he felt rising to his lips. He was wise enough to hold back his feelings when they dealt with such a powerful being as this. Better to live another day than to assault and insult a being who was equal to his goddess...perhaps even greater – if such a thing could be believed.

"I did as I said I would," came Galba's simple reply.

"Well, you could at least have helped," Rowan muttered.

"She didn't have the authority to, Rowan," Clara cupped Rowan's armored shoulder with her gentle hand. "Remember?"

"Yes, I remember, but...but," Rowan pushed through the storm of thoughts and emotions growing inside him, "I just don't understand any of this. This whole thing is just madness."

"In time, you will understand the reasons and workings behind this day." Galba's voice was like a peaceful breeze now. It was as if she truly felt bad she couldn't share more than she had, and wanted to encourage them all to stay true to their current plans despite their unease. "But not quite yet."

"I don't like it any more than you do, Rowan, but we have to try to stop The Master as best we can." Clara's words calmed the Nordican's blood.

"So then I can take us out of here with a spell?" Cadrissa asked Galba.

"I will not hinder you." Galba motioned to a nearby stone portal with her hand. "Cast your magic on that portal there. You will find success with it."

"However," she moved closer to the body of Gilban. "The dead shall stay. Only the living may leave this place."

"But Gilban–" Clara started.

"Will be taken care of with the others who were slain in the battle." Galba interrupted.

Clara moved to speak again, but was halted again by Galba's words.

"Let life be for the living. What is dead has now passed on to take part in a new journey. You have your own to undertake at a later time. For now, if you wish to be free of the circle, free to enact your plans, then your way is clear." Galba's fine alabaster hand pointed to the portal.

"Can I at least say goodbye?" Clara's eyes had become wet, her lips were thin and tight.

Galba bowed her head slightly. "Certainly."

Clara moved to the body of Gilban, her mentor, her friend, and in many ways…her inspiration. The journey seemed to take years, though he was mere feet away from her. His body, still cold, still lifeless seemed so frail, so simple. The man, in life had seemed to be so much more than the housing of flesh that had contained him. She didn't want to remember him how he looked now. No, she wanted to recall him as the kind and wise man who had been so much to her, who had served his nation and his goddess admirably in this life and would in the life to come.

Clara bent down to smooth out the messed robes of the priest. Tears started to flow from her eyes. She knew he was gone now and she had to go on, that there was little time to grieve for losses…but she also wanted to stay right by the priest's side for a while…maybe forever. She had to lead now, she knew that. The plan was still forming and weak at best, but she had to do something, try and stop this thing she had helped unleash…even if unknowingly.

She had to put it behind her for the moment. Place the pain, the emptiness behind a wall so she could do what needed to be done. The moment called for action, not the mourning of things that had faded away. The mantle of leadership was heavier than she thought she could bear but when she looked down upon the fallen elder elf, she drew strength from his example and life.

"Safe journey friend," she whispered.

She remained there for some time, at least it seemed so to her, until she heard the soft footfalls come up from behind.

"Its time to go." Rowan placed his hand upon the elf. His voice was calm and soft.

Clara turned and looked over her shoulder toward the young knight, tears staining her face. "I know." She wiped the tears from her checks, sucking back the gathering mucus in her nose. "I know." It was then that Clara noticed how much Rowan had grown over their time together – how much more *mature* he'd become. And there was still so much more potential for him to tap into and develop. When he did reach the apex of his manhood, he would be a stunning figure, that was for sure.

"You'll make sure his body is taken back to the temple?" Clara asked Galba as Rowan helped her stand up.

Galba had adopted the face of a loving mother who shared in the pain of her child's grief. "I shall."

"Thank you." The elf's smile was brief and bitter sweet.

"Now go." Galba's voice was incredibly soft and soothing to the elf's emotional wounds. "Your place is not here among the dead, but with the living."

Rowan placed his arm around the crestfallen elf as he silently led her back to Cadrissa.

"You know the spell." Galba told Cadrissa. "Speak it now and be gone from here."

Cadrissa watched the portal before her turn black and empty, void of any image at all. Her attention changed toward the couple as they neared her.

"Rowan, grab my hand." Cadrissa held out her hand to the knight. "Now take Clara's." She added after he had done what she had said.

"You sure this is going to work?" He shot a nervous glance across to Cadrissa.

"The worse thing that could happen is we miss the library and head toward a more familiar area that might be stronger in her mind at the time. So you need to keep the image of the library inside your head at all times. Focus all your conscious will upon it and we should get there."

"What do I do then?" The knight asked.

"Just close your eyes, and clear your mind of any thoughts other than going to the library then follow me through the portal." Said Cadrissa.

"But I don't know what it looks like," he rebutted.

"It doesn't matter," Cadrissa bit back a portion of rising frustration, "the thought alone has weight, and will see you carried there on the strength of Clara's will. Just concentrate on my voice and the spell I will invoke in a moment. Don't open your eyes until I say so though or the spell will be ruined."

Both closed their eyes and tightened the grip on the other's hand. Taking a breath, Cadrissa tried to clear her head, but found it still cluttered. On a whim, more so out of a strange urging she could not explain than anything else, she reached out to the medallion with her mind, focusing what mental energy she could upon it. Even with the fragile tendril she was able to muster, she wasn't prepared for the surge of energy which shot back into her greater than lightning or the spark of true love upon first sight.

There were no whispers this time, just a steady, almost addictive hum of mystical power. Infused with this energy she heard herself speak the words to a spell, but she herself was far away, as if her spirit hovered over her body overlooking it all. It was then, as the words of the spell came to her mind, before they bubbled to her lips, that Cadrissa felt the surge of arcane might increase even more. Her whole frame shook with it's discovery, her mind raced in fearful awe and the hidden medallion blazed like the furnace of the pit beside her body. It was too late to wonder if this had been the right thing to do for she was compelled by it more now than anything else.

A voice echoed the words which came out of her own lips seconds before.

"*Kanree loth ra. Ambi-lo-deen. Uth vos angri.*" The spell released itself from Cadrissa's grip with a mind of its own. Birthed of a nature the mage felt frightened of and excited by at the same time, the spell not only worked, but at such a level of power it astonished her.

Before her the portal Galba had directed them to began to spin and twirl as a kaleidoscope; colors and patterns blooming and fading into one another until a familiar scene materialized between the posts and lintel: a tranquil park like setting with fresh water lakes and a leafy canopy of trees nearby. The mage quietly watched as the image became clearer, more refined, then spoke to the others.

"I'm going to start moving." Cadrissa cautioned them as she began her first tittering steps toward the portal. It was hard to move, almost as if she was drunk. The energy released and sustained throughout her body was just short of euphoric. The others followed slowly behind her, eyes still clenched tight in mental concentration.

Cadrissa stepped up to the flat image, then into it, and through it with one simple stride. It looked to any who would have seen it as if she had stepped into a puddle. Her entrance into the image sent only ripples bouncing back from the posts framing the portal. With another step Cadrissa's body vanished from view completely, being sucked in whole with only her hand sticking out of scene which pulled the Nordican fast behind her, and Clara behind him. Following their exit the image in the portal faded from sight between the two standing stones, the images of all the portals merging into a soft gray haze.

Only Galba remained.

The body of Gilban resting at her feet.

Silence anointed the circle with heavy, syrupy waves. Alone in the scattered field of death he seemed to slumber in a restful sleep. Galba peered down at the elf with a face devoid of emotion. Suddenly a nimbus of light shined forth from the middle of Galba, spreading outward in a tidal wave of consuming brilliance swallowing up all inside the circle. This light even shone out of the stone circle itself causing anyone who might have seen it to imagine the area to be home to a star rather than an ancient monument.

Then it was gone.

As fast as it had come, it left again with nothing in its wake. Only the throne and its platform remained. Gilban's body, the remains of the battle with The Master and Galba herself were nowhere to be seen.

Chapter 17

Dugan awoke and discovered he was no longer in pain. The wounds he'd suffered from – to the point of death – had departed, leaving him in a strange sense of numbness. It was an odd sensation but a welcome one after his torturous death. His eyes moved up to the gray, lifeless canopy of sky above him. No cloud sailed the dismal dome nor any source of light seemed to radiate in the heaven. Only the persistent glow of the day, which came at either twilight or predawn, ruled the sky. The Telborian was uncertain which condition currently dominated.

He also noticed everything around him was silent. No wind or even the sound of his own breathing disrupted this dead stillness. It was both a dreadful and a peaceful place. It was also then that Dugan noticed he didn't have any breath. He wasn't breathing and yet he lived! Placing his hand on his chest he noticed two things: first, he felt that his heart no longer beat in his chest, second, he now wore a robe.

The Telborian observed the new garment for a better look and saw that it was a long-sleeved, red robe with what looked to be an orange, flame type of embroidery around the hem and cuffs. The garment went down to his ankles where the former gladiator was glad to see he still had his boots…there was some small comfort in that familiar dress.

So where was he and what was going on? Dugan surveyed the broken, gray land which stretched on for endless expanse all around him. Miles upon miles in all directions he spied shattered columns – petrified trees in a strange and unsettling forest; toppled statuary, scattered open scrolls and books lay about the stubbly stones like dry hides – flaking and crumbling; tearing to minute debris. Here and there were a few open areas where now and then the cluttering of ruins gave way to small puddles – even lakes of dust. The same dust covered all in a thick, undisturbed layer, like a gray cloth smothering out all life beneath its folds.

There was no sign of life, no wind, not even the sensation of air itself. All of it smelled of dust, and was so dry as to cause the Telborian's mouth to lose all moisture and his eyes to grow itchy. If he was dead – truly dead – then was this the realm of Rheminas?

He didn't see any fire.

Could he have been sent somewhere else by The Master, perhaps before his death? He didn't think so because he recalled the death priest praying for his safe passage into death. No, this was someplace else…but where?

The Telborian stooped to pick up a fragment of what looked to be the remains of a shattered statue. The chunk of granite appeared to bear the visage of a comely woman, probably of human lineage, with flecks of red paint still on her lips and green paint around her eyes. Dugan studied it a little bit longer and then dropped it to the ground. Even the sound of the stone hitting the ground was muffled to the point of near nonexistence – as if the noise was swallowed whole almost as soon as it manifested.

Seeing nothing before him to direct his path, for all was the same or seemingly the same in all directions, the Telborian chose a direction at random and began to tred down it; booted feet leaving no trace of his movements. He walked on for what seemed like miles without seeing any signs of life. The ruins changed here and there – cultural differences the Telborian thought, but nothing living came into his field of vision. He didn't stop to look at much of any of it – didn't want to. There was no reason to, and he felt little urge to do little more than continue his long trek.

After what he was sure to be hours, the Telborian stopped. Looking up at the sky he saw it still held the same shade, neither fading to a deeper twilight or brightening to a shimmering dawn. Further, he didn't feel as if he had traveled for any great distance at all. Had it not been for the scenery changing around him he wouldn't have known that he had moved anywhere at all. With no heartbeat or breath it seemed his body was able to go on as if undisturbed by anything indefinitely. He realized then it mattered little how long he traveled – he could walk from now until the end of the cosmos and still not grow tired, nor the sky above him change. If this was what it was like to be dead, then he wasn't looking forward to his afterlife.

This couldn't be the home of Rheminas so where was he and why was he here? The Telborian turned to the left and spotted a tall statue which seemed more intact than the others he had seen. There seemed to be some writing on it too which he could barely make out from his present location. Perhaps it was a marker he could use for directions.

Moving through the rocky, dusty soil, he made his way to what he came to see as an image of a woman sitting on a throne. The statue had to be about double his height he guessed and carved of some cold, dead, gray stone. Still smooth to the touch and in relatively pristine detail, he took in what appeared to be a single word, carved in a large, strange script at the base of the seated woman who appeared dressed for war. Dugan was unable to read the script and it was like nothing he had seen before – though in truth that meant little since he hadn't seen much of any writing outside of Elonum and Telborous.

Giving up on the word he decided to look up to the woman in the throne. She was young and stern, even Dugan could see the battle hardened features about her face. This was a warrior who had seen many a fight and lived to tell the tale. He was unable to discern what race she was, though he was sure it was some type of human. Probably Telborian from the looks of it. Dressed in plate armor as she was, it was hard to tell the rest of her features, and in short order Dugan gave up on the effort. If this was a sign post, he couldn't make heads or tails of what it meant.

"Ah, there you are…" The voice spun the Telborian around. "It seems you wandered off by yourself." Tebow smiled. Beside him was Cracius. They both looked different though, somehow more life-like than before. He couldn't put his finger on it but they were dressed as they had been when he last saw them only there was something about their eyes…

"It's not a wise idea to go wandering in Mortis for very long by yourself." Tebow continued.

"Mortis?" Dugan panned the scene behind the priests once more with his eyes. "*This* is *Mortis*?"

"That's right, the realm of Asorlok." Cracius now added to the conversation.

"I'm dead then right?" Dugan questioned the older priest.

"Yes." Tebow nodded.

"How can I be alive then if I'm dead?" Dugan held out his hands before them to help him contemplate as he spoke. "I can move, speak, even see and hear. I can even taste still, but my heart's stopped and I can't breathe."

"You're seeing your true self." Tebow spoke to the Telborian's concerns. "All beings created by the gods have a true self, that is to say the spiritual body. It is the truest part of the being which is encased in flesh. Further it is how you really are – for many who were once lovely in their physical bodies were not too fetching in their spiritual forms and the reverse is true also."

"So this is the *real* me?" Dugan studied his hands more closely, closing and opening the appendages. "I don't look that different – don't feel that different – apart from not having breath or having a heartbeat."

"Not all have that many differences between these two bodies if they have strived to live an authentic life," said Cracius. "There are some differences on your person, but only minor ones that I can see."

"So *everyone* has two bodies then?" Dugan lowered his hands to focus his attention on the two death priests.

"Three actually." Tebow corrected.

"*Three?*" The former gladiator's eyes widened with this revelation.

"Your physical body, soul, and spirit," Tebow counted each off on a finger.

"Soul?" Dugan's gaze moved toward Cracius. "Isn't that the same as your spirit?"

The young priest held up three fingers before him. "Spiritual body." He motioned his index finger forward. "Mental body, which is called the soul," he wiggled his ring finger, "and the physical body," moving his third finger forward.

"All three" he combined all three fingers into one mass of digits, "form the existence we call life. Such was the way of our creation. When one body goes away – like when the physical body passes on," the priest moved his third finger away from the other two which he still left combined. "Then the other two go on without it, for the spirit and the soul are eternal. In fact, they are so tightly intertwined that people can say soul and mean spirit and vice versa."

Dugan's mind began to race at this new understanding.

"So if someone were to sell their soul, then it wouldn't be their *spirit*, but *mind* they were selling?"

"That depends," Tebow's eyes took in Dugan more attentively than before.

"Depends on what?" Dugan had grown hungrier for an answer.

"Depends," Tebow continued, "on how such a deal was brokered – such things, if done, are very tricky indeed."

"How could you know if you were missing your soul then?" Dugan's face grew even more studious.

"Not all the creatures that inhabit Tralodren, and indeed the cosmos, are so blessed as those who have a spirit, which possesses a soul, and inhabit a body. All mortalkind, giants, monsterous races, their descendents, dragons and linnorms are so created. The rest of the creatures you see have only a physical body that is inhabited by a soul." Cracius answered the Telborian.

"When one's physical body is destroyed it sets the spirit free to it's final destination and body – an *immortal* body which all possess through their afterlife." Cracius pointed at Dugan now with a single finger, "You, and us as well, are on such a journey now and are set to meet up with your final, eternal body quite soon, only after your judgement."

"I thought you said *this* is the real me." Dugan looked down at his hands which he closed and opened into fists in his contemplation. "So this isn't real then?"

Tebow moved to clarify the matter when he noticed the growing confusion in Dugan's face. "You're in the transition between the old body and the new, as are we, and as are all who lose their mortal body. Mortis is the great gate which all must pass through in order to reach their eternal destination.

"All those who pass through the gate are then sent to one of the realms and there are given an eternal physical body to house their mind and spirit forever. This new body will be suited to the realm in which it is to reside just as our old bodies were made for life in the realm of mortalkind."

Tebow let out a sigh when he saw his words were doing little but adding to the furrows on Dugan's forehead. "Perhaps it is best to let that matter rest for the moment." Taking a small, airless breath, the dead death priest tried a new angle of explanation.

"The body is made of flesh, bone and blood; the soul contains our mind, will and emotions; the spirit holds our wisdom, ability to commune with higher levels of reality, and our conscience. The soul is able to animate the body of flesh and keep it alive, and it provides intelligence to function and operate in the physical world, as we see many animals do, but it is a spirit which raises creatures to greatness. For it is the spirit that provides the understanding of right and wrong, good and evil and gives a sense to a time and place outside ourselves. In short, it makes us aware of both a spiritual reality and our need for a place in it. It also is the furnace from which higher civilization stems. This is why we have been raised up beyond the common animal in terms of building civilizations and producing art, recording history and having the power to create and destroy whole new realities in the cosmos; all of which the common creatures are forever barred."

"So if I lost my soul, then I wouldn't be able to think?" Dugan was still puzzled.

"Yes," Cracius nodded in agreement, "but you didn't lose your soul, you asked what would happen if you *sold* it. There is a difference."

"There is?" Dugan wanted to hear this.

"Yes." Tebow now spoke. "Whenever a soul or spirit is sold then they are collected at the end of the physical life, but you already gathered as much before we met I believe."

Dugan's face grew sterner as he was able to get his thoughts together.

"You've been chosen by Rheminas Dugan," Tebow's voice grew a bit more consoling to the former gladiator, "and there's no way out of it."

"I see," were all Dugan's tight lips would allow him to say.

"He has your body, soul and spirit," the older priest continued, "I could see it when we were on Tralodren, and it's even plainer now to my sight."

"Body, soul *and* spirit?" Dugan's blue eyes grew predatory in a flash of thought. "How can that be? I only sold him my soul."

"No, he's laid claim to all three parts of your life." Tebow's voice was more subdued and relenting than below. "Of that much I am certain."

"But how?" Dugan growled. He was beginning to embrace the rage that was swelling upon this new information. Of course he knew he'd been used before, but the old feelings of hatred and black anger rose to the surface yet again anyway.

Cracius looked at Tebow, face ripe with uncertainty. The two seemed to stare at each other in silent contemplation before Tebow gave a nod to Cracius who then turned to Dugan and addressed his concerns.

"Because we have moved beyond our mortal bodies we can see things more clearly than before and have been given much greater knowledge to do our duty here in Mortis."

"One thing I know for certain in looking at you, into your soul and spirit, is that you didn't sell your soul to Rheminas, but gave it to him long ago. It was this act that called him to you and allowed him to take your spirit as well. Your body simply followed where your spirit and soul told it to go."

"But he said his payment was my *soul*." Dugan's anger flared out of his nostrils in what would have been a large, bull-like release of pent up rage but was instead an empty, airless gesture. The more his anger grew though, the more Dugan thought back to the past. The images of his life flew before his mind like leaves in the wind. He watched them in a new light though, a light that seemed clearer than he had been able to see them with before. Perhaps what the death priests said was true after all – perhaps physical death did bring a greater clarity to one's thinking.

He saw how he gave himself to Rheminas with his oath – swearing his allegiance to the dark god before he even came to him in his weakest moment and took advantage of his desperation…

"He's not one who is known for his trustworthiness." Tebow's words tried to consul the Telborian, but were of little effect. "He took what he wanted."

"And I let him…" Dugan hung his head in what would have been another, heavy sigh.

"So why am I here then and not with Rheminas?" Dugan raised his head with a defeated expression. His red hot rage fell into gray, cold ash.

"We've been sent to take you to your destination." Cracius answered. "You've already been judged as to your final destination." He motioned to the robe Dugan wore causing the former gladiator to take it in once more with his eyes.

"You wandered away before we could come to collect you." Tebow started to explain. "You don't want to do that here. Mortis is no friend to those who wander away from the path."

"I didn't see any path." Dugan looked around for anything that might remotely be considered a trail of some kind. "I just started to wander and hoped to find another living person."

"You would have wandered long and not found such a thing." Tebow was solemn. "If you veer off the path you will never go to your destination. That is how spirits have been known to enter into the realm of the living."

"You mean *ghosts*?" Dugan's face wondered alongside his words.

Tebow motioned the curious question away with a bat of his had. "We must go now Dugan."

"So where is this path then?" Dugan still wasn't seeing any pathway around them.

"You will see in time," answered Tebow.

"Wait," Dugan turned to point toward the statue behind him. "Who is that? I tried to read the inscription on the base but I couldn't make any sense of it. It's the only chunk of rock around here that seems to be in the best shape I've seen so far."

There was a silence then as both priests looked toward the each other in a means of wordless exchange. When this had finished, it was Cracius who spoke. "That is Sidra."

"Who's that?" Dugan continued to look at the statue now with added interest.

"She was the first real threat to the Pantheon long before Tralodren was formed." The younger priest continued, albeit slightly hesitantly.

"So she's dead then?" Dugan turned around to face the death priests again.

"Indeed." Cracius made an effort to dust off his robes.

"So what did she try to do?" The former gladiator continued to study the statue.

"Kill the gods." Tebow now took up the conversation with a curt tone. Clearly he wanted them to be moving onward.

Dugan though was wide eyed at this statement. "Kill the gods? She didn't succeed though, huh?"

"No." Cracius returned. "Though she did come close…"

"How close?" Dugan was suddenly fascinated beyond words.

"Close enough," said the younger priest.

"We really have to get moving now Dugan." Tebow's patience was now slipping.

"*Both* of you need to escort me to Rheminas?" Dugan looked up at them with amusement. "I must be very precious cargo indeed."

"We're not here to escort you anywhere but to Sheol." Tebow's frustration to move on was mounting. "From there you'll be sent to your final destination."

"Sheol?" Dugan shook his head. This was all a little too much for him to take in so rapidly.

"The city of Asorlok and where the twelve gates reside." Tebow spoke as if that should be common knowledge to anyone. "Everyone who dies has to travel to Sheol, and then on toward their afterlife as they are so judged."

"So where are the others then?" Dugan made a show of looking about himself for more people who obviously weren't there. He didn't think this made much sense. If this was where all the people of the cosmos came upon death then they had to be more populated than this. More over, what about the fellows he had just seen in battle? He knew that he couldn't have been the only one to have died in that fight…

"If you're referring to the other mercenaries who had joined us in the battle, not all have died yet and those few who have besides us have already passed on to their destination…" Tebow turned in the opposite direction he was facing then proceeded to walk away from the gathering. "…and they stuck to the path."

"If you are referring to the other beings who have died and still are dying with each passing moment, when we get closer to the city you will see the large throng about it. Out here we are too removed from most people and the priests who serve our god by helping to process all who come here. Come Dugan, it is time."

Dugan took what would have been a breath for a sigh but turned into a breathless muscle reflex instead, then joined the two priests.

"So how did she die?"

"Sidra?" Tebow raised an eyebrow.

"Yeah." Dugan replied.

"Her father killed her." The older priest answered.

"Who was her father?" Dugan took a look over his shoulder back at the statue and was surprised to see how far it had now fallen behind them.

"Gurthghol." Cracius kept his attention ahead of him.

"And how do you two know all this stuff?" Dugan plodded beside the two priests of the god of death.

"As priests of Asorlok we have been given all this knowledge upon our arrival." Cracius continued to keep to the path that only he and Tebow could see. "It's our purpose to usher those who have died to Sheol, and run the great city of our god as he directs. Such information is needed to help us in our tasks."

"So how far is it till we get to Sheol?" Dugan tried to scan the direction they were heading but saw nothing but more ruins.

"You wandered far from the path but we will be there soon enough." Tebow kept an even pace with Cracius. "Once you start to move along the path again you will find it pulls you forward and compresses even the most drawn out of journeys into a simple trek."

Chapter 18

It seemed like forever, at least it felt that way for the Telborian since they had started their trek down a path he still couldn't see. He didn't like this uncertain place where time itself seemed to stand still and any sense of purpose and reason faded away from his existence. He'd already been ready for the fiery greeting of his death, but this constant stream of interludes was very anticlimactic and draining on the gladiator in a way that had become tiresome. It was a series of hills and valleys he wished to just end. Why he couldn't even have an afterlife ending as a true, flat, straight path he didn't know but it was starting to irritate him.

"How long till we get there then?" Dugan asked merely to strike up a new conversation against the oppressive silence. It was something to do until he met his new owner.

"We'll be there before you know it." Cracius gave answer without turning back.

"So why is this place full of ruins and dust?" Dugan tended to the conversational kindling. "I thought Mortis was filled with ghosts and ghouls."

Tebow chuckled. "More misconceptions of our faith and god. What most people don't understand is that all things have a lifespan. Even things without a soul or spirit pass away. Though they may not be the same type of span for life as living, breathing creatures have, all things have an allotted span of existence. Once that time has expired they fade from the cosmos – dying if you will, and end up here."

Dugan looked up to his left to see a shattered bust whose shoulders were the only things to remain intact, the head above them long since shattered away. "So even art comes here to 'die'?"

"Yes," said Tebow. "Artwork, bricks, houses, palaces, planets, stars, even whole empires when they've meet their demise end up here. The world may see them as falling to flame, rust, moth, war or some other such thing but even as their remains are scattered over Tralodren and the cosmos, their very nature – their concept of design and purpose come here. This isn't just for tangible things either. Ideas end up here too. When they have been forgotten or abandoned or suppressed – philosophies and understandings dying the slow death of dark ages, all come to Mortis in the end."

"So Mortis is one massive graveyard." Dugan took more in from the stark scenery around them. He found himself wondering just how many ages sat here in the dust. How many layers of time had not only come to rest from Tralodren but from other spots all over the cosmos. How many stars contributed to the dry dust he was walking on now?

"Yes," the older priest answered.

"If I wasn't already promised to Rheminas, then where would I go?" Dugan's brain – at least his spiritual version of it he supposed...or was that his soul – blast these priests for muddling his thoughts, was bubbling a line of questioning to a boil. "Priests have always said that if you hold to no deity as your own, you don't get an afterlife. I didn't hold to any deity in life – so would I be here if not for Rheminas?"

There was silence for a small part of the the journey.

Dugan found it unpleasant and uncomfortable until Tebow broke it. "Why does this all concern you now Dugan? You can't change anything that happened once you've come to Mortis."

"It's something to pass the time, and I find it fascinating." Dugan replied in truth. "If it can't help me then fine, but at least I can have something to think about as I live out my existence with Rheminas."

"Very well," Tebow held his face stern and forward as he walked onward.

"So then what happens to a person who dies without holding to a particular deity?" The Telborian repeated.

"Your afterlife is determined entirely by what you held to in belief while you lived in your physical body." Cracius stated. "If you held to a certain god then to him you would go, if you held to more than one – as is the cause in some areas of the world who worship the light gods together, then you have a potential set of options for an afterlife – which I'll get back to in a moment." The young priest rose a pointed finger before him as if to remind himself to do so.

"Now, to those who held to no god in their mortal life…well, they are sent to the Abyss."

"*The Abyss?*" Dugan's face went white from both shock and rage. "What kind of reward is that?"

"A true one," Tebow added flatly.

"So a man who lived a good life but was not that beholden to a god would still end up in the Abyss?" Dugan couldn't believe it. Where was the justice in that?

"All who have made their way into the Abyss have done so for one of two reasons and sometimes both reasons," Tebow craned his neck to take in a sideways glance of the Telborian behind them who was still chewing on some raw anger. "They have either warred against the gods or they have denied them their due as powers greater than themselves."

"So I would have gone to the Abyss?" Dugan's fear had subsided a little now with his rage, but it still clung about his face and thoughts for a little while longer. Had he still had a heartbeat it would have been pumping quite heavily…the warlust might even have been coming upon him.

"Don't trouble yourself about it, Dugan." Cracius took up the conversation. "It's been decreed since the dawn of creation and there is nothing any can do to change it. Just be thankful you are going to Helii and not the Abyss. Though Helii is a harsh realm, the Abyss is far, far worse."

"Yes." Tebow looked behind himself to see how Dugan was doing with all this new revelation of knowledge. "A small hope but at least you won't have to know the despair and horrors of that realm. Even many of the gods shun the Abyss."

"I still don't find it fair that one has to be made to worship a god to have an afterlife out of the Abyss." Dugan wouldn't let his sense of injustice die down just yet.

"The gods created Tralodren and all things in it Dugan, I think it fair that they make the rules of their own creation." Tebow shifted his head forward once more.

"What about those that hold to more than one god." Dugan's hope rose. Perhaps he had found at least some small part of common sense to this seeming disparity of justice. "Where do they go then?"

"Well," Cracius slowed a bit in his gait to let the Telborian come up beside him as he spoke, "That is for the Lords of Death to decide. They judge all who pass their way into death and determine where they best are suited to pass into based upon what they believed and how they lived out that belief. So most go to one of the gods they worshipped. Whichever deity matched their strongest beliefs – they are sent to for eternity. You can tell these right away because they don't have a robe. Neither they nor those destined for the Abyss wear a robe."

"So that's it?" Dugan looked across at the young priest.

"Yes." Cracius returned the gaze. "Were you thinking this matter more complicated than it really is?"

"I guess so." Dugan returned his gaze to his feet as he continued to shuffle onward.

"Well…" Cracius' voice brought Dugan's eyes back on him, "there *is* the matter of Paradise. Since we've shared just about the whole process of how the afterlife works, I might as well share that with you too."

"What about it? I heard a song about it in the arena a long time ago. Isn't it suppose to be the most splendid place in the cosmos or something."

"Just as the Abyss is unclaimed – for no god claims it as his own, Paradise is also unclaimed by any god." Cracius began to explain. "It is here that good is manifested and those who have done some incredibly noble and righteous deed have been known to ascend from time to time – both robed and unrobed creatures alike."

"Even if they didn't believe in the gods?" Dugan pressed the thought forward again.

"No, they have to believe in the gods or a god, that is a constant truth." Cracius answered. "If they hold to a god though and do a noble and good deed which brings about their death then they have been known to enter into Paradise, but the judge who grants passage into that gate – the twelfth gate, is a hard one to pass."

"Who's the judge?" Dugan wondered for himself as well as in a general sense. Though he knew he wasn't destined for the twelfth gate, he was still curious.

"Asorlok." Tebow was curt, and slowed down so now he stood beside Dugan on the opposite side.

"The god of death is the judge?" Dugan snorted. "How fair is that?"

"He is an impartial judge who doesn't judge by his own authority but by the authority given him from another greater than himself." Tebow now stopped.

Cracius followed his example.

"What are you talking about?" Dugan grumbled as he too stopped after a few more steps forward. He was getting upset with all this mystical, cryptic speech, which priests tended to sprinkle their words. "Just speak plainly. I'm dead. You don't need to keep up with these mysteries."

"We've told you all that you need to know. It is a matter that doesn't concern you nor will effect you where you are going." Tebow sounded a little bit irritated now as if he had grown tired of the former gladiator's company. It wasn't cold, but it was certainly formal and meant to put an end to any further inquiries into the matter.

"And besides, we have reached our destination." Tebow pointed ahead of them causing Dugan to follow the priest's lead to look before him. In the distance he could see a huge gray mountain ascend into the dim sky. At its peak, stood the bone colored walls and silver capped towers of Sheol, the city of Asorlok, The Lord of Mortis. Millions of people pooled around the mountains base, snaking up its rocky trials and streaming in from beyond like living rivers. They came in all shapes and sizes, from all races that covered the world. Rich and poor, old and young, beautiful and hideous – all had been made the same in death. Each had to wait for their own audience with the Sovereign Lord of the Silent Slumber and learn of their eternal fate. Many of the throng were bedecked in robes ranging in color to form an unimaginable spectrum whose myriad multitude washed the gray mount in vibrant brilliance.

Dugan couldn't believe they were so many people in all the world. He had never even heard of, let alone seen. many of the creatures who now waited in line for an audience with the Judge of the Spirit. More amazing still was the fact that still more seemed to come out of the scenery, as Dugan and the two priests had just done, to add to the back of the congested mass. It seemed an eternal progress of bodies and the Telborian found maddening to even try and figure out just how it all worked or the sheer volume of what he was seeing. This itself had to be a miracle for he didn't have words to explain what he felt or thought. How could he when he was witnessing the whole dead population of Tralodren, *and the entire cosmos,* converging at the base of a mountain for their final judgment…

"Come." Tebow resumed his previous pace. "We should be there shortly."

Chapter 19

~⊙~⊙~

𝕬 lazy orange sun reflected off the high bronze dome of the grandest and oldest building in Cleithious, capital of the Republic of Rexatious. The Great Library was a sight to behold even for The City of Wonders itself. Said to have been built even before the palace outline was drawn out across the dirt, it safeguarded all the knowledge and history that the Patrious had collected over their long series of generations. Recently added to the collection was what Gilban had brought back from his mission to Takta Lu Lama.

The Great Library was under the control of the Dradinites, the most powerful of faiths on Rexatious, who followed Dradin, god of learning, literacy and magic. His temple, called The Temple of the Eternal Book, was the largest to the god in all the world. His priests, more numerous than bees, busied themselves on various tasks from copying old manuscripts, maintaining the library and recording new knowledge in the form of historical accounts, day to day events and other fare alongside their religious duties.

The temple was very close to the library, but not connected. The Dradinites were a cautious bunch when it came to protecting the library. Keeping it free any other buildings, though there was a small shrine to Dradin inside, that helped safeguard the books from fire or structural failure of another sort. Having a grand botanical encampment around the library also added a hedge of protection.

A marvel in its own right, the lush grounds sported tall shade trees, bubbling fountains both of the geometrical and humanoid type, soft green grass and cobble stone pathways for travelers to wander the rainbow hued flower beds and various shrub mazes. If that wasn't enough to enhance the beauty of the place, their were several small artificial lakes that dotted the landscape; more ponds than extensive expanses of water, they had been arranged at strategic points to serve as natural fire breaks should the worse come the library's way. Many of these ponds had small footbridges, others were left more 'natural' but all were the destinations of many waterfowl that had come to make much of this park their home over the decades and centuries.

All this of course was mere dressing; a necklace around the neck of the real beauty: the library itself. Even amid the tallest trees it stood out higher; its gigantic golden dome rising above them all to shimmer in the sun. A wide array of architectural wonders had been compelled in unison to create such a building, more than any one person untrained in a mason's craft could discern, but all could understand size well enough. The full height of the dome was two hundred ten feet and the measurements of the library itself were two hundred sixty by two hundred seventy feet.

There was more than that to see with his eyes as the whole structure was a visual feast. A series of smaller domes rose up all around it's base like mushrooms or soap bubbles. There were two in the front, two to each side and two in the back. Each of these were topped with copper, gray granite was the whole exterior of these buildings, along with the Great Library which they encircled. Most eyes though fell from the central dome to the eight red marble caryatids which supported the overhang of the pediment of stone and roof tile fifty feet above the white marble steps leading to two massive, gold plated, doors some thirty feet from where the pediment began.

The caryatid were spread out amid the sixty-foot entrance way under the pediment which had been carved with the image of a cloaked man holding up an open book. Six of the caryatid were chiseled to resemble attractive Patrician maidens wrapped in an himation; ampyx crowning each of their heads. Together the three stood back to back; hands lifted above them to capture the roof and keep it aloft. Their sandaled feet resting upon a platform of smooth red marble some five feet off the ground.

Two other caryatids followed the clustered three, these being opposite each other and between the doorway, which was arched to a forty-five foot height to allow the tall doors to open, and the clustered column. Each of these two singular columns was the mirror of the other: a himation, sandal- and ampyx -dressed elven maid, but these held the weight of the roof with their head. Each also faced the patron as they climbed the steps inside with a congenial face and subtle smile. They also held a rolled scroll in each hand crossed over their breasts so as to form an "x".

At the base of the library, near the very steps themselves, were three people appearing from the air; coming into greater clarity like a solidifying smoke. Surprisingly, their arrival was not noticed by any of the Patrious who milled about the stone roads who seemed too diligent in their tasks and goings. Many were too snared by the beauty around them and their own daily routines – their internal thoughts. These did little more than walk past them, looking up at them with distant eyes which told them someone was there that should be stepped around to avoid collision, but that was all.

A few, though, took notice of the newcomers as two of them were humans amid a predominately Patrician world. Those who took particular notice were two Patrician maids who came from behind the newly arrived trio, both of whom turned a curious eye toward Rowan as they passed him on route to the library's great marble steps. They looked no more than sixteen winters to the Nordican (though he knew they had to be five or even ten times older than that) who felt himself grow flush with their stares and girlish giggles.

Clara, watching it from his side, gave the young knight a sly smile. "I don't think a Nordican has ever come this far. You're quite a sight to behold."

"An oddity, then." The knight gave the woman he was learning to love a sideways glance.

"I think those two showed good taste, though." She drew closer to Rowan, smile deepening all the way.

"So, I'm the only Nordican that's ever been here?" The knight sidestepped the comment with his own thoughts.

"The only one that I've ever heard of coming on shore." The elf answered.

"Then won't I cause too much attention to us – mess up the task at hand?" He looked around then, fearful of causing a disturbance or hinder them in any way.

"Rowan," Clara giggled, " We're here to do research work, I don't think your being the stranger here would interfere with that. If anything, it might help us."

"I don't understand how." He kept up his looking around, though at a lesser degree than before when he saw just about everyone seemed to pay him little mind.

"Preferential treatment for the first visitor of your race." Clara added matter of factly, as if the thought should have been in the knights head as soon as she brought up the point.

"I don't know–" Rowan started.

"Usually my people don't give out special treatment to anyone beyond their rank." Clara causally commented. "They tend to treat everyone just about the same. However, if one of the curators of the library wishes to do you an honor or favor because of your unique presence, I think it would not be too unwise to take them up on such an offer."

"Of course," she sighed, "most here might not even pay us that much mind. They *are* scholars and bookworms to a man, and probably couldn't care less about who we are, just as long as we don't interrupt their studies."

Clara rousted the youth's hair with her hand. "Besides, with that tan you look more Telborian than Nordican, and we see our fair share of Telborians in this part of the world."

"I see." Rowan's sunburn he'd received a few months ago had faded away for the most part, but the lingering traits of a tan, refreshed from his recent sea voyage to Arid Land, did darken his skin a bit more than the pale snowy shade most of his race were known to possess. Confident he could handle whatever came his way, he turned back to look at the impressive building. "So this is where all the knowledge of the world can be found, huh?"

"Well, all the knowledge that has been written down, yes." Clara joined his gaze toward the scintillating dome. "There are still secrets that have yet to be tapped, but everything that has happened since recorded time and even before is inside."

"So with all this knowledge why don't you do anything with it?" Rowan asked the elf.

"What do you mean?" She turned to face the youth.

"I mean, why not use it to build up an empire or pass it on to the world so that everyone could have it and benefit from it?"

"Well…I-I don't know really." Clara stammered with the ideology she had come to accept in her youth. "The idea behind the library is to store all the knowledge and keep it safe."

"Safe from what?" Rowan moved to stand before the elf; eyes alight with questions.

"From falling into the wrong hands." Clara spoke as if the answer was self-evident.

"*Whose* hands though are the wrong hands?" Rowan crossed his arms. The knight saw some holes in this thought process. Why keep knowledge from those who could benefit from it? It made little sense to him.

Clara didn't answer, she knew where the knight was going with this line of questioning and she didn't want to journey down that path with him. It wasn't the time for such a discussion, they had work to do and little time in which to do it.

"We really don't have time for this discussion right now." Clara started to move briskly toward the library.

"I see," was all that Rowan said before he lowered his arms and cleared himself from Clara's path.

"You ready Cadrissa?" Clara moved her gaze to the mage.

"It's more beautiful than I could have ever imagined." The mage stood transfixed outside the large building. She had been mesmerized by it during the couple's entire conversation. It was a true wonder of the world, and she was standing outside it – the very seat of all collected knowledge of Tralodren…If only she could live here for the rest of her life and absorb all that was inside it…all the knowledge she could ever want or need…

"You okay?" Rowan's touch on the mage's back brought her back from her gaping daydream.

"Huh – yeah. I just can't believe we are here is all…it's just so *huge.*"

"Yes it is." Clara added. "You can take years in just one section of it alone if you wanted to and still not read everything there."

"And we're suppose to find this information about the scepter in *there*?" Rowan shook his head slightly. "If it takes years just to go through one section how are we going to *locate*, let alone *read* the information we're looking for?"

"He's right, Cadrissa." Clara added. "Do you have any idea where to start?"

"Inside is always a good place to begin." The mage began to make her way toward the white marble steps. "They should have a directory of what materials are stored where, correct? All the same information about a certain topic in one area?"

"Yes, they do have a directory," Clara joined the mage in her ascent up the steps and past the tall caryatids, "but that's pretty large too, and a lot of it can only be found by the help of the curators anyway."

"Then we better get started." Cadrissa moved toward the great gold covered doors that were double her size in both height and width. Rowan found himself drawn to the caryatids on either side for a moment, admiring their beauty and comparing it to Clara's own charms, and then back to his task at hand. Through the open portal filtered out Patrician men and woman, scholars and priests, even a few wizards, all who had come in and were going into the Great Library for greater insight.

They passed all these without incident and weren't even hindered from entrance by the two silver scale mail covered guards standing on either side of the great opening. Each donned a green silk cape attached over their shoulders and fastened onto their silver coat; carrying a long spear in hand. Their feet were garbed in black leather sandals, where a medium oblong shield, painted with the image of an open book rested not too far away. These guards only eyed Rowan with some slight interest, and possibly suspicion, but let him pass with the others. They hadn't even taken notice of the scepter at Cadrissa's side. He supposed he might have expected more from them, but was happy with their lax interest. Perhaps he was indeed more Telborian than Nordican now as Clara has said. When he reached the inside of the building though, he could scarcely believe his eyes.

All was like a vision before the young knight. It was as if he had passed into the realms beyond and was in the very chamber of some god. Gilt was everywhere. Candelabras hung down on shimmering chains high above the domed ceilings which held not candles, but slender crystal rods of light – enchanted items crafted by aid of mages and Dradin's favor. Daylight poured in from stained glassed windows, which spread across walls of the upper- or middle-level where galleries snaked around the whole building. These brought in a rainbow hue which mixed with the silver rods of the candelabra in a most exquisitely breathtaking way.

Added to this light was the illumination which fell from even higher, arched windows – the collar of the great dome. Numbering forty-seven in all, these windows were crafted to hold golden tinted glass which served to enrich the already splendid light dancing about the library's interior. This rich light only accented the luscious mosaics covering all of the ceiling and dripped down to form renditions of past philanthropists and rulers who had added to the greatness of the library.

The strong aroma of cedar and other strange perfumes hung heavy in the area; wafting from specially crafted incense burners dangling from the ceiling. It was an almost overpowering mix that mingled with the tang of the dry leather and time-aged pages of the countless tomes, scrolls, and sheets that filled every opening of the gigantic shelves that seemed to take the place of walls inside the library. The further he walked into the great entrance chamber the more he felt his tongue and mouth go dry; his eyes grew sore and itchy.

"The books pages suck all the moisture from the air. Your eyes will get used to it shortly." Clara gave some explanation to Rowan's rubbing of his reddened eyes.

"What's that smell?" Rowan's nose had wrinkled farther up his face the further they entered into the antechamber.

"Cedar shelves help keep some vermin away and the incense is a special mixture the Dradinites make to keep the other pests, who would destroy the pages stored here, from coming inside," said Clara.

"And we're going to have to be here for *how* long?" Rowan was reminded of the strong perfume that the harlot wore who had harassed him when he first came to Elandor. It wasn't a fond memory.

"As long as it takes. You'll get used to the smell, too." Cadrissa answered as she drew near to a tall wooden cabinet, lined with perhaps a hundred small wooden drawers, then stopped. The cabinet was as tall as the mage and perhaps twice that in width. It stood at the base of a man-sized statue of a middled aged Patrious elf dressed in some archaic armor. Some twenty feet away from the stone figure there were rows of ten foot tall cedar shelves going onward for as far as the eye could see, dotted with the odd statue or pieces of crumbled sculpture placed in alcoves like relics on display.

Here and there as well were long, oak tables and chairs along with some shorter, more intimate collections of tables and chairs that were populated with a smattering of scribes and common folk alike.

"The directory." Cadrissa pulled out one of the square drawers at chest level like a child opening a box full of candy. Inside was a worm of parchment sheets cut to neatly stand upright within the drawer. The mage's fingerless golden gloved digits dug into them instantly moving down the line like dominoes.

Rowan lifted his head higher to look at another level above him still. Being allowed access to the sight via archways opening up the wall, he spied yet more of the same that made up the lower level. It was a world of books and scrolls and strange smelling incense. A world in which Rowan felt very much the stranger.

"We're going to have to locate the section on the Wizard Kings and narrow it down from there. I'm going to focus on the Third and Fourth Ages as those would be the key times such an item could be crafted. Maybe even the Wars of Magic too…" Cadrissa stopped when she pulled out a card. "Clara, is everything here in Collonus?"

Collonus was the ancient base tongue of the elven race or rather it was believed to be; at least for the Patrious and Elyellium. These two of the four known races of elves shared it in history but the other two races of elves on Tralodren did not seem to come from the same language tree.

"Everything but the source documents, yes." She had joined the mage at the directory.

"That could be a problem then." The mage turned to the elf.

"It's one of the few languages I can't read." The mage's shoulders sunk in with a sigh. I guess you won't be able to help out too much either, Rowan unless, it's written in a human dialect." Cadrissa turned to face the knight, who was staring at the statute of the anciently armored elf in thought.

"I'll do what I can, but if it's not in a human dialect then I won't be able to translate it, no." He raised a finger to the statue. "Who is this?"

"Cleseth," Clara joined him before the stone figure. "He's the founder of our nation, the one who built all this up and was the first ruler of Rexatious."

"Hmph," came Rowan's reply.

"Since I can't read the directory," Cadrissa turned to the elf, "You'll have to find what we're looking for: some books on the Fourth Age of the Wizard Kings."

"Okay." Clara trotted off to the directory again. "Give me a moment and I should be able to find something. I was taught how to use this system when I was younger."

Rowan made his way across the mosaic floor behind the statue, below the dome, stopping to gaze down at the image portrayed: a wizen, green garbed, Patrious bent over a table writing in a book. Quill in hand and an inkwell at his side, the figure was a bit of mystery to the knight.

"Who is this?" He asked the mage who had followed him.

Cadrissa looked down at the mosaic. "That's Dradin."

"Dradin?" Rowan returned to face the wizardress. "I didn't know he was an elf."

"It's how the Dradinites, his followers, see him here. This whole library is owned and kept up by them as a service to their god, the Great Chronicler."

"So this is a temple then?" Rowan lifted his head to take in the high domed ceiling once more and saw the dark images of green clad figures in some kind of collected pose amid the various other geometric and figurative mosaics which spread over the entire ceiling.

"To a follower of Dradin, all places of knowledge are holy sites." Cadrissa joined the knight in looking up at the dome. It really was a lovely sight, and she never would grow tired of looking at it. For indeed, here was her shrine. For someone who loved knowledge, where else could she go? Would she even dare to leave such a place in the first place? If not for the threat of The Master she probably won't. In fact she would be content to live out all her days in this place and…she felt her head growing numb again and the medallion at her side flaring to life.

At least the whispers had stopped.

That was a blessing.

Had she been forced to suffer through that experience any longer she might have been driven to the doorway of insanity. It was an odd and frightening thing to hear all those faint echoes climbing around her head like spiders on their web; building a net around her consciousness, hampering her thought.

What was it anyway? Far from a simple, enchanted bauble, that was for sure. She was also now almost certain it was tied to the events that had taken place so far. Starting with the stone circle–

"So Dradin's your god, right?" Rowan inquisitiveness jarred her from her thoughts.

"Found it." Clara's interjection brought the two around to see the elf closing up the drawer with a look of triumph. "I think the section we want is on the second floor toward the back of the library." The elf then made her way toward the set of wide marble stairs, lined with gold worked railings nestled to the left side of a corridor alongside the library; its twin to the far right. Both Rowan and Cadrissa followed.

"Can you tell me anything more about what Gilban shared with you regarding the scepter?" The mage asked along their way.

"Not much more than I did already. He told me it could be used to stop a god. Then, of course, he told all of us it can only be used once in a lifetime."

"Yes, that once in a lifetime clause again…" Cadrissa traced her finger along the scepter's plain head with her free hand as she walked. As she did so she felt the medallion at her side flare up with an intense heat – even hotter than before and felt a painful spike invade her head. She managed to force it aside though, and in a moment both the heat and pain faded away.

"I don't think Gilban meant it could only be used once in a gen-eration. The Wizard Kings wouldn't have put so heavy a restriction on the item – of that I'm sure. So I think it best to assume that it can be used only once in the lifetime of the wielder."

"Are you sure?" Rowan followed behind the two women.

"I just have a hunch." Cadrissa returned the scepter to her side. She didn't want to say anything about how she felt different, how everything arcane and mystical about her and around here seemed to be amplified beyond her own natural ability of understanding. She felt as though she had stepped into a pair of shoes that were much to large for her, but with each passing moment, her feet were learning to grow into them.

"So what do we do then?" Rowan asked as they reached the foot of the grand staircase populated with ascending and descending Patrious.

"I guess, just start looking through the books and scrolls to see what we can figure out." The mage climbed the first step. "And pray the gods are merciful in leading us to what we seek."

"So let's get started." Clara followed.

Chapter 20

"What do you want with me?" The Master's voice fell flat before him, as if all the force of his words dissipated as soon as they left his mouth, unable or unwilling to continue their existence.

"You will serve my purpose." The voice returned, though the dark god continued to have a hard time in trying to figure out from where it came amid the placid fields of pitch surrounding him. "I wouldn't have been so direct, but you aren't going to get to the place I need you to be without this intervention and seeing how my opponent has made a rather direct intervention of sorts as well– "

"I serve no one!" The Master turned to where he guessed the voice might be coming.

Laughter.

"I am The Master! I am a *god*!"

"You are my pawn and part of my plan." Came the cold reply of the phantom voice.

"Show yourself! Your speech is bold, but you've made no effort to reveal your form. Where's your courage?" Cadrith continued to search for his heckler in vain.

"Where's yours?" Came the cold voice's rebuke. "I have no need to boast, as some do. I know who I am. Arrogance is just a front for stupidity…and often…cowardice."

"To the Abyss with you and your games! Release me now!" Cadrith's rage was hot.

Laughter once more came to The Master's ears. It seemed to encircle him, swimming about his head and mind and echoing out of time with itself as to make a seeming chorus of ridicule; a wreath of mockery about his head.

"You are as arrogant as you are naive. Did you really think you could have earned the right to the godhood you now hold? Did you really think you were skilled enough; that you were worthy for such responsibility? Mortals have been searching for that privilege since the beginning. Even the so-called gods stole what they possess; no more deserving of your own attempt, but even in their theft they are of higher worth than you."

"It was I who freed you from your prison, and set you on the Path of Power which lead you to Galba. I also kept you alive in your trials where you would have disbursed into the cosmos. I've watched over you for quite some time, knowing you and planning your purpose since you were a mortal man. You are my tool, and I have one last use for you and then I am finished."

The Master listened to the words coming to his mind and ears. He didn't want to believe, couldn't believe, what was being told to him. Had he really not been able to do all he thought he was? Was his whole life, his whole desire for power and his dream of gaining godhood simply the urging and creation of this formless being? Was he really nothing more than a pawn in some game?

"Lies." The Master spat. "What you're telling me is possible to only the most powerful of gods. I have studied the Pantheon and there are none who would have done all that you have said. None would even bother themselves with me until now, when I pose a threat to them.

"You'd make the bards happy with your tales, but I don't believe them. It was a good story really and I almost believed it...almost."

The Master was regaining some of his confidence again. This had to be a pathetic attempt to slow him down to hinder him or trap him. Maybe it was even the work of Endarien to keep him from defeating the winged god.

Yes, that had to be it...

"The gods must indeed be worried if they are beginning to perform such actions." The Master believed he had figured this situation out. "So who are you *really* then? Gurthghol? Asorlok? One of you must have come with Endarien."

"You think that the gods are the highest beings in the cosmos?" The voice countered. "Didn't you just finish meeting with a being who could grant godhood to mortals? A being who was more powerful than gods themselves-"

"Galba!" The Master's eyes blazed hot blue flames. "This is *your* work? You swore you'd have no more to do with me."

"Idiot!" The voice returned as a hate-filled, cutting tone resonating around the dark god "Galba is nothing – a form that is taken on much like gods when they wish to walk Tralodren since it is barred from their true form. The force behind Galba's true form is something else."

"You also studied us Cadrith. I made sure of that. You had to have some knowledge of us to get this far. You were never given the true picture of things, no, but enough to begin to understand and prepare you for the work I'd have you do. You couldn't have done what you did without knowledge of us, that was what led you to Galba in the first place."

Suddenly a thought began to germinate in The Master's mind. It shot up quickly taking root from his understanding of what the voice was telling him. He couldn't believe it though...it seemed too impossible. If correct, then he had become the biggest fool ever and he was indeed in more danger than he thought.

"Galba *was* the Positive Energy." The Master's tone was hushed in the revelation.

"A representative of it." The voice toyed with the dark god, letting the truth sink in slowly – layer by layer.

"Then...you are the *Negative* Energy." The Master didn't like where this was leading.

"Now you begin to understand." The voice was rich with sardonic mirth. Like the tired teacher who is happy his slow student has finally grasped the most basic of concepts after years of lecture on it.

"Wh-what do you wish of me?" The Master, for the first time in his long life, had dread seep into his bones. Fearful in the understanding that he really had no control over his life or death anymore – that his movements have been calculated prior to it all starting. Such revelations revealed to him the great emptiness of his future…the barren potential in trying to achieve his plans and dreams…What was the purpose now if everything had been preordained.

"Not so arrogant now, eh?" The voice gloated. "Now listen to what I have brought you here to undertake."

Endarien had left The Master's island in a stormy wrath. He was still vexed over how The Master had survived his attack. It should have killed him outright, dissipating his being totally. He had used the will of his grandfather, the most powerful of gods and still The Master had survived. The lich's patron was truly a force which with to be reckoned.

Endarien flew over the Northlands in his search: Valkoria, Baltan, Frigia, and Troll Island. They seemed empty of the dark god's presence. Endarien's own sharp vision revealing to him all that passed below him in clear minute detail. Where could he be? For good measure he flew over Arid Land, over Galba's circle. Nothing there as well. So where was he? It was as if he fled from the world which Endarien knew was impossible…or was it? The dark god's patron could very well do such a thing if he already had saved Cadrith from destruction…

Endarien's wings beat thick turrets of clouds like rolling surf in the sky as he turned toward the Midlands in his frustration. A thick slate gray thunderhead proceeded him, a long stretch of brilliant white cumulus clouds followed in his wake. Should he fail to find and defeat The Master before Vkar's essesence left him Endarien would be trapped on Tralodren…forever. That was a fate he'd have to avoid no matter if he found Cadrith or not. His revenge was important to him but not so much as he would jeopardize his chances at being free from the confines of Tralodren.

Time was not on his side.

The Storm Lord hovered over Talatheal.

Nothing.

None of the birds he had released found sight of the dark god either.Colloni, Draladon, also revealed nothing of The Master as the great weather based parade flew onward. It was fast becoming a pointless search. Frustration mounting to a pinnacle as he thought about what he should do next. What he could do next… and the options were not pleasing.

The Master had finished listening to the voice's plan.

He was speechless.

It was brilliant to say the least, and dwarfed anything the dark god could have thought of himself; that was certain. The scope, the implications were beyond anything he had known, every thought possible under his own increased understanding of things by divine insight.

"Now you understand your place." The voice from the darkness echoed in The Master's head.

"It seems I have little choice." The Master returned.

"You always have a choice – everyone does. In any choice you make, however, my plan is still laid, and you still serve me."

"You don't think anyone else will be able to stop you then?" The Master needed to make sure he understood all the angles.

"Only one, but they will be unable. What I have told you shall come to be."

"What do *I* get out of all this though?" The Master scanned the empty shadows before him. "You've told me what I have to do, but what do I get out of all if it? If I do as you say or if I refuse you've said the event will happen as planned anyway, so what is my incentive to work with you?"

"Your boldness returns it seems." The voice chuckled. "You want something to motivate you? How about your continued existence? I will let you exist when this is all over...should you survive."

"That's not enough." The Master stated dryly.

"You presume much, Cadrith." The tone of the voice had grown flat.

"Your prize is too fleeting." The Master pressed for all that he could get out of the offer before him. "I need more than my existence to move me toward your side. I want–"

"Power." The voice echoed from all over the darkness. "So be it. I shall grant you greater insights into the power you seek. You shall learn things that few of the gods know or dare to seek out should you survive. Does this satisfy your urgings then?"

"Yes. It will do nicely." The Master said smugly. "So now that we are agreed, how do you want me to start your plan then?"

"I will return you to the world you left," said the voice,"and then you are to start immediately performing what I have set you to be about.

"You know what you must do and how it should be done. I will aid you no more. You will have my mantle resting upon you and that is all. Should you die then so be it, the plan will still be completed as I have told you it must...even in your death. Once back on your world you are on your own, but I will be watching you. Succeed and live, and you will be given access to the secrets and increased power you seek, as well as keeping your existence."

Without warning The Master found himself on Tralodren once more. Far from his keep he rested in what he understood to be a desert, but what desert and at what time he didn't know. He felt the presence of the dark entity on him as well now, heavy and strong like a yoke attached to a weighty stone. It was in that domineering weight though that The Master found the pool of power which now fueled him to a greater place than he had been before, even with his recent status of god.

The large disc of the sun blazed down upon him with a furious glare, his dark clothed frame alone in the empty expanse stretched on for miles. He knew what he had to do if he was to serve the voice. Though he didn't enjoy the servitude, he would submit to it this once. He had another plan brewing in his mind – a failsafe he had put in place when he rose to godhood. He would yet be master again of his own fate should things not go to his liking.

He didn't know if he could trust The Darkness. It offered him no real assurance save its words, and even those were not backed by anything of substance. Further, it seemed odd to The Master that he would be promised anything if even in his death he would accomplish the will of this entity.

Why even give him anything in the first place?

No, it was better to play along for now, to give it what it wanted, and then to keep his back door open for escape should events not befall him in a manner he enjoyed. That was his only real security. That was where he could only draw forth his comfort about anything now. Though he feared the entity, he also had no true reason to trust it, not yet. He'd survive to make his way to the goals he wished to complete on his own terms. For now he had to plan, to bide his time, and enact the plan that had been given him. In the meantime he would have to get to work.

Looking around the desert, he examined the horizon for any familiar spots he might have known. He didn't find any but felt drawn to the east. Something was there he'd need to seek out. Something that was vital to the entity's plan. He didn't have the ability yet to transport himself there as he didn't really know where it was exactly or what he was looking for; only that it was there before him in the east. It waited for him; called out to him. And so all he could do was tread sand in his trek forward.

High above Tralodren Endarien stopped. He hovered over the northern hemisphere in thought. He had felt something – a jolt of energy like a ripple in a pond, told him The Master had again surfaced on the world.

"I sense you, Cadrith." Endarien called out, the heavens quaking with his glee.

"You shouldn't have come back – should have kept your tail between your legs and stayed in hiding." Endarien extended Heaven's Wrath above his head in a triumph salute; raising Storm's Eye before him as if the god was preparing to defend himself from a charge. "You'll soon be dust in the wind and I and the Pantheon will finally be vindicated."

The Storm Lord fell from the sky toward where he knew The Master to be. His majestic presence surging with the remaining remnants of Vkar's blessing; his very flesh pulsating with increased strength and ability that was birthed in rage and war.

"Your death comes on swift wings godling!" The sky god screamed over a symphonic eruption of thunder and lighting overhead.

"Your death comes on swift wings!"

Chapter 21

Dugan, Cracius and Tebow had made their way toward the back of the massive sea of creatures around the base of Sheol. From his slightly higher vantage point, where he had come to stand astride a broken mound of columns amid the throng, the former gladiator could see the collected masses of goblins, giants, humans, elves, and all manner of creatures that called Tralodren home. Some Dugan knew only from stories and some he didn't know at all. Some with robes. Some without the colorful garments.

Everyone of them continued to stand still and silent, waiting for their chance to ascend the mountain to the city, and from there go off to their afterlife. It didn't matter if the person would be going to a favorable end or not, all were silent and still in the massive, fleshy press. And that was another thing which struck the Telborian as odd. He was still surprised at how 'solid' their frames were. Now that he understood the whole process a bit better regarding the nature of soul and spirit, he could make some sense of it but it was still odd to think that your spirit could be as solid as your flesh. It could be as real, if not more real than your physical form.

Dugan pondered this as he surveyed the swath of mortalkind around him, others have already filled in behind him and were extending the sea to still further banks. How did these people all come here anyway? He didn't see any marks on their person at all that could tell him if it was a sword, or sickness. Moreover, none of them were old either. All were either at the prime of their life in appearance or younger. This was very odd indeed and a bit unnerving to the hardened slayer of men and beasts. He saw not an old face in the crowd. How he could be sure of the longer lived nonhuman creatures he was uncertain, but the humans all seemed to be no older than middle aged, and extremely vigorous in appearance.

When he finished looking about he stepped down from the crumbling mound to join the two death priests. When he did so he seemed to think he had moved forward more, but knew he hadn't taken a step forward. He had stood in line this whole time and no one in front of him nor behind him moved forward. He seemed to be closer to Sheol than before, and the scenery around him reflected he had indeed moved forward.

"Did we just move?" Dugan was perplexed.

"Though it looks long, the line itself is rather swift." Tebow cocked his head to one side in answer. "Asorlok and his lords are very efficient judges."

Dugan let the silence settle in again before he began to think of new thoughts to pass the time while he waited, though it might not be as long a wait as he thought hearing Tebow tell it. No new thoughts came though. His mind was as still as the scene about him. What could he do but wait? He was pretty much boxed in now amid the group of beings who had pressed up against him from behind and all around…More and more from who knows where and how. It was a seemingly endless process of the dead, which Dugan knew would go on long after he had passed this way and would go on for all eternity.

"If this is the amount who are dying, won't the realms where they're going be filled up soon?"

"No." Cracius answered. "The realms of the gods are very large in theory, they could be filled in time, albeit a very long time, but it will never get to that point."

"Why not?" Dugan looked over at the priests, happy for some conversation again.

"The Great End." Cracius returned matter-of-factly.

"What's that?" Dugan didn't like the sound of that.

"The time when all of Tralodren and the Pantheon is destroyed," said the younger priest.

"He didn't need to know that, Cracius," Tebow scolded the younger priest. "Such information is meant only for us to know for it will just trouble those who pass our way. He has enough to contend with in his mind before this enlightenment came to him."

Dugan stood still for a moment and watched the priests in their discussion. He was trying to make sense of what he was just told. It was too incredible and dreadful to believe. The Asorlins stopped their palaver to look over at the Telborian who had just then finally gotten his lower jaw back under control and promptly closed it.

"Since you started this matter," Tebow instructed Cracius, "you will have to finish it."

Finally, Dugan asked the question that all three had been waiting for. "You mean even if the world is saved from The Master it will be destroyed anyway and the gods with it?"

"All things will fade away," was Cracius' reply.

"So what does *that* mean?" Dugan wasn't totally sure he wanted an answer.

"You must understand that all life, in fact all existence as you understand it, is really in a downward spiral, funneling to an ending point where nothing more can be spun lower, and then everything stops." Cracius began to explain.

"You mean the whole world, the gods, even this afterlife everyone here is going to – is coming to an end?" Dugan's eyes went wide.

"Yes, the cycles are spinning lower to their enviable end." Cracius spoke the gloomy decree with a fleeting, dismissive tone.

"That doesn't make any sense." Dugan tried to grasp the idea of the whole cosmos winding down, then finally stop, to be nothing…he couldn't even begin to comprehend it. "I thought you said those who die and pass on go to an new eternal life. How can it all end then?"

"No it doesn't make sense to most mortals," Cracius stated, "they live in the spiral and it's only really when you get outside of it that you begin to see more clearly. Either that or look toward history more with an open mind; embracing legends and myths as having more truth than most folks give them today and you can start to decipher the underlying reality of the cosmos."

"That things are getting *weaker*?" Dugan didn't like the sound of that. Tebow was right, he was happier before he heard this. "So wherever we go in death, it won't be *forever*?"

"It will seem like forever to those who reside there," Dugan noticed they'd moved closer still to the mountains base as Cracius answered his query. "But in time all things will fade away into nothingness."

"Even me?" Asked Dugan.

"Even us." Cracius nodded.

"So why aren't you two not worried about any of this?" Dugan to find some hope to this dark revelation…if there was any.

The younger priest shook a strong, finger in the air, "Because, there is something to come after this destruction."

"And what's that?" If Dugan still had a beating heart he knew it would be pumping away quite rigorously right about now.

Cracius looked toward Tebow whose face grew even more haggard as he hesitantly nodded permission for the younger priest to proceed. "Let me just say there has to be something in existence all the time for there to be nothingness. The cosmos never can be totally destroyed for it would violate…well, it can't be done and won't happen."

Dugan's face was clouded now with even more confusion.

"It is a confusing thing for a mortal mind to grasp – even in Mortis – I know, but it is true. You should have no fear of these last days – whenever they come for only Saredhel knows when they'll come for she prophesied the doom of the Pantheon a long time ago. Just know that something better comes after this reality which we now know."

"So this whole thing with The Master isn't the Great End?" Dugan had almost returned to a basic place of understanding matters.

"No," Tebow spoke now. "Although it can certainly be a way to hurry things along in that direction."

Dugan shook his head in an attempt to clear it of the clutter with which the two priests were filling it. "Maybe it's best if I don't know anymore. I'll have plenty to occupy myself, I'm sure, when I get to Helii."

"Still it is fascinating to realize that all of creation is on a downward slope," Cracius still continued his mini-lecture. "Not rapidly of course, but subtlety, every generation weaker than the one before it in some way or the other. Would it shock you to learn that humanity once lived as long a span of years as the longest lived elf does today?"

Dugan said nothing, only looked around him to again notice the scenery had changed once more and all three of them now were at the base of the mountain on the long, flat path ascending the gray rock. He'd be happy to be done with all of this and soon. All this strangeness and delay was too much for a man who just wanted to die and get his afterlife over with."

The young priest continued. "Truth is all the races lived longer, and had keener insights, abilities and traits that have been weakened, depleted or faded away all together. The same is true with magic. It was purer back then, less corrupted."

"What is going to happen to the scepter now?" Dugan finally found a way to change the subject. If the priest was going to blab, at least it might be on something not so esoteric and dismal for the former gladiator's tastes.

"That," Tebow lifted up a warning hand silencing Tebow and the rest of the conversation for sometime after, "is none of our concern.

"We are dead, and the dead no longer have to trouble themselves with the affairs of the living."

Each then settled into a little silence of their own aside the soft, occasional murmur of others in their own weak conversations as the scenery changed and they drew closer to the top of the mountain.

Dugan wasn't sure how long it took to get to the top but it seemed like nothing at all once they got there. It also seemed like time was dead here anyway. Perhaps time could die like other ideas and wound up here in the end with everything else...

Before him and thousands of others were the open silver doors of Sheol, the great city of Asorlok, Sovereign Lord of the Silent Slumber, as Tebow and Cracius knew him. They stretched for an insane height above them, perhaps to accommodate beings of all sizes who would walk through them, Dugan supposed. The Telborian looked at the walls, which were built in a large circle around the city, as he passed nearer and then between them in the supernatural flow of bodies. They were comprised of fat blocks at least as tall as the Telborian and twice that in width; sheered smooth as glass. Now that he saw them up close he noticed their resemblance to bleached bone – the color richly running through all the walls. This fleshy tone did much to contrast the gray mountain all around them, helping the structure stand out even more amid the landscape like a cairn of bones.

All passed beyond these walls in silence, the whole gateway was filled with it; hovering over all gathered. This was a sacred place and all knew it. This was the place of their final end so to speak, the gateway which would ultimately lead them to another which would usher them into their afterlife. All had a reason for silent inner contemplation. Dugan had done his introspection already – at least as much as he wanted, and so studied the doors before him instead. On each was a relief carving of a lecring skull flanked on either side by a sickle and a circular ring of keys under the jaw. The images weren't frightening but they weren't that comforting or inviting either. Dugan passed the doors and moved into the interior of the city which the Telborian thought was rather drab when compared to other cities he had seen in his short life of freedom. It was parchment colored inside with only a few trappings of red cloth here and there. Bone-hued robed figures (the other priests of Asorlok) broke up the scenery. It seemed a far cry from the glorious displays Dugan thought should have been present in a god's city.

The Asorlins looked down at them from a higher set of balconies sticking out overhead from the tall buildings along this very wide cobblestone road. These priests, at least the ones Dugan could see, were incredibly observant, like a farmer inspecting his cattle as they passed before his eye. They neither showed any mind to the creatures passing before them, under them or above them. Giants, gnomes, and even a few dragons (which towered over these balconies but not the walls of the city) all made their entrance silently beside and before and behind the Telborian. It was a grim parade if ever there was one.

Dugan was also far from impressed on the quality of the inside of the city. It was well maintained and looked newly constructed, though Dugan knew it wasn't. It was also very plain: with no open carvings, no statues, no artwork of any kind. All was as lifeless and uniform; unitarian as a common tool. Then the Telborian turned around a corner and entered into the center of the most wonderful sight of his mortal life.

At the end of the cobblestone roadway he'd been traveling all seemed to stop in what seemed to be a central hub like that of a wheel, the road he had just come there on being one of what looked like fourteen spokes – each spoke being of a different color. Each went off in another direction, but only people who wore the same colored garb traveling the path. Red robes going down a ruby-and-red-silk decorated roadway; amber robed beings going down an amber lined and lighted thoroughfare. So it was with all of the fourteen roads save the one on which Dugan had entered into Sheol with all the others, which was the most drab and spartan. Even those without robes went to their own spoke/road. All of the inner workings of Sheol were a sign of machine-like efficiency managed by bureaucracy.

In the center of this hub stood a tall tower which seemed to have a base carved out of the same bone-hued rock as the city and walls to look like piled human skulls, which changed into a series of keys the higher they ascended as they covered the rest of the tower to it's silver-capped top. All along this tower were some dark, narrow, windows where beige-robed Asorlins watched the throng below move off into their assigned destinations. This assigning was conducted by a handful of priests who now had drawn closer to Dugan – or had he moved closer to them? He never would figure out how that worked.

Dugan now stood before a muscular Celetor dressed in the parchment robes of an Asorlin, red sash at his waist and silver medallion around his neck. Behind his tall, dark skinned frame were two more similarly dressed priests of Asorlok, one an Elyellium, the other a Telborian. These were the three who seemed to take notice of him out of the seven gathered there. Each of these three appeared to be middle aged, but also ageless at the same time, like all the priests who populated the realm of Asorlok. They seemed to stand apart from the rest of the dead moving past them. As with the eyes of the others Dugan had come into contact, these priest's eyes had the same other worldly quality about them which the former gladiator couldn't place. And it still unnerved him to see it.

The Celetor looked over Dugan for a moment with a practiced, assessing gaze then spoke.

"You have an audience with Helii and its god." The Celetor's clean shaven face was stoic.

"So I'm told." Dugan's words sounded strangely flat and lifeless before when compared to the Celetor before him.

Tebow looked over at Dugan now. "Here is where we part." He placed a hand on his shoulder. "May you find peace at the end of your journey."

Dugan said nothing as Tebow left to talk with the Elyelmic priest, Cracius made his way toward the Telborian preist, speaking to Dugan in parting. "Safe journey, Dugan."

"You too." Dugan felt foolish saying it but could really think of nothing else to say at such a time and to such a person anyway, but he felt he had to say something.

"Go your way now." The Celetor jabbed a figure in the same direction his eyes were drawn. Both lead to a roadway where others who wore the same robe Dugan was wearing had been gathered and were making their progress down their own great path. "Helii awaits."

Dugan then felt himself move.

He himself didn't really move, but rather everything else did and aligned itself in relation toward him so that he stood at the beginning of this new roadway. A roadway that was made of black basalt for both walkway and walls and studded with red rubies, yellow topaz, amber and some type of orange gem he'd never seen before but sparkled wickedly like living flame.

Here it was that many races, both mortal and monstrous and everything else in between had come to stand. Beside a few giants and even what looked like a handful of lizardmen, Dugan squinted his eyes trying to see what was at the end of this seemingly unending passage. As he did this he was moved further into an amber light which grew brighter and brighter until it was all around him.

When his eyes had grown accustomed to the light Dugan found himself standing inside a large chamber which rose for a staggering, undiscernible height from the floor to the top of a domed ceiling and covered in precious gems of the same type lining the roadway that brought him here. Though it was large, this chamber was still full to the point of immobility by what appeared to be a large number of Celetors, Telborians and even a few Nordicans, Elyellium, Patrious, dwarves, and gnomes, halflings and many, many goblinoid races mixed amid giants and other kinds of creatures Dugan had never seen before. All of them had on the same robe Dugan wore, and all were standing in line before what seemed to be a large disc of light built into the dark, gem studded wall a good distance ahead of him.

This was the gate to Helii, one of twelve watched over by the Lords of Death. The longer he looked at it Dugan believed he saw the lip of the massive opening lined in what appeared to be some kind of gemstone which seemed to mimic the affects of flame. The light spilling out of the opening was the same in hue, but somehow seemed to be a bit more organic than the glittering gems encompassing it. It was into this opening people and creatures continued to move silently toward, and then through, at a fairly moderate pace.

There was something else though, something just outside the realm of his vision and inside the light from the gate. Something he thought he saw besides the gate; a shifting form he just couldn't get a solid view from his current position amid the gathering. This was something he felt uneasy about as he drew closer to the gate; without willing himself to do so naturally. A person before him seemed to stop before and bow toward this undiscernable figure before moving through the gate.

As Dugan drew nearer he could see better than before and the indiscernible form now had shape. What he saw filled him with a deep sense of dread. The figure the former gladiator beheld was fifteen feet in height and covered in a long, flowing robe and hooded cloak which hung over all his features. Thin to the point of emaciated, the black cloth covering the being seemed a ghostly bundle of fabric hovering under its own power rather than being supported by anything of substantial weight underneath. The few aspects of the figure's body which Dugan could see though gave him even less comfort.

Bony, long nailed fingers crept out from behind velvet cuffs directing the petitioning person before it into the amber portal. That wasn't what made Dugan tremble in his stomach. It was the unnatural nature of the skin covering those hands. It was of a strange incandescent whose cold sheen was reflected by the hard, white, icicle-like fingernails. Further, it was translucent as to allow the viewer to actually see the beings bones, displayed in a dark, almost charcoal gray.

"What is that?" Dugan's words came out in a hushed fearful reverence.

"Charbis," A Celetor beside the Telborian answered with equal reverence; his whisper being nearly swalllowed whole by the heavy silence in the chamber. "The Lord of Death who keeps the Helii Gate."

Dugan barely heard the answer, as he couldn't take his eyes off of the divinity. It was just such a surreal sight but also invoked such powerful emotions in him. Fear and worry, charged over him like a stampede of horses. These emotions seemed to be emanating off of the cosmic being like an outgoing wave and then he found himself just outside the seemingly tangible aura of this dark clothed judge. Only one Elyellium stood between Dugan and this being now – a woman who seemed to be of a war-like disposition.

He noticed now too how the light of the gate was really caused by flame flickering all about and through the opening, though the heat of it didn't do anything to those who stood before it or by it, such as the Lord of Death it seemed...

Looking up at Charbis, Dugan could see that the lord did indeed have a face under his hood. Like his hands the face was a strange and awful sight. Charbis' dark gray skull was clearly revealed from under his transparent, shimmering face. Inside his eye sockets rested two orbs that had what should have been the whites of his eye being a medium shade of gray; both his irises and pupils glowing a pure white. Though Dugan could see Charbis' face, the lord did not seem to acknowledge the Telborian at his feet.

When the elf before Dugan had finished her business she bowed her head and then moved through the gate to disappear from his sight. Charbis then drew his hooded head down to the small figure of Dugan before him as the Telborian came to stand where the elf had been just moments before. Dugan could see farther back into Charbis hood now – past the swimming shadows. Under this hood stringy, flat and lifeless strands of pure white, phosphorescent hair fell from underneath a wrought iron circlet crackling with black energy like an ebony serpent twisting around his brow. It was a sight that would stay with the Telborian forever.

Dugan then felt himself being pierced by a thousand spears under the Lord of Death's gaze. It was as if he was looking all the way through him, past even his soul and spirit to where Dugan felt he needed to cover himself from the sheer nakedness he felt. However, he had nothing with which to hide from the lord's sight.

"I have been expecting you." Charbis' voice was as a withered whisper which, though still a whisper, seemed to fill the entire room as if it were the loudest of shouts.

Dugan couldn't help but quake at that statement.

"You," Charbis pointed down toward Dugan with his skeletal digit, "have been already claimed by the god of Helii. To him you must go."

The gate to Helii seemed to grow hotter as if a blast furnace behind the opening had been opened up before the mortal man. Had he been a physical body sweat would have poured from his brow in small rivers and his chest would have felt constricted from what he could smell now were harsh, metallic vapors – noxious fumes one could find near a forge or in the heart of some volcano. Dugan felt himself pulled forward; feet and legs moving into the flaring gate under their own independent direction. He could do nothing but be a spectator of his own body as it made the passage up to the gate and then into it. All was a flash before him and the heat he felt beyond searing, even without a physical body, and then it was all over.

The light.

The heat.

Everything.

Chapter 22

"Where are we?" Hoodwink looked around what appeared to be a large collection of labyrinthian tunnels. They had emerged out of the darkness suddenly or had Hoodwink appeared there? He wasn't quite sure about that.

"You've been brought closer to your destiny." Gilban stood before him, ghostly and sighted as the moment before when the goblin hadn't been here in the first place but instead somewhere else all together.

"So how come everyone seems to know so much about my destiny except me?" He kept his eyes searching about the seemingly endless underground corridors. When Gilban gave him no response, he turned around to look at him. The priest was silent and still, head cocked and seemingly waiting to hear something which the goblin wasn't able to appropriate to himself.

"What is it?" Hoodwink asked at last.

"The battle is about ready to start."

"Battle?" Hoodwink dared another look around a bit fearful now of hordes of attackers rushing at him from all over the honeycombed rock in which he stood. "Here?"

"Not here." Gilban raised his staff above him to touch the ceiling and then pass through it true to his insubstantial nature. "Up there."

Hoodwink raised his head to the ceiling. "Where are we?"

Gilban peered down at the goblin with gentle, eyes. "Thangaria – well under it at least."

227

"Thangaria?" Hoodwink tried the word out on his tongue. "Where's that?"

Gilban grinned. "The former home, now council seat of the Pantheon."

"The Pantheon?" Hoodwink's eyes went wide. "What kinda destiny you think I have anyway? I'm not a god and–"

"As I said," Gilban interrupted, "you've been brought closer to your destiny."

"Which lies here?" The goblin jabbed the earth beneath him with his heel.

"Yes...well above us really." The priest corrected.

Hoodwink still wasn't used to seeing Gilban with his vision restored or as some ghost and caused a slight shiver to grip and shake his stomach when Gilban smiled at the goblin.

"So I still have a choice, huh?" Hoodwink took a good hard look at the transparent elf. "Even though you brought me closer to my destiny I can still *refuse* it right?"

"You always have a choice." Came the now familiar reply.

"Yeah, you keep saying that – you *all* do, but I'm beginning to think that it really isn't true." Hoodwink huffed out a small bit of his frustrations.

"You do?" Gilban took on a slight concerned tone now as he drew a step closer to the goblin. "What would life be without free will to chose our own course?"

Hoodwink didn't answer, but turned his gaze to the dusty floor to get away from those strange eyes and the unsettling feeling they caused him. He trekked a short distance from the ghostly priest while keeping his head down. The silence that followed this action grew in presence to be almost stifling upon the goblin. Still he held to his thoughts a little longer, for they were big thoughts – important thoughts. Almost too great to have come from a small creature.

"So you won't tell me what my destiny is then?" The green-skinned mortal said at last. "You're just going to bring me closer to it?"

"Did I tell you when you wanted to know your death?" Gilban was as still as a tombstone.

"Then how do I know that I want this destiny?" Hoodwink looked back up at the priest, seeing through his ether-like frame to the sprawling tunnels beyond. Tunnels that could have allowed a giant easy access through them without so much as scraping the top of his head.

"By having faith that you are able to endure the mantle that waits to be placed over your shoulders." The ghost's words were soft now, but still potent; his manner was still as rugged as stone, however.

Hoodwink drew within himself again. This was a far cry from where he had seen himself in those nights he'd sat amid his own private area amid the ruins where he'd come to dwell. Once he had dreamed of being great, of finding his way out of the jungle and ruins and the tribe that oppressed him to seek his…Suddenly everything slowed in the goblin's mind as he came to understand how everything had just lined up to view before him. It had happened so fast he was unable to think or do little else. The gravity of the revelation seemed to still all around and inside him; warping time all about him. Had he really been looking for this – this destiny that was now before him?

"Seems like we all have our personal fate which has been linked in dealing with The Master, and there's nothing else." Hoodwink shared his thoughts with the dead priest. "That doesn't sound like free will to me."

Gilban remained silent after the goblin's comment. Hoodwink didn't like the silence and so spoke again. "So what happens if I refuse to do what you brought me here to do?" Again the goblin found himself looking both at and through the former priest.

"Then you will not fulfill this destiny and instead walk into another." The priest's new, sighted eyes found an anchor in their gazing amid Hoodwink's own orbs and stayed there for a moment; the weight of what he was saying touching his heart. "A choice, one you are free to make–"

"So you aren't going to tell me what the other destiny would be either, huh?" Hoodwink broke away from that strange stare to hover his gaze at Gilban's center. He was glad to be free of it, for he felt it tugging him into one line of thinking. A line of reason that marched boldly into the dark chasm of uncertainty with the strength of faith he was doing the right thing leading him onward. Such feelings and thoughts were troublesome to the goblin at the moment, he just wanted to get some illumination into that dark chasm.

"If I told you, you would be given an unfair advantage in making up your mind. It could hardly be a choice you could have made fairly – which you need to do with such a matter as this task you are called to do. No one knows what their choices will hold in and of themselves. One may guess and perhaps rightly surmise some of the outcome, but there is much more to every choice we make. All choices come to form a life and the destiny which is part of that life."

"But you said all of us have already been chosen to deal with The Master. We're champions who are supposed to stop him." The goblin squinted as he tried to take a closer look at his spirit, trying to make sense of what he was saying and what he had said. "So if I've already been chosen, then how can I have a choice in the matter on what I'm supposed to do then? Why choose me anyway?"

Gilban smiled.

"What now?" Hoodwink had grown a bit perturbed by the priest's seeming smugness which still clung to him in the afterlife.

"You have asked a very wise question." The priest's smile widened. "There are currently two great forces in the cosmos, Hoodwink. For the sake of time and ease of explanation, I shall call them Light and Darkness. They are old and have been since the beginning of all. They also have a pact to which each subscribes. This agreement grants them the right to destroy a world and the time has come for Tralodren to meet this timely fate."

"However," Gilban held up a lone, transparent hand, "They have also decided to give each world a chance to save itself from destruction. It was a clause put in by The Light, which is never interested in destruction but in finding ways to preserve the cosmos. To this end, The Light has called its champions to fight for this world – to save it from the ending that hangs over it even now."

"So we're *The Light's* champions then?" Hoodwink's face wrinkled even more in thought.

"Yes." Hoodwink was amazed Gilban had given him such a simple answer.

"And we're supposed to save the world?" At this the goblin's brow grew even more furrowed. He was beginning to understand things a little better. "So The Master is The Darkness' champion then?"

"Correct." Gilban gave the goblin a nod.

"So we have to stop The Master from winning so The Darkness doesn't win and Tralodren is destroyed?" Hoodwink tried to keep his attention on the transient figure before him and not the scenery he could see through him. "And you didn't know any of this until you were dead?"

"Not all of it, no." Gilban was still. "Once I crossed over though, many things became clearer to me."

"So how does the Pantheon getting destroyed come into all this?" As long as Gilban was less cryptic in his replys Hoodwink thought he'd press for more answers. "I thought you said it was just Tralodren The Darkness wants to destroy."

"Another matter," Gilban said almost dismissively, "but tied to all this none the less."

"It had something to do with Sidra right?" Hoodwink's eyes glimmered now as he was beginning to make some more sense of all this the longer he reasoned it out with the deceased elf. It was still out there in the esoteric field of reasoning but he was gleaning from a good handful of sheaves here and there. "That was what

Saredhel said when I saw that giantess kill that other giant on the throne."

Gilban gave Hoodwink another nod. "Sidra was the first champion of The Darkness and she tried to kill off the whole Pantheon then–"

"The *first* champion?"

Gilban continued, unaffected by the goblin's outburst. "The first world The Darkness came to destroy was Thangaria, killing the gods was just an added side effect to that end. When she served her purpose, she was destroyed."

"But we're on Thangaria now." Hoodwink just stared at the priest, trying to make sure he had just heard him correctly.

"Well, *under* it to be more precise," Gilban again corrected the goblin. "A small fragment of the world survives housing the council where they are right now above us getting ready for war."

"With The Master?" Hoodwink craned his head up to take in the rocky roof above him.

"Yes. They know The Master will come to them as did Sidra and try to kill them off as she once had done. The Master craves and is driven by the same thing."

"So why is he attacking the gods then?" Lowered his gaze back to Gilban.

"Any action that would be taken against Tralodren would be blocked by the Pantheon. They're the natural protectors of the planet – it's one of the few things they all agree upon. So you have to remove the Pantheon if you want to do anything to Tralodren. Either before or during your tampering as you're going to meet up with them at some point along the way. That is why we are here – why *you* are here." The ghost pointed the goblin out with a semi-vaporous finger.

Hoodwink thought he felt a tremor in the rock around him. It was faint, but he could have sworn – another one shook the tunnels a little harder. So much so that dust and tiny pebbles spilled down from above them.

"What was that?" Hoodwink's eyes widened.

There came another rumble, this one much louder and forceful than before – actually shaking all of the tunnel system from top to bottom as it rained down more fine bits of debris.

"The battle has started." Hoodwink's body grew cold at how fatalistic Gilban's words sounded. "I have to attend to another matter, but I'll be back before you have to make your choice – though deciding it now would be much easier than waiting to the last moment."

"Wait." Hoodwink tried to reach out to the ghost as he began to fade from sight. "You're just going to leave me here?"

"I will return, have no fear." Gilban's gray, misty being faded completely from view and was no more.

"But–"Hoodwink stammered.

"Make your decision now," the fleeing, disembodied voice of Gilban whispered in his ear, "because when the time comes to act you best be ready."

Chapter 23

"**H**ow about this one?" Rowan turned toward Clara. The youth held a dark purple tome in his hand, the binding was made of some type of scaled hide which he had never seen. The elf herself stood in front of a small reading table on the upper gallery of the Great Library. Tucked away from the main collection of bodies who populated the institution, the three had taken to a collection of books like a pack of wolves to sheep.

Though Rowan couldn't read any of these texts, as they were composed chiefly in Collonus, with a few other non-human languages coming up now and then he could, however, play gopher to the mage and Clara who were busy scurrying through the text and scrolls looking for something worthwhile to their cause. Cadrissa was beside her; piling a small hill of scrolls before her tired eyes and the scepter on the table before her.

They had been there for hours now and still nothing had been discovered in the texts to aid them about the scepter. Clara was really the one doing most of the work, having to skim the texts for anything mentioning Wizard Kings in the Third or Fourth Age, and then asking Cadrissa if what she had found was relevant or not. It was tedious and tiresome, but needed to be done. The texts Cadrissa had been able to read on her own were far from helpful either.

"Let me see," Clara looked up from her reading to take up the meaty volume that was about about half the breath of her hand in width. Turning it over to see the cover, she saw that it was devoid of a title.

"So how much longer you think this is going to take?" Rowan asked as Clara opened the book with a dry crackle.

"As long as it takes." She responded without even raising her gaze from the vellum pages.

"Thought you'd say that." The knight returned to a nearby book case with a worn, but preserving frame, like a champion athlete who has run a great distance and maintains his course as he enters the final lap and draws near the finish line.

"If you want to take a break–" Clara started.

"No, we have to find the answer. There's no time to rest when we don't have that much time to begin with." Rowan interrupted the elven maid.

"I can make some of these out as they are source documents, but nothing is coming up here of interest." Cadrissa made her way through more scrolls. The small puffs of dust birthed by this action caused her eyes to water and nose to twitch.

"There's nothing here either." Clara released a sigh at the mounting frustration of the task of trying to gain the answer that eluded them. "Just more biographies of the Patrious who opposed the Wizard Kings." She set the book down among the others on the table.

"What if the answer isn't in the library?" Clara asked Cadrissa. "What then? Are there any other places we can look?"

"*Not* in the library?" The wizardress was shocked by the statement from the elf. If it wasn't in this vault of the world's knowledge then were could it be? "If it isn't here then we aren't going to find it anywhere else, I assure you."

Rowan wasn't listening to their conversation. He had made his way back to the library shelves cluttered with the strange, spidery written language of the Patrious and the hard lined, blocky Collonus. He realized just how hopeless this was, how frustrating it was. It was worse than trying to find a needle in a haystack. At least then he knew what he was looking for, but here…here he couldn't even make sense of the scribbles put out in front of him even if he tried. Sighing, he tried to locate a book which he felt might be closer to what they needed. He might just as well close his eyes and pick at random. It would be just as effective the way they were going.

Rowan.

Rowan jerked himself free from his melancholy thoughts and spun around the gallery looking for the source of the voice.

Rowan. This time the voice, which was still in his head, attached itself to a gray furred panther that had appeared before the knight as silent as the grave.

Follow. Was all the feminine voice spoke in his head before the panther made it's way down the aisle of bookcases. Rowan did as it bid, taking his steps close behind the great cat which lead him through the gallery's wide assortments of texts and towering shelves; a virtual forest of knowledge all about him. He had no idea where he was going, only that he needed to stay close to this vision…at least he was sure it was a vision.

The panther lead him for a little while more, actually walking him past a wall of stain glass windows showing a collection of Patrious from a time long before Rowan could even imagine. Here they were posing amid their daily tasks: farming, building cities, assembling to fight some kind of giant as well as marrying and yes, recording history and reading scrolls and books. He didn't stop to study them long – couldn't really as the panther led him onward.

He passed some silent Patrician scholars who merely kept to their own work, never even acknowledging the knight or his guide. Could they even see the panther? Rowan thought not. He had become comfortable enough with visions and portents now from Panthor to know when something was real and when it wasn't.

He was sure of that much at least. What he wasn't sure of was why he was being lead around the library to what looked like the opposite gallery from where he had been previously. He supposed he would get an answer soon enough…

And so they continued, the panther leading the knight, until he came to stop before a single bookshelf stacked tight against a wall rising far into the ceiling above. The area around it was empty of anyone and seemed almost like a deserted piece of the building – neglected for some reason. His guide though had curled itself up at the base of the lone bookcase, like some smaller feline beside the warmth of a fire, and waited for the knight to draw near.

"What now?" Rowan quietly asked the panther.

The cat did nothing save open it's mouth to yawn, revealing it's deadly teeth. Seeing no help there he focused on the books and scrolls. When he caught sight of the text, he smiled. It was Nordic. The familiar runic shapes cheered his soul to no end. Not only because he felt like he could be useful again but for what one of the books titles was: 'The History of the Valkorian Knights'.

Read and begin to understand.

Rowan spun around to see what he thought would be his goddess. He was sure she was standing right behind him – had to be. When he turned around though he saw that nothing was there to greet him, and when he'd returned his attention back to the bookcase, he found the panther had fled as well.

No matter.

The creature had done it's job and brought him here.

The youth made his way to the shelf, withdrew the rather fat leather clad volume, and began reading. Though it was of an older time period, the text reflecting a few anachronisms, Rowan could read it quite easily from his own training, which had covered all the human dialects and languages.

Thumbing a few pages into the main body of pages he stopped when something caught his eye:

The location and nature of the Northlands have long been both aid and hindrance to the Nordican. Aiding in the sense that it has helped foster the independence each Nordican craves and thrives in while also stopping the softness of civilization, common to the southern lands and races, from taking root. It is a hindrance because this semi-isolationism has prevented any strong form of unity to take place amid the Nordic people.

We have been little more than packs of wolves striving for our own causes, pitting ourselves against the other for countless generations. Only with the coming of the Knighthood could we start to make a better future for ourselves. For here is an institution which unites the common Nordican rather than splinter him. It is a gathering of men from all sides of the continent and then even beyond Valkoria's shores to other northern lands to unite and bind them in one brotherhood. In this unity I see a great and glorious future for my race.

And to think we owe this new beginning to the elf. For more so than Panthor did the elf give the builders of the Knighthood the energy to follow through on their commitment. For it has been told to me by some elderly knights, who have also come to see themselves as scholars, that in 3000 B.V. a group of Telborian refugees fleeing the devastation of their home city of Gondad made their way to Valkoria.

Here it was that they made up a small camp and with the aid of the local tribes who took some pity for their plight, survived through the winter. They were mostly men, the woman and childern having succumbed to some of the hardships of refugee life before they made it to Valkoria's shores. The men who survived were convinced that they were in danger of elven aggression from the south and started to build a walled village to protect themselves.

Added to this, they took up arms and the art of warfare to further defend themselves, teaching it to their children, some now created from the mixed unions of Nordican and Telborian. They were even able to convince some of their neighbors of the threat of this coming elven invasion who joined them in their walled town which soon became a minor tribe to itself.

More years passed and the elves did not come, but the Knighthood of Valkoria had been born. They saw the time they had as an opportunity to reach other Nordicans and recruit them for their growing army to stand against the elven aggressors who were soon to come upon Nordic shores hungry for imperial expansion.

In a generation, the Knighthood had swelled in number and the trace of their once Telborian founders had washed away to be replaced with a Nordic face. A generation more and these Nordicans began to believe they had founded the Knighthood themselves. The purpose though: protection from elven invasion, remained. That is until it was challenged by another migration from the south.

Once again a group of Telborians came up from the Midlands to visit Valkoria. These though were of another stripe – missionaries for the new goddess Panthor. Said to be a goddess for all of humanity, the faith took root around the Knighthood, making converts as the martial dedication of the knights merged with the spiritual devotion of the Panians, as they were called. The faith took root so quickly that in one generation the Knighthood had dedicated itself to Panthor and the protection and unification of all the Northlands and to a lesser extent, the whole of humanity.

Once more the Telborian blood ran thin and the Nordican dominance over the Knighthood returned, but the new mission and purpose stayed. And in time, as with the matter of its founding, those who lived in the Northlands soon forgot its foreign foundations and took it wholly as a native construction. Save for the few elders to whom I spoke and the scraps of ancient history I've been able to discover and save here and there I would be in the same belief with them.

It is my hope that by writing this book I will keep this knowledge alive for those who still wish to learn the true history of the Knights of Valkoria...

Rowan stopped reading.

He couldn't go on with any more text at the moment. His mind was frozen in what he had just read. Here was the whole history of his Knighthood in a nutshell and it was nothing like he was told it had been. There were no brave souls of the far north who had seen a vision of the goddess and moved to the south of Valkoria to build her a place of worship and a knighthood to honor her.

It was all lies.

All lies.

He had given himself in service to a lie…

No, that wasn't quite true. He had given himself in service to Panthor, to serve her. The Knighthood had just been a vehicle by which he could achieve his pledge. However, Panthor's words now made much more sense to him. She hadn't built the Knighthood, but allowed the people there to follow her because she could use them to spread her influence. She might have sent the priests, but certainly not the first band of refugees to found the Knighthood in the first place.

So where did this put him then and his calling his goddess placed upon him? She said he had a great purpose in life, but what was it and what was he to do with the Knighthood now that he knew its true origins. Should he even go back to them in the first place knowing what he knew now?

Sadly, he knew he had little time to dwell upon these matters, and so opted to read just a little bit more – glean what he could, for he didn't believe he'd ever have a chance to get to learn this information in his life after today. He planned to make use of the rare gift, yet another of his goddess' blessings she had granted him, while he could.

Cadrissa looked up from the scrolls she was reading. "How long has Rowan been gone?"

Clara stopped her own studying of a new book to answer. "I don't know." The elf tried to see down the aisle he had disappeared down when last she had seen him, but saw no sign of him. "How long has it been since you last saw him?"

"Maybe no more than a third of an hour ago," replied the mage.

"You think he might have found something?" Clara turned her attention fully to the matter at hand.

"More likely he got lost," Cadrissa smirked. "I think he would have brought something back to us to check out if he found something."

"Perhaps he's resting." Clara stood up and stretched her back and arms. "We did have a long, eventful day so far."

Clara's face went wide with wonder at what she had just said. "Has it only been one day?"

"Yes, it has." Cadrissa assured her, though she too was amazed at what had been achieved in that one day.

The elven warrior thought about this for a moment and then let out a breath to clear her mind, She needed to stay on task. "Do you think you could go look for him; make sure he's all right?"

"Sure." Cadrissa nodded. "I'm not much help right now as it is anyway."

"Thanks." Clara returned to her seat to continue her search as the mage began to wander the aisles of books for a lost Nordican. At least he shouldn't be too hard to find. He'd stick out quite easily in the group assembled here in the library.

It took the mage close to an hour to find just where the knight had wandered off to. She had made her way all around the galleries and was about to check to see if he might be downstairs when she caught sight of him from the corner of her eye near an older bookcase stacked in the corner of the library, almost hidden away from even diligently seeking eyes. She made her way toward him quickly, not sure what to make of his absence, what he was doing here, and what Clara must be thinking by her own extended absence.

"Rowan?" She quietly asked as she drew closer to the youth.

He turned to face her, and it was then that Cadrissa noticed he held a book in his hand. A rather large book the knight had been reading.

"How is the search going?" The knight turned all the way around to face the mage, finger holding his place inside the book he'd been reading as he closed it over the digit.

"I don't know." Cadrissa was a bit frustrated at having spent so much time looking for the youth. "I've been looking for you."

"I haven't been gone *that* long." Rowan batted the mage's comment away with his words.

"Over an hour at least." Cadrissa's tone was flat.

"An hour?" Rowan's face was smeared in wonderment.

"What are you reading?" She motioned to the book with a nod of her head.

"I found it over in that bookcase." He pointed to the lonely bookcase. "They're all in Nordic. I guess I must have gotten into what I was reading and lost track of time." Though it was a feeble apology since he knew he wasn't being that helpful with the search in the first place.

"Anything good?" Cadrissa wandered closer to the bookcase for a peek. As long as she was here she might as well see what she could see. This was the Great Library after all, and who knew how soon she might be able to return here again…if ever?

"I don't know yet," Rowan followed behind her. "I've just been reading this one book so far. I did notice that there are books on various areas of the Northlands and tribes–"

Cadrissa stopped him by pulling a slender, green hide covered book from a lower shelf. "And it seems a possible few that might be of some interest to us."

The wizardress hurriedly opened the volume and began to thumb through the vellum pages with some speed – though not so rapidly as to risk damaging the volume. She wasn't reading so much as skimming the contents; her smile growing wider as the fatigue and frustration of the day's search had seemingly come to an end.

"What is it?" Rowan curious of Cadrissa's grin and renewed energy.

"I think this is it." She continued to flip through the volume as delicately and speedily as she could.

Suddenly she stopped; head bolting up into Rowan's face.

"We need to tell Clara." The wizardress began to briskly walk back to where she had come from. It almost burst into a jog now and then but remained just under such a pace for the whole span between the wizardress and the opposite gallery.

"Tell her what?" Rowan asked after her as the mage flew down the wilderness of books and a spattering of patrons who paid both her and the knight little if any mind.

Cadrissa didn't reply, only continued on her way.

Rowan sighed, removed his finger from the book he'd been reading, and placed it back from where he got it. He supposed he'd read enough to get a clearer image – a truer understanding of just what Panthor had been saying about the Knighthood. Now that he knew it, things began to make much more sense than ever before…but he couldn't concentrate on that now. He had to finish what he had come to do in the first place.

One mission at a time.

That was all he could do.

Turning from the bookcase his goddess had lead him to, the knight started to jog off after the mage who was now a good distance ahead of him. He was curious to hear what Cadrissa had found. Even more curious of the fact his goddess had shown him to the bookcase which contained not only what he needed to know about the Knighthood, but possibly something relating to their search as well. Truly Panthor was watching over him, and that increased Rowan's faith in a favorable outcome.

Chapter 24

A long trail of shuffled sand shadowed The Master's tracks. It had been hours and the sun still wouldn't relent its attack, nor the desert give up for what the dark god was searching. All around him for miles was dry, lifeless sand; beige waves of granulated death undulated like a camel's back in the canary sun. He had already tried to use his new-found talents to locate his goal, but as soon as he attempted to do so, nothing would happen. It reminded him of the encounter with Galba, and how his arcane insight had been blocked the further he went into the mystical circle. This was different though, this time he felt as though it was simply an impossibility. He couldn't find what he'd been told to seek out with divine insight no matter how hard he tried. Surprised at the limitations on a god, The Master contemplated its meaning. All he had to go on then was his own internal urgings, birthed by The Darkness, which had given him the task of seeking this destination out in the first place.

It was very strange indeed. He was getting closer though, he could feel that much and as another hour came and went, he felt he was very near to the place. Around him though was still desert – sprawling, lifeless desert. With a few more steps he finally stopped at the base of a dune which looked no different than any other around him. Something here though piqued his interest.

He jabbed his ebony staff into the dune.

It was swallowed by the sand, but underneath the unsteady covering struck something. Something hard and metallic. The echo of the strike almost sang to him, vibrating his bones. Though

244

he didn't know what it was yet, a deeper part of himself, the nature that was totally emerged in the new powers he possessed, told him he had reached his destination. The dark god retrieved his staff with a smile, then motioned before himself as if he was parting a curtain.

Mimicking the action, the dune split down the middle, falling off to either side as if it had been a discarded orange peel. Beneath the dune was something even The Master found stunning. Under the sand was a granite dome polished to a smooth surface to look like wet glass in the sunlight. The dome went down a bit further into the sand, but was plain save for a steel door resting in front of the structure.

The door was the height of a man and covered in a relief which portrayed a breathtaking woman of unknown descent with serpentine curls and flowing toga. Her expression was an invitation to ecstasy, her smile beyond divine. The Master was unable to do anything but stare at the door. What could this be? What could it mean? He knew he was supposed to go inside, but what was he walking into now? Did he really want to go through with what he had been told? Play along Cadrith, and it will all work out well in the end. He always had that safeguard if things got too dangerous after all…

Speaking of that, he felt a twinge in his consciousness and knew that Cadrissa and those still with her were doing something against him. He wasn't quite sure what it was but he could tell it wasn't good for him. The small amount of his spirit which he placed in the wizardress upon his ascension told him that much at least. It should have been telling him much more than it was but that was another matter all together. For now it aided him in what he needed to know. He'd implanted it into the mage thinking that if he had used her once before then she might make another worthy vessel should he need one later. It was one of the reasons why he had wanted her to survive his rise to godhood in the first place.

At the moment he didn't want to deal with the plotting of the mage and any of her allies. No, this was not the time to be distracted by them and their plans. He had too much to deal with in just completing what The Darkness had told him to do. The Master would deal with them soon enough, but after he had finished the matters at hand.

That being the case, he took the initiative and reached out to what he felt of her spell and tried to intervene; pulling the implanted piece of his spirit up from within the wizardress hindering her in getting too far along in her casting.

The dark god was quite surprised as well to discover she had such power still remaining in her to cast such a spell. Seeing how he should have drained her dry on route to Galba before his rise to godhood, feeling the immense pool of energy within her – still even now was something of a wonder. He was sure that this constant flow of mystical energy and his limited access to the wizardress were connected. He'd investigate that too soon enough. He also learned they were looking to secure the operation of the scepter to use against him. Cadrith had read that much from her mind and found the idea a worthy one and adopted it into his own plans...and if he could get rid of the knight and the elf along the way, so much the better. So he tried to interfere in Cadrissa's spell to bring this all about.

The more he tried to intervene though the more he felt a barrier coming against him. It was the oddest thing – akin to Galba's hindrance of his mortal magic. But this force was much weaker; it was strong enough to hold him at bay, even push him aside from time to time as he tried to get a good grip on the situation. And then there came a great heat and a strong shove pushing him away from everything. In frustration The Master lashed out once more and then he lost his hold on the matter.

Standing for a moment in the sun, he was confident he had at least hindered their progress somewhat, but he didn't know how much time that had bought him to complete his assignment. It would be enough. He'd make it be. The dark god was more concerned over what had pushed him away and what had generated the fire he'd felt. Surely not Cadrissa…so who? The lich was suddenly roused back to his senses with the sound of a coming windstorm. Turning, he spied a tall funnel cloud coming toward him.

"Endarien," he cursed.

He had to be fast then, get this over with and done before he had to fight with the god once more. Striking the door with his staff the steel melted away as if it were a poisoned arrow wound in flesh. The dark god stepped through the door and was swallowed by the gloom which it had kept at bay as the cloud of desert sand drew closer. The sand storm leapt about the dome, sucking up more sand into its maw and twirling it about, clearing off more of the dome as well, revealing the whole clean, and plain structure underneath.

"Cadrith!" The wind howled.

Inside the dome The Master lit his way by the incandescence of his staff, the large black pearl sending out a faint purple light about him. It was enough to reveal the stairway he was now jogging down, but little else. In truth the dark god didn't care what might linger in the gloom around him.

Faster.

He had to go faster.

With but a thought his body lifted into the air so that it hovered a few inches from the stone steps, then began to fly down the spiral staircase as it wound about like a coiling serpent toward the very object which he was drawn toward like a magnet. He could feel himself growing closer, a sense of accomplished purpose and fulfillment coming to his inner self.

In a rapid movement he had flown down all the stairs coming to a stop at a sturdy iron door with an attached iron wheel on its front; like the wheel of a ship. The door itself, and the attached wheel, were very large – the door at least twenty feet in height and half that in width.

The door was tall and empty of any design. It seemed only made for its function: keeping all back from what it sealed off behind it. Yet it was what was behind that door that The Master needed. Above him, at the top of the stairs near the entrance of the dome, The Master could hear the shifting sand come to an end. The storm had abated and the heavy tread of another was taking its place.

"Cadrith!" Endarien's voice echoed around the stair well and to his ears.

"There is nowhere you can hide from me!"

The Master paid the boastful god no heed, instead focusing his attention to the wheel on the door. It was too big to be able to use himself, the mechanism at least eight, maybe ten feet around and the poles which radiated outward as thick as his own arm. No, he would have to use other methods. Above him the roof shook.

Tiny shafts of sand and pebbles rained down upon him.

He had to hurry.

"There is no escape godling."

The Master closed his eyes and tried to focus on the door before him. He willed it to open, the wheel turning around to unlock the barrier. It took all his effort for the door was strong, almost alive in some ways, and fought against the dark god's attempts but it couldn't win…it wouldn't win.

Another shudder from above.

This time louder and more violent.

Sweat began to stream down the dark god's forehead.

Another explosion.

Dust and sand belched down the stairs behind him, covering all in the minute debris.

The Master paid it all no mind – his will had almost got it…almost.

A sudden jerk rattled the great door, then the massive wheel turned and spun about counterclockwise, the lock it once had held fast releasing under the dark god's will. Cadrith opened his eyes and let out a deep breath. He had done it, but now Endarien was fast behind, ready to pounce upon him at any moment. Wasting not a breath, The Master flung up his hand as the massive iron door squealed open before him. Behind him a wall of force shimmered into being with a yellow energy, then turned transparent, almost blending in with all around it as to better cloak it from sight.

The Master then moved into the deep darkness, which the doorway revealed, as the last great explosion rocked the room. This one bringing a waterfall of sand and rock as well as Endarien himself who landed just outside the barrier The Master had erected, Heaven's Wrath poised to strike.

"You can't run anymore godling. It's over!" Endarien shouted with animalistic glee.

The Master said nothing as the dark doorway he'd just opened swallowed him whole. He had to be about his task if he wanted to work out the angle that had come to him in the presence of The Darkness. Part of that plan was to survive the upcoming encounter and avoid any conflict with Endarien as this would certainly slow him down and might indeed be the death of him as the Darkness had told him or in the very least, wound him enough to slow his plan down or even end it completely.

Charging with a guttural cry, the sky god ran face first into the invisible barrier, slamming into it full force from his wrath. Angered, he pushed himself back from the barrier, hands using the invisible wall as leverage, and cursed.

"Damn you godling! Your insolence only fuels more of my wrath!"

Endarien jabbed Heaven's Wrath into the invisible wall. A symphony of yellow sparks and electrical pulses, like veins, flared all over the wall, traveling all the way up to the ceiling and down to the floor and walls. These sparks showed that the barrier had sealed off the rest of the room from passage.

The barrier still held.

Endarien screamed.

"This won't stop me! You can't hinder what is coming to you!"

Behind the iron door The Master heard the god only faintly now, his mind was elsewhere as he had finally found what he had been told to seek. Now the true moment of testing would come. Could what The Darkness said be trusted?

The square room was still dim, pools of swaying pitch in the corners, but his staff was able to grant him enough dark lavender light to see where he needed to go, what he needed to do. True, the wall of force he had erected wouldn't hold back Endarien forever, but he knew he would be done here before the god could break through the barrier he'd erected…at least he hoped that was the case. He still hadn't figured out exactly what he needed to do with the object he sought. The Darkness had told him what to do but not how to do it.

Cadrith carefully trod a few more steps until the image of what he sought came better into view, emerging from the shadows that fled before his staff. The dark god took in the shape before him and tried to bring to mind some semblance as to what would help him understand it better – have it make sense to him in some way other than the charcoal colored, twisted array of mummified flesh before him. All he could discern is the body was that of a humanoid long since dead. The flesh was preserved in leathery fashion, holding together the bones of what appeared to be a fourteen-foot tall frame should it be able to stand again, rather than slouch in a heap on the empty floor as it did now. The sex of the body The Master decided was female. He stepped closer, sticking the glowing globe which capped his staff outward before him to reveal the shrunken and dehydrated breasts and swan like neck of the body, all of which was encased – at least in part, by ebony pieces of armor.

"I'm here. So what now?" The dark god lifted his head. "I don't understand what I'm supposed to do."

A soft shudder rippled across the darkness around The Master. It parted around the mummified woman and the dark god before her. It held itself at bay at the same time it seemed to be breathing, swelling larger, then waxing leaner at a rythmatic pace over the shriveled corpse.

"Idiot." The familiar dark voice returned, though it was all around Cadrith now and even seemed to be more real and tangible than before. "You call yourself a god?

"Use your mind. Picture yourself doing what you have been told to do. You're a god now and part of my mantle is already with you. Take the last remnants of the old mantle and come into your full potential of power."

Outside the room The Master's barrier finally fell. Endarien wasted no time but charged forward, Heaven's Wrath set to skewer anything before it. He burst through the open door and into the room to see The Master standing before a blackened corpse. It didn't matter who it was or what was going on. The god was blinded by rage and a lust for bloodshed. He would have his revenge and have it before the substance of his grandfather had fled his system entirely. The Master turned at the rampaging god's assault, spinning about narrowly missing the thrust of the long spear as it crackled next to his chest cursing the dark god's very life with each hot spark.

"Fight me if you can, but I will not be denied." Endarien thrust forth the spear again.

The Master countered with his staff, deflecting it away from his person.

"I've beat you before and now have an ally greater than any god who will not see me die. Leave me while you yet still live."

Endarien chuckled.

"Your ally is far from what it would seem to be. I know it of old and its true nature and plans." Bright blue beams shot from the god's eyes into The Master's chest. The dark god hunched over from the blow, clutching the bloodless wound with his left hand, his right hand holding out his staff with a death grip.

"I know its plans and am happy to bring them about." A twisting serpent uncoiled from the inky pearl on top The Master's staff and flung itself around Endarien, sinking its teeth into his neck and coiling about his throat. Endarien grimaced as he wrenched the serpent free, leaving behind a bloody and burned neck. He threw the serpent to the ground where it shattered into sparks and dust.

Do it now! The Darkness vented its rage into The Master's mind. *You don't have time to waste in this petty squabble. Absorb the body!*

The Master ignored the direction for a moment. He wanted to engage in this 'petty squabble' a little while longer.

"Clever." Endarien stepped back a moment, raising Storm's Eye as he did so. "You *learn* it seems, but you don't know everything. Do you really know what your *ally* plans?"

"I know when I'm on the winning side." The Master gloated.

"Really?" Endarien's eyes flashed a bright amber.

"I've been told what is to come, and your fright over it more than confirms its truth then." The Master took even greater delight in his gloating. "You and your wretched Pantheon will fade from existence, and there will be no one left to oppose my will."

"Tralodren will also be gone." Endarien sized up the room, pacing about the dark god who also seemed to be sizing up his opponent.

"A small matter." The Master pushed such concerns from his mind. "I am god of this world now and I will still remain to be god of other worlds."

"*If* you survive." Endarien let lose a verbal barb. "I would surmise that your usefulness to your *ally* has just about come to an end."

The Master sliced his hands across the air with a violent sideways chop, unleashing a silent burst of force gauging the rock walls about him on their path toward Endarien where Storm's Eye weathered the blow, but was unable to stop the god from topping to his back from the impact; bits of pebbles raining down upon him.

The dark god gloated. "I've heard enough of your empty boasts and baseless claims. Now it is time to end this."

Indeed. The Darkness hovered around the lich. *Do as I have said or die here.*

The Master chanced a glance back to the emancipated figure behind him, though ever mindful with one eye toward the toppled frame of Endarien. He wasn't in the best of positions. Either do as The Darkness said, or allow himself the indulgence of finally getting to kill Endarien…The dark god made up his mind, willing the withered corpse – the last pieces of Sidra still carrying the tatters of The Darkness even in her bones, into his own body. It was a simple matter to do once he put his mind to it – easier than what he thought it should have been, but then again, he was just getting used to his new abilities as a god. No sooner had he finished this absorption than Endarien struck.

Faster than lightning, Endarien threw Heaven's Wrath at The Master, sheathing it deep into his heart to burst forth from his back, splattering black blood all about and behind him in an inky spray. Blood continued to splattered everywhere as The Master staggered about, focusing his mind on the storm god who had now righted himself and stepped nearer the dark god with a pleasant sparkle in his eye.

"At last it ends." Endarien took a great sense of pleasure in his grisley work. At last he had nearly come to putting the upstart mage under heel.

"Yes." The Master returned with a sinister smile. His face had changed now – had grown even more cruel as his wound began to close of its own accord. The Master's smile deepened as Heaven's Wrath fell through his body to land on the floor with a small rattle – passing through the lich's flesh as if it were ether .

"At last it ends." The lich shimmered with a dark aura now, as he grew in size to match Endarien's own height. "And I finally get to be rid of you." Cadrith was now even in height to the god of the air so that he could look him in the eye with a mocking glare.

Endarien made a grab for Heaven's Wrath, but was only able to get his hand around it before Cadrith's boot connected violently with his jaw lifting him up into the air – just far enough to allow the dark god to connect again to his jaw with a clenched fist. This upper cut sent Endarien crashing through the roof above and into the sky beyond that, soaring heavenward like a shooting star in reverse. The Master laughed a wicked mirth as he watched a waterfall of sand pour in from the hole created by the Storm Lord's passing.

It was now time to rise to his glory.

Endarien sailed past the sky and into the star speckled mantle of space where he struck the protective barrier around Tralodren, broke through it, and then continued his flight without slowing his ascent. He'd been rendered unconscious by Cadrith's blow and was unable to stop his hurtling path taking him straight toward the sun.

Each passing eye blink saw the helpless god soaring through the stars; shining brighter and brighter as sweat glistened over his body birthed by the heat of the approaching sun. He would have been flung into the burning star and quite possibly destroyed, since he was still unconscious and unable to will himself to heal and stay alive in the blazing furnace, had a hand not stopped his momentum. Of course, the essence of Vkar would have preserved him for a small amount of time too, but it had almost run its course through his body and then there would be nothing left of the first god.

The hand that had stopped Endarien's path to destruction was a plum colored hand with black nails like talons. The god of the sky stopped before the ball of fire to just hover in silence as the same hand, which had halted his certain doom drained him of the last remnants of Vkar, which still yet pulsed through his veins. When the last of this energy was gone, the hand and the figure to whom it belonged shot off toward Tralodren like a comet, disappearing behind the protective barrier rippling with his passage, leaving Endarien behind to float unconscious in space.

Back in what had been Sidra's tomb, Cadrith became accustomed to his larger, more augmented nature. Flexing his arm, he finished looking around the room. There was nothing of value here for him to use. He had what he had come for.

"Weakling." He cursed beneath his breath. "They're all weaklings."

"Yes," The Darkness agreed, again seeming more tangible than before and speaking outside the mind of the lich. "They all are. You can see that now Cadrith – so go finish them off as was my command. You should have no trouble at all in vanquishing every last one of them."

"I'll need to prepare first." The Master lied. He knew just what to do. He'd absorbed that knowledge with Sidra's remains. He wanted to get a few things in order though now to help his cause, should the events following his successful vanquishing of the Pantheon not go to his liking.

"Treachery will get you killed." The Darkness reminded the dark god with the deepest of hate. "Serve well and you may yet live."

"I just need to have some time to understand this new strength I have–"

He suddenly hunched over in pain with a stabbing sensation in his stomach.

"What was that?" He turned to The Darkness.

"Learn quickly," replied The Darkness. "The battlefield is already nearing the completion; the battle will be fast upon you... Gurthghol has come to Galba in search of your doom. So recover your strength quickly." The Darkness' tone grew sardonic with the last sentence.

It seemed The Master didn't have as much time as he would have liked then. Pity, but he would make do with what he could muster. He was a god after all. That had to afford him some extra moments to work out his final strategies...

Chapter 25

The gods of Tralodren were silent around the scrying pool. They had watched the battle, had seen Endarien fly into the sky (but not the hand which stilled him from entering the sun), and knew now what awaited them. Instead of the hand that had stilled Endarien's progress, all the gods saw Endarien's momentum slow of a seemingly natural pace to a dead stop before the blazing ball of fire. None thought more about it either as there were other matters before them. A dead silence hovered over all of them, a silence that only magnified their own internal ponderings and fears.

"So now what?" Drued's face lifted from the pool.

"We prepare for war." Khuthon also lifted his gaze.

"War?" Panthor asked, "Isn't there some other way to defeat this threat?"

"No." Olthon joined the conversation. "We have to raise arms in defense or be laid waste as were Vkar and Xora."

"What about the words given to us by Saredhel?" Panthor persisted. "That has got to be the answer to victory. Maybe there is another meaning we've missed."

"Well, they didn't seem to help us in stopping Cadrith now did it?" Gurthghol grumbled. "I've little time to debate the meaning of riddles right now – we all don't have such luxury." The god of chaos was already finishing up the final pieces of his own interpretation of Saredel's fateful declaration to the Pantheon.

"We've weathered this threat before and won, so now it won't be that hard to do so again. We just need to raise an army and unite–" Khuthon was interrupted by Dradin's calm voice.

"When we last waged war against this similar threat it was a brutal battle – a bloody battle and then we survived only by the shed blood of our father and mother. We have none of that now and are facing this threat again. I am uncertain that all of us can survive such an onslaught…"

"Though pessimistic, I too have to error on the side of caution with this matter." Ganatar addressed the Pantheon gravely. "We have to think through what strategy will work best because I don't believe what we did before to defeat Sidra will work again with Cadrith…and the stakes are much higher this time since we have no room for redeeming any damage done."

"While we talk the threat grows. What we need is action, and fast." Khuthon grew more restless.

"Agreed." Rheminas nodded. "Needless discussion will only slow matters down."

"What then do you propose?" The Lord of Light asked.

"We gather our forces at one place to make a stand." The Vengeful One returned.

"But how do we know where he'll attack?" Aero asked.

"He will come to us." Gurthghol spoke up. "We needn't worry about seeking him out. Wherever we are, he will follow. He's been consumed by his dark patron, and has little choice but to carry out it's desires."

"Should we take up our priestly champions and followers on the world as well, call them to arms against this threat?" Panthor addressed the council.

"No." Dradin answered. "The mortal agents we now have in our service will be of little help against such a threat. Even our own armies will be hard pressed to find victory against such a challenge. It would be foolish and wasteful of their mortal lives to involve them in such a fight."

Rheminas' smile was saccharine as he listed to his uncle's words. "Right indeed, uncle. I think this battle is between the gods and the gods alone."

"Even though should we lose, and Tralodren is destroyed as well?" Shiril's voiced entered into the conversation.

"Even then." Ganatar's words were solemn and firm. "For what hope has Tralodren without its gods?"

"A point of discussion could be raised on such a topic." The Mage Lord spoke, "but at a later time…when things have been resolved."

"But we still haven't agreed upon where we should gather for the battle." Aero spoke up with growing unease. He also was one who didn't want to waste any time he'd been given.

"What about here?" Shiril asked.

The rest of the gods gathered fell silent at the suggestion.

"It has never been done before, the very laws of our own council forbid us from making our true presence known." Ganatar turned to the woman who appeared more living sculpture than goddess.

"Perhaps it is time to break those rules then to stand and fight for a greater purpose than old customs and habits which keep us from being in a disfavorable position when the attack comes." Shiril's words were as strong as her frame.

Ganatar and the Pantheon quietly contemplated the offer. None had seen this side of the Goddess of Minerals and Metals – the active, more engaged goddess who seemed to be more deeply persuaded upon these matters than anyone could have guessed. To many of them it served to show just how dire the situation was.

"Thangaria *is* an easily defendable area." Khuthon turned to Ganatar.

"It would be a wonderful place to extract our vengeance on the one who betrayed us here so long ago." Rheminas added with a wicked glee. "Irony is always a wonderful highlight to such settings."

"And the loss of life would be less if we kept it here, away from our own realms and off Tralodren as well." Asora took a little brighter view of the matter under her reasoning.

"Not to mention that our own realms would survive a little while longer rather than being the place of slaughter they would become in such a fight." Endarien mentioned dryly.

None would speak to his avatar of his recent defeat, at least not yet, and not to the guise of the god. Besides, it wouldn't make a difference any way. The battle was done, and that option was past. They all had to be focused on the task at hand: survival from the attack to come. None needed to discuss it yet, though they would, surely enough, should they each survive the fight to come. It wasn't the time to criticize or lay blame or heap up honor for that matter. Now was the time to rouse the flames of war. One god among the council, however, couldn't wait to drive a little barb into the Storm Lord's chest even if it was to his avatar.

"Will you even be ready to stand with us after such a disastrous confrontation?" Perlosa asked her gray cloaked cousin.

"I'll be more than ready to stand by all of you when the time comes." The Storm Lord flatly gave his answer; cloudy face turning a dark charcoal gray.

"If this is what you all wish then, so be it," Ganatar stated. "Who then agrees to this offer? Shall we then merge an army here to fight off our ancient foe and his new pawn?"

The gods all raised their hands in support for a unanimous vote.

"So be it then," said The Lord of Light. "Go and gather what forces you can and begin to place them outside the hall, we'll make our stand there."

The other gods then broke up from the circle overlooking the pool and moved toward various areas of the massive chamber to set up contact with the nebulous forces and allies they had under their leadership and command so as to bring everything they voted for to pass. Each was too absorbed with their own tasks to observe the others in their own personal matters, so they missed both

Rheminas' and Gurthghol's actions completely, along with a short palaver with a handful of some unexpected allies...

It was time to enact his plan, and so Gurthghol had managed to find a quiet, dark corner to think and to speak his mind freely. He'd been able to cloak his aid of Endarien quite easily. Since he'd sat on his father's throne for some time, he'd found that some of its abilities, though greatly reduced over the centuries, remained. One of them being the ability to hide his presence from the others in the pool. The pool, after all, was his mother's who, like Vkar, had drawn her power from the throne, and so the manipulation needed to cover his actions was quite easy to preform. He needed to keep his actions hidden for as long as he could.

A certain dawning of understanding to Saredhel's riddle had been growing in his mind since they had voted to send Endarien to his failure. Seeing that failure, mixed with the understanding and revelation on the word given, had prompted his current course of action. And he needed to be about the cloaked work quite rapidly...

Away from the others, he willed open a swirling black portal before him. From the other side of this mystical opening a multicolored image appeared to him, still blurry and incomplete in form to confuse anyone else who looked through the dark gate. The god, though, knew to whom he spoke.

"My lord," the blurred image bowed to his god.

"Listen to me very carefully, I have a mission for you and your kin. It will be dangerous, but should it succeed, the rewards will far outweigh the cost. I need you to gather four of each order of lords and take them to Arid Land. Have them meet me near the stone circle of Galba."

"Lord?" The blurry figured sheepishly inquired.

"Do as I say. I'm already on route." The god of darkness' voice was stern.

"Hurry and get those lords gathered, all the lords I requested gathered, and meet me there. I will have little time for any delays, and will need all your aid if my plans should succeed."

"Yes great Gurthghol." The image bowed again and then was gone.

The portal then faded away as well into nothingness.

Rheminas moved to where he thought he too could be in some privacy in the large room before he spoke to his own forces. He turned over his black-nailed hand to cup a bit of fire that sprang up from the appendage in a small, sputtering gout. It flickered before the god, who whispered into its confines, sounding like the hissing of a serpent.

"Is he ready?" Asked the god of revenge.

"Yes, lord." The flame responded with a small, slithering voice.

"Good, then you need to give him his first mission. It is very important, and we can't waste any time in him carrying it out. Have him bring the object to me. I'll be at Thangaria near the troops you are going to raise for me. Get the other lords to gather my forces, and send them to me there as well."

"What if he should fail my lord?" The flame flickered.

"He won't. I've seen him in action before. My enforcer will not be so easy to beat and can stand before even the most ardent of adversaries." A smile slithered its way across Rheminas' lips.

"But this foe is greater than any other." The flame countered and flickered.

"You have my orders, now carry them out." The god of fire was pert.

"Yes my lord." Submission once again behind the voice of the flame.

Rheminas extinguished his conjured flame by making a fist. He had to make himself ready. This battle would be a large war and he'd have to don the ancient armor and weapons in his keeping to stem the coming brutal onslaught...but he would also get a second chance at his own revenge and that was a fine taste the god savored.

"So you have your own plans then?" Asorlok peered into his nephew's face as he spun about to face the death god on his way out of the room.

"As you do – as we all do." The former glee of the Flame Lord reduced in intensity.

"But do we all plan as much as you I wonder?" Continued the god of death's questioning. "Who could match the retribution dreamed up by the Vengeful One's own revenge."

"What do you want?" A venomous disposition flooded up into Rheminas' face. "Endarien failed so now we're left to our own devices."

"There is still a chance for hope to prevail." Saredhel now entered into the conversation, Panthor and Endarien at her side.

"Then you make your own hope and I'll make mine." Rheminas pushed through the god to be about just that. The others watched him go, and when they were confident the others of the council couldn't hear them, they began their own conversation.

"Do you think he knows about what we're planning?" Panthor asked with some slight concern.

"He might." Asorlok stated plainly. "Doesn't matter now though. Besides, I'm sure everyone here is working on some angle of their own." He turned his gaze toward Panthor. "I recall telling you about that before. We're family after all."

"So what do you think *Rheminas* is planning?" Panthor didn't want to let this matter drop just yet. She had some unease about it still that just wouldn't go away no matter how hard she tried to get rid of it.

"Who knows, but it's bound to be something large enough in his mind to cause him to get so riled up over it when I pressed the issue a bit with him," said Asorlok. "That's not saying a whole lot since he's on such a small fuse all the time anyway. He's like a walking gnomish cannon."

"I'm more interested in what *you're* planning." Endarien brought all gathered to Saredhel. "What are we supposed to be doing now?"

Saredhel paused to collect her thoughts. Her pure white but not sightless eyes staring off into the distance before she spoke, "Each of us has called another, as directed, to fight in this battle for us and they have done their task in part, but some have yet to complete their full purpose. These have to be put into position to help bring the needed aid in this upcoming battle."

"So we can't avoid this battle then you're saying?" Endarien's hood fluttered in thought.

"There will be a battle," Saredhel answered, "and we will be called to fight…but so too will the last of our champions."

"So, somehow they're going to help us win then?" Asorlok raised an eyebrow in disbelief. "How can any mortal help us out now?"

"It's always the unexpected which takes place when no one is watching." Came the goddess' cryptic reply.

"So what does that mean?" Panthor pondered aloud.

"Nothing." Endarien's cloudy countenance had darkened. "We don't have time to unlock more riddles, only enough time to gather our forces and weather the storm to come."

"Agreed." Asorlok nodded slightly. "If we have help so be it, but I'm not about to sit here and waste what precious time we have trying to guess the meaning of another riddle."

Panthor looked discouraged by this grim assessment, but said nothing. She didn't think it wise to dismiss such wisdom out of hand. Granted, she knew they were all pressed for time, but she felt bad about turning away from such insight – even if it took some time to digest. But she had her own concerns too, and could understand. Her thoughts were elsewhere then, to the people and places she had to go to gather her own forces to be able to fight.

"So then it's all over for us?" Asorlok mused aloud.

"Only if you wish it to be." Saredhel returned with a soft, unreadable voice.

"Well I don't." The god of air and sky departed from their company. As he walked off, Asorlok took his leave. Only Panthor and Saredhel remained.

"The time grows short." Saredhel's face now took on a soft, maternal quality as she addressed Panthor. "You best make ready."

"Are we going to win?" The goddess of humanity asked the seer.

She simply smiled. "What do you believe?"

"That we will." Panthor plainly stated.

"Then let your belief lead you." Saredhel was unreadable in both her countence and voice.

"But you–" Panthor started to speak, but Saredhel turned away from her, ending their conversation.

"Let your belief lead you." Saredhel repeated.

Panthor could do nothing but watch her go. She had plans to make and forces to rally…and only a belief in victory to tie them to…it would have to be enough. It seemed the time of questions had come and gone.

Chapter 26

The darkness fled before Dugan as he opened his eyes.
He found himself in the midst of an incredible landscape. Somewhere he knew he couldn't have survived if he was still living in the manner to which he'd been previously accustomed. Here he stood amid fire and lava, smoking volcanoes and the intense heat of a sun radiating all about him, but oddly without any of that sun's light from the charcoal gray clouds overhead. Organish-red shades of molten rock splashed and splattered like rivers and pools amid byzantine ingenuous landscapes; glowing in a dirty yellow cast from the lava's glow and the periodic jets of fire which made its way up from below via tiny fissures.

Why anyone would want to spend eternity here was beyond Dugan. If he had mortal lungs they would have burned away long ago from the thick haze of oily fumes hovering over the realm in place of clean, natural air. However, he now found he had a new pair of lungs…and a heartbeat as well. Placing his hand over his chest he found it once again registered a familar rhythm, and he took small comfort in it.

To what he could see and feel Dugan seemed to have flesh again, or at least *felt* alive again as opposed to how he had felt in Mortis. Other than his flesh having a more bronzed appearance to it – as one might have who has spent their whole life under the sun, he didn't really feel or believed himself to appear different than from how he'd been in his mortal life.

The former gladiator was surprised by the rapid transition of his form to what was to him just seconds, but put further thoughts from his mind. He needed to figure out just what was going on and how he would deal with it. As far as Dugan looked he could see no one or anything populating this brimstone-caked expanse. All that seemed to go on for miles was more of the same, only being broken up here and there in the distance by craggy, reddish-brown mountians. If this was Helii, then it didn't seem he'd have much company during his stay. The Telborian's attention was lost in the wonder of the scene and he didn't hear the sound of the approaching creatures behind him who took him by one arm with a strong grip.

"Welcome to Helii, Dugan." A low, calm and measured voice entered into his left ear.

Dugan turned around to see who had spoken and was greeted with the fantastic sight of a man with the lower half of a serpent and head of a bull – a bull with a bristly black beard about his lower jaw. A pair of pearl black eyes also reflected back the Telborian's amazement.

What sort of horror was this? He'd seen enough already to last the rest of eternity. Could these be the faces of his tormentors then? If so, they wasted little time in getting acquainted.

Ebony bovine horns glistened in the constant firelight as the bull head nodded in greeting. "We have been expecting you." The mouth of the bull head spoke as plainly as any man, though it was more surreal than anything the Telborian could have dreamed.

"Who are you and how do you know my name?" Dugan's hands instinctively went to his waist to latch around a weapon but he quickly found he was defenseless. Nothing but his red robe graced his frame.

The light bluish-gray flesh of the bull-headed creature shined with thick gold necklaces, bracelets and a wide belt holding a great sword in its scabbard. Dugan paid special attention to the weapon. All of the jewelry had a painful motif to it: sharp, jagged edges which also seemed to mimic tongues of flame here and there. The sword was mostly hidden in the ruby studded scabbard, but the tiger eye pommel was quite impressive.

"We have been sent here to collect you upon your arrival."
Another voice answered. This one was much more animalistic and
hurried than the other bull-headed being, peppered with snarls and
even a growl.

"Are you Furies?" Dugan turned in the opposite direction to
see the other figure who held him. This one resembled a humanoid
wolf: bipedal with more wolf-like legs but a humanoid torso and
hands ending in sharp claws. Unsettling wild yellow eyes gleamed
as the creature smiled a predatory grin revealing its deadly teeth
and shaking its wispy goatee trailing from its muzzle.

"Yes," snarled the wolf-like one. "The servants of the Vengeful
One, working his will upon the cosmos."

"I thought you were just a legend." Dugan half spoke, half
whispered.

A full foot taller than Dugan (as was the case with the bull-
headed Fury) the wolf creature had to look down into the face of
the human allowing the Telborian to get a good view of its ram's
horns curling on either side of its head. The creature was naked
too, save for his gun-metal gray fur covering him from head to
clawed toe. He appeared as strong and well versed in physical
combat as his bull-headed companion – a paragon of physical
aggression for sure.

"We are very real Dugan," the wolf-headed Fury growled.
"and we take our assignments very seriously."

"So the legends say." The Telborian called to mind the old
tales he'd heard swapped in the arena about these beings. Creatures
whom the gladiators fighting for their lives often tried to invoke for
aid. He didn't know much about them save that he was told they
controlled the elemental emotion of fury and revenge, thus their
name. Whether they were free agents or enforcers of Rheminas'
will the tales he was told never seemed to clarify. Only the warriors' coveting their maddening endowments to help them get
through another bout was all that mattered. Ironically, it was this
introduction to the workings of Rheminas and his servants where

Dugan had found himself drawn to the idea of seeking Rheminas' aid in the first place. Now they were before him face to face...

"Rheminas sent you?" Dugan turned back to the other bull-head Fury.

"Yes." The bull-headed Fury smiled, revealing his own set of sharp teeth looking more frightening and surreal inside his bovine mouth.

Dugan struggled against their grip. "So why take me in force? Where else can I go now that I'm here?"

"You're not going to see Rheminas." The wolf-headed Fury growled.

"I'm not?" This didn't make any sense to Dugan. He'd been sold to the dark god, and was now here as his property, so why didn't he want to see his possession now that it had been delivered him? What further bump in the path to his final destiny would he have to endure? A beating? Another wardrobe change? The Telborian would just be happy with closure to this whole ordeal, but it seemed that such a release was still aloof for him.

"No, you have another destination you have to go to first," The bull-headed Fury slithered up before him to take the lead, tugging at Dugan to follow. "And we have a deadline to maintain."

"Come on," The wolf-like Fury growled.

Dugan could do little more than comply. Their grips were uncompromisingly sturdy and he knew he couldn't push past them no matter how hard he struggled for release. He followed between them then as they lead onward.

Two large brass doors opened into a bronze tiled room. The room was built like a cylinder, but with no ceiling to cap it off, leaving the orangish cast metal tiles to climb up into the hazy sky. The floor was polished black marble and shimmered with the reflection of the column of yellow flame standing in the center of the room flaming for at least twenty feet; the cylindrical walls climbing for twenty more.

Here it was where Dugan was escorted.

On either side were the Furies directing him in this path – his final march. They were silent, as was the Telborian, as they made their way through the doorway. It was as if they all knew their parts – the characters they were portraying in this play moving toward the close of the final act. All but the Telborian who wished he knew his role in this grand production.

Dugan could smell the sulfur from the flame as well as feel its intense heat, the hottest flame he'd yet felt in this world of fire. He paid it no mind though – not now. His end had come. He was certain of it now. It had come before in life at the circle of Galba and now it was to come to a close here in this place, his soul, spirit and new body being ushered into their final place. There would be no more waiting for his final resting place – he was being taken there now. There was no other option he could present himself with for he knew and believed his ending would be a grim and probably gruesome one.

The Furies stopped still some ways from the flame.

"Where are we?" Dugan turned to the bull-headed Fury who seemed to be the calmer of the two.

"The place where you are going to get your reward." He smiled, an unsettling grin on his bovine face; flashing more of these unnatural teeth to the Telborian.

"Reward?"

"Step into the flame." The bull-headed Fury pointed toward the burning column.

Dugan looked to his ordered destination with a clear mind. He tried to see into it, see past it even, but he could see nothing save the impenetrable core of the flame – the all consuming flame.

"Get moving." The wolf-headed Fury rudely shoved the Telborian forward. "Time is short."

Dugan stumbled forward after the shove and proceeded to march toward the column. It was a steady march. Nothing rapid nor too slow. Dugan stepped with purpose and took one last bit of fatalistic joy that these were the last steps he was making as a freeman. Once he moved into that column, and should he survive, then he would be shackled to Rheminas for all eternity. What and how that eternity was to be lived out he had no clue. He had always imagined himself being chained once more as he had been in the arena, tortured or locked away or something worse. In truth, he didn't know what might befall him, but it was too late to worry about that now.

It was ironic too as the heat grew closer, that the Telborian now found himself realizing he was the most free when he had been in Haven, looking for the release of his divine pact. There he served no man and wasn't in fear of the hunters coming to claim him for the arena, for he was far from Colloni and its gladiator schools.

It was ironic because in this most liberated condition he'd allowed his days to go sour in his vain quest for release from his spiritual obligations. It was this very search that had led him back to Rheminas again and again, like some dog returning to it's vomit. He could see that all now as if the column before him was illuminating him to this kernel of truth.

Even as he neared the very cusp of the flaming cylinder, he began to understand how he had lived his life as a slave, even when free. Hindsight was always the clearest of visions. It was also, perhaps one of the cruelest as it showed clearly what could have been, should have been done, but what wasn't, often attaching grief to this clear revelation along with sorrow for it was too late to fix what had passed on now.

As his robes began to spark and flame away from his person Dugan saw how he could have been free long ago. He never would have made his pact in the first place if he'd just understood then how freedom was a state of mind. He could have been freer than the guards of the coliseum if he'd so chosen to be. The freedom of his mind would have led to other avenues of liberation. He understood now too that being able to move about the world physically unhindered didn't mean someone was truly free, he had proven that to himself in Haven. His body was no longer shackled but his mind and spirit were just as fettered as he'd been in his cell.

Galba's words also brought more clarity and weight to him now as he reached out to touch the fire. He discovered it didn't feel like anything to his fingers. It was like reaching into empty air before him. Dugan saw now how he had chosen his whole life to be a slave even after he had attained physical freedom. How he had tended his thoughts was the key for that was the gateway, so he had learned from the two priests, to his spirit. It was too late to change where he had gone by living under their leadings, but not too late, at least for a moment, to reflect upon what might have happened if he never gave into revenge in the first place; didn't stew in the bitterness of the past hoping that it would somehow change the future…

He latched onto this clear and truly free vision as he stepped into the column of yellow flame. Keeping the thought tethered to his heart he closed his eyes and waited for what was to come as he felt his body begin to throb and groan. It was the last thought he had before all fell into darkness; the flames consuming all…

…and then he was aware once more.

"Arise."

Dugan didn't know who had said it or when, only that it had been spoken to him and he felt compelled to obey the command. He opened his eyes to see he was still inside the middle of the flaming column. It seemed as if he was coming to his senses after a deep, restful slumber as he peered outside the now strangely transparent fire to see the two Furies watching him from below. He seemed to be higher up than them, perhaps he was floating. No, he could feel his feet solidly on the ground.

"Come forth." The bull-headed Fury addressed Dugan.

Dugan watched a large bronze skinned leg step out of the flames. It was long and thick with muscle. Stranger still, it was his own! What sort of reward did Rheminas give him? This hardly seemed like what he'd been expecting.

"You've been purified for work in the service of our god." The bull-headed Fury answered the Telborian's thoughts. Dugan looked over his hands and took in their massive size – he was a giant now, a giant with bronze skin – no, actual bronze, the metal *was* his skin!

"Put these on." The wolf-headed Fury lifted up a pile of garments above his head toward the newly awaked Dugan. It was then Dugan understood he was naked. The Telborian dared a further, more in depth look down at himself and was overcome with a symphony of emotions. Indeed his flesh was now of bronze – as he was some kind of living, fluid statue. No hair remained on his frame, not even on his head, which he could feel was bald even without confirmation by a hand swipe over the cranium. However, he was surprised to see two new things about his person: he no longer had any genitalia and now had a set of peacock feathered wings adorning his back.

"Take them and get dressed." The wolf-headed Fury tossed them up toward Dugan's chest where he caught them before they fell.

"You are now a fellow servant of our god." The other Fury began to fill Dugan in as he looked over what had been handed him and started to dress himself. "This is the reward Rheminas has chosen to grant you. You're one of the elite servants who act as the avenger of the Pantheon. You are now one of the Galgallium."

Dugan donned a simple, white, sleeveless tunic which stopped at his knees; covering his feet in tall, black leather sandals which he found close beside him. The final piece of his dress rested beside the sandals. It was a gold, diamond encrusted, breastplate with glowing silver runes carved on the outer edges. He had no idea what the runes stood for, though he recognized the script from the statue of Sidra in Mortis. He felt they were important, and he should be proud in wearing them on his chest into wherever it is he may go. He affixed this piece of armor to his chest, thick leather straps fixing its form on his person between his new wings which were allowed to be free of his tunic via a set of clever slits in the cloth.

"Your sword is a tool of judgment." The bull-headed Fury lifted a massive blade which took both hands to get over his head toward Dugan's reach. It was a wonderful weapon to behold: a broad sword with a ruby-encrusted handle. It rested in a finely crafted, cordovan leather scabbard which was etched with some more runes Dugan couldn't decipher, yet recognized at least in style to the base of the statue of Sidra.

"Use it well." The Fury's dark eyes beamed with what Dugan supposed could be pride.

Dugan took the weapon, looked it over for a moment, then tied it about his waist. He felt more complete now somehow, like he was finding more of himself with each new piece of armor and dress given him; a puzzle coming closer to completion which each new piece brought forth.

The wolf-headed Fury tossed two large bracers up to Dugan with a huff. Dugan caught them with one hand and looked at them in wonder. These were of gold and studded with onyx, emerald and lapis lazuli. Amid the oval cut gems were spirals of shimmering gold arranged in a truly mesmerizing fashion. Dugan couldn't wait to put them on, feel them against his bronze skin. Somehow these were also very important to him – an important part of his personhood; his new identity.

"You've been called to this high position because Rheminas favors you," The bull-headed Fury continued. "This is your place from here until the end of all."

"This is what I sold my soul for?" Dugan didn't know what to say and was shocked at how he sounded. It was his voice, but at the same time it wasn't. Something new was there now – a resonance which was birthed in a sense of command the Telborian had never known in life. How could he say anything to what he'd been given? It was beyond him – beyond his realm of comprehension. He was to serve as the executor of the judgments of the Pantheon? Was this really what the Flame Lord had planned for him all along?

"No," The wolf-headed Fury snorted sarcastically, bursting the bubble of euphoria around the new Galgalli. "You were raised to this potion when you carried out Rheminas' wishes regarding the cult you dispatched when you were yet mortal. You were acting as a Galgalli then and your success impressed Rheminas."

Dugan tried to make sense of what he was hearing. "So by getting my own revenge against the cultists–"

"You were proving your worth for this position." The bull-headed Fury finished Dugan's sentence for him, rolling the thought further along with a twirling of his thick fingers.

"I see," said Dugan. Regardless of how he came to the position, the former Telborian found great delight in his new form. Somehow it just seemed to fit him…to be him.

"Here," the other Fury drew Dugan's attention with a black, silken object folded up in his outstretched hand. Even folded it seemed oversized for the Fury's palm. "Your final garb and your authority to complete your task."

"Authority?" Dugan bent down and picked up the silken object. Unfolding it revealed it to be a cowl. Similar to the hood of an executioner, this one had some fine writing on the space that covered the forehead. It was tiny and so artistically rendered that Dugan even wondered if they were words at all. They were there though, and he was sure they followed the same style of script as the rest of the writing he'd recently seen. And though he couldn't read it, he knew it was important.

"This cowl is what declares your authority to judge and to whom your judgment is set up against," The bull-headed Fury answered.

"Hurry." The other Fury nearly shouted. "Put it on. There is little time left. The judgment has been decreed and now has to be enforced."

Dugan pulled the cowl over his head, covering up his face with shadows and the dark fabric. Only the pure white glowing eyes of the Galgalli, piercing the shadows of the eye holes, allowed for any color and radiance on his bronze face; a small opening being cut away to his chin and mouth to be seen as well.

"Now listen to what the Pantheon has decreed and what you are to do." The bull-headed Fury spoke. "No Galgalli has ever failed in its mission of enforcement. However, should you fail in this execution of judgment, it will be the doom of all for none will be able to stand against that which is coming. All of the Pantheon is now gathering in Thangaria. They plan to fight a war against one whom they have marked for judgment. That judgment has been placed on your cowl. Cadrith, the newly arisen god, must die."

Dugan's eyes narrowed.

Somehow he could feel the words on his cowl burning into his head. When the bull-headed Fury read out this order it told him all he needed to know to find him and how to deal with him as the gods had decreed. It was at once an odd thing and a familiar thing. Like taking to an old hobby you had long left and forgotten about, only to find the skills and love of it growing anew when you take it up once again.

"I understand." Dugan nodded.

"Before you do this though," The bull-headed Fury continued, "Rheminas has some other tasks for you complete."

Chapter 27

"So this is what we're looking for?" Clara asked Cadrissa, who was giddier now than she had been before when she had first found the book.

"I'm certain of it." Cadrissa watched Clara turn the green book over in her hand. She couldn't read Nordican writing and so had to only rely on what the mage had begun to tell her since she and Rowan got back from finding it.

"Frigia though?" The elf raised her gaze over the book toward the mage.

"Frigia." She responded with so much excitement she could barely contain herself.

"I still can't believe it's the same place you wanted to go to find your Wizard King to help us with Cadrissa." Clara shook her head slowly.

"I know," Rowan added from beside the elf. It seemed the book Cadrissa picked up told about a Wizard King in the wilds of Frigia. where the book would have the reader believe the scepter they had been trying to decipher was crafted in the Third Age of the Wizard Kings. Coincidence? Rowan didn't think so, not after all he'd seen leading up this moment. It wasn't at all amusing that the Wizard King he was going to try and seek aid from before was the same one they now had to seek out for the answers to his scepter. Were things going in circles or just getting wrapped up? He didn't know…and that was beginning to grow more frustrating.

"That's a long ways from here and even less hospitable than Valkoria." Rowan continued to play with the circumstances in his head.

"Jarl Knorrsen?" Clara questioned aloud. "You sure about that?"

"It says that he was a powerful Wizard King or Ice King as they tended to call them in the Northlands." Cadrissa exuberantly added her insight on the matter. "Course I suppose it could be he was a worker of magic dealing with ice as well…" Cadrissa shrugged. "I didn't get that far."

"Well you're the one who is going to have to make sense of this then." Clara handed her the book.

Cadrissa gripped the book like a child receiving an extra large piece of pie. "This shouldn't take me too long to go through."

Clara turned to Rowan. "Now don't you go wandering off again."

Rowan returned the jest with a grin. "No this time I think I might disappear for some food."

"We can't stop for that now, there's too much to do." Clara allowed herself to briefly come into contact with her own growing hunger. She hadn't been fed since this morning with some porridge. How long ago was that now anyway? All this jumping around from place to place had really changed her reference to what time of day it really was and how much more daylight they had. All the more reason to get and keep things moving along faster and focused on the task at hand.

"All right, so what's left to do then?" If he couldn't eat then he'd have something to do to take his mind from the grinding in his gut.

"Put all these books away." Clara motioned to the pile of assorted tomes and scrolls on the table before them.

Rowan moved over to the table with a sigh as Clara began to pile the books into his arms. He had little time to react, as soon a small tower of bound texts had been assembled to his chin by the efficient elf.

"You can help." It came out more like a mild command than suggestion, but Rowan wasn't about to complain at the moment.

The elf then looked over to Cadrissa. "You think you want anything else then Cadrissa?"

The mage simply said nothing, nose buried deep in the book and reading it as fast as she could.

"I guess that's a no then." Rowan joked from behind the dry stack.

"We'll be back in a little while after we get all these books and scrolls back where they belong. You going to be all right?" Clara looked again to the studious wizardress.

This time a barely audible garbling mumble bubbled up from the pages.

"Okay." Clara moved to lead the youth, who followed her with slower, measured steps. "Let's get to work. I want to have these all put away and cleaned up before she's finished reading that book."

"Then we'll have to be faster than lightning as quickly as she's devouring it." Rowan did his best to follow behind the elven maid; eyes and head darting through and around the stack of books in front of him. It was something to take his mind from his hunger but he wasn't so sure it was the best option of things he could have done. At least they had their answer or were closer to it and that was a ray of light to bask in for a little while.

Cadrissa didn't really hear them leave, but she knew they were gone nonetheless. Her mind was racing as she was reading the book. She hadn't had a chance to read up on anything for what seemed to her to be ages. Though the spattering of text she could decipher with Clara hadn't been as filling to her, just getting the slim volume in her hand was like a slice of bread when at the point of starvation.

She couldn't get enough. She had to read it all fast and take more in, like a starving person trying to swallow and breathe at the same time. This wasn't the only thing going on with the mage, however. The medallion by her side flared into life again with an almost searing heat that almost overwhelmed her to the point of screaming. Then came the whispering voices and pressure she felt around her head as if a metal band was tightening more and more around the top of her skull. She tried to grit the pain away with her teeth, gnawing the sensations under her breath, but it wasn't working. The pain only increased. Soon she couldn't even concentrate on what she was reading. It took all her effort to hold back the fire in her brain which matched the blaze she felt at her side.

Cadrissa had to put down the book, focusing all her willpower to do just that, then turn to pull the medallion from her pocket. It took her a moment as she struggled with her fingers, wanting to stiffen up into a fist, but she managed to get them to obey in the end. She placed the medallion on the table and then rested from the effort.

Through pinched eyes she looked at the golden object that glistened now in a pure, bronze light on the table. What was it doing? Since she had pulled it out of its hidden pocket she felt it calling to her somehow, speaking to her with the scattered, web-like force of millions of voices. Each faint audible echo the strand in a growing net to ensnare her and the mage didn't know how to get out of the web in which she was wandering. Indeed, she felt compelled just like a moth to flame and couldn't stop herself, even if she wanted to. Part of her didn't want to either and that was what made her even more concerned.

Her fears grew when she watched her hand reach out for the medallion, pick it up, and then move it to her other hand where together they made ready to place it over her neck. She could do little but try and stay conscious as the medallion was brought closer and closer and then rose over her head. She felt it fall to her just above her collar bone with a thud which made it feel like a sack of bricks had been looped about her person instead of the light metallic object. Around her neck she felt a strangling sensation – like two hands had her tight about the throat and were trying to choke her out of life for but a moment and then it was over. The choking sensation left, the flash of heat fled her brow and mind and the whispers stilled. The pain then faded away into the background and she could think and move about freely once more.

Keeping still for just one moment more, she wanted to be sure it was all over; the strange event nothing more than some nightmarish scenario or some supernatural event whose meaning was more benign than sinister. She didn't have the luxury to delve very deeply into the matter, and so hoped for the best possible situation. When a few more moments passed and she still felt fine, she dared a breath, and moved for the book once again.

Nothing happened…she felt fine…letting out a soft sigh, she proceeded to read the text again, trying to bury what had just happened to her into a corner of her mind. She had to because there wasn't any time to analyze everything. Besides, she wouldn't allow herself to focus on the matter until the book was read unless she unleashed something worse than what had just occurred. She wasn't about to relive it again anytime soon, and she needed that information in the book – they all did. It terrified her too. Part of her perhaps thought that as long as it was out of sight and out of mind then all as well for the moment. Part of her believed that anyway.

And so she read…

After about an hour, Clara and Rowan had managed to return all of the books and scrolls to their locations. Why the librarians didn't do this Rowan didn't know. Upon his questioning of Clara upon this matter, she replied that it was only common courtesy to return what one could. It just so happened, however, that they could return all of the materials. Rowan didn't really mind as there was little else he could do but think while he waited for Cadrissa to finish reading. He didn't want to think right now. There were just too many things to ponder. Life kept getting harder and harder for the youth the more he strayed from his home it seemed. Or was it the longer he stayed with Clara…or the more he learned the truth about his calling from his goddess…

At any rate, the books got put away and they managed to return to Cadrissa who was just finishing up the thin tome. Her eyes were alight with flames though her body was still calm and reserved.

"I think I know where we go next." Cadrissa turned toward the others.

"The Wizard King's tower." Rowan answered the statement with strong confidence. "We already know that."

"Yes, but I know now where it is located and what we will need to get inside and past its defenses." The mage raised a finger as she corrected the youth. "His tower still stands because of the defenses that were put in place to help keep it unspoiled."

"It also helped, I would imagine too," Rowan slumped down into a wooden chair for a break, "that it's in Frigia where there isn't anything but giants, snow and ice."

"If anything," the mage closed the book, "those things would have destroyed the tower long ago. Nothing lasts forever."

"You sure about that?" Rowan gave the mage a doubting stare. He'd seen a lot since he had come south that would give rise to a few doubts in regards to that statement.

She didn't answer.

"So where is his tower then?" Clara rested her hands behind the knight's chair.

Cadrissa pointed to her temple. "I have a map of it in here. I just need to cast a simple spell, like the one that took us all here, and we can be there instantly."

"So when do we leave?" Rowan looked first at Cadrissa then craned his head up and back toward Clara.

"How about now?" The mage's withheld excitement was starting to leap out of her grasp now.

"You're going to need some warm cloaks and gear if you're going to head up that far north." Rowan stated.

"I can get us right inside the tower. We won't have to have any special gear other than what we already have." The mage's excitement was growing.

"You sure about that?" Clara was still a bit reserved by all this information, however. She wasn't about to do something foolish, even if there wasn't any time or enough coin on their person to get the supplies and gear they would need to trek about in such a cold climate.

"Positive." The mage's lips parted ever so slightly. "I've got it all locked in place. We can be there instantly. Get the information on the scepter and then move on to where we need to go next."

Clara sighed.

It was a decent plan if not a bit rushed. If it worked, it would be simple and effective in getting them to where they needed to be and done with the final leg work in what she hoped was the last bit of hoop jumping for whatever game in which Galba had them participating. She would have liked to have had more time to think things through, but that wasn't going to be an option, not now. Even though they may have gained a few hours of daylight by heading to the far west of Tralodren, the day itself was still expiring. Somehow Clara felt deep inside herself that it was important to get all these things resolved before the day had ended. It was a sense of urgency which somehow just felt right.

"Fine." Clara removed herself from the back of Rowan's chair. "What do we need to do to get there?"

"Just what we did before we came here, save I'll use Rowan and myself as an anchor and we won't have a portal to walk through," said the mage. "It probably will be better to cast this spell outside the library though to avoid any counterspells that might be in place here."

"All right," Clara began to make her way toward the stairs to the lower level. "Then let's get moving."

Rowan and Cadrissa rose and followed. Cadrissa stopped to look at the book one last time and then picked up the scepter from the table. Absently she rubbed her side temple. There was a sharp cold pain there, a pain she had felt once before...

"That medallion's new." Clara noted as all three of them walked down the stairs.

"Yeah." Cadrissa smiled softly. "I finally put it on. It was something I got from the ruins in the jungle."

"You think that was wise?" Asked the elf. "I heard tales about objects being enchanted and the user putting them on to their own hurt at times."

Cadrissa hid her face from them as they reached the ground floor. "No wiser than Rowan picking up and using that shield he found or his own necklace."

"I was given this amulet by my goddess," Rowan defended his gift. "I don't think it could prove worrisome."

"Well, this medallion is fine. If anything, it will help us get done what we need to get done, and I think it has been helping me and our goal all along, even before we met up again inside Galba."

"We don't need anything else against us–" Clara started to say.

"It's fine, Clara." The mage then picked up her pace to out distance them as she made a beeline outside the Great Library. Clara turned to Rowan, who looked at her with a similarly confused expression which each passed away between them for the time being. They have more important matters to contend with at the moment, and so both hurried after the rapid-moving mage.

Outside the Great Library, in a safely semi-secluded cluster of trees, the three of them were holding hands as Cadrissa cast her spell. Suddenly the pain she had recently been feeling as she left the library grew. She felt even colder now as the chill had made its way into her spine and legs, traveling down her arms and up her neck and head. Bone cracking frost licked the internal side of her skin giving her goose bumps even though it was a nice mildly warm day in the park.

Rowan and Clara didn't notice the mage's struggle with this matter. Each had their eyes closed and focused on the upcoming spell. Cadrissa tried to push the familiar grip out of her mind and she could for a few seconds, but it returned, desperate to gain control of her as it had before. Fear was threatening to swallow her whole and end the spell as well. What was happening and why now? Why would The Master come after her when he was already a god and she far beneath him? Did he know their plan?

"*Grastal yorn-leem. Rasbin ulchre ione qatre.*" Cadrissa forced the words from her mouth and drew in a hard breath to uncap the still amazingly filled reservoir of mystical might she somehow still possessed to fuel the spell. In fact, she thought that there was actually more inside her now than what she had last felt…before she had donned the medallion.

It wasn't natural and she knew it, but she was starting to like it too…the sensation of unlimited energy for whatever she wanted to use it for. To have such power at her fingertips was tempting indeed and she was certain that it was one of the factors why she was able to hold out against the cold clutches threatening to overtake her before the spell had ended.

"*Resbin ulchre ichore tress.*" She forced out the words again and then the world was black around her. She saw the night sky wrap about about her and realized she was looking out over the vast expanse above Tralodren as she had seen it from on top the Roc not that long ago. She, Clara and Rowan were floating amidst it; holding hands and concentrating upon where they were going save Cadrissa. Her eyes were focused on the growing specter of an image which was drawing closer to her – almost racing toward her at an incredible speed.

It was The Master.

It wasn't The Master though in the flesh, but in the guise of his lich form, the form which had most frightened her when she'd been his prisoner for those long weeks.

His skeletal hands reached out for her; ghostly frame towering over everything else like some giant of death. Cadrissa could do nothing, say nothing. All her energy was tied to the spell, keeping it focused on reaching its destination. She couldn't react to The Master's presence without jeopardizing all their lives. Knowing this as she waited for the grim figure to draw closer was a terrible thing.

She tried to speed up the spell, force it to end in Frigia, but something wasn't right. She could do nothing but stay and watch as The Master's hand ensnared the mage. Vise like, yet ethereal, it's arctic encompassing shook Cadrissa to her very spirit. She could feel her mind being pulled from her, like a child being tugged away from the tight grip of a mother's hand. She could feel The Master entering into her body, mind and spirit; possessing her with his own dark nature.

She could also feel something else though, too. The medallion around her neck was heating up and sending the chill of The Master away from her. In fact, the heat was soon radiating over her whole body and around her head and then out of her hands to fill up both Clara and Rowan as well. And then Cadrissa felt a strong force move upon her stomach – almost as if she had been punched there…and hard.

The blow set off a chain reaction all around the trio in which The Master and the night sky faded from sight in a shower of rainbow colored sparks. She was falling too. They all were falling like a comet toward the planet. Cadrissa could see the continents swim under them as they grew closer and closer to the Northlands and then she clammed her eyes tight – everything went black. Only

in her mind did she still see the image she wanted to: the Wizard King's tower.

The *inside* of the Wizard King's tower.

Chapter 28

$\mathfrak{I}$t was a black rock that blazed from heaven to earth. A black rock with a fiery tail the shade of plum. From high above the heavens it burst forth, scattering clouds on its descent that took it closer and closer to Tralodren. It sunk lower in the sky over the stupid-eyed faces of creatures and mortals alike who wondered at its passing presence with curious minds and fearful ponderings.

Though not small, the heavenly rock was far from massive, being larger than a man in diameter as the fires around it continued to gnaw away at its edges – incinerating any small pebbles it could chip away by its efforts. Behind it a trail of oily smoke slithered away into the atmosphere and would soon be gone all together, with nothing left to even mark the passing of such an event save the silent wonder of those who had seen it pass over head.

Its arc of descent took it over Talatheal and Colloni and the deep Yoan Ocean until it grew lazy, drifting lower to scrape the mountain tops of Arid Land, scattering ancient pines and mountain top boulders as well as cremating the nearest objects in its brief interactions. Finally, it landed with an incredible earth shaking explosion just outside the stone circle of Galba, spitting debris, dust and flame all about the stone circle which alone was unmoved and unrattled in the ensuing quake.

The silence which followed the impact was deafening.

As the dust settled, snowing from above in small drifts of ash and dirt like sifted flour being poured out from the sky. The thirty-foot crater was just yards away from the timeless stones. The ageless trees that had feared to approach the glade had been swallowed by this crater as it expanded outward. The rough edges crumbling still in the dwindling silence around the glade that still seemed to dominate all.

Near the immediate outskirts of the crater, more trees had been toppled, sprawled out like warriors laid low on their backs – defeated and harmless. Even with all that had just happened, the sanctity of the glade still held. Even with the dark blot of burnt earth near its center, the peace still emanated from within the ring of stones. The presence and majesty that was Galba still remained amid the flickering flames which crouched between the fallen pines – waiting breathless for the following moments.

Outside the circle the crater's center smoldered and spat, crackled and sputtered. Then, amid the churning fire, which was all that was left of the cosmic debris, something moved. A shadow at first; insubstantial and fleeting, it danced amid the flames but then grew more substance and rigid as it rose up and above the blackened, rough hewn walls of the crater. This shade became the semblance of a man who grew more massive and spectacular the closer he drew to the crater's lip.

Upon reaching this location he took hold of the edge itself; clawed plum colored hands digging into some remaining green grass and pulled his frame free and into the light.

He was tall.

A giant more than a man for sure – fifteen feet at his full height. He pushed his long, black, silken locks from his face to clear his vision. His eyes were a strange thing to behold; black where most other eyes are white and a deep purple iris and black pupil. These strange orbs took in the surrounding scene with a cautious, but determined air.

The being who had risen from the crater stepped forward with his bare feet ending in black talon-like nails, the same as his hands, and the earth shook again. The great stone circle was shaking…was moving. In a handful of heartbeats, the stone structure shot up to a staggering height, matching that of the new figure's.

The figure did nothing in reaction to this but stroke his black handlebar moustache with a soft smile. He was dressed for war and ready for anything. A sleeveless suit of black scale mail was wrapped about his body, falling from his neck to just above his ankles; slit up both sides to his waist where a black leather belt held it fast. The coat of scales seemed to be more organic than metallic and could well have been the hide of some animal or beast. His shoulders were capped with wrought iron carved to resemble the upper portion of a dragon's head, appearing as if they were devouring the arm underneath. Similar motifs could be found on the wrought iron grieves and gauntlets which covered his frame, save these were of linnorms.

This was Gurthghol in his true form.

"You know why I am here." The god's voice was strong and clear. At his right side a morning star hung ready for use on his belt. On the opposite side rested a silver khopesh. As with The Great Eye revealing Endarien's whereabouts, Gurthghol hid his current actions from the others now. None would see this upcoming encounter – none could if he wanted to work out his plan successfully.

"Very well. If that is how you wish to have it be, then you leave me little choice." Gurthghol continued.

Seeing he was not getting anywhere, the god beckoned the air with his left hand. Out of the shadows of the trees and stones around him emerged four beings of similar size to the god. They appeared to be humans with shaved heads and deep violet eyes and dusty, grayish-purple skin which seemed to grow grayer tinted in the light and more purple in the shadows as they moved to stand before Gurthghol.

Each of the four wore a dark and somber robe. The color was like liquid shade which darkened and lightened as they moved, making it impossible to determine its actual hue. On top of these robes was a charcoal gray cloak, the hood of each drawn, masking their faces their faces in a constant pool of shadow. They approached with silence; long robes hiding their feet and making them appear to hover on the air itself as they came to stand by their lord.

"Make ready. The time is almost here." Gurthghol had a hunch he wanted to explore. Well, it was more of a burning conviction than hunch he figured. In order to make it work though, he would need to have some help. He hoped it didn't come to that really, but figured it would as Galba wasn't going to be the least bit friendly to his demands. If she was though, Gurthghol would have wondered at the validity of Saredhel's prophecy.

The armored god motioned again and this time there was the sound of a million whispers being spoken at once. The screams of the mad shot through this noise like lightning and then silence. Before Gurthghol stood four more beings, but these were much different then the previous four he'd summoned. Similar in height and shape to their predecessors, they seemed to be pure bedlam incarnate. Hair the color of wildflowers sprouted from their heads as two different colored eyes, which seemed to change at whim, stared out of each head as they looked at their god, each pupil being disproportionate to the other.

Their dress and flesh were all a patchwork of color and texture and shape. Here were bits of armor sown into goat hide, pieces of old cloth stitched into worn leather. Their faces and bodies were tattooed and painted in all manner of strange designs and colors and shapes. Their ears, eyebrows, nose, tongue, and any other likely spot of their anatomy which remained uncovered by their motley dress were pierced a multiple of times; dangling bones, jewels and worked precious metals like the cart of a vendor at a bizarre. In all this insanity though was the uniform nature of their weapon. Each had strapped to his side a silver scimitar, enlarged to match their wielder's frame, and deadly enough to lay waste to anything it would come up against. Each of these new four greeted their lord with a smile which seemed to be laced with an insane, drug-induced, euphoria.

"Welcome," Gurthghol said as they took their places beside him and the four others.

"Now we are ready." The plum skinned deity clapped his hands and instantly, a wrought iron helmet appeared level with his chest. It allowed for the covering of the head, but not the face. A nose guard and a limited extension of metal at the sides created some cheek guards of a sort, but that was all. At its crest a ridge of sharp spikes much like that of a lizard's spine, followed the curve of the helmet from the nose guard, where they started off small, growing in size climbing the top of the helmet to the back where they became small again. There were also openings for the ear which allowed Gurthghol's own pointed, purple ears to stick out from underneath – a small black iron ridge covering the appendages with a cap of worn, dark forged metal.

He donned his helmet. "You know what to do."

The eight were silent, only nodded.

"Then let us begin. Time is short."

Together they walked toward the stone circle, behind and between its posts the image of a soft tranquil glade continued to appear to them as it had to all who had come before, but Gurthghol knew more. He knew what it really was and why he was now seeking it. He and Galba had made a deal and he doubted if Galba would go back on it now after so many millennia had passed. In truth, he wasn't really relishing trying to lay claim to it again either, but then where would be the sacrifice?

As he took a stride toward the circle he drew his morning star, the chain falling from the wooden handle like a chime, the spiked metal ball the size of a goblin dangling free about the god's knees. The four armed men were Lords of Chaos, beings in service to both the chaotic force of the cosmos and the force's god. They were rapid in their approach as they drew their scimitars, smiling at the conflict to come. Their grins bordered on maniacal delusion as they rushed forward but quickly vanished when they came face to face with the invisible barrier.

They wanted to be sure their next action was in line with their god.

All four raised their swords high and then looked back toward their god and the four others, the cloaked Lords of Darkness.

Gurthghol simply nodded.

The Lords of Darkness then began to wield a spell. Velvet blackness flew from their outstretched fingers and toward the barrier where it clung and spread like oil in water. In moments the entire barrier, once invisible, appeared as a round half globe, shading what was underneath. When the darkness had consumed its prey the Lords of Chaos struck.

Each screamed a cry that would shatter the soul of any creature – the very words and manner of madness distilled, Chaos' song in the cosmos. In addition to this shout, their blades rung true and struck the black barrier with a thick *thud*, as if they were chopping wood. Though the effect of their attack seemed to be negated, they still continued to raise their weapons in a wild frenzy and hack away at the dark dome before them. For a few moments more this bedlam continued until Gurthghol came to join them. Upon seeing their god draw near, the lords stopped their attack, then turned to their orchid skinned deity.

"That should give me enough reach." The god of chaos and darkness began to swing his great morning star overhead, both hands on the thick hilt. Gurthghol's face darkened, his eyes squinted and brow furrowed under the effort it took to build up the force he'd need to break open the dome before him. His strong upper body didn't fail him in that effort and soon he had conjured a vortex of darkness above his head.

With a great grunt the god unleashed the brunt of his strength and the weapon itself to strike first into the barrier, and then the force behind the barrier. The attack was massive in nature, first rippling the black dome with the vibration of its impact and then shattering it all together the following second. The dome's destruction mimicked the shattering of glass, but was magnified to an unearthly pitch so as to seem to slice the air itself into atomic fragments.

All gathered near the circle as shards of night exploded around and past them in a cacophony and force only a god and his chosen could have survived with their existence intact. Behind the dome the standing stones returned to leer over those who fought to enter inside them; to take part in what lay beyond them. Gurthghol would have no such hindrance, however. The first born of Vkar and Xora, he was the best suited to do this task since he had once used the power which Galba watched over before. None of the others gods knew what they would have been getting into, should they have taken up this task, but he also knew what they were facing better than they. After all, he'd dealt with the first pawn the dark entity had used, sacrificing much there too for their victory.

Cadrith would be a challenge to defeat.

"Galba. Your fight is in vain." Gurthghol bellowed.

"Why battle me now when you know what is at stake?" Gurthghol lowered his weapon, then proceeded to step through one of the stone portals and inside the circle.

"Can you really afford to waste such time when the life of Tralodren itself may be ending?" The god entered into the circle's center, his eyes lusting after the throne before him on the dais. The throne he had once controlled for many years before giving it up for his freedom.

"The life of this planet is insignificant when compared to the whole of the cosmos." Galba's disembodied voice rebuked the god.

"Think of the creatures inhabiting it, the mortals and the gods who lay claim to it, and nurture its and their own development." Gurthghol grew closer to Vkar's throne. "Recall our own pact to make it safe from interference–"

"No." Galba appeared before him then.

She had grown in size to match his own; green eyes flaring with a stern aura. Her left hand rested upon his armored chest, holding him at bay. The delicate appendage was stronger than even Khuthon; stopping Gurthghol's progression.

"You forget that though you may be gods, you are not, nor ever will be our equal." Galba's voice was as strong as her blocking hand. "You are the creation and I and my counterpart are the creators. If it were not for the throne of your father we wouldn't even be here now. You and your kin would have gone the way of all created things eons ago. But you *did* suffer and you *did* survive, and now that reprieve has ended and things must work their course." Her words were sharper than a sword.

"Or you use those you can to bring about your wishes." Gurthghol curled his lip in disgusted anger. "Be they god or mortal."

"Fighting me will not reverse Sidra's choice. She made her choice freely. All have a choice."

Gurthghol flinched at the mention of his daughter for a moment. After all these centuries a part of him still missed her and...perhaps a sliver of guilt still hung over his heart for what he had to do–

"Don't make this more difficult than it has to be, Galba...move aside." The god, sometimes called the Shifting One, tightened his grip on the morning star.

"You are strong Gurthghol as all first born are, but you are not your father and even he was limited by the throne as much as he was its prisoner. You are not Vkar, and you will not have his throne again." Galba didn't move her hand or stance. "Claiming the throne again will just make matters worse – your pain greater and even bring greater doom upon the Pantheon." Gurthghol said nothing, merely gave a mental command and his eight lords rushed in to join their god and stand by his cause.

The Lords of Chaos rallied against Galba, blades striking her soft alabaster flesh, but never drinking of the ichor behind her skin or even shredding her gown by their strikes. The Lords of Darkness met with similar resistance as they launched their black daggers, pulled from under their cloaks, trying to puncture her with wicked delight. Amid all these assaults the great being held her ground, being immobile to any and all attacks leveled against her.

Only her green eyes moved, seeking out Gurthghol. who had backed up during the beginnings of the assault and now slowly made his way toward the throne of his father. She continued to do nothing but watch as the god drew up to the white marble dais with all the regal manner of an ageless monarch as his minions unsuccessfully attempted to slay her. She waited a moment more, then began her move.

With but a thought Galba vanished from the ensnaring circle of attackers to appear before Gurthghol once more. She appeared right in his path, only one step above him, a white pillar with flaming red hair. The lords who had been attacking her rapidly fell into and on top of each other, tumbling in a pile of swords and mismatched colors and shadows. The Lords of Darkness halted their attack, but kept their gaze ever focused on Gurthghol to gauge their next action. The Lords of Chaos did their best to withhold their anxious twitches to slaughter. As they righted themselves, each looked to be holding back a seizure with varying degrees of success.

"It is not yours to claim." Her full lips spoke.

"Nor yours to bar." The god returned.

"Remember the pact we made Gurthghol." Galba's face was as stern as it was lovely.

"You let a mere mortal aided by your darker aspect sit upon it, letting him take hold of its promises and gifts but yet you halt the advance of myself, the rightful heir, from taking it back?" The god of chaos searched around Galba for some pathway around her, but he knew he could only gain the throne by going through her. It would be a waste of time, but he'd have to do it – have to suffer through the process to claim his prize.

"You even break your own rule Gurthghol in a rush to shatter our pact. The Pantheon cannot be here in their true form, they are forbidden from entering their creation in such a manner." Galba followed those wandering eyes of the god whom some called Father Chaos.

"It is my nature to challenge rules." He gave the woman a broad grin, showing off his sharp canine teeth.

Galba continued to reason with the god. "But it is not in your nature to defy the will of what must be – to defy change."

"You speak of change yes, but your change is nothing but the destruction of all. I never agreed to that, nor did the others. We thought we were through of your meddling after we defeated Sidra. We didn't expect you to mark us out as prey once again for–"

Galba interrupted. "Change is something I thought you would favor Gurthghol. After all, here is the time and place to see all things change, to witness a new age being born, a shaking up and off of the old things to give birth to the new, be they a new age or whole world."

"*Your* game," Gurthghol placed one foot up on the stone step and drew his strong body forward so that his face was inches from Galba's, "will have no winners if allowed to continue. I will not allow something I helped to create suffer destruction before I wish it."

"Are you still referring to *Sidra* or *Tralodren?*" Galba gently questioned.

Gurthghol's countenance darkened in his silence.

"So I see." Galba grew crestfallen then. "You favor change only if you originated it – if it comes from within your understanding…your control." She was a representative of the very creative force of creation itself and so abhorred the slaughter of life, but if she was left with no choice, she would have to fight and ultimately destroy Gurthghol. "You must understand Gurthghol that even as mighty and wonderful as your divine family is, there is still and always will be something greater."

Gurthghol stared into her deep green eyes with his own black and purple orbs. For a moment he simply peered deeply into the forest green pools that swam in an emerald light as they pulled him deeper and still deeper into the truth of her words. He could see the veil being pulled from them so they became windows to the things even beyond the gods, even Titans, their forbearers. He knew then the fathomless reaches of nothingness and everything being combined into one location, one reality...

He felt himself being pulled away with this feeling. After all, who was he – what was he – to contend with a force that had given life to all the cosmos?

Compared to it he was nothing; he was...his thoughts stopped when he saw the faint outline of an outstretched hand amid that churning mix of Light and Darkness. It was the hand of his father, Vkar, reaching for the very things that gave him existence – the very things from which he stole and crafted his own divinity; passing it on as a legacy for his offspring to form the Pantheon. The very hand of the first rebel who reached for something far outside his station.

Seeing that image fueled Gurthghol with the resolve he needed to snap the spell of disillusionment which swam before his eyes. He could see the endless cycle returning to Tralodren and other worlds. Even if the world was spared and the Pantheon victorious, they would have to stand up against the threat once again, but then they would be weaker than they were now and would surely be destroyed at some point for sure if they managed to just survive this time.

No, his father had been right. Vkar had sought out knowledge and power from the throne by dominating the two entities who had created all the cosmos. Gurthghol would do much better than this. He would supersede even his father's unrealized goals and not only dominate, but absorb the two forces to keep Tralodren and other worlds safe from their endless game. He could only do this though if he got to claim his father's throne once more. This was his plan; the reality of the cryptic words spoken by Saredhel to the others before Endarien failed in his fight. The very thing he once believed was his prison eons ago he know sought out with near reckless abandon. He found the irony to his liking.

"Out of my way." Gurthghol introduced the back of his hand to Galba's smooth cheek. There was a peal of thunder from the strike and Galba fell to the ground before him, looking up at her attacker with eyes rimmed in anger.

Galba didn't remain down for long, however, rising to her feet like a flash of lightning and then appearing beside Gurthghol once more in the twinkling of an eye. "There are bigger things afoot here than this foolish action." Galba's sudden arrival beside the god of chaos and darkness allowed her to keep in time with Gurthghol's advance to the next step on the dais; matching him step for step as she made her way to stand before him to block his path once again.

"Your coming war on Thangaria is a distraction as is this." Galba held her ground.

"A distraction to whom?" The god of darkness swung his morning star toward the cosmic woman, only to pass right through her, biting into the ground in anger over its failure to land a blow on its intended victim.

Galba rose off the ground then; a few feet above where the shattered steps cradled the black pointed ball of Gurthghol's weapon. The lords were watching the battle with great interest, ready to obey their god however he directed...and direct them he did – the Lords of Chaos barely able to keep themselves away. Then another mental command came. Their god had requested their aid. The Lords of Darkness began to cast a spell at the keeper of the circle while the Lords of Chaos made their reckless charge forward, happy to be free to slaughter once more. Galba paid them no mind, instead focusing her attention firmly on Gurthghol, the real threat.

"If you want to fight then we shall fight," she said.

"To the winner goes the throne." The dark god clenched his teeth in a snarl.

"If that is what you wish..." Galba waved her hand before her, and the eight lords vanished from sight. "...but only you and I shall fight, your minions have no place in this battle. If I am being forced to kill this day, then I wish it only to be one and not nine."

"Agreed." Gurthghol didn't even turn around. He knew they were gone, placed back to where they had been summoned. She would never kill them, just return them from whence they'd came. It was probably better anyway since they could be used for troops at Thangaria where they were needed more than at this battle.

Gurthghol tightened his grip on the handle of his morning star. "So let it begin."

Chapter 29

Snow and ice flew in the gales around the young Nordican as the fat white flakes swirled past his eyes and mind too fast to fathom. His body was rigid, though he didn't feel the cold zephyrs tear into him as some might who didn't share his blood. Like all Nordicans, Rowan was able to fend off some of the cold climate that made up his homeland. But as all mortals, he wasn't immune to the terrible turrets of cold forever. Though he was presently surviving, he had no idea where in the Northlands he was.

He tried to make sense one last time of what had happened to him recently to help him get some mental bearings; his thoughts getting lost in the white haze of his breath which quickly scattered about his head.

He recalled the spell Cadrissa cast at the Great Library. It had started well he supposed, since he didn't really know how to gauge the success of any spell. However, something had gone wrong. He wasn't inside the tower, and he didn't have any idea where Clara or the mage were at all – let alone where he might be.

The next thing he could recall after the spell was cast was suddenly opening his eyes in the frozen wastelands where even few Nordicans came if they could help it. Even though of hearty stock, many preferred the more temperate and fertile land to the south.

He came to believe he had been in the white wilderness no more than an hour now. To add even more hardship upon him, no sooner had he appeared in the snowy tundra than it started to snow. It was soft and gentle at first, like baby's breath, but soon increased into a torrential storm that swallowed up the knight whole before he had time to react. Now he felt as though he'd been walking in circles ever since.

He knew he probably wouldn't survive the night. Without food, the proper gear and a basic understanding of where he was, he didn't stand much of a chance. He knew Cadrissa and Clara wouldn't either if they were here with him. Once more he dared to shout their names against the storm. Once more he received nothing back but the harsh slap of Perlosa. Rowan knew if he wandered far enough north he'd come into the territory of Jotun and Trolls: two races of giant that have warred with the Nordicans off and on for centuries. If he did survive the night he might find out he had wandered straight into their territory, and without proper aid and equipment he'd be dead for sure. Frigia, especially the more northern areas, where the tower resided, was not known to be hospitable to any form of mortalkind.

The bleak thoughts were all that kept Rowan comforted on his silent trek amid the fury of Perlosa around him. His feet sank deeper into the snow beneath him with each step and each movement forward was harder and slower than the last. It was then that the youth knew his strength was failing him – the snow winning the day in this battle of life and will.

Had it been a clear sky, Rowan would have seen the soft pink light of dusk, but instead a dim gray blanket covered the atmospheric vault. Rowan continued to scan the landscape for any shapes he could recognize, any area he would be looking to find some shelter from the storm. He was hoping against hope he hadn't been that lost after the spell and Clara and Cadrissa were just around the next burst of flakes cheering him on to find them and safe harbor for the night.

He wondered in his heart and soul where his goddess was. Why she had left him to die in this desolate place? Ironically, a place so close to home and yet so far from where he felt he had to be; so far from the purposes she had told him he had yet to accomplish. Where was she? What was her plan? Had he failed her, and now this was her punishment to her champion? His ponderings were unanswered – only the wind dared give him a reply, buffeting him with shards of ice and freezing his skin and muscles to his bones.

He was thankful he still held his cloak but it did little to stop his blood from feeling like a glacier filled river. His hands had become so numb he couldn't feel them any more, and his face felt as though it had been crafted from marble, immobile and lifeless. Even his eyes were like glass orbs in his head. Rowan's boots had stopped working a short while ago, the cold snow finally managing to claw into them and coating his feet with a cold garment, robbing them of feeling with each passing step.

The end was near.

Fatalism was a trait all Nordicans shared on some level of their subconscious. They were wild in that sense – savage in their outlook of nature and the cosmos around them. Where other humans saw things differently in such situations, Nordicans believed in fate and fortune. The predisposed destiny of all things; a hold over from their mysticism that was being replaced by the light of Panthor and civilizing efforts by the priests and Knighthood. It was believed men could do little about their fate. If a person was fated to die, they died. One could not change destiny. Why bother, when one is fated so. Man could be fated for many things; to marry, grow old, sick, and die; he could be fated to be a great chieftain or warrior, or even robber or poor. While other humans would say you can make your own destiny, many Nordicans were unsure and doubtful and it was into this familiar philosophy that Rowan found himself sinking as his uncertain wandering increased.

He had given up looking ahead, and just let his head and shoulders slump forward to ponder his feet, concentrating on them to keep moving even though he began to stop feeling them-losing all sense of movement whatsoever. His mind turned to Clara for a moment. Her face, her eyes, her gentle spirit. What a woman she was and indeed he felt he would have liked to have learned more of her, settle down with her and possibly even have come to love her as wife, but these were fleeting hopeless thoughts. Whims of a desperate mind trying to stoke what fires it could, from wherever it could, to rouse the embers of life for a few more steps.

She was probably dead or lost somewhere now. This snow would see to that if not the spell itself. He was probably all that remained and soon he'd be dead, a soft white grave swallowing him whole before morning came. It was all so fruitless. Why had he done any of it? Why had his goddess allowed him to join the Knighthood, to go on this mission? Why fill his head with such confusion and mysteries as to what she had planned for him – a destiny that he seemed fated to do? Perhaps men could change their destinies after all...

He thought of his mother and father then. They would never know where their son was buried; where to find him or what happened to him. Never know if he had been successful on his first mission or what fate befell him. He knew such lack of knowledge would be devastating to his mother and probably deeply grieve his father as well. But there was nothing he could do about it, nowhere he could go, and no one he could plead to who would hear him – let alone help.

Darkness did indeed come, faster than he had thought possible, swallowing up what light remained like a wolf. His claw-like hands clasped at his cloak and could not move either. He had become a frozen statue, and it was then that Rowan fell. His six-foot frame tumbled into the thick snow, denting it with his weight. The knight couldn't go on any further. His will was gone and his life would soon follow. In what strength remained he grasped onto the amulet around his neck, as the snow started to bury him, he said a simple prayer to Panthor to watch over his soul when he died and to take care of his loved ones.

Then his eyes closed and silence reigned.

"Keep moving." Clara forced the words out of her chattering teeth. "We have to keep moving."

Cadrissa said nothing. She was too busy trying to keep from freezing to death in the inappropriate clothing she was wearing to be wandering around the snowy wastes of Frigia. Hands clasped tightly inside her cloak to hold back the cold as best she could, she tried to think about what had gone wrong in her spell. She still had the scepter clutched tight in one hand inside her cloak and the medallion around her neck, so there was that small comfort.

It had to be The Master. She was sure of it. Somehow he had been able to alter the spell, sending them here, outside the tower rather than within and separating them from Rowan. At least the mage hoped they were just separated, and nothing worse had befallen the knight.

They had been walking now for what seemed to be an hour. An hour in a storm of ice and snow that pounded their frames with all it had, intent on bringing their doom. Since that time Cadrissa had been hard at work wracking her mind for spells to ease the conditions to give them a fighting chance against such hostile elements. So far she had been able to come up with nothing. She could feel the icy fingers of The Master still lingering inside her and knew they were blocking any attempt she made to remedy this situation.

"How are you holding up?" Clara took a good look at the mage. Her silver hair was frosted now under her hood, tear streaked face lined with small rivers of ice; snot frozen around her nose. Her garments were little better than Cadrissa's, but managed to hold her own as best she could. The hardest pain for her to endure was trying to find Rowan in the storm…if they could…

"I'm still alive," Came the mage's curt reply.

"Any spells yet?" The elf looked a little more hopeful; snowy eyebrows raised in eager anticipation.

"Nothing." Clara turned back to the blizzard before her with resolute resolve. She wasn't going to die easy, that was for sure. She'd put up as strong a fight as she could, even though her body felt like it was a moving statue from the cold. She would press on – had to press on. Now and then between breaths slicing her lungs with barbs of ice she thought of Rowan, and what his fate had been. Was he out here wandering through this storm as well? If so, how did he fare, and how close was he to them? It would be truly ironic if they all wound up dying in close proximity to each other, but not know it due to the storm.

Stop it.

She had to think more positive thoughts, believe the best and hope for the best. It could still all work out if they found the tower and could get inside it. If they could hold out a little longer and push onward they might be able to see it soon and then get away from this storm and their slow deaths.

Clara stopped then in her tracks.

"What is it?" Cadrissa asked.

Clara said nothing, merely stared at a lump of dark snow before them. Cadrissa followed the gaze to see what looked like a pile of snow gathering on what could have been a rock or...a cloak. Both women hurried toward the shape to discover it was indeed a cloak with a familiar dragon-crested shield slung over the occupant's back but more than that, it was Rowan as well. His face was half buried in the snow and was quickly being swallowed up by the fat, falling flakes. He didn't look dead – at least as far as they could tell, but he didn't look that far from it either.

"You get one arm and I'll get the other," Clara ordered.

Cadrissa did as she was told as Clara took the other arm after dusting off his face. "We'll pull him as long as we can," she said, then began to do just that; dragging him across the snow.

Unable to hold their cloaks closed, they flapped wildly in the wind; daggers of frost jabbing into their ribs, breasts and thighs with each snowy gust. If they had been cold before, then they were beyond cold now. Both knew they couldn't keep this up for much longer and hope to live through the next hour, if not half hour. Something had to be done.

"Anytime you get a spell–"

"I'll use it." Cadrissa cut off the elf with the same degree of frustration.

Clara nodded solidly and then focused all her effort on the matter of pulling and walking, pulling and walking. As the elf did this, Cadrissa begin to feel the heat of the medallion rise up around her neck, growing in intensity until it felt like a ring of fire encircling her shoulders and base of her head. With this heat, the cold melted from her bones, and her mind became clearer. So clear in fact that the whispers which now came to her head could be partly discerned. They were telling her what could be done, giving her options to the situation she now faced.

Cadrissa listened intently, completely ignoring the other part of her mind which spoke out to her at just how convenient this all was. This part of her mind also wondered why the medallion seemed to have a mind and perhaps even life of its own – almost as if it was some self-aware, living thing...but she ignored that part of her mind, for it was becoming drowned out in the whispers.

While all this was going on Clara looked behind her to the unconscious Nordican she was dragging. She was happy to have found him, that much was true, but did it really matter since they would probably all die together anyway in this tundra? At least they would be together when that happened. Walking amidst such pessimistic thoughts, Clara began to understand something about herself – things she hadn't had the time to ponder until now. Life and death issues had a way of bringing truth to light, prioritizing where one's real loyalties and self lie.

What she saw now in that clear light of pre-demise reason astonished her. It challenged some preconceived notions of herself which she had felt were secure and grounded and showed her just what it was that lead her to love the young human she was dragging behind her. It was so obvious now, why hadn't she see it before? Why–

"I got something." Cadrissa's voice interrupted the elf's thoughts.

There was a whispering of some indiscernible words which were stolen in the wind, and then the wind and cold stopped. All three of them were held a short distance above the ground in a red tinted bubble. Clara looked over at the mage, who smiled.

"We can let him go now." The wizardress dropped Rowan's arm, letting it fall to the concave floor of the bubble, which was as solid as normal earth and even though slightly curved uninhibiting to any movement. "It will carry all three of us easily enough."

Clara let the knight's other hand go gently to the floor, bending at the knees – which had now started to warm up quite dramatically. "The heat?"

"It's all inside and will keep us from freezing while we're looking for the tower." The mage continued to smile.

"So you got access to your spells again?"

"Thanks to the medallion." Cadrissa looked over to Rowan then. "If he can warm up enough, I think he'll be fine."

"I hope so." Clara peered down at the Nordican, who appeared now to be slumbering more than dying. She didn't want to say what she thought about that medallion – that it might be the cause of their misdirection of location – at the moment, lest it cause come unneeded strife.

"He's a Nordican." Cadrissa passed off his recovery as more than certain. "They live in this kind of weather all the time. He'll be fine."

Clara wasn't going to argue with the mage's optimism either. "So you think you can find the tower?" She looked back over at Cadrissa.

"I'm sure." Cadrissa's free hand went to the medallion tightly encased it in the gold-gloved flesh. "We'll find it soon enough, and then we'll figure out how to work this" She raised the silver scepter at her side, "and be out of this wasteland."

Cadrissa closed her eyes again as she kept her hand on the medallion.

Clara thought it wise to brave at least one question about Cadrissa's new accessory, especially in light of how quickly she had seemed to become attached to it. Cadrissa looked like the drunkard who loved his bottle more than life itself. "You said you think that medallion's trying to help us out – to get us to achieve our mission. Why do you say that?"

"Because it has been talking to me, and telling me how we need to get to the tower and what we need to do once we get there." The mage didn't change her pose, but her voice was growing more distant now – like one in a trance. "I didn't understand it at first, but now it is talking to me clearer and clearer. It has been the reason why I've been able to keep casting spells as I have. I've been drawing on the power of the medallion." Her face then washed over with delight. "...so much power..."

"Cadrissa?" Clara dared a gentle hand on her shoulder. The action pulled her back from her trance so she could look into the elf's eyes. "You all right?"

"Fine." The mage replied as if indeed nothing were amiss.

Clara looked at her skeptically for a moment longer.

Cadrissa let out a nervous laugh. "I'm fine Clara, really. In fact, I know where the tower is now. We'll be there very soon, so why not just rest and warm up and we'll all be ready to deal with whatever we face when we get there." She smiled again but it didn't seem quite right to the elf.

It seemed like the smile of a liar.

Clara wanted to ask the mage what she thought they'd find there – what the medallion had told her, but she thought against it. The same feeling of unease that washed over her whenever Cadrissa grasped the medallion in her hand held her back from commenting. Clara tried to stop herself from feeling this way, but as much as she tried to bury the unease, a small flake of it, like unmelted snow still fluttered about her mind. She didn't like that medallion, or the whole matter of what she felt it was doing to Cadrissa.

Had she intended to dump them in the snow all along with her spell, Clara wondered? Was she trying to kill them? Was that what the medallion wanted her to do to them? Clara had known of drunks doing many things outside their normal character if they could but gain access to more drink. Was this the same with Cadrissa and the medallion?

Clara bent down to look over Rowan. If anything was going to happen to them by the mage's hand, compelled by the medallion she now wore or not, Clara would feel much better with Rowan at her side. Another sword arm would help, even if they would be waging a war against magic. Keeping one eye on the knight whom she wrapped up in his cloak, and one weary eye on Cadrissa she tended her thoughts and suspicions as the red tinted bubble moved through the air like a silent cloud.

One thing was sure. If Cadrissa grew more influenced by the medallion – Clara was sure that was the case – then they might very well be looking at being stranded in this land. All the more reason to watch her carefully, even more so in a tower where her access to even more spells and potential dangers could grow. All the more reason to rouse Rowan and get him ready for anything to come.

Amid the snowy lands beyond the Stomikja Mountains of Frigia resided the Frigian Wastes. Here in this land, hidden away from all prying eyes, giants and the few other beings that called the tundra home, stood the majestic ice palace of a long forgotten Wizard King, Jarl Knorrsen.

The palace was large and splendid beyond words, looking like solid diamond when the light of dawn hit upon its walls and minarets. It was built in concentric circles, radiating outward like a ripple on water. Three circles enclosed themselves, each with four slender towers built upon each circular wall. They seemed to look like inverted icicles erupting from the snowy wastes. Each of these first towers was aligned to the north, south, east and west. The second set of four towers were higher and rested on a taller wall and aligned with the northeast, southeast, northwest, and southwest. The last set of towers were more slender and reached farther into the frosty receding day than the rest; following the orientation of the first towers. It was a strange construction, as it had few windows to speak of, save a collection here or there on the towers highest levels, but the walls were thick and seamless ice.

A large, heavy gate served to allow entrance into the structure below which was created to look like reinforced wood though it too was formed of solid bluish ice. Like the rest of the outside of the palace, it was simple and functional. The ring of walls were connected with simple ice walkways that crisscrossed the circular structures and latched into the towers like a spider's web. Snow capped and empty, they showed no signs of occupation. It was to the very gate of this ancient tower that the red tinted bubble carried the three adventurers. Hovering like a stalled cloud, it came to rest right before the doors of the massive structure. As it did, Cadrissa began to study the door intently, fingers tapping on the medallion as she did so.

"Rowan." Clara knelt over his chest peering into his fluttering eyes.

"He's waking up." The elf stood up allowing Cadrissa to see the youth garble out words and flap his eyelids until some sense of cognitive awareness returned to his face. She noted it like a simple fact and then returned to her study of the door.

"You've been unconscious for a while." Clara began to help the young knight sit up. "You all right?"

"How did you find me?" He managed to sit up without aid, rubbing his eyes to clear them of the debris that had found harbor there since his passing into sleep.

"The favor of the gods," said the elf with a warm, thin smile. "If we didn't happen upon you like we did, you might have lain there forever!"

Rowan looked down around him, saw the red tinted bubble and was more than a little amazed. "Where are we?"

"At the tower." Clara answered.

"How?" He stood up now to get a better look at the structure before them.

"Cadrissa," said the elf and then she whispered into the Nordican's ear: "I think something isn't right with her, she seems unlike herself and I think it's because of that medallion she started wearing."

Rowan said nothing, only nodded ever so slightly as he watched the mage with a prudent eye – observing her finger the medallion as her dreamy eyes stared straight ahead toward the tower…looking right through the tower.

"How long have we been here?" He asked Clara while keeping his eyes on the mage.

"I woke you as soon as we got here." Clara mimicked the knight's gaze as she spoke to him.

"So what now?" He spoke loud enough for Cadrissa to hear him, and she did, turning to greet him with a face that seemed all her own and full of understanding. The dreamy quality was gone from her face and her hand no longer rested on the medallion.

"We'll get inside." The mage's visage and voice were clear and focused once again.

"I thought you said there were spells protecting it from anyone getting inside." Rowan stated. "How did you plan on getting into a tower protected by spells cast by a Wizard King?"

"You're awake!" Cadrissa seemed surprised to see the Nordican up and about as if she had been elsewhere when she had watched the youth rise from slumber. Rowan and Clara suspected she had…

"Yeah," Rowan held back his concern at Cadrissa's remarks, "and surprised we all wound up here when you said you'd take us *inside* the tower." The knight studied the mage, looking for any signs about Clara's warnings of her change in personality.

He didn't see any at the moment.

"Something must have happened in the spell." The mage didn't want to tell them what, not yet anyway. It wasn't helpful in getting them inside and would probably raise more questions and concerns then needed.

"Obviously," Rowan turned his view to the gate into the tower. "Now that we're here though, how are we going to get inside? It's huge. Looks more like a castle than tower to me, too."

"From what I've read, Jarl was a bit of a recluse who took to protecting his tower from anything as common as a wandering animal to the storms we all got to walk through to get here. He did these spells in layers it seems and so it will be just a matter of pulling them back layer by layer, until we have our way open."

"But he was a *Wizard King*," Rowan voiced his concern again. "Are you sure you could get rid of them? Won't they be too strong?"

Cadrissa smiled. When she did, her face turned dreamy again and Rowan could see that other world stare looking back at him and then he knew the extent of Clara's concerns.

"I have that covered," said the mage.

"Good." Rowan cautiously made his way closer to Clara, giving himself a little bit more room between the mage and himself. He looked to Clara to see her already staring at him with eyes that seemed to say: "*I told you.*"

Cadrissa turned around to face the gate and started to mumble in the strange language of magic, her free hand rising up to clasp itself around the medallion once more. Rowan and Clara said nothing, merely kept an eye on the mage and each other as the wizardress continued her low, slightly mumbled, chanting. It seemed to go on for ages, but then...

"Rowan, look," Clara jabbed the knight in his side which drew his full attention to the door of the tower. It had started to shimmer with a golden light – a golden aura enveloping all of it.

"Open," Cadrissa whispered amid the murmurs in her head. The mage drew in a sharp breath, then let it out in an even sigh.

Focus, you have to focus Cadrissa, the wizardress told herself, feel the words as they are spoken. She felt as though she were on fire, inside to outside being consumed by an incredible heat. So much heat in fact that she had started to break out in a sweat.

Nothing happened.

"Open" Cadrissa spoke the word again, this time with greater volume that drew the attention of Rowan and Clara. She paid them no mind as it took all of hers to hold back what she felt growing inside her as some kind of large tidal wave of power. So much power she wasn't be able to keep it back much longer – even if she wanted too.

Even though this revelation was alarming, it was was also very intoxicating. She could understand why The Master and many of those who had followed the Path of Power were so consumed with it.

To wield such power in one's veins made you feel like some kind of divinity. Cadrissa felt like she could do anything. With but a whim and a word she could enjoy seeing her will manifest all around her, rising her claim of worth in the cosmos to the heels of the gods themselves…

Shaking her head she caught herself in mid-thought. These weren't her thoughts…at least not the ones she had wanted to concentrate on. She would always follow the Path of Knowledge, she could never be tempted into the Path of Power…never. She felt her eyes focus again on the door, could see it now in her vision.

Nothing had happened.

"Open." Cadrissa repeated again, this time at higher volume still, almost near a shout. When she did she felt the tidal wave behind her surge up as if getting ready for a massive crash.

Still the gateway to the tower remained barred.

"Cadrissa…" Clara moved slowly toward the mage. "…are you all-"

And then it fell.

Amid Cadrissa's frustration, the wave inside her fell – and there was an outpouring of such magnitude she couldn't believe it was all stored up inside her…though it wasn't that, was it? No, it had been – and still was stored in the medallion. She wasn't doing any of this. It was the medallion using her as The Master had used her. She understood now as she collapsed into darkness.

While Cadrissa had this further epiphany Clara and Rowan had to contend with a surge of force that shoved them to the back of the bubble. The same shove shattered the bubble, causing them to land in the snow below as the nimbus of energy, now shimmering like liquid bronze, made its way toward the tower. In similar fashion the wave besieged the tower, ramming into the protective barriers surrounding it; creating a rainbow as these protective barriers fell like dominoes.

Rowan and Clara managed to right themselves from their small drop in time to see this spectacle of lights. Four eyes saw the barriers over the tower that had been invisible before shatter into a display of star dust. Four eyes watched in wonder as the door to the tower melted away like butter in an oven's heat. Ice and bits of precious stones that once had called the door home all retreated like a fleeing tide from the beach to leave behind a sinister looking opening.

Both stood there in the biting wind as it tore at them and the ringing in their ears began to fade. They stood there in amazement and fear, in awe of what had just happened. They had witnessed something neither would forget as long as they lived. They had seen the magnitude of the force that was trying to or perhaps had now gained total control over Cadrissa.

Finally, Clara broke their silence. "Let's get inside before we freeze solid again."

Rowan made his way to the downed mage, who had landed on her side like a crumbled snow angel. The knight brushed her off, and slung her over his shoulder as he made his way to the dark opening.

"No. No…" Cadrissa's voice was faint and weak. "…put me down Dugan."

"Hang on." Rowan plowed through the mild dunes around the tower following the path Clara already had cleared before him with her own foot traffic. "We'll be out of this snow soon."

Together all three entered the tower, happy to be free of the storm, but knowing they could also be walking into something far worse…

Chapter 30

Once inside, Clara had taken to looking around the spacious chamber. Rowan had managed to deposit Cadrissa, who was still a little out of it but coming around with each passing moment, against the doorframe. He too was lost in the wonder that was the interior. It seemed at once a strangely beautiful and anticlimactic locale.

"*This* is the tower?" The knight took a few tentative steps around the plain, white marble block walls of the dim room. Save for a few faint sconces giving off some odd, icy light, the room swam in pitch puddles. Though large, it wasn't endless and the knight could see a set of double doors – white pine by the look of them, just on the edge of the darkness. The ceiling was another matter. He surmised it had to be at least twenty feet or more in height, and most of it hidden beyond the light of the flickering sconces. They seemed more like stars in the expanse of the night sky as he stared heavenward.

"You sound disappointed." Clara made her way back to the knight.

"I just thought it wouldn't be so...*empty*." Rowan made his way closer to the elf as well.

"It's been deserted for some time." Clara now came to stand beside him. "I'm surprised it has stood this long – especially after Cadrissa's performance."

Rowan looked over his shoulder again to see the mage still struggling between unconsciousness and consciousness. "Do you think it was all from the medallion?"

"My guess is yes." Said the elf.

Rowan nodded. "It looked that way to me too. Do you think she's possessed by it then or something? She looked like she was in a trance there for a little while..."

"I don't know what to make it of it yet." Clara now took a careful survey of the crumpled mage. "But I'm not going to take any chances either. She's found something that can help us...or at least it has so far. We should still be careful about what she does though – watch our backs. I won't put my trust in something with that strong a hold over her as being benign."

"Agreed." Rowan nodded again. "So where do we go now? This place is huge."

"We'll have to just start combing each room, hoping we'll find something to help us," Clara said with only a slight bit of weariness in her voice. She had hidden much of the real weariness she felt. "And hopefully Cadrissa can help keep us on the right path."

"That's a pretty big gamble." Rowan returned his full attention to the gray tinted face of the elf.

"It's also about all we have." Clara tried to keep herself optimistic about their present situation but it was proving more a struggle with each breath she took.

"She's right." Both turned to see Cadrissa struggling to stand up against the wall.

"Cadrissa," Clara instinctively went to aid the mage in her struggles to gain vertical stature. "You should be resting a little more. That last spell you cast took a lot out of you."

"Out of *all* of us." Rowan muttered beneath his breath.

"I'll be fine." She shooed away the elf's hand as she managed to stand on solid feet once more. "The longer we stay here, the more chance we have of any dangers this place might hold finding us."

"Dangers?" Rowan's hand moved to his sword hilt.

"I have broken the counterspells in this tower which will allow us to move about freely without magical impairment, but it also means all spells that were at work in this tower have been removed."

"So what does that mean?" Rowan grew a little unsettled by his surroundings.

"It means that any spell that was used to say, hold up a load bearing wall or keep a creature that had been held prisoner for research or some such thing has now been removed." The mage dusted the few flakes remaining in her hair away with a hand stroke.

"Great." Rowan's face grew emotionless.

"Not much we can do about it now." Clara copied the mage in dusting off the few stray white flakes remaining on her person. "So let's just get looking." She turned to Cadrissa once more. "You sure you're up to this? If you like we can wait a little–"

"I'll make it." Cadrissa was resolved to see everything through.

Clara was amazed at how much better the mage already looked to her. She wondered just how much influence that medallion had over her. What was its real power and had they seen it – seen all of it yet? Not much she could do about that either. She couldn't very well take it from Cadrissa, not now. No, best to just do what they came here to do and be done with it all as soon as possible.

"Did you want me to hold the scepter at least?" Clara braved the question.

"No." Cadrissa returned. "I've got it."

Rowan pulled out his sword, Clara mirroring his example. "Then let's go."

"What are we looking for here exactly?" Rowan asked Cadrissa, who was in front of him, leading him down a dark, marble hallway; Clara was beside the mage. It was cold inside the tower, but not as cold as it had been outside. They could still see their breath, but it wasn't as bone chilling as the wilderness around the tower. "Relics? Books? Scrolls?"

He was struck by how amazing the structure was, and also how sparse it was. No decoration of any kind adorned the walls of the hallway, not even relief carvings sprung from the walls to greet him on his way. It was cold and silent and empty. Like some bleak tomb. A shudder shook his frame when the thought entered into his head. It was quickly followed by his concern for Clara. She had taken to wander beside Cadrissa: the mage whom both he and Clara were growing more suspicious of with each challenge they faced. What kind of harm could befall them here? If Cadrissa was already under the influence of one magical trinket, then what might happen should they run into a whole room of them?

"Probably all of that and more." Answered the wizardress. "Anything that can point us to what we're looking for will help us."

"You still think it would be a book then?" The knight gave the hallway one more survey; making sure he didn't miss anything that might have been there. It seemed to stretch on forever, but Rowan knew that to be an illusion. It had to be. "It seems kind of foolish to keep the instructions on how to make such a weapon doesn't it?"

"Not really." A strange chipperness momentarily overcame the mage. "Most wizards record their work in order to study it and see if they can improve upon it."

"How could you improve such a weapon?" Clara wondered aloud.

"Well," Cadrissa lifted the scepter before her, "Making it *lethal* to gods would be a start I suppose."

Rowan didn't think he liked the tone in Cadrissa's voice. Was he reading too much into her actions now? Was he worrying too much about nothing?

"At least it isn't as cold in here." He tried to change the subject.

"So where do you think we have to go?" Clara turned to Cadrissa.

"Probably upstairs. From what I read about Jarl, and other Wizard Kings, the lower levels were for their warriors and servants, they didn't do much of anything in them and kept them practical and common. If we want to find anything it will be upstairs."

Silence fell upon them then as they made their way in search of some stairs. Only occasionally would there be a small sound to break the stillness. Rowan found himself looking over his shoulder more than once as he thought he heard the sound of a muffled footfall behind him. The swaying darkness beyond him didn't allow him to guess what, if anything, it would be. After the fourth time of turning his head to find nothing he assumed it was just the wind. The storm was strong out there still and this castle/tower didn't have a front door anymore…

In time the trio had found a flight of stairs spiraling up into the higher levels of the ancient tower. These they climbed, under Cadrissa's direction, till they reached the sixth floor. Then they departed down another hallway, illuminated with the spotty gleam of the sconces which were common about the place; still eerily burning after all this time, even after Cadrissa's magic has allowed them entrance.

After what seemed like forever, they stopped behind Cadrissa in front of a tall iron shod, wooden door. The door itself was simple and plain, almost rustic. Cadrissa had opened the door with minimal effort, pushing them into the room, sconces on the walls coming to light as they entered.

The room itself, like the door, was practical and simple, a place set up for conversations rather than anything else. A fireplace was built into the wall opposite the door, a collection of simple wooden chairs rested around a circular table sitting on top a carpet made to look like a mosaic of a battle scene between two human nations. The two other walls held tapestries of red emblazed with a golden dragon, flowing to the floor. Other than this a small bookcase sat beside the door itself, a few old scrolls and dusty tomes resting in it, a bronze statue of some kind of fiendish creature resting upon the top of the bookcase.

"This could be something worthwhile." Cadrissa made a bee-line for the bookcase. Clara and Rowan though were a bit more cautious in their assessment. Steady eyes covered what was, in truth a very dark room. Though there were a fair number of sconces in the room only two, one on the wall opposite the doorway and another on an adjacent wall, flickered to life upon their entry. When they felt all was well, they turned their attention back to the mage and her feverish digging through the bookcase; fingers and eyes groping all before them.

"Anything there?" Rowan kept his distance from the mage.

"Oh there's a lot of stuff here," Cadrissa was more than a little excited with the prospect of getting into such knowledge, "but nothing that can help us it looks like." She turned around to face them. "This was an understudy's collection."

"So Jarl had apprentices?" Clara asked. "Do you know how many? We don't want to be looking into their rooms and wasting more time."

"I'm not sure on how many," Cadrissa spoke amid her wild rummaging, "but he had to have at least a dozen."

"A dozen?" Rowan was shocked.

"Magic was more common then." Cadrissa moved past them on her way out of the room. "And was a sort of status symbol too. Most Wizard Kings didn't teach too much to their apprentices lest they started to outshine them and possibly covet their station for their own. Having a bunch of apprentices though showed that the Wizard King wasn't too worried about those he trained raising to his skill level and also demonstrated how powerful he was too because of the desire for so many to be instructed under him."

"Really?" Rowan watched the mage closely as she passed. She seemed to be acting like her normal self and he was thankful for that. He'd thought that something might happen to her when she touched the books or went inside the room or something. "It must have been a very different time."

"Night and day when compared to this modern age." Cadrissa agreed.

"So then how much higher do you think we have to climb?" Clara followed Rowan out of the room. She wasn't looking forward to searching all over this place but would if that was what it took.

"I'm not sure." Cadrissa's face turned contemplative, "Maybe all the way to the top. These corridors all go on forever it seems and the stairs just seem to climb endlessly. It's like a maze within a maze." Cadrissa rested her hand around the medallion, fingering it absently with her thoughts.

"I thought the same thing." Rowan kept an eye on this action, looking to Clara as well with a quick glance to see that she too was abreast of the situation. "So how are we going to–"

All three fell silent then as they heard a noise from the darkness of the hallway. As they peered into the direction they had traveled from, none of them saw anything, but they all heard the second noise that followed. It was muffled, but louder than what they had heard just moments before. Rowan motioned them behind him with his hand, taking his sword in his right and removing the shield he had slung over his back with his left. Clara readied her own weapon and stood just a few steps behind the knight, Cadrissa behind that.

They stood still for a moment longer; hearts beating like drums and muscles tight until the sound came again, this time closer. The swimming darkness didn't allow them any more of a view of what was making the noise but it sounded fairly good sized.

"Get going up those stairs." Rowan whispered to the two women behind him. "I'll be right behind you."

For a moment neither woman moved. Cadrissa was too frightened to and Clara wasn't about to leave Rowan behind. "Go!" Rowan motioned them on with his shield. "Take Cadrissa and go!"

With that, Clara started to move. She had just begun to pull the mage behind her, tugging her with her free arm and encouraging her to follow when the wizardress screamed. This was followed by a cavernous roar spinning the elven warrioress around in time to see Rowan defending himself from a Troll's frenzied attack.

"Go!" He shouted. "I'll hold it off as long as I can–" The Troll raised his other meaty claw in a swing only to be blocked with the shield again. The force of the blow was so strong that it actually caused the young knight to be pushed back a few steps.

It was Cadrissa now who led Clara, hand like a vise on the elf's as she pulled her along in her own run toward the stairs and away from the menacing creature. Clara looked back once more at Rowan and then took to a run to keep from stumbling behind the mage's own fear charged gallop. Then the deep shadow swallowed up the two combatants from view leaving only the sound of the shouts and strikes to echo down the corridor.

The Troll didn't hold back his attack even as Rowan dared a sword swing into his abdomen. The blade did little but nick the creature's hard flesh drawing out only the tiniest river of dark red blood. Rowan though had to use a great deal of muscle to hold back the giant's counter strike; sliding back a few paces even from the blow. He knew he couldn't keep this up for much longer. Either his shield would break or he'd be shoved onto his back. It was foolish to think he could defeat the Troll. Not even the best Nordic warrior would take up a fight with the race of giants without some great consideration. Fierce combatants with an even wilder bloodlust, Trolls were one of the few things the bravest of Nordican warriors feared.

He saw the Troll's curled horns when he struck, smelled his rancid breath and felt his hot gusts upon his neck and face. It sapped what little strength he'd been able to maintain against the creature; the long journey he'd been on so far taking it's toll more upon him with each passing heartbeat. A claw followed another snarl. Rowan raised his dragon-crested shield in time to block it, but was unable to hold his ground, sliding back another span of feet once again.

The Troll laughed, creating a misty, foul smelling vapor.

It was toying with him now – enjoying his rag doll before he sank his teeth around the neck for the kill. It knew it had the advantage, and was just enjoying that truth as he rubbed it in the knight's face again and again. Rowan knew when he was beaten and now began to look for a way out of the conflict. If he could get to a better position – a more defendable position where he could have some options, maybe even put his back to the wall, then he'd stand a better chance at defending Cadrissa and Clara. If he died here he'd be of little use to them. So he opted to run.

Nordic logic aiding the choice.

Swinging and jabbing hard into the towering monster, Rowan felt himself gain a few good wounds, though it didn't make any sign it had been wounded. In the fraction of time it took for the Troll to draw a breath before he continued his attack, Rowan made his move. The knight ran as fast as he could backwards, keeping his shield and sword leveled before him until he came to feel he had enough of a lead, and then turned to run for the stairs. Any lead he thought he had quickly evaporated as the Troll came after him, ready to rend and eat the warm insides of his fleeing prey.

Pushing himself as far as he could and never looking back, the knight vaulted up the steps, joints aching and body wet with per-spiration. Lungs burning with each breath throbbed in rhythm to his frantic heart which pounded away faster than the Troll's foot-falls behind him. The Troll was still gaining though, and no matter how hard Rowan willed his legs further forward, he could feel himself reaching the point of total collapse. The cold, the emotional load he'd had to bear and the physical stress on his body these last few weeks were starting to add up and into a negative account on his person…and then the bolt came.

The bright flash of greenish light rushed over his shoulder so quickly he nearly lost his footing on the stairs as all he could see were incandescent spots before his eyes. It had barely missed him, but struck home hard into the Troll who, upon being struck straight in the chest, rolled backward with the momentum of the blast to somersault down the steps.

Rowan couldn't move. He couldn't do anything but drop to his hands and knees to support his hunched over frame as he panted like a dog in the desert. Heart thumping in his ears and eyes still dancing with tiny green globes of light before them, Rowan didn't notice Clara and Cadrissa coming down to meet him. Only when the elven maid put her hand to the shoulder of the young knight did he take notice of anything other than his physical condition.

"You all right?" She peered at the youth with motherly concern as Cadrissa wandered a few steps down lost in her own thoughts as she fingered the medallion around her neck.

"Just lemme…catch my breath." The panting had lessened a little but he still was far from his normal rate of breathing.

"Is it dead?" Clara looked up to Cadrissa who hadn't moved from her place; eyes searching out the oily darkness below with trance-like eyes.

"Yes." The mage then returned to her full senses, hand dropping from the medallion as she came back to Rowan and Clara.

"So why didn't you do that earlier?" Rowan huffed out between gulfs of steamy breath.

"I didn't know I could until just then." Cadrissa smiled faintly which caused the knight to shudder a bit inside from the odd disconnect between that smile and her face.

"Do you think…there's any more?" Rowan made an effort to stand, Clara helping him along the way, and came to look the mage in the eye.

It was then that she came back to her full senses once again; her normal self looking back into the still slightly spotty vision of the knight. "Probably."

"Then we can't afford to stand around wasting time." Rowan drew himself together, wiped his slick brow with his arm, then arched his back to stretch it. A few more moments and his vision would be normal once again.

"Right," Clara added as the knight finished his stretch. "You up to it?"

Rowan smiled a grin born of pure male bravado. "You joking?"

Clara shook her head with a loving grin as she turned to Cadrissa.

"Where too then?"

"Up." Cadrissa turned back around in the direction of the ascending stairway they had started to climb in their recent escape. After she passed, Rowan took a moment to speak to Clara before they started to follow.

"She all right?"

"She was until that bolt of green light she cast." Clara kept her voice low as they climbed a fair number of steps behind the mage.

"Trance again?" Rowan feared he already knew the answer.

"Yeah," said Clara. "The medallion's definitely got some kind of hold over her…might even be growing stronger too."

"Great. So what do you want to do?" Rowan took one last gaze behind him as they climbed. Content that nothing was following them – at least as far as he could gather, he moved his gaze forward again.

"Continue to keep an eye on her, but nothing else yet. We need her to find the incantation to activate the scepter."

"What if she isn't able to?" Rowan kept his voice low. "What if the medallion won't let her?"

"Then we deal with it as best we can." Clara took in the knight's dark blue eyes with a gentle smile. She really did love him and the man he would soon become. "We can't have our attention diverted on more than one topic here. Let's focus on getting this information and then moving from there."

"Okay?" A soft shimmer of pearlescence appeared between the elf's parted lips.

"Okay." The knight agreed with his own soft grin. Together they drew closer to the mage, silently climbing the tower steps. In front of them Cadrissa moved as if in a dream. She heard the soft whispers around and in her head growing clearer and then fading again to mix with the whirlpool of others. These distinct voices were telling her many things – *urging* her to do *many* things. For now Cadrissa pushed past their demands while at the same time searching them out for any insight as to where she should search next for what she sought.

This too rose to her in time. Like cream coming to the top, Cadrissa was able to blend the various bits and pieces of information she was able to gather from the whispers. It was all coming together now, she rubbed the medallion as she walked and thought.

Yes, it was all coming together.

Chapter 31

ndarien's unconscious frame floated silently in orbit outside the sun. Here he drifted for a good amount of time
and would have remained longer too had it not been for another
who came to his aid. Surprisingly, this being came from the sun
itself. Birthed from a massive solar flare, which spat him out away
from the massive ball of flame. This new being who flew toward
the incapacitated deity was Dugan, now transformed into the servant of Rheminas. Moving quickly, he roused Endarien by kicking
him in the arm.

Nothing happened.

Dugan tried again and met up with similar success.

Growing impatient he drew his large sword, the blade hissing
in the vacuum of space and then sparking into a flaming mixture
of steel and white fire. He used this weapon to strike Endarien,
moving all the way down his arm and leaving small slash lines,
like burn marks on wood on the deity's skin. After the fourth strike
the god arose.

"So you've been sent to judge me then, eh?" His sleepy eyes
focusing on the Galgalli. Then, like lightning, Endarien righted
himself in his orbit and focused his avian eyes upon his would be
attacker. "I suppose it was voted for fairly, though I didn't think
I'd be held guilty for my failure with Cadrith."

The hawk helmed god bowed his head in defeat. "Go ahead
and get it over with then."

The Galgalli simply stood before Endarien in silence. When the god raised his head again in question to the silence, Dugan spoke.

"Brave Endarien." The words of the Galgalli boomed across the solar system, "I have been sent to rouse you and tell you to seek your kin who make ready for battle in Thangaria, not judge you. The Pantheon doesn't wish you to die but help them in the coming battle."

"Who has sent you?" Endarien drew a sharp focus on the half hidden face of the Galgallium. "I haven't seen your likeness among the Galgalli."

"It was your cousin Rheminas." Dugan answered.

"I did not know he cared." Endarien snorted. "I suppose they figured I'll probably die in the battle with them anyway. So why use your talents when they can make use of mine one last time?"

Dugan said nothing, merely stood stoically before the winged god.

When he saw that he wasn't going to get any more information unless he pried it from the agent of divine retribution himself, the god began to speak again.

"Has Cadrith left the world yet?" Endarien then craned his head over to take in Tralodren, some distance from his location but still visible to his keen eyes. "The last thing I can recall he was still on the planet."

"He is still there now, but he will be free soon enough and then you must stand with the other gods who are now assembling their forces in Thangaria." Dugan sheathed his sword, extinguishing the flames in the process.

"I am to go seek out another matter for Rheminas. This won't be a long lived venture so make ready what you can and prepare for the onslaught to come." He flew to stand beside the winged god.

"Bah. The fight will be bold and bloody, but we will prevail. Our collective might has beaten his predecessor before and will do the same to him." Endarien's wings stretched to their full span.

"Whatever you can do to still him for a few moments more will help greatly. That will let us gain some time to set up our strategies. After that, he won't be much more of a threat to contend with anymore." The god smiled at his own boasting.

"If you are well and can return to your own realm to rouse your troops then I must hurry to Tralodren to complete my mission," said Dugan.

"I'm fine and will recover. I don't need you to help me hobble back home. Now off with you."

"I will need a small favor from you Mover of the Clouds," said Dugan. "I will need a small portion of Vkar's essence in you so I can enter Tralodren for the mission I've been called to undertake."

Endarien's head went low with a sigh that, even in the vaccum of space, sounded like the rush of a mighty zephyr escaping his lips. "I guess I've proven to be a spoiler of such a boon. It seems that most of it has already left me, but what still remains I'll give to you. It might as well go to someone who can make better use of it than me."

The god of the winds held out his hand, palm facing the Galgallium and expelled the last of Vkar's essence from his body in a red bolt of crackling energy which flew into Dugan's chest.

"I thank you." Dugan bowed his head, spread his peacock wings and then left for Tralodren at an incredible pace. Endarien watched his departure for a moment and then turned from the direction of the world he helped form to enter into his own realm: flying into a vortex of cumulus clouds which suddenly opened up before him, some short distance from the sun. He wasn't really wounded, just worn out from the power that had been inside him for so long and the battles with Cadrith.

What a waste. He wished he had some of Vkar's power left over to face the lich again with the others. Pity since he knew the wounds he'd inflict would be with the wounded forever, barring some boon of which the Storm Lord was not aware. Since Cadrith, as with Sidra, was backed by the darker aspect of creation, the blows dealt by him now were quite serious and deadly. Sidra had killed his grandparents after all and they were the most powerful of gods...

As he flew through the vortex, Endarien began to form his plans. Stark realities or not, he would fight and be counted among his kin. Either alone or united he would fight, but at least in uniting they would stand a much better chance of surviving.

Something didn't sit well with him as the vortex he had summoned swallowed him up and faded away into space like so much steam. He couldn't help but feel devastated by what he had just done or rather not been able to do. He felt used and angry. Could another have done better? Khuthon perhaps or maybe he should have taken Rheminas up on his offer of personal retribution, he was quite skilled in the matter that was certain...

No, he'd made his choice, and now would have to live with it as would the rest of the Pantheon. For good or ill he had made a decision, they all had by vote, and so made clear their intent to bear the burden of such a choice. He didn't have the time to feel sorry for himself or wallow in the possibilities that could have been. He had work to do and a short matter of time in which to do it.

The battle was close at hand.

Chapter 32

Cadrissa ran down the strangely familiar hallway of the great keep of Jarl. She felt she'd traveled down it many times before. She was aware it was the work of the medallion which had taken hold of her once more, compelling her forward into this mad dash, but she was far from fearful. Instead, she was happy though rushed, to try and get to her destination before some unknown deadline she felt in her head had expired.

Her ears managed to hear the rapid footfalls of Clara and Rowan behind her over the constant whispers in her head, but her main focus was on where she was going, what she was doing. Her thoughts were feverish and driven – compelled to one end: finding the information which currently eluded her. Everything to this goal had finally fallen into place and was growing stronger in that connection with each passing second.

"Am I the only one with some apprehensions about running through this tower?" Rowan asked Clara who ran beside him.

"Just follow her," Clara huffed. "We can't do anything else at the moment."

"But where are we going?" He asked through his own deep breaths.

"Hopefully to where we need to be." Clara then concentrated all her attention on keeping up with the mage, who seemed to be boundless in physical endurance as well as magical potential. They had climbed flights of stairs in this mad run, and still the mage seemed unhindered by scaling more. Whatever drove her, Cadrissa prayed it would aid them in finding what they all sought, and that it was the same thing. For who knew what the medallion was compelling the mage toward...

Cadrissa gripped the scepter tighter in her right hand as she ran. It felt good there, like it belonged there and she had no intention of letting it go anytime soon. Not when they were getting close to their destination – she was sure of it. She could feel herself getting closer...so much closer. She could barely contain her excitement. The endless levels they had to ascend barely registered with her now. She'd climb however many levels were required to get to her destination and sensed the medallion was deeply pleased with this commitment...as if it was a living thing able to have feelings...

After a few more floors the mage slowed and than stopped before a wooden door. She felt something in here – something that might be of use to her...and she smiled. She placed her hand upon the door, letting it touch the rough, dry wood, soaking in the hope that it offered.

"You found something?" Rowan came jogging up behind the mage shortly after, Clara at his side.

"I think so." The mage pulled her hand back from the door, letting out a gentle, visible breath.

"Is it safe to enter?" Clara drew a little closer to the mage, but still left some room between them should anything suddenly transpire.

"I think so." Cadrissa repeated in a slightly dreamy tone that caused both Rowan and Clara to eye each other with some slight concern.

"If it's another Troll," said Rowan, "just let it have another one of those blasts you did on the last one." The knight turned to Clara. "I'm not in any shape to fight another one."

"You ready?" Clara turned to Cadrissa.

The mage nodded.

Rowan moved forward and pushed on the door with the point of his blade. It opened up silently before them. "Remember what I said." Rowan told Cadrissa as he donned his shield over his left arm. Cadrissa did nothing but nod sleepily as she made her way into the room beside the knight while her fingers caressed the medallion in her left hand; Clara bringing up the rear.

Behind the icy walls and the door was a world of opulence. Polar bear hide, wolf skins and other rich tapestries hung over the inner walls amid crystal chandeliers, bronze braziers and golden statues of young Nordic male and female warriors. White and silver carpets covered the floors and the very room choked on other rare and wonderful artistic endowments that seemed unimaginable. Indeed amid such craftings of bronze and gold, silver and brass, one who saw them could forget where they were, but Cadrissa didn't forget.

The circular room beyond was spacious, more so than what Rowan had even seen in any of the Nordic halls or his own knighthood. Above him was a chandelier crafted of shimmering crystal holding a hundred white tapered candles all aglow. Around the walls were more sconces, and a great fireplace opposite the doorway that was as wide as he was tall and twice his own height, cold and dead like the rest of the Wizard King's home.

In the center of the room was a massive dark oak round table, stained a deep reddish brown which seemed to draw the mage to it like a moth to flame.

"Cadrissa?" Clara cautiously made her way inside. "What are we looking for? I don't see any books or scrolls."

"We're close." She stopped in front of the table. She stood there for what seemed a little too long for her companions liking and then pointed with the scepter to the opposite side of the room. "There."

Rowan and Clara both turned to see that she pointed to nothing but a solid wall, and a statue of a rather savage looking Nordic male dressed for battle that stood before it. This statue held up a hand axe in hostile greeting.

"Cadrissa are you–" Clara started to ask, but was cut short by the mage who hurried to the statue's base.

"We're *very* close." The mage continued to fondle the medallion.

"So where are we then?" Rowan made his own way cautiously around the table.

"In one of the private chambers of Jarl by the looks of it." Cadrissa kept her focus on the statue; hand fumbling with the medallion all the while in an increasingly faster pace. "You can see that it was his by the way it is decorated."

"Yeah." Rowan had no insight into this reasoning at all. He'd just have to keep trusting in Cadrissa...Cadrissa over the medallion. "So what do you mean that what we're looking for is here?" Rowan finished his trek toward the statue.

Cadrissa didn't answer, merely stood transfixed before the white marble sculpture. The knight was going to say something when he felt Clara's gentle hand on his shoulder hold him back from doing so. Rowan glanced beside him to see the elf deep in thought. She stayed this way for a little while longer, weighing the options. Though this mental evaluation was far too rapid for her liking, she was giving them at least some type of contemplation.

As Clara thought and Rowan watched, the mage came up beside them and raised her left hand to the statue, touching the nose and face of the figure ever so slightly, and then let out a sigh laced with a mystical phrase. "*Grah rah themena.*"

Before anyone could do anything else, the statue had begun to melt like snow in the sun; fine, lifelike details fading and falling into a homogeneous blob of white goo. Within moments the incredible sculpture was a puddle of pearlescent ooze at the trio's feet. Cadrissa stepped over this mess to stand before the wall behind it and there to trace her fingers along the cold marble surface.

"We're very close now." Her voice was faint.

The whispers in her head were louder. Louder than they had ever been. They told her what to do next, compelled and commanded her in what she had to do next. There was little choice, she had to do what they willed...the medallion had finally gained control, and it was then that Cadrissa learned the truth of the object she wore around her neck – it was very much alive.

"*Bjorak fren yiploth.*" Cadrissa spoke the words of magic and brought forth the outline of a door.

"How–" Rowan started to ask but Clara's hand reached over his shoulder; pulling him back from the statement.

"She's not herself." The elf whispered to the youth, hopeful that only he could hear her for the moment. "Look at her movements, and when you see her eyes they're alive, but not with the same person who used to live in that body."

"So what do we do now?" Rowan whispered back, but kept his gaze firmly fixed on the mage before them.

"Be ready for anything." The elf's grip on her sword tightened. "We have to follow this through, but be ready for anything. If we're close to where we need to be then we just have to ride it out."

Rowan gave her a look that was worrisome. He didn't want to use Cadrissa for their own advantage, there was something not all together right about such an action…but…Did he have a choice?

"*Yopek.*" The mage spoke with a solid, authoritative voice that didn't seem to be her own entirely – as if there was something else underneath it; a serpent making ripples under a silken sheet. Nevertheless, the outline of the door grew into a solid door crafted out of the same stone as the wall.

"I thought all the counterspells were taken care of." Rowan addressed the elf beside him in whisper.

"So did I."

Cadrissa motioned with her hands and the door opened into darkness. She wasted no time in claiming entrance. Rowan looked to Clara, both saw the others' resolved face, and then followed the mage inside the shadowy opening.

Clara, Cadrissa and Rowan found themselves in a rather plain white pine paneled room in the same dim illumination common throughout the rest of the Wizard King's domain. The room itself was well-furnished compared to the rest of the spartan tower complex, but not as majestic as the room they had just come from. Some oak square tables with matching chairs whose backs had been done up into a snowflake design, were covered in a thin film of dust.

Cadrissa though was more concerned with a tall desk resting on a wooden dais. She was drawn to it, pulled to it like a fish on the line, for on top of it was a fat tome. Nearly running to it in her excitement, her eyes opened wide when she saw the golden insignia emblazoned in the white scale hide. It was the sigil of Jarl, she was sure of it. The whispers told her it was. All that knowledge at her fingers…all that power…

"Is that what we're looking for?" Rowan asked the mage, then added in quieter tones to Clara: "Seems too easy doesn't it?"

"It is," said the mage in a voice that sounded like a homesick child happy to see her parents again.

"Easier than I would have thought." Clara returned the knight's whispered response.

Cadrissa touched the insignia on the book and before anyone could say or do anything further, the medallion around her neck blazed into a shimmering golden nimbus. This aura of light turned into a column covering the wizadress fully, and spreading out to envelope the dais where the desk rested.

"Cadrissa!" Rowan started to run toward her, but Clara's shout stopped him in mid-stride.

"No Rowan! We don't know what's happening. Don't chance *anything* yet."

So the two waited in tense anticipation as Cadrissa continued to hold her pose as if she was frozen. The light stayed too, but it didn't seem to want to venture outside the area immediately surrounding the dais. Inside this cylinder of illumination Cadrissa listened to a single strong voice pounding into her head and finally, mentally shoving her aside. Suddenly she felt like she was sick. It was like she was unable to do anything now, not even think, as what she had come to believe was the medallion's presence – the fierce heat it tended to emit on various occasions flooded into her veins, heart and brain and then pooled in her eyes.

It was unbearable – like molten lead coursing through her body and she screamed in agony.

In her mind, Cadrissa could see herself being surrounded by shadows. Shadows with grasping, clinging hands seeking her with reckless abandonment – content on holding her fast and pulling her into them.

"Let me go!" She struggled the best she knew how but it wasn't enough as one hand grasped her ankle. Then another found a sure grip on her thigh and then the others followed suit grabbing whatever opening they could to pull her in and hold her down in the darkness which was rapidly enveloping her. All the while she could hear the chattering words of thousands of whispers scuttling about like cockroaches on cobblestone.

Don't fight us. She heard a single voice being formed from a collection of smaller voices. *You can't win and will only risk bringing greater harm to yourself.*

"What do you want?"

A vessel. The words came back to her like a spike of ice shoved into her spine. For a split second she thought of her former capture but this wasn't his work. This was something far darker…and involved more than one being. Indeed, Cadrissa could sense them all around her, heard their whispers still – faint scraping on glass. There had to be dozens of them, if not more given how many hands where now assailing her – pinning her down and grabbing her firmly in any open spot on her body that didn't yet have a grip.

"Who are you?" She fought away a new claw that tried to cover her mouth.

"They are my new servants." Cadrissa felt the ice in her spine explode throughout her entire body as she saw The Master emerge out of the darkness. He was as she had seen him upon his ascension but changed in garb, now dressed in black with a black staff beside him. His smile though was still the same bone chilling evil she had come to loathe and fear.

"I thought you were done with me." She cried out. "What more do you want?"

The Master drew closer then, shadowy beings scurrying from his advance like rats before the light of a torch. "Oh I want many things and right now I want you to be my champion."

"What–" Was all Cadrissa could get out.

"You didn't really think I'd let you live this long for any sense of *mercy* or *obligation* did you?" The Master came to stand inches from the shadow wrapped wizardress. His smile faded as he continued to speak.

"I needed someone of your talents to use to claim godhood and someone after I got it to help clean up any loose ends."

"But you're a god," Cadrissa rebutted. She didn't understand any of this.

"Yes, I am now, but there are a few things I will have need of if I want to follow through on my plans." The Master held up Cadrissa's face with his hand, looking over it as if he were admiring the finer traits in an animal he might be purchasing. "I didn't know what they all might have been before I ascended, but I kept you alive nevertheless, should I have need of you in overcoming them. And I'm glad I did."

The dark god released Cadrissa's face only to allow a single finger to trickle down her neck where it stopped at its base. "The medallion was an added bonus."

"How could I ever help a god?" Cadrissa tried her best not to squirm too much under his touch. She didn't want to give him any added pleasure.

"I implanted a portion of myself inside you, but this little trinket," He jabbed the mage where he had rested his finger, then pulled it away, "made it a bit of a challenge to do much influencing over you. So it's good to finally see you face to face again, to get my hold back over you and over the medallion."

Cadrissa suddenly became aware of the larger picture that was before her. "The fight at Galba's circle...I wasn't wounded."

"No. I didn't kill you, only implanted you for further use – branded you like they do cattle."

Cadrissa didn't like that analogy at all. She doubted Dugan would either and for a moment, indulged her feelings of loss over the Telborian's passing.

"The medallion was meant to hold spirits and mystical energy." The dark god motioned at the shadowy beings gathered around them. "That's why these are here, but I've modified it to help magnify my own essence so I can have increased control over my vessel – as it is now."

"Why me?" Cadrissa felt the familiar twinge of dread rising from her stomach and into her throat.

"I can't be the most powerful mage on Tralodren. I was of little use to you when you were mortal, and now can't be any better to you now that you are a god."

"You really don't know do you?" The Master smirked now. The gesture was filled with mockery. "Pity."

The dark god then motioned for one of the shadowy beings to come forward. Even when he did Cadrissa couldn't make much of the being out. It was still a roughly hewn frame of humanoid design, but perhaps seven or eight feet in height. "This is your new ally." The lich looked the being over as if it were his son.

"They tried to fight me off at first, but once I showed them I had the same agenda as they did, they came to my side in the end."

"The trip from the Great Library." Cadrissa's eyes widened in a sudden ephinany. "You were fighting the medallion."

"Ah," the dark god chuckled. "so you *do* understand some things. The medallion was created to hold the spirits of some fifty Dranors who were looking to escape the Abyss and be reborn again to continue their war against the gods. You just happened to stumble onto it when you were in those ruins where I used you to release me. It actually worked out better than I thought, for I planned to implant you with a small portion of my ascended form, but didn't see the advantage of the medallion until later, after I'd discovered it."

"With this small army behind me." The Master gestured to the shadowy beings of the nearly forgotten Dranor spirits, " and the scepter you have been able to discover-" he nodded to the wizadress in a form of thanks, "an added boon I never had figured into my plans and for which I thank you, the gods will fall and then The Darkness will follow." The dark god ground his teeth at his last statement. "Then I will be free and possess all the power in the cosmos."

And it will be a new day for Dranors, who will reclaim what the gods stole from us long ago. The coal colored spirit beside The Master spoke into her mind.

"Yes." The dark god's eyes sparkled in wicked delight. A claw tried to cup her mouth again and this time succeeded before the mage could say anymore.

"And now it's time for you to fulfill my wishes." The Master drew nearer as Cadrissa's eyes grew wider. "Serve me well and I might let you reclaim your body. Fight me and…well you might not even have a spirit left to inhabit it."

Then it was over. Her eyes were covered over with the pitch shaded hand and all turned to blackness…

Clara and Rowan saw the burst of golden light fade away as Cadrissa fell unceremoniously to the floor in a heap of white satin robe and crushed golden cloak. Clara ran to the mage's side with the knight following suit, both still cautious about what was going on and trying to be prepared for anything, though that was always easier said than done.

Clara managed to turn Cadrissa over and was ministering to her as best she could. Rowan came to squat across from the elf, making his own assessment of the mage's condition…and it wasn't good. Cadrissa seemed to be unconscious, though she moaned and rolled her head from side to side a bit, sweating and at the same time shivering as if from extreme cold. It appeared to both as if she had come under the effects of some illness, though each knew better. Rowan noticed the scepter was still tightly clutched in Cadrissa's hand, medallion clutched in the other. The elf and knight looked at each other, unsure of what to do and fearful at the prospects of what was happening before them.

Clara placed her hand on the mage's moist head. "She's burning up and her hands are ice cold."

"Don't get so close Clara," Rowan warned. "We don't know what is going on and-"

"*Ugh.*" Cadrissa's suffering pulled the knight's full attention back to the mage.

"Cadrissa." Clara gently brushed a few slick, sable strands away from the mage's face, "Are you able to hear me?"

Cadrissa let out another groan.

"Cadris–" Before anyone could react, Cadrissa eye's flashed open at the same time her fist hit Clara in the stomach, flinging the elf across the room to be introduced to the solid wall with a jarring impact. The blow was so strong as to crack the pine paneling and even the marble behind it as Clara cascaded down its surface to slump up against it; unconscious and gravely wounded. Rowan leapt back with reflexes birthed from his years of training as Cadrissa rose to her feet on shaky legs. The eyes that greeted him were far from human, and laced with an incredible cruelty.

"We meet again Nordican." Cadrissa began to admire her own body with bright blue eyes, like a farmer sizing up a prize animal up for sale. Though it sounded like the voice of the mage, Rowan knew it was another speaking through her. The medallion it seemed, had finally won. Rowan dared another quick glance toward Clara.

She seemed alive...for now.

If he was going to do anything he would need to do it soon or he might not be in the best shape to try and save Clara himself.

"Cadrissa?" Rowan cautiously spoke the mage's name while at the same time taking a step back; sword casually pointed toward her, shield raised before him.

"*Gone.*" Cadrissa drew closer to Rowan with a sultry step. The voice was growing more flat by the moment. "And you still seem as if you don't know when to die." The voice had now taken on more of a familiar air again...

"Who are you?" He dared.

Cadrissa only smiled. It was a hideous thing – with too much teeth and eyes that were dim like a corpses' "An old friend." Rowan's eyes narrowed to slits and his body became flush with blood as he understood who was now speaking to him, who had possessed the mage.

"Release her." Rowan commanded.

The Master laughed through his vessel.

"Why torment her?" Rowan moved to keep some space between them to allow him some room when he needed to make his move...whatever it might be. "You're a god now, why bother with her...with us?"

"You're annoying pests who I should have dealt with before in the circle." Cadrissa took another step forward, keeping the grin plastered to her face. "And that will have to be corrected before I can take care of the few loose threads that remain. The cleaner the board, the easier and faster I can win."

She then lunged toward the knight. Rowan swung his blade, but found it ineffective in his hand partly because he didn't really want to harm Cadrissa and partly because the thing inside the mage was an apt combatant. The opening Rowan's weak strike created allowed the mage to strike with a fist to Rowan's face, which he couldn't block in time with his shield, and sent a shower of sparks across the young knight's vision.

Rowan staggered away from his attacker as she continued to press him. Another blow to the face split his lip, which was followed by another that dug deep into the knight's stomach. Cadrissa was moving too quickly to get an accurate eye on her to anticipate her movements. The knight bent over from the strike. It was then that a mystical charge of energy ran up and down his body as Cadrissa clamped both hands on either shoulder to release a spell.

As she chanted, Rowan peered into her blue eyes and saw they had gone dead. The woman whom he had once quested to save was nowhere in sight. It was then, in that rapid instant as Cadrissa spoke the words to her spell, that the knight was making up his mind. Would he kill Cadrissa to save Clara? Honestly, he couldn't see any way out of this situation without attacking Cadrissa. He didn't want to give up hope though, even as he felt the tendrils of pain snake down his arms and chest like lightning.

Rowan's time had run out however, as he shook violently, he dropped both his shield and sword, then collapsed before Cadrissa into a twitching heap. He couldn't move his body, but he could still think and see all that was going on before him. The mage let out some haunting, unnatural laughter which froze the room.

The knight could do nothing but watch as the possessed wizardress peered down at him with dark, hooded eyes. "Your plan would never have worked anyway. Rest easy though in knowing that *my* plans, now that I have the scepter, *will*."

Everything that resembled Cadrissa's flesh – everything marking her as her own person melted away as the cruel visage of The Master seemed to glare down at the helpless knight below. "And now," she took a step closer to Rowan, "It's finally time for you to die…and then…" an emotionless smile eased over the mage's lips, "that elf as well."

Suddenly there was a loud, thunderous explosion.

Neither Rowan nor Clara, who was slowly regaining a little consciousness, saw what happened next clearly. Neither did the being who possessed Cadrissa until it found itself face to face with a Galgalli.

The avenging angel stood before the smaller woman, debris, dying light and snow falling down from the roof and ceiling above where the massive agent of vengeance had made his entrance. Miraculously the falling rock and timber and other building materials hadn't fallen on or near the three persons inside, but did a good work of demolishing the room in compensation.

"So," Cadrissa was unphased by the Galgalli's dramatic arrival, pressing on like a cat slinking toward its prey. "They think you will stop me?" She lifted up the scepter with a hearty air of defiance. "Come and judge me, Galgalli – if you dare."

Dugan did nothing; peacock feathered wings folding behind him as he merely looked down at the possessed mage. The tension between these two figures was so heavy Clara felt it as she weaved in and out of consciousness.

"Hear my words." Dugan's stern voice rattled the room even as the words written on his cowl began to glow a searing white. "I have been given the authority to judge you for your trespasses against the Pantheon, and the inhabitants of Tralodren.

"You have defied the god of death by seeking lichdom, slaughtered many in your pursuit of self promotion and power, have possessed this woman and others to use for your own ends, stolen, cheated and defiled burial sites for your own pursuits along with seeking to challenge the Pantheon itself by siding with your current dark patron."

"For these crimes – which have become legion over the centuries, you have been sentenced to death, your spirit and soul sent to the Abyss for eternal torture and imprisonment."

"And they call *me* arrogant!" The Master's voice erupted from inside Cadrissa. "Let's see if you're as bold as your words Gal-"

Dugan acted in an instant, drawing his sword and slashing it across the vision of the possessed mage and then sheathing the weapon again at his side in one smooth action – white flame igniting and extinguishing on the blade in one brief breath. Cadrissa's voice was cut short by a series of spasms shaking her suddenly, driving the mage to her knees, and then to the floor where she continued to flay about like a fresh caught fish. As she did so the medallion fell free from her body; necklace holding it around the mage's neck having been severed by the Galgalli's strike…as was his intent.

"I will judge you face to face," said Dugan. "Not through the guise of this innocent woman."

As soon as Cadrissa fell, Rowan felt himself able to move again and took advantage of the situation to pick up his sword and shield with still slightly numb digits and quickly run toward Clara. He could see she was conscious now, though it was more like a dreamy state of consciousness. She had some blood dripping out of the corner of her mouth and her face seemed paler than good health should allow.

"Rowan?" The weak voice of Clara fluttered toward his ear.

The knight bent down beside the elf. "How badly are you hurt?

"A fair sum." She let out a moist, raspy sigh.

"Do you think you can stand?" Rowan looked over his shoulder to the possessed mage. She had stopped her shaking now, and was just lying still…too still for Rowan's liking. Clara made a low groan, which brought the knight back to her.

"Our battle is done." She ended her speech with a violent series of bloody coughs. Rowan did the best he could to ease her suffering, but knew that she was bleeding from the inside and there was little to nothing he could do to stop it.

"Better to save yourself while you can than try and save me. I'd never make it out of this tower, let alone into the wilderness around us."

Before he could think any further, Rowan was drawn back toward's Cadrissa who started to shake once again while uttering some strange language that the knight had never heard before.

Before this macabre display, the winged creature, which Rowan had grown to become more concerned about than the previous situation with the possessed Cadrissa, merely stood silently by in observance – pure white eyes taking it all in.

The mage arched upwards from the floor and expelled a pale blue mist from between her lips. Rowan and Clara both watched as the mist twisted and twirled into the faint semblance of some humanoid shape and then faded away; its last impression reaching out to those who saw it in silent screams of frustrated desperation. Violent shudders then shook Cadrissa's body once more. Rowan and Clara could do nothing but watch transfixed at the spectacle.

After the shaking, Cadrissa stood still as a pillar; eyes and mouth open wide like some drooling idiot. There was then a blast of blackness and green shards of light erupted from her body and then Cadrissa collapsed to her knees, then face first onto the floor.

The Galgalli then turned toward the tensed Rowan and struggling Clara.

"What did you do to her?" Rowan rose with sword and shield in hand, making sure to defend Clara as much as he could should this towering figure choose to attack. He didn't know if he could though. He had regained feeling again in his body, but he wasn't sure he could hope to even scratch this incredible being. As soon as the Galgalli's eyes washed over him he felt as if he had been laid open for all to see. He could hide nothing back, contain nothing of himself within the normal confines of mind, body and spirit – it just all spilled out of him…and was seen by this…this agent of judgment.

"Have no fear, I mean you no harm." The words were softer now, but still resounded with the strong authority the Galgallium carried. "I have begun the judgment of Cadrith and those who would ally themselves with him."

Rowan shivered and then realized just how cold it was getting with the large hole in the roof and portions of the wall – snow had even come to gather under tables and corners. He still felt like he was naked before this being but it wasn't as bad as it first was when Dugan had set his eyes upon him.

"Who-who are – what are you?" The knight braved.

Chapter 33

"**I** am a Galgalli," said Dugan.

"What's that?" Rowan held his blade and shield level, keeping one eye on Clara, continuing to monitor her degrading condition. She was still awake though; there was that small bit of good news at least.

"An executor of the Pantheon's wrath," Dugan returned flatly.

"So how do you fit into all this?" The knight peered up at the Galgalli. He still wasn't feeling the best from the recent attack, and felt somewhat defenseless before the Galgalli, but enough Nordic blood flowed through his veins to see him through to get some answers.

"I have been charged with judging Cadrith for his trespasses against the Pantheon. That is why I have come here."

Rowan shook his head. "Why?"

"You have something I need to finish up my judgment."

"The scepter." Rowan looked past the Galgalli to Cadrissa where the object lay beside her.

"Yes." The Galgalli nodded.

"What did you do to Cadrissa?" Rowan braved.

"I freed her from the domination of the medallion. It had corrupted her along with the touch of Cadrith which had been simmering inside her for quite some time." The Galgalli simply stated.

"So The Master was inside her?" Rowan was more than a little amazed. Had he known that he wouldn't have treated the whole matter so lightly. He would have ripped it off the mage at his earliest chance.

"Yes." Came the Galgalli's reply.

"So he's defeated now?" Rowan questioned with some small portion of hope tinting his voice. Could it really be that easy to have defeated this new dark god who nearly destroyed all of them when he met them just recently.

"No." The Galgalli looked around the room now. "The portion of his spirit which was there has been driven away, but he still remains unharmed as he readies his coming attack. So bring me the scepter so that I can depart."

"The attack against the Pantheon…" Rowan looked over toward Clara, saw her condition and was cheered for a moment by the faint sliver of a smile she could muster on her lips. She could still make him believe if he was able to get her to some healers – priests or others trained in the medical arts…"That's the *real* battle then isn't it? So what was the purpose of us being used to get here when they sent you to us?"

"I'm a Galgalli, not a seer or sage." Dugan's tone had become a little rough. "I don't have your answers, merely obeying my orders."

"Galba already told us why we've all been called together to fight this new god, and we're not about to give up yet." Brave words, even for Rowan. Clara was near death, Cadrissa was probably dead for all he knew, and he didn't feel so well himself.

"We were able to get this far on our own – get the scepter…we were doing this because Galba told us to, because we realized we had to do it." The fire behind the knight's words was dying, fading back into his veins from whence it had been spawned as he once again regained composure over himself.

"Why are we being treated this way? Why are you dishonoring our efforts, our sacrifices? We're all that remains out of the ten of us who were assembled to undertake this purpose. We may have been compelled to join ranks, but each of us did our best. Why are we being deserted after all that?" Rowan's eyes were misting over now. He couldn't hold back the tumoil or emotions; chaos had come to reign in his heart.

"You are not being forsaken," Dugan's face seemed to soften just slightly at this, "but saved so that you can live."

"We won't live much longer if you don't help us or take us to someone who will." Rowan was shaking a little now as he tried to keep the last shredding tethers of reign on the tidal wave of feelings. "Or take us with you. There has to be someone who could help Clara."

"You assume much." Dugan ruffled his feathers slightly. Clara set loose another string of bloody coughs, drawing Rowan away from the conversation.

"If you're on our side then, can you heal Clara? I don't think she'll make it much longer without some healers or divine healing." The youth returned to the look up into the plain white eyes of the angel of retribution. Eyes that allowed nothing to be read from them; blank slates facing out to the world.

"I cannot heal." These words struck Rowan harder than a sword strike to the heart. "I am sent to judge and bring about retribution, not heal and comfort."

"Then we're just supposed to die here?" Rowan's face grew hard. He had to fight back the rage that was growing in him from his Nordic blood. "We're just some game pieces who no longer are needed, and now it's time to clear the board?"

"I have my duty." Dugan returned coldly.

"And so do I." Rowan shouted.

The Galgalli was silent.

Rowan held his breath and then let it out to regain some composure. He now needed all the skills in diplomacy he had been taught. What he fought for was the most important thing in his life…second to his faith in his goddess of course…but a close second.

"If we give you the scepter and the way to activate it, then you must take us with you." Rowan attempted what he hoped would be a strong barter.

The Galgalli didn't move, only pondered the mortal's statement. Clara wheezed closer to Mortis and Cadrissa still didn't stir.

The only noise in the chamber was the slow, stress induced fragmenting of the marble around them and the galloping heart of the youth.

After seemingly far too long, the Galgalli spoke.

"I don't think you understand where I'm going to go. Even now all of the Pantheon is gathering to face this threat to their continued existence and the world itself. I'm going to a battlefield the likes of which you've never seen nor will in your lifetime."

"If there is going to be a battlefield, then there are going to be healers – probably priests." Rowan took in the withering state of Clara again. She was paler still, head nodding forward to her chest sleepily. "We don't have much more time." He turned to face Dugan again. "I'm speaking for all of us and this is what we want.

"Now, do we have a deal?"

Dugan looked from the knight toward the dying elf, then toward the motionless mage. He stared at them for a moment, almost as if he was looking through them. When he was satisfied with this he came back to Rowan.

"Very well." The tall bronze being bent his hand down to the knight. "Give me the scepter then."

"Cadrissa had the scepter before she was overcome by the medallion. I think she found the information she was looking for about the incantation to make it work but I don't know if she got it and I don't know how you're going to get it out of her when she's–"

"Leave that to me." The Galgalli finished the knight's sentence.

The Galgalli turned toward the mage with a flap of his wings. Suddenly there was a flash of light about him. Following this flash of light Dugan stood before all eyes present, dressed in the same garb he wore as a Galgalli minus the dark hood and in his former, mortal dimensions.

"Dugan?" Rowan could say nothing more. It couldn't be the dead gladiator, but there he stood before him. How had that happened and what sort of twisted game was this that still forced people to play even after death? Rowan could conceive of no answer to his question, but his heart sank at the wheels within wheels that were turning around like gears in some great clock that they were all just helping move along as the time passed on.

It was amazing now, in looking back, that he didn't see any of the threads as they were gathered up to make this tapestry... but Clara had. He prayed that the Galgalli, Dugan or whatever it was, found what he sought for all their sakes. The knight dreaded to think about what could happen should Cadrissa not have the answers...Rowan put such dark thoughts far from his mind and watched...and waited...and prayed.

Gently the Telborian made his way beside the mage, stooping low to place a strong hand upon her delicate back. A soft nudging rub seemed to rouse a low moan from deep within her. Persistence in this tactic caused her head to lift up from the floor. Fluttering her eyes, the mage managed to roll, with Dugan's gentle assistance, over to her back and look up into the face of the last man she thought she'd ever see again.

"Dugan?" She hoarsely whispered. "I thought you were dead." And then a thought came to her. "Am *I* dead?"

"No," A thin slit of a grin cut his face. "Not yet."

"Then what—" Dugan put a finger to Cadrissa's lips.

"Shh. Rest easy. I need your help Cadrissa. "You have something I need to know, some knowledge that is very important to everyone who calls Tralodren home." He removed his finger from her lips. Cadrissa wished he would have left it longer, but enjoyed the brief stay nonetheless.

"You look better in this outfit than with that black one with the face paint." A half delirious smile bloomed over her face. "Course you'd look good in anything...especially that loin cloth-"

"Cadrissa, I need you to focus." Dugan's blue eyes blazed into the mage's own green orbs.

Eyelids fluttered again and some greater sense of understanding returned to her. "I don't hear the voices anymore."

"They're gone now," said Dugan.

"The Master—" Sudden realization of what had happened to her flooded her mind then as she bolted up from her seat. It had all come back to her.

"Is gone now." Dugan gripped her shoulders firmly, but gently to help steady the mage. "You're safe."

"I need you to tell me how to make the scepter work." Dugan's eyes shimmered with an intense sparkle in the light. "I need the incantation."

Cadrissa just looked at him, absorbing all that he said.

"Cadrissa." Dugan's words had an edge to them now, an edge that pulled the wizardress out of her stupor rather sharply. Her eyes had a strong focus behind them now; a reflection of cognitive awareness molding itself into her face as she looked up into Dugan's.

"Do you know how to operate the scepter?"

Cadrissa noticed a difference in his eyes. She couldn't quite place the change but knew that the Telborian standing before her was no longer the same Dugan she had once known.

"How did you get here?" It seemed she had finally returned to herself as everything became clear and fell into place once more.

"Cadrissa." Dugan shook the wizardress slightly to help emphasize his point about being in a hurry. She nervously cleared her throat, then regained her composure under the Telborian's grip.

"I-I was able to read The Master's thoughts, as well as the others inside the medallion," Cadrissa shuddered at the recent memory, "while it was happening I overheard the incantation in The Master's mind to make the scepter work."

"No doubt to use it against the gods." Dugan released the wizardress from his grip. "I need that incantation, Cadrissa, and I can't afford that much more time in getting it either." Dugan picked up the scepter from the ground, then rose to his feet, tightly gripping his new acquisition in his hand. As he did so Cadrissa was able to have a short revelation. As much as she wanted Dugan to be alive–

"You're not Dugan." She immediately rose to her feet and took a step away from the former gladiator. "I saw him die. Who are you?"

"Right now, an ally." The Galgalli's voice was calm, yet authoritative.

Cadrissa nodded her head slowly, letting the words sink in as far as they needed to. She supposed that would be as much information as she would be allowed.

"The incantation." Dugan's voice had an irritated edge to it now.

"He said he'd take us with him if we gave him the scepter and the way to activate it." Rowan shouted over to the mage. "It's Clara's only hope of making it out of this alive!"

Suddenly Cadrissa remembered that she wasn't alone in this tower. "Rowan?" She turned and saw the knight beside Clara… who looked terrible. "What happened to–"

"You have to hurry, Cadrissa." Rowan pleaded. "She doesn't have much time."

Cadrissa knew Rowan was right, she could hear Clara's slow, labored breathing even from where she stood. She also knew more now about who this person was before her as well…Why not give 'Dugan' what he wanted. He had freed her from the grip of the medallion and The Master hadn't he? What did she need with it now anyway? She wasn't in any condition to fight anyone. With the medallion now removed from her she felt as she truly should from such an ordeal: exhausted. All the mystical energy of the well inside her was gone, with only a deep hole remaining that would come to be filled in by rest, and distance between her and this whole recent ordeal. No, she'd come to the end of this battle or quest – or whatever it was. It was time to let it go and if Dugan wanted to pick up the slack she was dropping, then so be it.

Cadrissa closed her eyes then and concentrated on the image of the scepter, pulling it into her mind as she searched for the incantation to activate it, pushing by the unease she felt when she recalled that she was going inside The Master's thoughts – well, the memories of those thoughts, to retrieve her answer. Frantically she searched over the many mounds of other words and phrases and spells which now crowded her mind. When she found it hidden away in some dark corner of thought, she felt a burden released from her person and sighed.

"You can only use it once in your lifetime." The mage's voice was small as she opened her eyes toward the figure of Dugan before her.

"Once is all I will need," he said.

Cadrissa swallowed and began to move toward the former gladiator turned avenging angel of the gods. "You'll have to speak the incantation before you strike. Once spoken, you'll have to use it or risk having your one chance lost if you don't strike after the incantation is spoken."

"How much time will I be allowed from speaking the incantation till my opportunity to use it passes?" Dugan's strange eyes blazed into the mage's soul.

"Only about an hour I believe, maybe less." Cadrissa suddenly felt very insignificant in the former gladiator's stare.

"More than enough time." A grim smile appeared on Dugan's face.

"You think you'll be able to remember it? Right, of course you will." She responded to Dugan's now other worldly stare, then repeated the incantation:

"Coo at limbea. Estorin gablin moor."

"Uthran-koth. Uthran-koth. Japeth real!"

"Akeem. Akeem. Akeem. Yorn toth osiri latas!"

"Thank you." Dugan bowed his head.

Before anyone could get any closer to him, Dugan changed back into his former form with a flash of white light. Scepter now grown in size to match the new relation to his increased body mass, the Galgalli fluttered his wings, preparing for flight; causing white flakes and small pieces of rubble from his entrance to leap about the air.

Cadrissa was speechless regarding the transformation and, like Rowan before her, felt the pressure of his gaze upon her for a moment, felt the terror of being layed so bare before another being and then sighed in relief when the intensity of that look had faded from her. She still felt in a state of undress around him – a deep mental and spiritual nudity more so than anything physical but she could deal with the uncomfortable feeling for the time being.

"Are you sure you wish to go with me?" The Galgalli looked down at Rowan.

The knight's face was set. "Yes."

"And you?" The great hooded head of the angel of judgment turned toward the mage beside him, and she shuddered for a moment under those eyes.

"I'm not going to stay here," she managed to say.

"Very well." Dugan flapped his wings, sweeping the room with a feathery gust of still more scattered flakes and debris "I will take you with me as was our deal. Your safety, though, once you get there will be your own concern."

"Agreed." Rowan gently began to pick up the wounded Clara.

"Wh-what happened to her?" Cadrissa asked the knight.

He peered back at her with hurt eyes. Eyes that didn't reveal more – didn't want to reveal more than their suffering.

"Rowan?" The wizardress didn't like the unease she felt growing thicker in the room by the minute.

"We have to hurry." He pushed the question away from them. "She's getting worse with each passing breath."

Cadrissa only nodded blankly, then turned her gaze back to the dais and the book…the book which held the insights to the mental workings of a Wizard King…and she was leaving it behind…such knowledge…such waste…

Chapter 34

Thangaria had been readied for war. The rocky debris of the shattered world orbited around the central body of forces assembled by the Pantheon in the courtyard of Vkar's Hall. Ancient laws and customs suspended, the place of meeting that had always been a neutral ground of peace was now littered with the forces of war, the Pantheon itself willfully leading it.

Not wasting much time between their votes, each god took to assembling their forces. While not marshaling their whole army, each god took the best of their troops, knowing that only the strongest could stand against the coming threat and even hope to survive. Some of the Pantheon brought more than others, but all brought something to the fight besides themselves. Though it went unspoken, each had assembled their own followers in their own respected realm to fend off any attack should their god fall at Thangaria. All the deities of Tralodren came in their true forms as well. Their various guises would be but a passing shadow against the approaching threat. To face down the same power that had killed their grandsire by another champion they'd need to be present in the truest substance, for this enemy would spare nothing on them.

From behind the courtyard walls they gathered and waited. The gate was now closed and watchmen had been posted for both new arrivals and the threat itself (for they had no idea when it might show up). The divinities, gods and assembled warriors prepared themselves in this tense atmosphere. Whereas before each might have been the others' enemy when times were less perilous, they now held to each other, uniting across philosophical divides and various allegiances to form as solid a resistance as possible. Even the gods did so as they made their plans, waiting for all their number to be gathered. It was the way it had to be if they would survive this challenge – for in unity there is always strength.

Shiril watched all this from on top the wall, her surveying gaze taking in the activity silently. She had been one of the first to arrive at the hall, bringing with her some Lords of Earth to fight along side her. The smallest force gathered, even when compared to Asora's allies who rallied behind her, Shiril was still as passionate about this fight as any other.

The goddess of earth and minerals was a sight to behold with a semblance of a fourteen foot tall athletic human woman, whose skin was the shade of dried wood, and cascading black hair the color of freshly turned earth. She stood watch over all below with eyes of solid, living gold; irises a sterling silver with copper-yellow pupils. Around her neck was a string of rough hewn gems – emeralds, rubies, topaz and diamonds, ripped raw from the planet's flesh. Though unworked, they still caught the light of strange illumination of the realm; their fire adding to the splendor of the goddess who wore them. A rose tinted marble circlet with a princess cut sapphire the size of a man's fist, crowned her as the goddess of the earth.

"My great goddess, more have arrived." The voice was gravely and low. It belonged to one of Shiril's Lords of the Earth – a handful of allies that called the rocky terrain of Boda, the realm of Shiril, home.

"Who now?" The goddess turned around to see the great gate being opened to allow a new host entry, letting a crystal earring swing back and forth as she did so. A form fitting, fine scroll worked steel breastplate rested above her black steel spiked leather belt, blossoming outward with her bust. Each bulge of steel holding a breast was emblazed with a bronze disk – a circular shield capping off each endowment.

"Rheminas has come with his troops." The lord replied.

The lord was a stern figure, in many respects looking like a human male of the same size and shape as Shiril-perhaps a little taller but with bitumen eyes, short-cropped black hair and a reddish umber skin. His dress was of a simple utilitarian affair: leather breeches, wide brown belt, and dusty chestnut shirt with small tracks of various metals attached to his garments and the toes of his boots. The only finery on him was a bronze, jewel studded circlet sparkling in some of the rays of light it managed to capture.

"I see." She watched the ragtag group of Furies, Lords of Fire, Lords of Magma, and even a few other denizens she didn't recognize readily march through the gates. She knew that Rheminas himself would be eager to join the others in their plotting of strategy. He had a love of such things after all.

"How much he is like his father." The goddess shifted the weight of her feet that showcased her strong legs, each encased in steel bands riding from her trim waist to her ankles; steel capped black shoes covering her feet. These bands had been forged by the goddess to move with her, flexing and sliding in amongst themselves to allow for a total range of motion, unhindered by the apparent restriction one would think such defenses would allow. Her arms were covered in the same steel bands, these going down to her wrist.

"How are you and your kin holding up?" She brought her attention now to the lord.

"We bide fine mistress." The lord bowed his head slightly at her concern.

"I suppose I should see what aid I can offer then to my family before it becomes too crowded." Shiril thought aloud. "Rheminas' arrival already makes it much more uncomfortable."

"Yes my lady, they await your insight for making plans for the battle to come."

"If we win this battle it will be a miracle in itself." The goddess confided to the lord. "Even in crisis our family is far from united. I assume my uncle has already been elected to lead the troops."

The Lord of Earth nodded. "Yes, he has been."

"Ah, then the plan has been laid. They just need me to vote on it." Shiril turned back to the scene below her; watching the troops of Rheminas make their way inside the courtyard to form their own unit of warriors among those already gathered; the gate closing once more behind them. It was becoming quite a motley host indeed.

"See to the comfort and care of your own." Shiril's normally stotic visage became a bit more compassionate with these words. "I will be unable to help you in the battle to come. My place will be beside the Pantheon and my own defense." Her words were as smooth and soft as talcum.

"I understand." The Lord of Earth bowed again.

Then Shiril faded from sight.

Shiril appeared outside the entrance to the chamber of the Great Eye. Now guarded by two Guardians, she made her way past them with a soft, self-assured grace. Though about half her size the entire race was well known for their attention to duty and strength in combat against any foe. The pair watched her with their flaming eyes; pure white skin shimmering off their golden armor and spears. Allowing her entrance, they watched her pass by in silence into the great chamber beyond; hawk-like wings rustling softly in studious observation. As their name implied, these were the guardians of the remains of Thangaria and an honor guard of sorts to the Pantheon, though they served the Lords of Good, who are seen as a power to themselves besides the Pantheon

The chamber beyond the guarded doors was the same as it was when they had watched the battle with Endarien and Cadrith but it now had a gargantuan wooden table standing as tall as most mortal men and spread out in a rectangular design over a fair amount of the open space. It was around this that a good many of the gods were gathered in discussion.

"Greetings cousin." Rheminas had turned to greet Shiril upon her entry.

He seemed a human male with a copper-yellowish caste to his skin and bright orange hair standing up all over, appearing to be like living flame; red eyes beaming with the upcoming pleasure of revenge.

"It's so nice to see you in person again." Rheminas' grin widened like the baring of a wolf's teeth. "It's been ages." Like his uncle, Asorlok, Rheminas had a flare for style when the situation called for it. Silver studded, red leather armor sleeves and pants jutted out of a mid-thigh length coat of bronze ring-mail. For flare, the god had also donned an orange half cape emblazed with his own symbol: the sun with the silhouette of a dagger buried up to the hilt. Tall black boots, which also doubled as bronze grieves, with a fire motif that matched his bronze bracers, completed his basic attire.

"Rheminas." Shiril's tone was dry, yet cordial.

The Flame Lord's wolfish grin turned to a smirk as she passed. The two had never been that close, the god of fire wasn't keen on any of his cousins save maybe Causilla who pleased his eye. All the others he argued with, even hindered at times. To Shiril he was actually rather indifferent. Since she made no moves against him or his plans, keeping to herself, he had nothing to hold against her…yet.

He had to admit though that Thangaria was a wonderful place for a battle. A great place to let the blood of gods flow with that of the other divinities who followed them. Like his father, Khuthon, Rheminas had grown to appreciate the taste of battle and bloodletting but unlike his father who did so for the love of domination and destruction of the weak, Rheminas favored vengeance as his impetus for slaughter.

"You were right," The giant body of Khuthon looked down at his earth-ruling niece, "This land is very well suited to wage a war. Already we have a great advantage in the terrain."

"And we'll need all the advantages we can get." Causilla spoke in low melody beside the god of war. Not a warrior by nature, she would fight in the defense of the Pantheon never the less. Though she had dressed for war the charm of her figure and, indeed, the nature of her armor, seemed more decorative than protective: thigh high brown leather boots rose up the shapely limbs of the goddess of art. A slit on the right side of her skirt rose to her waist opposite the slender sword she held holstered at her left hip. Like her dress, the weapon seemed more ornamental than practical and was covered in jewels and twisting thorny vines; handle and hilt being a mixture of thorn and leaf to end in a pommel shaped like a flowering rose.

She was a goddess to whom all were captivated. The daughter of Ganatar and Olthon was the most lovely, the most breath-taking being in all of the cosmos. How such beauty could be conceived of, let alone represented in a living being, was a wonder even for the divine mind. Though, like her cousins, she was equal to Shiril in height but seemed more a standard for a great epitome of womanly grace and splendor rather than some great hulking figure as her stature might have suggested to others not so tall. Soft olive skin shimmered with youth and health even in the mixed lighting of the chamber. Her bright hazel eyes shined with an innocence that added to her appeal and tied her long serpentine curled, red-tinted, chestnut hair into a bow about her face.

A silver, form-fitting, breastplate cover had been carved with thorns wrapping around the metal with two full rose blooms etched into the convexity of her breasts. Attached to this piece of armor was a clinging, gossamer-like material, which flowed to her shoulders and hands, looping around her fingers as to make a sort of attached, fingerless glove and medium length skirt which ended at her knees. The material, which was made of some substance akin to tiny scalemail, shimmered in the light like liquid mercury poured over the goddess' skin.

"I'm sure you have chosen a fine spot to battle, Khuthon." Shiril drew near the great table; the others gathered there, making room for her.

"I've chosen many fronts." The god of war's appetites were wet now and he looked like some lone wolf getting ready to stalk his prize kill. We will attack on at least three sides and then close ranks on a fourth to surround him and then destroy him."

"Do you think we can count on the others showing up to make this defense?" The goddess of metals turned to Ganatar as she took her place at the table. "I don't see my father or mother nor a good many of the others yet."

"Peace." The Father of Law spoke to his niece. His face was fatherly and wise with gentle blue eyes, and straight white hair that ended in a square cut mane about his neck. White stubbly hair also made a neat oval under his nose and around his mouth and chin.

"The others will show up in time. They have yet to rally their troops and get all things in order." He too was dressed for war, but carried a regal veneer over his regalia that none of the others gathered or who would later come, possessed. Though he looked to be a fifteen foot tall Telborian knight, the subtle touches of his dress added to his refinement. These were the shining golden plate mail, the black silken cape attached over each shoulder by means of a golden gavel affixing it to the armor, and the black plumed golden helm resting beside him near the map of Thangaria on the table.

"What about Gurthghol?" Shiril asked.

All the eyes present moved slightly toward Ganatar's direction, interested in what he had to say upon the matter. The nature of Gurthghol on this matter was, after all this time, still a very sore subject with Ganatar. Stemming from the beginning of the last conflict with their enemy to the present, the wound never truly did heal completely.

"Gurthghol will be here to fight this threat as he did once before," was all the god of law said.

"I don't think we have to worry about anyone not being able to come to the aid of the Pantheon against this threat," Olthon added from beside her husband.

Like Ganatar, she was dressed in solid plate mail, her's though was form-fitting silver, over which a white tunic covered much of the finely worked armor and was tied off with a silken green sash. She had no helmet, however, but wore a golden laurel crown. She resembled her husband in height and racial appearance, save in her possession of white dove-like wings and blond curled locks dangling from her forehead, entwining her neck. Her soft flesh was pink with health which added all the more life to her bright green eyes which beamed with an great inner peace.

"That's right." Rheminas spoke up. "I think everyone has something to settle with this enemy."

"Don't be too sure of that." Khuthon cautioned his son, "Your mother isn't as dedicated to the eradication of this threat."

"No, she isn't." The great door to the chamber opened once more to let Asora inside. Of similar height and build to Olthon, she was great with child, which she managed to handle rather well in her gait and posture. Bright green eyes complimented her fiery red hair that curled about her neck and face. She made no attempt to hide her unease upon the whole matter of warfare and the slaughter to come. If her lack to fully dress to engage the battle itself was not a strong enough expression, then her choice of weapon and indeed her physical condition made the rest of the points clearly enough. She wore only a form-fitting white gown that stopped at her knees, allowing brown leather boots to take over from there to the floor. At her side she held a large wooden club, a rough hewn and almost ugly thing when compared next to her graceful presence.

"I'm not interested in killing another creature but I am not above self preservation and when you figure out how many more will suffer – will die if I don't act, the choice becomes quite clear. I do this for the protection of the Pantheon and all living things on Tralodren."

"How many troops did you bring with you?" Khuthon asked his wife.

"Enough to help, mostly Lords of Life under my command but a few Lords of Animals and Plants came of their own willingness as well. A total of some twenty-five persons in all."

"Twenty-five?" Khuthon shot out a half-cocked smile. "I'm impressed."

"Don't be." Asora was pert. "This isn't about bloodshed and slaughter."

"Believe what you will." The god of war turned back to his map as his wife drew near the others. "So with these new troops we are now posed to start building up our other fronts."

"Who will lead the assault?" Asora found her place around the table beside her husband. Khuthon turned to his wife with an expression she had known far too well over their long years of marriage. His eyes danced with the upcoming possibility of conquest and his lips parted to savor the joys of open combat.

"I thought as much." She muttered.

"Where's Saredhel?" Olthon peered over toward Shiril.

"Obviously not in attendance yet, but she should be here shortly I would think."

"She better," Khuthon growled. "I'm going to need her insight to help finish up this plan, and if she can't tell me when the enemy is going to appear that makes things a bit more challenging."

"What should happen though if this plan doesn't work?" Causilla looked up with her alluring eyes at Khuthon.

"My plans don't fail." His face darkened.

"But we suffered a great loss when we faced a similar threat before and only were able to stop it by–" Causilla continued.

"We are *going* to win." His face grew darker and sterner still, the very cauldron of slaughter and warfare staring back at the goddess with full fury.

"But do you have a contingency plan in case–" The goddess of love continued to press her concerns forward for consideration.

"We are going to *win*." Khuthon's jaw locked hard when he repeated his conviction by slamming his fist onto the table.

In the midst of the rapidly crowding courtyard, three more gods appeared. Aerotription, Drued and Panthor exited a tunnel of light which had brought them and their troops to Thangaria in a silent, yet regal procession that each would have understood and appreciated from their former mortal lives.

With Drued came some of his dwarven champions and priests – all former mortal men who had served the god in life and had volunteered to serve him again in this battle in their afterlives. They came from a wide span of years, yet each looking relatively the same. All were armored and carried axes and shields; they were bearded and crowned with shining helms. They followed their god into the courtyard, into the war to come.

The god who led them wasn't that discernible from his troops in many respects save height. Standing more more than twelve feet tall, long flowing silver beard ushering out of his partially open faced steel helmet, he seemed to be an enlarged version of a mortal dwarf. His armor wasn't auspicious but practical, hard forged steel platemail shining in the gray sky of Thangaria. A wolf hide cape fluttered from behind the race god as he walked toward the large assembly already gathered from his summoned host who made their way through the tunnel of light like well oiled machines of war. At his side swung his axe, and on top of the wolf hide cape itself rested his great steel round shield.

"Make rest here, and I will come back to tell you how we are to fight this battle." Drued addressed his troops.

"Hail Krieg Herr!" Came the dwarven chant.

"You do likewise." Aerotription stopped and turned around to address his own soldiers who were congealing into their own distinct mass amid the motley warriors like the mixture of oil and water.

As with Drued and Panthor's troops, his were comprised chiefly of followers who had passed away in the mortal realm in service to him. These had been his priests and faithfully devoted adherents. All Elyellium, they wore the same uniform for battle: gold studded leather strips forming a skirt from their waist to their knees; brown leather, open toed sandals covered their feet; leather breastplates affixed with silver reliefs of two griffins facing the other on their chests, and a crimson wool cape which fell from their shoulders.

Each carried a large rectangular shield emblazoned with the symbol of their god in one hand and a gladius in the other. Their helmets were of tough leather, straps on the side of their head tying beneath their chins to keep the cap-like hats held fast. The priests wore similar attire save under their armor they wore a purple tunic and had a deep purple cape and a plumed helmet with a fin-like brush of white colored horse hair sliding down their metal open face helmets.

"Hail Aerotription!" Came the shout from his troops, some three hundred in all, who banged on their shields with their swords to further augment their appreciation and veneration of their god.

Aero himself wore his own battle attire, which mirrored his troop's dress closely. His was pure shining silver banded mail sloping over his shoulders and down his chest to where black, brass studded leather strips formed a skirt about his legs. His cape was a deep purple silk matching the tunic he wore under his armor. His helmet was like his priest's though the plume was larger and purple in hue.

"Make ready here and prepare for the battle to come. We will be victorious and your generations shall live long on Tralodren, your valor protecting them, saving them from this dark hour which has now come upon us." The elven god's short cropped black hair contrasted his soft brown eyes which burned with a strong inner focus.

"Hail!" Each thrust their gladius into the air in salute.

The twelve-foot Aero then turned with a flourish of shimmering purple and silver and left to follow Drued to the chamber where the others had gathered. Panthor watched it and thought it amusing at how little the god had changed when it came to pageantry since he had lived once as a mortal man. The long feuds which had brought the world to near ruin long ago between the three race gods had long died out and the three had been reconciled to each other as had most of their people, but these small idiosyncrasies remained.

She didn't bring such a large force, as had her two companions, merely one hundred humans of mixed gender and race, for she knew that the cause was a costly one and she didn't want to dishonor the rest of those who had come to follow her to certain doom. She would fight sure enough, for the cause was a true one, but she would encourage those with her in keeping to be slaughtered when they might yet live beyond the grasp of this returning threat.

Panthor was the only race god, next to Drued, who didn't change her image even slightly from life upon rising up to godhood (save for her increase in size). Drued had highlighted a few minor areas, mostly his beard and hair, but the rest he left as true as he was in life, save for the increased size, a testament to dwarven tradition that even extended to their deities. Panthor appeared as she had in meeting chambers of Saredhel not that long ago. For dress it was a rag-tag collection of hide and cured leather stitched together to form a simple sleeveless and short dress. Other than this she wore hide boots tied up with strips of leather, carried a simple short sword and hide covered leather shield.

Her troops were as eclectic as her dress: wild barbarians from the savage north when it was yet populated with the race that would later come to be called the Nordicans, tribal Celetor next to scimitar wielding desert nomads and even a few handfuls of Telborians who had come to see and follow the edicts of the goddess of humanity in life and so gained a place near her in death.

It was to these human spirits that she now turned and spoke but a few simple words before turning onward again toward the pavilion to join up with her fellow race gods.

"Rest here until I return. The battle will be hard fought and you are indeed brave to come with me this far, but enjoy the beauty of this calm peace before the rising clash of blades comes to take you."

They all nodded in silent unison upon the truth of those words.

Each knew they would probably not be coming back from this place but thought the price a fair one if it would halt the destruction that would come to the mortal world they had once loved and lived. Their troops assembled, the race gods left to join the others inside the hall.

"...we have come nevertheless." The cold tone of Perlosa's words finished her greeting to the gathered gods. She wore no armor, but instead donned a fine white mink trimmed gown of shimmering white silk that blended in with her smooth alabaster skin. Form fitting and augmented by diamonds of blue and white shade, it told all who saw her that Perlosa was not looking to fight at all.

"So I see," Khuthon growled, "but no troops? Not even your mother is resigned to defeat that she'd hold back sword arms against this threat."

"As we have said," Perlosa drew up to her father's displeasing face, "they would not come."

"Would not or *could* not?" Rheminas chided his sister with a mocking tone and glare.

"They would not set foot on the realm. They hold it too sacred and remind us many times of the ancient oath we all took in coming here with weapons, troops and even in our true bodily form." Her ice blue eyes crackled with a chilling rage that remained subdued beneath her smooth visage. "An oath which we are all breaking and they felt to be a bad omen should they face such a threat here."

"Still, the Lords of Water–" Olthon started, but was cut short by the snide sneer of her niece, Perlosa.

"Have stated their displeasure with this plan as well," Perlosa shared in a tone that was well beyond condescending,"and we are not about to waste our followers in a vain battle that will serve us only one purpose."

In a violent flash of rage the god of war reached out toward his daughter and dealt her a blow from the back of his hand. The thunderclap from the strike creating a rolling echo in the chamber. Perlosa toppled to the floor in a rude fall; humiliation much more damaging than the slap.

"You go back to your realm and get those insubordinate worms you call subjects and bring them here." Khuthon gnawed the very words from his mouth in his rage. "They *will* fight and they *will* defend this Pantheon and Tralodren.

"I will not have my own daughter mock me to my face when even her own mother finds and brings warriors to this battle and pledges to wage it along side us all." Khuthon's eyes became slits of rage. "Get out of my sight."

Perlosa got up with a jerk, rubbing her jaw in cold disdain. All the while her icy hatred never left her father.

"I would tend to agree." The doors opened again to allow Endarien entrance. He had removed his helmet to carry it at his side; Heaven's Wrath in the other while Storm's Eye decorated the same arm. "If you won't fight with us then you have slid even to a deeper depth than which I once held you, cousin."

"If you had lived up to your boasting we wouldn't be facing this challenge now." Perlosa snarled her greeting to the sky god as both passed the other in their separate directions.

"If words are your only weapon, cousin, then pity be upon you when greater trouble looms for even your words are dull and fall flat before their target." The god of air's comment followed the goddess as the chamber door closed behind her. This tiff behind them, the business of the Pantheon moved on once again.

"It's good to see you again." Olthon greeted her son.

"Had I known just what was being planned now by our enemy, I might have acted with a little more prudence." Endarien told the gods as he joined their number around the table.

"Hah." Rheminas snorted. "You would have gone after that lich anyway. You wanted your revenge, and nearly got it."

Endarien smiled. "I'm grateful you have spared me too." Endarien turned toward the Flame Lord.

Rheminas nodded in acknowledgement.

"Saved you?" Causilla was bewildered "I don't understand brother."

"It was a servant of Rheminas that saved me from further injury, maybe even death." Endarien drew closer to the table.

"Really?" Khuthon's stare penetrated into his fiery son.

"I had to buy us some time and so I did what I could. We probably will be able to get troops and the lines ready for the battle, but it won't be enough to stop the attack itself." Rheminas returned his father's gaze.

"What are you working on, Rheminas?" Ganatar asked.

"We can't have secretive agendas now – not when we have to be of one mind and body to defeat this threat."

"Very well." Rheminas relented. "It is time to tell my plans, but not before the rest get here for I only want to explain myself once.

In the middle of the crowded courtyard another arrival to the battle appeared. Singular, he was a force to himself. Flying down on his majestic peacock feathered wings all eyes of those stalwart warriors gathered fell silent as the shadow of the avenging angel fell over them.

Around his feet, holding onto the straps of his sandals, stood Rowan and Cadrissa. The Galgalli held the wounded Clara gently in the palm of his meaty right hand, scepter in the other. He had flown them through the gulf of galaxies, to the very center of the cosmos where the forces and gods had gathered. True to his word the Galgalli had brought the three mortals here, now their fate was up to them. He landed safely amid the others gathered who made a path for him to do so. Once his feet where on the ground Rowan and Cadrissa dropped off his sandal straps.

"Here I must leave you." Dugan's voice thundered over the strange silence now present around them. All gathered had hushed at the Galgalli's arrival for he was a representative of each of the gods and so deserved their honor and respect. Dugan knelt to place Clara down beside the worrisome knight.

"Thank you for honoring your word." Rowan nodded toward Dugan.

Clara stirred briefly, muttering something to herself and then fell back into unconsciousness.

"If you want to live, stay away from the battle to come." Dugan stood up, then began to make his way to where all the gods were gathered. "You may have been foolish to request to be taken here, but you'd be truly stupid to wish to stay here when the din of war begins."

Rowan watched him fly away for a moment more and then turned to the bizarre and wonderful figures gathered around him. "I need your help," he beseeched them. "This woman is dying, and we need a priest or healer to bring her back to health."

His eyes searched the varied faces that were still turned around them, trying to make sense of these new arrivals who had come with the Pantheon's executioner.

No one came forth.

"Please." Rowan pleaded. "She doesn't have much longer."

A man then unlike any other emerged from the gathered host. Equal in stature to the Galgalli that brought them, he seemed eternally youthful though his eyes spoke of a wisdom gained from many a year of life. His clean, smooth skin and dark brown hair had the sheen of eternal health to them. His blue eyes were clearer than any sky and soft with concern.

"You have come to an odd place to ask for healing." His words were as gentle as his eyes.

"I've come to the only place I could to get her help." Rowan watched the man draw closer, his white robe tied about his waist; a green silken sash whispering as he bent down low toward the shorter knight and prone elf beside him.

"Then let us see what help can be rendered to one so brave as to come to the field of a battle where gods and their servants would make war." The man took in the lingering life inside Clara with obvious sadness. The bronze circlet he wore on his head, sparking with white energy, making his expression all the clearer to Rowan.

"Can you help her?" Rowan watched him closely.

"I'm a *Lord* of Life, the very *servant* of Asora." The lord's eyes drifted toward the knight. "If her time has not come, as it must for all things, then I will do what I can to save her." The lord then drew his full attention back to Clara.

"Rowan." Cadrissa placed her hand upon the knight's shoulder. "I wanted to – wanted to say I'm sorry."

"For what?" The knight turned his head to the side to speak to the mage.

"If I wouldn't have given into the medallion–" Cadrissa did her best to hold back the water in her eyes welling up behind her quivering lids. She had figured out what had happened on the trip to Thangaria. It didn't take a genius to place the pieces of the puzzle together and it filled Cadrissa up with a the sickest of feelings she'd ever known. The guilt alone was almost unbearable. Not just for what she had done, but in being shown how weak she was in resisting the opposing path.

"No matter what you feel, you didn't attack Clara on purpose. You weren't yourself, Cadrissa. You were possessed." Rowan was troubled by the mage's words. "It wasn't you who attacked Clara."

"I know but still–" Cadrissa wouldn't let the matter drop. Though it wasn't her who had hurt Clara, the thought of what Rowan and Clara must have seen and now had to endure…

"Let it go." The knight returned to look over the woman he had come to love. "You'll never be able to forgive yourself if you don't. I don't hold anything against you and I know Clara doesn't either." At that, the dam holding Cadrissa's tears back broke and her face was flooded with a deluge of wild emotion and quiet sobs.

"I have done all that I can for her." The lord faced the solemn knight.

Rowan didn't see any discernible change in her condition. "She doesn't look any better."

"Her wounds were deep and grievous," said the Lord of Life. "Further, there is a strong call of Asorlok upon her."

Fear then settled and took deep root in the knight's soul and face. "What do you mean?"

"It means that she is very close to the appointed time of her death," answered the lord. "It might be too late to save her from Mortis and its god."

The Lord of Life's countenance further melted when it took in the pain his words cause the Nordican. "Rest easy, for there is still a chance she has yet the ability to live through this. We will just have to wait and see what transpires these next few moments. Don't let hope die just yet when there is still fruit on the vine."

Chapter 35

Gurthghol spun his head back to face Galba. Red blood trailed from a split purple lip which the god wiped away with the back of his hand.

"Not bad." His smile smeared more red over his white teeth.

Gurthghol threw his weight behind his morning star. Like a small asteroid it sought collision with Galba, who simply side stepped the swing with startling speed.

"Your father couldn't take me, so how could you?" Galba remained calm, her body fluid but straight – like a coiled serpent ready to strike.

Gurthghol swung his weapon again.

Again Galba moved from its strike faster than the eye could see.

The god of chaos and darkness gave out a shout of rage which accompanied his morning star as it flew into, and then through, a nearby stone. The damaged object collapsed from the hole inside its center to topple to the ground below, the top flat lintel it had once supported with its twin post, drifting into a diagonal descent with it.

"You really would seek to kill me?" Galba moved parallel to the god.

"If you stand in my way, yes." His words were strong and sharp.

"What you are seeking to do I cannot let you do." Galba's words were of equal strength.

"So you let us die as you did before?" Gurthghol drew forth his khopesh.

"There are rules Gurthghol, and you are not to have this throne. Would you threaten everything you created with your fellow gods – this world by seeking out this throne?"

Gurthghol lunged forward in a stabbing gesture, nipping Galba's gown, tearing off a piece of fabric which fluttered to the ground. She countered with another fist to the god's face, this one directed toward his nose – which stuck hard and fast. The sound that followed was like a tree limb snapping off a trunk. Warm crimson blood spurted and sprayed from the wound, trailing down his lip, coating his moustache in the slick humor. Gurthghol's unusual eyes blurred a powerful sapphire for a moment, then the god was joined by five duplicates of himself, each facing Galba to surround the keeper of the throne with a deadly khopesh in hand.

Galba did nothing, merely stood amid the bodies, waiting for them to attack. When they did, it was a flurry of swords and screams. Each of the six blades found a sheath in the protector's flesh, but there was no blood, and she made no cry of pain; merely stood still and dug deep into the dark eyes of Gurthghol with her own unwavering gaze.

Seeing that she didn't move, Gurthghol closed his eyes to change locations, willing himself from where he had been to stand before the base of the dais to the opposite side instead. With no hesitation he started to take his ascent then heard Galba shout her defiance. In a matter of a breath Galba jumped out from between her attackers and flipped in the air to land on her feet before the dark god, blocking his progress yet again. The five remaining duplicates were amazed with the action, staring dumbfounded at the white clothed being, before they faded away back into the nothingness from which they were spawned.

"Recall what happened to you before." She exhaled. "You wanted nothing more than to shed it from yourself when you sat in it once before. Do you really want to pick it up again so readily?"

"Your rules don't concern me." Gurthghol had grown angrier now. He knew that little time remained. This battle was a pointless exercise and had to be over with very soon for everyone's sake. "I will not be played by either of you like we were last time. This is not a game. We are fighting against one of your own creations–"

Galba's eyes watched Gurthghol closely. "It wasn't I who–"

"You're just as guilty." The dark god spat back.

"Yet you still won out." Galba's face remained stern.

"Only by a great sacrifice." The god's tone was dripping with subdued wrath. "We have nothing left now, no net to catch us should we fall…and we will–"

Galba's face softened as she heard the heart cry of the god of chaos for she knew it was the desire of all the Pantheon. They were fighting for their lives alongside the lives of their creation. She could understand and respect that. "Then leave Tralodren. The stakes are only one world, you could go and find or create another."

For a moment Gurthghol stopped in place, frozen at what he heard. Abandon the very jewel of his creation? Would he even be allowed to be tempted by such a thought? Would he really be willing to run away like some battered dog who hoped to live another day? Could he?

No.

In his heart he knew there was really no where to run. He would be tracked down and called out to fight this threat as he was here, but perhaps without the same face that presently stood before him. He supposed Ganatar would find his mindset very noble, but the dark god knew the truth. In his heart, Gurthghol knew that it wouldn't really end with Tralodren. It would only grow and spread over time and eventually the whole cosmos would be in jeopardy. To be true to himself and what he believed, the prophecy Saredhel had seen, he needed to take the throne and put an end to two entities once and for all.

"There are other worlds, Gurthghol." Galba continued her refrain.

"But there is only *one* Tralodren." The dark god's jaw was set and resolute. He knew where he stood and would not be shaken.

"What is your existence when compared to such a world filled with lesser life, weaker beings who would go on for generations before they could come as close to you and your kin have risen in rank?"

It was a good question, but Gurthghol would hear none of it. He had decided his action. It was time to see it through.

"The time for debate is over." He prepared himself in a battle stance, khopesh poised to strike Galba down in the next instant.

"So it is." Galba's countenance saddened. She had no love of destruction but she would do what she had to in order to defend the throne and the circle. And defend it she did with a hard push into the chest of Gurthghol which sent him sprawling to the ground with an earth shaking fall.

Gurthghol rose up and charged Galba head on, shoving his shoulder into her collarbone with a violent force. The impact jarred the shimmering woman enough to cause her to lose her balance for just a moment. It was in that moment though, that Gurthghol took his advantage. He seized Galba's neck with his hands and began to squeeze.

Immediately Galba attempted to claw the plum hands away from her throat, but the dark god held her fast. Then he used the last bit of the energy of Vkar still coursing through him to drain away the substance and power of Galba and absorb it into himself.

Galba's eyes grew wide and panicked. "What are you doing?"

"What my father should have done eons ago." Gurthghol tightened his grip so Galba began to fall to her knees. She could feel the power ebbing from her body and into the hands and frame of her attacker. She knew that though she was still strong enough to defeat the dark god, she would be weakened a fair amount in a very short matter of time if she stayed as she was.

This had to end and she knew just how to do that.

"If you...break your word..." Galba's raspy voice assured Gurthghol through his strangling grip, "then I...am...not bound to...our agreement."

The form of Galba melted away to fold into a expansive cloud of white light blinding the dark god upon its first inception. The blindness lasted only for a moment, but the strangle hold Gurthghol had Galba in was now useless as the living energy flowed and fell right through his fingers; swimming away as easily as oil through water. When his vision returned to him the dark god saw that he now stood before a huge ball of white light blocking his way to the throne, presenting itself with a milky aura which spilled out even up to Gurthghol's bare feet.

"Even now there is still time to turn back from your intended action." The voice was like Galba's, but also different – more expansive and regal and less feminine – but not yet totally devoid of the softer undercurrents of the gender's tone.

"I have no intention of turning back," Gurthghol snarled back at the eminence before him. Nothing would stop him from doing what he felt had to be done.

"You were warned." The Light shimmered out all about Gurthghol in a blinding shower of dagger-like rays. It covered everything around him, even filling up the whole interior circle to spill outside the stone posts into the empty glade beyond. Gurthghol shaded his eyes with his arms and took one step closer to the throne.

The light was intensely corrosive upon his flesh and dress. He could feel it digging into him and bubbling away his person, defeating his will and spirit, more and more. Even gaining just one step closer to the throne made him feel the full force of this fragment of one of the two entities who had created the cosmos. If he had stood before the whole presence of The Light then Gurthghol would be no more in an instant. Here though, in its fragmented form, the dark god at least stood a chance.

Even with this chance though he wouldn't be able to hold out for long against such an onslaught. However, he could still feel a tingle of the remaining presence of his father, Vkar within him. Amazingly, Endarien's foolishness and the attempt to drain Galba had not used up all of it yet. The trace amounts of what he could siphon off of Galba were still present as well. He had to use what was left of them to make it to his goal, or die in the process, for even now Gurthghol struggled to hold himself together under the onslaught.

"Father, grant me victory." Gurthghol raised his voice toward the sky as he tapped into the last bit of his sire's essence and mingled it with the pilfered pieces of Galba. The dark god then glowed a fiery red – his whole body and even armor cast in a crimson shimmering of light flickering about and off of him like fire. It was under this red glow that Gurthghol took another heavy step forward, then another. Each time he was fighting against what felt like a wall growing more spongy as he pushed to move through it. There weren't any more caustic sensations now, just the oppressive barrier.

Gurthghol's eyes narrowed and his brow began to perspire under the focused pressure he continued to push himself through, but when he forced his way into the center of the white globe, into the very heart of his opposition, he let out a roaring shout of defiance. For behind that globe was the throne and it was all that mattered now.

Gurthghol pushed himself into the globe, and then was swallowed whole by it. For a long series of moments all that remained on the top of the dais was the resplendid, ever-present, all-consuming Light. Then there came a hand from the back of the globe reaching out for the throne of Vkar behind it. This was followed by another hand, and then a head looking upon the object of his maddening devotion with a painful grin. He was almost there. Though his body had the look of being marred and wounded as if gnawed by wild animals after a deadly physical fight, Gurthghol yet lived and continued his push forward.

"Turn back Gurthghol," The Light told him as he passed through its mysterious confines. "I don't want to destroy you."

Gurthghol brought a foot through, planting it with a thunderous clap, which then pulled the rest of his body behind him out of the mire-like light clinging to him and tried to pull him back as if Gurthghol was prying himself free from a tar pit. Another foot and he was almost free of the luminous tendrils. He could feel the last of the extra power of his father fading away with the lessening intensity of the red aura about him.

Even as Gurthghol freed the last of his person from its hold, The Light shook and quaked like a bowl of jelly. Gurthghol spied the wondrous gems of the throne beckoning to him with their enchanting call which he had heard and followed long ago. He saw the familiar stone seat on which he had sat for countless millennia; shackled to it like the drunkard to his bottle. If there was any other way he would had done it, for this was truly a sacrifice for the god, he would have pursued that option in a second. If Saredhel's prophecy was to be true, then Gurthghol had to follow through with his plan. For only by this sacrifice could the Pantheon and Tralodren be saved. Gurthghol took one last step forward, turned then seated himself upon his father's throne.

There was was a hush which seemed to be the sum total of all life in the cosmos drawing in a deep, fretful breath, and then the whole circle shook. Gurthghol could feel the familiar sensations of being connected with the whole of the cosmos once again, and felt the deep loathing the two entities released upon him as they felt the throne knitting himself into their beings once more.

"You have made a very grievous error." The Light continued to quiver before the seated god. It seemed now to be more like a pillar of snowy flame whose voice was solid discontented rising rage.

"Let's hope not." Gurthghol closed his eyes and the whole scene around him changed. Stepping into the throne again was like putting on a pair of well worn shoes. The fit was comfortable and familiar, more than easy enough for him to make full use of the thrones powers instantly – even after his long absence.

The ring of stones crumbled away with a massive earthquake toppling the sturdy rock so it fell away from what it had somehow been able to camouflage from anyone's sight: twelve thrones of lesser decoration but similar design to the one on which Gurthghol sat. Each empty throne faced the dais as if in anticipation for what was to come. Once each throne had held the whole Pantheon, but now they would serve another purpose as Gurthghol enacted his plan.

"You have set yourself against us now, Gurthghol." The pillar of white light chastised the god of chaos and darkness, but he wasn't listening.

The earth shook again and the thrones uprooted themselves from their ancient locations with the sound of breaking bones to fly straight toward the center throne. As they neared, they grew more transparent until they were faint flickerings merging into the central throne – one after the other in rapid succession. Gurthghol felt every throne lose itself in the majesty of his seat. As buckets filled the pond, so too did the absorption of the lesser thrones serve to augment Vkar's throne.

When the last of the twelve had been absorbed, Gurthghol opened his eyes. Around him was the glade and the pine trees encircling it where the ruinous crater created by his arrival still smoldered. The circle that had stood there for so long was now gone. Only the central throne and dais remained.

"You have no idea what you've done." The white fire persisted in its condemnation.

The god of chaos merely smiled, opened his mouth and drew the flaming light into him with a deep inhale. Another simple action for Gurthghol who was now augmented beyond the natural abilities of any god since his father who had stolen his godhood from his creators. When this was done he looked around one last time to make sure his plan was a success. He had achieved the throne and gotten rid of Galba. All his objectives had been completed and with the sacrifice he had now made, he felt confident he had fulfilled Saredhel's prophetic decree. He had only one final task to complete and than it was all over.

The god willed the throne upright to hover above the dais. Turning around in midair to take one final look at the dais and the two statues standing upon it, he waved his hand and melted the marble forms as though they were frosting in the bright heat of day. The statues of his mother and father congealed into a soupy mass seeping into the earth along with the rest of the dais.

When he was satisfied with the result, Gurthghol took off toward Thangaria faster than a shooting star, hitting the barrier as if it were nothing, for now it had no effect over him. He hurried toward the coming battle and hopefully salvation for his kindred...and perhaps even redemption for himself. Behind him he left nothing but the hollow echo of memories, which danced amid the flickering puddles of flame and dying smoke of the ruins which had once been the circle of Galba.

Chapter 36

"We waited long enough," Khuthon grumbled. He spoke for the majority of gods who had made their way around the table waiting for the last of their number to arrive. So far the only hold out was Gurthghol. Ganatar urged them to wait a little longer and give his absent brother a chance to show up, but in time he too began to doubt that was happening. Soon frayed nerves and escalating concerns took hold of the council.

"I agree." Asorlok, wearing skull motif covered silver plate mail over a richly adorned outfit, added his voice to the conversation. "Gurthghol's obviously not going to appear, so why waste any more time hoping he will?" The plate mail wasn't a whole suit, but pieces overlaid the luxurious fabrics at strategic places: his chest, the front of his legs, his shoulders, and forearms, with a pair of tall black leather gloves matching his leather hooded cloak completing his outfit.

The god of death seemed to carry no weapon to war – at least nothing the other gods could discern on his person. While this was far from alarming, it was a bit odd for one to prepare for battle with no weapon, but no one really paid it much more than a passing thought. For now was the time to worry about their own safety and protection over others.

"We will all stand against this threat." Saredhel was calm and appeared as she was in her chambers where Asorlok had spoken to her a short time ago.

Neither she, nor her husband, Dradin, wore any armor nor carried any weapon for battle. Neither of the two more esoteric gods of the council had been a strong warrior; they disciplined their minds over their bodies.

"What's that suppose to mean?" Khuthon snapped. "Is he coming then?"

Saredhel remained silent, head bowed and eyes on the copious amount of parchment and plans on the table. Her husband was silent beside her, body cloaked in dark green robes and hood. Only his well trimmed white beard could be seen from under the hood's shadow; his emerald eyes reflecting the sparking light of his strange, wonderful staff.

"While at least we have made *our* presence known." Perlosa tilted her nose toward the ceiling. The goddess of ice, waves and moon had returned to the council a fair amount of time after her departure with the requested aid in the courtyard with the others... meager though it might be.

"Please sister," Rheminas scolded Perlosa, "Father is angry enough without your goading him into a deeper rage."

"We were merely stating–" Perlosa had at least donned armor and weapon now for the battle. Her armor was of silver and molded to fit snugly on her upper body. It shined over her torso to her shoulders. Her legs were naked as her snow white arms; waist encircled with a silver skirt made of sharp, jabbing points of metal matching the style of the diamond icicles hanging over them for extra protection. In her fur lined boots she had placed a dagger (one for each boot), and carried a long spear at her side.

"You're fortunate enough to remain here as it is." Khuthon clenched his jaw tight against his daughter. "That pathetic force you brought back with you will do little to–"

"Enough!" Ganatar's decree rang out through the chamber.

All fell silent at the rebuke.

When the tensions had reduced, the Just One spoke. "We don't have time for this bickering. Rheminas has said he has a way in place to end this conflict and we have all waited to hear it, so let us do so.

Ganatar motioned for Rheminas to begin, "Rheminas."

"Thank you uncle," The god of revenge nodded.

"While we have all been watching events unfold, I have been making some events of my own should we face this very situation. Since the last time we battled this threat, we have never lived in much concern of great catastrophe for we still retained enough of Vkar's essence to remedy any grievous thing that would ever befall us. With its recent loss, we are now more vulnerable than we have been before and the threat more deadly therefore than it need be. Since to fight outright is to risk certain death, the answer lies therefore in not fighting."

"I can't believe I have raised a coward from my loins." Khuthon shook his head in disgust.

"No father," Rheminas continued, "no coward, but a wise warrior. I have created a new Galgalli to be our champion in facing this threat. With him taking up this fight for us the risks are greatly reduced."

"He'd fall just as any of the other divinities we have out there to war with us," said Endarien dismissively. "This isn't much of a plan, Rheminas."

"It won't be, no," A toothy grin made its way over The Flame Lord's dark face. "But I've added a few matters to make it that much more successful."

"We all saw the defeat of Endarien and that mortal rising to godhood in Galba." Rheminas looked toward Panthor, then Asorlok, and finally Saredhel. "It was then that I had an idea for another plan, similar to the one in which you all have been engaged."

"What are you talking about?" Aero's eyes hooded over in the shadow of speculation.

"Ask Saredhel…" Rheminas' gaze drew all of their attention to the seer.

"...if you want details. Once I saw what was going on I decided to hedge the bet."

"Saredhel?" Ganatar's face was focused on getting answers.

"Let it be." She held up a warding hand. "Time enough for explanations after this coming conflict. Too much time has been spent in waiting for Rheminas to say his piece."

"As I was saying," Rheminas waited for the others to grow silent; the goddess' words sinking into all of them before he said anything again. "I took one already destined for my service and rose him up to a Galgalli upon death. Then gave him the very scepter which the same group of mercenaries (assembled in part by Saredhel) who had released Cadrith in the first place, now came to possess."

"So?" Drued's tired word spoke for many of the Pantheon.

"This scepter is the very same one crafted by the Wizard Kings as they sought to take our power and placement in the cosmos." Rheminas grew slightly frustrated with the seeming lack of under-standing for what he was proposing. With it, our champion should have a tremendous advantage against our enemy."

"He might even slay him outright."

"We doubt that." Perlosa scoffed. "We are more concerned with the matter of this secret plotting behind our back."

"Whose side are you on anyway?" Panthor's eyes narrowed to slits as she took a good hard look at Perlosa. "Don't you ever get tired of looking for something to criticize?" Steely resolve met with icy waves. The goddess of the moon simply shot back a frigid face of hate, then retreated from the race god's gaze.

"How confident are you in the abilities of this Galgalli?" Khuthon raked his goatee with his finger.

"I would think him good enough to take on the task or at least help *tenderize* our opponent to give us a significant advantage. I've already tested him when he was mortal, and he did very well. With this new rank he should be a worthwhile opponent."

Khuthon chuckled to himself. "I should have known my son would not let me down." Perlosa rolled her eyes at this but nobody seemed to notice…or care if they did. "You've been listening to me after all." Khuthon's face was cheered by his revelation.

"More so than you know." Rheminas beamed in his father's praise.

"I'm afraid I don't understand this then." Aerotription raised his voice to the assembly. "We're going to let this battle now all hinge on one warrior? I thought we just did that with Endarien? So I've just brought good strong warriors here for nothing?" The elf god's anger was starting to rise.

"No, not nothing." Rheminas motioned for the elf to let his rising rage cool. "As a safety net should the Galgalli fail. We tried working with the word Saredhel had given us, but it didn't work out. We either misunderstood the word or–"

"Or he wasn't strong enough to do what was expected of him." Perlosa's comment drew hot ire of all around table and the bared teeth of a snarl from Endarien. Before more words could be exchanged, the god of the dwarves spoke.

"Foolishness if you ask me." Drued's pragmatism showed in his face. "If one warrior couldn't defeat the first pawn of this dark entity and Endarien, who had the boon of Vkar's essence, couldn't do it then why send out this new avenging angel to fight?"

Rheminas opened his mouth to respond but was interrupted by the large chamber doors opening up to present the very Galgalli of whom they spoke.

"Ah, welcome Dugan. Please enter." Rheminas ushered him inside. "I trust you were successful in retrieving the scepter then." All eyes followed the angel as he came to stand next to them.

"I was." The Galgalli replied.

"And the incantation to use it?" The Flame Lord continued.

"I have it as well," said the avenging angel.

"This is what is going to stand before Cadrith?" Perlosa snipped with obvious disapproval.

"If you wish to take his place, you are more than free to do so." The Flame Lord mockingly made an inviting gesture to his sister which brought a round of low laughter from the table causing Perlosa to finally huff herself into a frosty silence.

"So it seems we are agreed with this option then, since I've heard no real opposition to it as presented." Ganatar pulled them back to the matter at hand. "Let us put it to a vote then and be done with it."

The High Judge's eyes surveyed the faces of all those around him. "Who is in favor of letting this Galgalli fight as our champion in the coming battle?"

All present raised their hand.

"It has been decided then." Ganatar lowered his own hand, others following his example.

"We're still using the same plans that I've laid out," said Khuthon, "but wait until *after* the fate of our champion has been determined before we put them into action."

"Very well." Ganatar nodded in agreement. "If this Galgalli should fail, it would be a sound course of action."

"What about Saredhel's prophecy?" Panthor called all eyes to herself.

"What about it?" Endarien asked. "I already proved we didn't have the right interpretation."

"I thought it spoke of us being able to stop–" There was a great rumble across the room.

"He's here." Asorlok's statement brought a veil of soft dread upon the assembly.

"You know what to do." Rheminas looked deep into Dugan's white eyes.

There was another rumble then, this one larger than the previous one.

"I do." Dugan knew his place and purpose.

"Then fight well." Khuthon's words were a mixture of command and blessing.

Dugan ran out of the room then as still another rumble and the sound of nearby fighting was starting to draw near. He was through the doors and on his way to combat within the blink of an eye, leaving the gods alone in the chamber once more to wrestle with the sounds of rising conflict and the matter of their own recent vote. Would the Galgalli be enough to help them win? None wanted to debate that issue just yet…if ever.

"Well," Khuthon slapped his hands together. "It's time to join the fray, even if we are behind the lines of battle."

"What about watching it from in here?" Asora pointed out the reflecting pool of the Great Eye in the center of the room.

"No," Dradin startled a few by his sudden words. "Some things need to be done in person." The glowing globe on top of his staff increased in its intensity.

"Indeed." Khuthon's chuckle merged with a smirk.

Chapter 37

"She's not getting any better." The knight's stomach grew sour in his fear. He, along with Cadrissa and the Lord of Life– even a fair number of those gathered in the courtyard, had been watching the progress of Clara's healing. Only those who had come from mortal stock seemed to be the chief watchmen among the gathered host. The rest made ready for the battle while the others manning the walls kept their external vigil. For this moment this matter of life and death with Rowan and the woman he had come to love, drew these extra eyes to it as if it was the focus of their true concern and not the nearing warfare which had called them here in the first place.

"No, she is not." The lord responded in kind.

"Why can't you do anything?" The knight's eyes began to grow incredibly moist.

"I have done all I can." The Lord of Life empathized with Rowan, "As I told you, she was very close to Asorlok's grasp. I might not have been able to pull her from that grip."

"This can't happen! This–" Suddenly everything started to shake, accompanied by deep roars of thunder. The warriors gathered now looked toward the walls and the watchers who manned them.

"The enemy is upon us!" Came a shout from one of the watchers on the wall. "To arms!"

"To arms!" This shout of another watcher was followed by trumpet blasts which mixed amid the din of rushing feet, clashing armor and arms as these assembled troops made ready for war... probably their final battle in existence.

"It is too late for her." The lord stood up and began to hurriedly look around for a place to take his stand. "Best to let the living deal with the matters of life. If you value your own then you'd get far from this place." The Lord of Life left them then to rest amid the wave of shouting bodies.

Rowan's chin fell into his chest as tears began to flow. "This isn't right."

Cadrissa put her hand upon the youth's shoulder, her own face solemn at the present situation.

"Rowan..." Clara's weak words pulled the knight from his myopic melancholy.

"Clara?" The youth's face brightened if just for a moment. She had opened her eyes, but she was far from awake – at least in the cognitive sense.

Her breathing had slowed and her skin had turned the palest he had yet seen. Even her eyelids were dropping as if trying to fight back sleep. This was not natural sleep though, but the rest of eternity. The blood around her mouth, which had dripped down her chin and neck and splattered over her breasts in tiny droplets, told him that much. The wet, slurping sound of the breaths she did take told him the rest. Clara's eyes looked over at the youth, but there was hardly a force of life behind them at all.

"Hang on." Rowan pleaded. "I'll get you out of here and take you to a healer who can–"

Clara's head moved slowly from side to side; weakly declaring her mindset to the youth.

"Yes. There's still hope." Rowan's eyes continued to overflow in tears. Clara took a deeper breath, which sounded as if she was a water logged bellows, then closed her eyes.

"Rowan." Cadrissa's words from behind him were softer than silk. She had managed to stop her tears but the crestfallen expression of her face still remained.

"No!" He shrugged off her hand and words. "I'm not going to give up. Not now. Not on her."

Rowan grabbed the panther claw amulet around his neck then closed his eyes in prayer. If there was ever a time he needed his goddess, it was now. Even though Clara was an elf and his training had told him Panthor was the goddess of humanity only, he had to believe that she could do something. After all, didn't he have some great destiny or purpose? So he grounded his faith on hope and hope alone since there was nothing in his religion to support his faith.

"Oh, Queen of Valkoria hear me." Rowan pleaded in tears. "If I have ever been found worthy in your sight, if you have ever shown your favor upon me and my adherence to your faith, then I ask you to save this woman from death."

"Guardian of Gondad hear my prayer and look to this woman, this brave woman, who has given all in this fight against even your enemy. Bring her back from the point of death, bring her back to me."

Rowan continued to hold himself in reverence as he waited for his miracle to come, as he had asked his goddess to do. As he waited though he heard Clara slip away more and more, her breathing growing fainter, her spirit being unshackled from her body...

"*Panthor.*" The knight could only whisper the name of his goddess through his tears.

Why was she not answering?

What mockery was this?

To make him hopeful of the future but rob of him of one of the very lights of that future as well?

He then heard Clara breathe her last; heard the rattle of her chest, the stale, expired breath empty out of her lungs and the stillness of death come upon her as a shroud. In that final moment, the knight took up Clara in his arms and crushed her with an embrace – tears washing them both.

Cadrissa could do nothing but watch and try and stay out of the way of the commotion around them. Things had grown even more frenzied about them. There came another shaking, and what sounded like an explosion of some kind very near them now. The frenetic bodies around them didn't stop their rush to and fro; their tall frames preventing the shorter mortals amid them from seeing what was happening. It was only by some great miracle the trio hadn't been stomped to death in the stampede. Cadrissa didn't believe that such fortune would stay with them forever, however.

"Rowan, it's not safe here, we should seek shelter inside..." She took in the youth once more with sorrow laced eyes. "Unless you want to stay and fight." She didn't even know why she'd said it, but it came out just the same.

Rowan held the woman he had loved for what seemed like a lifetime, but in the end let the cooling flesh release itself from his arms to take his attention back to the chaotic situation at hand.

There came another loud explosion followed by some acrid smoke which drifted into the courtyard. There were screams now too, some being war chants, others the sound of death claiming another soul. Rowan looked swiftly over this escalating melee. Watching forests of armed warriors rush out of the gates at the threat that came to claim the Pantheon, he saw the futility of it all – the futility of his own self among them. He was a dot amid the sun. It had been very foolish to come here as Dugan had said...his hope...his faith had been a vanity.

"What do we do now?" Cadrissa was heart broken by the knight's disheartened features when he turned to her for guidance.

"You find ourselves some shelter and live."

Both Cadrissa and Rowan turned toward the sound of the familiar voice.

"Gilban?" The mage was as amazed as the knight to spy the lone priest looking back at them with eyes that now were clear and whole – though his body was a lifeless, transparent gray mist.

"This isn't your fight, not anymore." He made his way closer to the pair, staff clicking on the ground as if it was solid wood instead of crafted of ghostly vapors. "We have all done our part now. Not every hero goes off to war. Some battles are fought on more familiar soil. Nor does every deed need to be great to bring about good."

"Why are you here?" Cadrissa drew closer to the priest, ignoring the chaos around her and the oddity of his greeting for a moment in her curiosity.

"To help *you* finish *your* path."Gilban calmly returned.

Cadrissa wasn't totally understanding everything. "But you just said–"

Gilban raised a hand in interruption of the young mage. "I said you have finished your part in *this* matter. You both have lives of your own to lead, should this battle be resolved in our favor, and you won't be able to live them out if you don't survive to take part in them."

The elven priest motioned them toward the hall. "Come now, take shelter and live. You can't win this fight for it isn't yours to wage."

"So we just run and *hide* then?" Rowan's face grew dark as rage flooded his previous sorrow; mixing with it for a deadly concoction. It felt so cowardly, so against his Nordic concept of being a warrior – a knight for his Knighthood.

"You are free to do as you wish," Gilban's sighted eyes rested on the knight with some slight weight behind them. "for each man helps mold his own fate. I just came to help guide you to a slightly better end before I come into *my* eternal rest."

Bedlam was breaking out around them but Rowan was calm in its midst. Even as a handful of the giant warriors fell to their death around him causing minor tremors of their own. The calmness seemed to come from somewhere deep within; deeper than he thought was possible. It was from this calmness that a foundation was laid to allow him to build the beginnings of the truth to what Gilban and Cadrissa advised.

A wise man knows when to run and when to fight. He heard his father's words in his head. He turned his head toward Clara's body and sighed. It felt like the weight of the world, a weight he'd been carrying with him for sometime – since longer than he could remember fell from his shoulders.

Cadrissa grew more tense, scouting quick glimpses of the war raging around her. Though it was an interesting affair, self preservation was winning out over her curiosity.

"I'm not going to stay to get slaughtered, Rowan." She pulled up her robes to above her knees. "If you want to stay out here, that's your business. I'm sorry for your loss, but not much more harm can be done to Clara. We though are not so invulnerable." The mage then made her way to the hall and what shelter and safety she could find there; dancing amid the armored giants and shorter warriors as she did so.

Rowan watched her go – ground trembling more frequently and screams increasing around him all the while. It would be too late to try and get away soon he realized. He had to make up his mind and make it up quickly.

"She's right." Rowan spun his head around to see Clara now beside Gilban. She seemed to be composed of the same substance as the elder elf, but was every bit as beautiful – in fact more so than in life. Rowan reached out to touch her but his hand passed through her intangible frame instead.

"Let me go Rowan – let it all go." Her eyes were more loving than the knight remembered; somehow more real than himself…

"This isn't right–" Rowan shook his head in the sorrowful disagreement with the reality presented before him.

"Don't dare to judge until you've seen the larger picture in which we all live." Gilban cut off Rowan.

"My time has come, but yours hasn't." Clara's eyes now pleaded with the knight. "You have such a great purpose on your life. I can see that now – I can see many things now and you will too once your spirit has been freed from the body and its limitations."

"Clara…" Rowan tried to interrupt.

"You never really loved me, Rowan. Deep down, you know that." Clara's words dug deep into the youth. "Deep down you know that what you were attracted to. What you loved wasn't me, but the very thing you had been taught not to love: elves."

"That's not tru–" Rowan didn't want to agree with that even though part of himself let him know that Clara was speaking the truth.

"It *is* true and you know it," Clara strongly countered, "and will come to understand it even more in time...*after* you have survived this battle. I'm dead now, let me go and move on. *You* move on and live to fulfill *your* destiny."

"But you loved me too." The knight staggered with his words as if he was bleeding to death from a knife wound to the heart. It didn't matter to him about deciding to stay or go, the chaos around him for the chaos that now rose inside him was just as deadly, if not more so. He felt as if his whole world has been turned upside down – the last thread holding his reality together being cut away by violent force.

"No." Clara shook her head; the vaporous nature of her hair going from insubstantial to definition during the action. "I see that clearly now too. I began to understand it before I died and I see it very clearly now. I wasn't in love with you Rowan, just infatuated with the idea of your potential, though I couldn't articulate it then. You can see the truth of things much easier once you've removed the veil of physical sight from your vision. We had respect for each other if nothing else, but any love we thought we might have felt for one another was grossly exaggerated."

Rowan's fought back the urge to go berserk from the maelstrom of emotions inside him as the former calm he had known burned away in this internal cauldron. Around him he heard the shattering of gates by some great force, and the clamor of bloodletting and weapons crossing to prevent it...but it was still distant from his thoughts.

"*Go*," said Clara. "Go and live." Rowan didn't know what to think any more, but something greater than thoughts, self preservation, clawed its way into his head and grappled control of his thoughts. The condition around him was also drastically changing – getting far too deadly for any hope of him staying unharmed. It was time to go.

"Destined for something more?" Rowan bent down beside Clara's corpse, wiped his nose on his sleeve and then picked up the body. He wouldn't leave her corpse to be trampled.

"You already know this though." Gilban tried to be sympathetic, but it didn't seem to help.

"So what am I supposed to do that is so great then?" The knight turned to the two ghosts with the body of Clara in his arms. "Can you tell me that at least?"

Gilban shook his head.

"I thought as much." The knight began to make his way toward the hall then, dodging what bodies he could, running into those whom he couldn't. Both Clara and Gilban watched him for a moment, then the elven priest shouted a final message to him before he and Clara faded away and the din of war muffled any other sounds.

"Not all the battles we face are with flesh and blood, but with the matters of an unseen realm – the residents of our heart and head taking up arms against us." Gilban's words sunk deep into the knight's head and heart. "Not all battles are waged by sword and spear either, for through faith comes all victories; in it all things are rooted securely."

Rowan heard this strange saying but didn't turn back to see the two elven shades fade away as he knew they would. He wanted to remember Clara as she had been in life, even though what she had just spoken to him wounded him greatly. It was a small token of comfort, if he could accept it, amid all this mess.

He then heard the flap of massive wings and looked up to see Dugan flying above him, shadowing the knight below as the Galgalli went out to face the enemy. Rowan had enough of gods and wars and secret agendas for quite a long while. Let those called to fight the battle do the warring. He would find a place to sit and think about what he'd heard and seen and what he would do next…at least let the wound in his heart and mind slow their bleeding for a while.

Chapter 38

Cadrith had found Thangaria easy enough with The Darkness and the memories of Sidra to help guide him. He never felt so much energy coursing through his veins as he did now. When he had reached godhood he thought he had found the pinnacle of his being, but now he knew there was something else beyond him, bigger than he was and he both feared and craved it at the same time.

He could do little else now but obey. It mattered little that he wanted to do what he had been ordered to do, only that he had been told to do it and had little option but in carrying that order out…for now. Even as he traveled to Thangaria and made ready for an outright war against the gods in hope of destroying them all, he was searching his mind for ways to unleash himself from the grip of The Darkness who now held him in his grip – held him all along he came to now understand.

He had hoped to use the scepter as a tool toward his path to self-liberation when he'd become informed about it from Cadrissa, but that plan had been thwarted. No matter, he was a god now and imbued with even more potential power than that. Now he had confidence in his ability in finding some way to rule. For now he had to concentrate on the end of his prize.

It took him very little time to make his way toward the outer walls of the hall where he took delight in the assorted collection of beings who had been gathered there to oppose his entrance. This was almost too easy…With black staff in hand he flew toward the gate by sheer power of will, ready for the coming collapse of the Pantheon.

Within moments the assembled horde fell upon Cadrith and for a split second he was reminded of the attack dealt to him in Arid Land with the Syvani outside of Galba. These minor annoyances would be disposed of much more expediently than they. Galba wasn't here to hinder him or his abilities and he was eager to unleash the full might of his divine augmentations. In fact a wicked glee overcame him as he came to stand before the first wave of defenders who so foolishly tried to stand before him.

And so the battle began…

It mattered little if his victims were lords or other divinities, even followers of a god now risen to divine warriors – all fed his dark ambition as he pushed his way closer to the hall and the gods inside. None had even gotten close enough to Cadrith to strike. He was flush now with the potency of both the remains of the negative energy inside Sidra's husk and his own dark mantle he wore on top of his godhood. If this wasn't power at it's best he didn't know what was. And he planned to make the fullest use of it as well.

Taking the gate was easy; easier than it had been for him to slay his attackers. It fell before him in a crumbling heap, displaying the insides of the courtyard around the Hall of Vkar like the entrails of some freshly splayed animal. Bolt, and sword, spell and scream tried their hand at assailing the dark god, but nothing won out in the end. Cadrith conquered all by his force of will or staff which he came to use as a crude club and cudgel of sorts partly for his own amusement.

A volley of arrows descended upon him from behind the decimated barricade. This drew his ire toward the band of Elyelmic archers who had released them. Not Syvani, but close enough. Cadrith's eyes shimmered with an inky blackness and then shot a pitch hued beam out of his sockets toward them – disintegrating the elves like fat in the fire. They didn't even have time to scream. After the ocular blast nothing remained of them: no bow, no armor or arrow, not even a plume from their helms. All had been devoured; as would the world of Tralodren once Cadrith had removed the Pantheon, from hindering his goal.

How he savored this experience.

A Lord of Life then rose up against him on his side as the dark god made his way inside the gate and beyond it. A thrust of Cadrith's midnight staff impaled him before he could react. Face aghast from the shock and searing pain, the Lord of Life slid down the ebony shaft until The Master flung him free with the twist of his wrists. The lord was dead before he touched the ground; pieces of his insides and vermilion gore still spilling out of their cooling container. Another Lord of Life, who had risen up right behind the fallen lord, joined his companion in death by meeting up with a host of sinister black daggers which suddenly appeared and dug into him like suicidal ravens, making him look like a pincushion as he fell dead to the ground.

There were many more he had slaughtered. Humans and a few giants, some other divinities, but he couldn't keep track of them all – he didn't really care to. After all, these things were so far beneath him – flies that needed to be swatted; why concern himself too much with them as he cleaned them away from his over all goal. It wasn't important who he squashed under his heal, ripped asunder with his own two hands, blasted with his strength of will, impaled and wounded with this staff or what he did to still many, many more. What was important, was getting closer to the hall and the gods inside.

Cadrith had become so entranced by his bloodletting and the focus of his single pursuit that he didn't immediately notice the shadow that darkened the sky above and ground below until its creator landed before him. When he did so all combat stopped; all the clamorous noise ceased. For here was a Galgalli, here was the executor of the judgment of the Pantheon and all feared and respected any and all of their order. Even Cadrith was forced to still his hostilities. This cessation wasn't based out of fear or respect (though he could feel those pure white eyes looking deep into him; peeling all he was away to evaluate every little thing about him) but out of calculation in how to defeat a more challenging adversary. He knew though that the avenging angel was far from unbeatable.

No words were exchanged on the battlefield but everyone now collectively gave the Galgalli and Cadrith a wide girth, forming an arena-like opening of sorts in the midst of them so the Galgalli could do his job without their hindrance. They also knew their time to battle had ended, for the Galgalli was mightier than them and – each recognized the duty the avenging angel had to do in the upcoming moments; each now waiting for it to commence with the tensest of muscles and latching on to the highest heights of hope at his success.

Cadrith noticed the Galgalli held the silver scepter at his side and knew at once the creature was the same one he had faced by proxy in the Wizard King's tower in Frigia. He also knew that should the Galgalli try to use the scepter against him he'd fail. The lich had already planned for just such an occurrence happening, though not by the Galgalli's hand – that part could be improvised, however. This should be fun…a little more of a challenge but not much more than a slightly larger tree askew in the road. He'd climb up and over it in short order on route to the hall once more.

"We meet again." Cadrith's eyes narrowed. "Still want to challenge me?" The dark god tightened his grip on his bloody staff. "I'll break you without even raising a sweat. I've toppled this so called *army* your masters have assembled as if they were twigs trying to stand upright against a hurricane. What chance do you think you have against me?"

"I am your judgment and your doom." Dugan's words were dry and firm as he kept the scepter in his left hand before him.

"I'm surprised you can say that with a straight face." Cadrith released some callous mirth.

"I have been given the right to enact the full punishment afforded me by the Pantheon: your total demise." Dugan then drew his sword with his right hand, the weapon leaping into a white tongue of flame which encased the whole blade as soon as it had been drawn.

Cadrith's humorless smile widened. "So they really have sent you to die before me then?"

"Pathetic," Cadrith spat out his disgust. "They can't even stand against me themselves in battle. If you're the best they have to offer, then their fate will be swift and lasting."

"*Coo at limbea. Estorin gablin moor.*" As Dugan began the incantation as the silver scepter began to glow white hot. Tiny letters, too small to be seen fully by mortal eye, but not missed by Cadrith or Dugan, appeared all over the device in shinning golden radiance.

"You're wasting your time," the dark god mocked.

"*Uthran-koth. Uthran-koth. Japeth real!*" As the words of the spell continued to pour from the Galgalli's mouth the scepter's white light increased in its intensity till it exploded in a prismatic aura which covered the entire object before fading away to leave the scepter as plain as it was before.

"*Akeem. Akeem. Akeem. Yorn toth osiri latas!*"

"You know you can't win." The lich continued. "You're not fighting a simple godling, but someone with the backing of a being greater than you could even fathom. By facing me you're facing annihilation itself."

Dugan charged forward with silent effort, his strong body forcing it's way into Cadrith's personal space. The Galgalli had said the incantation, he and the scepter were ready. It was now the time to put the weapon to the task for which it had been created. For his part, The Master simply stood before the oncoming Galgalli. Calm and seemingly unconcerned, he waited for Dugan to come closer into his presence...closer to his demise.

He didn't have to wait long as the Galgalli was upon him with a flutter of wing and flash of blazing sword. Cadrith blocked this sword strike solidly with his black staff; the dark object before his face blocking the blow faster than then the blink of an eye. Reacting just as quickly, Dugan brought the scepter into play. Before he could defeat the descending arc, however, The Master vanished from before him, which caused the Galgalli to stumble forward a step as he regained his balance. Before he had totally done just that, he was attacked from behind by a burst of purple energy. The blast shot into him like a tidal wave, causing Dugan to fall to the ground; singed feathers scattering all about him.

"You're out of your league Galgalli." Cadrith boasted. "If you want to live leave now."

Dugan was wounded, but not too grievously. He knew that his back had been burned, wings bruised and scalded, but he still had the scepter, the strength to stand and his judgment to carry out. Dugan leapt up and spun around to swing his blade at this foe. The dark god was quick though and stepped back from the strike which would have sliced wide open his intestines. Dugan tried again, this time by thrusting his flaming sword forward in hopes of skewering Cadrith upon it. This too failed as the lich simply sidestepped the action with the simplest of ease and most condescending of smiles.

The Master then made his own attack by bringing the end of his staff to bear upon Dugan. With a swift slice through the air he had managed to cut into Dugan's forearm as he tried to parry the attack with his sword. Cadrith took delight in the wound – savoring it like a lover's embrace. Dugan ignored it, for his attention was focused tightly on getting the opening he needed to hit the dark god with the scepter. He knew The Master was toying with him, and it would be only a matter of moments before he could make use of this arrogant attitude to find a weak point in which to use the scepter. Once The Master was through with his sport, Dugan knew he'd make the job of his demise as swift and painful as possible. It wasn't him the lich was after anyway, but the Pantheon.

"One last chance." The Master stepped to the side of the Galgalli, pacing about the angel slowly like a lion preparing to pounce. Dugan though was watching and studying the dark god's moves, looking for an opening to exploit. He was so engrossed in this task he'd failed to see the Pantheon come out to watch the battle. A safe distance from the two combatants, the gods and the divinities gave them plenty of breadth to engage in their violent activities.

"Flee or fall forever." Cadrith snarled at the last word of his statement. Dugan had no intention of falling for he had found the opening he needed and moved rapidly to exploit it.

"Your judgment is at hand." Dugan's pure white eyes shined forth from under his dark hood, as in the same instant he brought forth the scepter. Swinging it down to connect with The Master just where the Galgalli had envisioned. At least it would have had it not been for the supernatural speed with which The Master deflected the strike with this staff. Before Dugan could register what had happened, the scepter had been knocked free from his grip and was flying through the air where it eventually fell deep into the rocky earth beneath him.

His advantage was gone in an twinkling of an eye.

Then came the flurry of fists.

Dugan was able to block some, but not all of the whirlwind strikes. Soon he dripped blood from shoulders and even places on his wings. They were almost too rapid for him; like an avalanche of comets pummeling him into a pulp, and he could do nothing against it.

As soon as he rose to defend himself from one, another would follow behind it elsewhere. They were too fast, and he wouldn't be able to stand up to much more of this. It was then that the Galgalli recalled his training at the hands of the cultists when he'd been a mortal in Haven. He focused his mind to slow the world around him down in order to better master his own reflexes and observations. Even as an agent of judgment, the training held up quite well, allowing him to create his opening to avoid the crescendo of fists.

In a heartbeat Dugan was able to better block the seemingly endless attacks with growing ease. A moment more and he found himself being able to deflect the blows, and make attacks of his own. Though not at the same pace of The Master's speedy assaults, they did the job in keeping the dark god on his toes...or did long enough for Cadrith to grab the flaming sword of the Galgalli to still the Galgalli's actions.

"Your masters' await, and I don't want to tarry too long if they're already expecting me." Cadrith's eyes dug into the white orbs of Dugan, hate spilling over into judgment; retribution into wanton destruction.

"Mayhap you've overestimated yourself." The Galgalli rolled his head back with a scowl.

Cadrith growled at his answer. "Don't you think I would have planned for that scepter being used against me. I was the one who was going to use it against the Pantheon in the first place." Cadrith gave a hefty tug on the sword, pulling the weapon closer toward him, Dugan along with it.

"Let's hope you die better than you fought–" Cadrith stopped himself and turned his head behind him, keeping Dugan at bay and in his grip. He had felt something there, something very strong, and when he had turned he caught sight of the Pantheon. All decked out in armor no less, making their appearance behind their army some distance from him and Dugan.

What cowards! What decrepit things they had become to cower and creep behind beings that were not fit to stand in their shadow. Oh, they were ripe for dissolution and he would bring it to them post haste...and then deal with his *patron* as well. For there were other worlds true enough...and he would be Master of them all.

"Finally come out of your hole?" The dark god mocked them. "You saved me the time of having to go inside and rustle you out like the rodents you are."

Dugan tried to pull away, to move to strike again in this wonderful opportunity, but he couldn't. Something held him back, held him to his current position. It was at that moment that the Galgalli saw a glimmer of The Master's patron and was overcome with the grisly revelation. It was too horrible to even attempt to flesh out with detail, for doing so would burn more of it into his mind more than had already entered in – the image of a million ravenous mouths in a great span of darkness would forever be in his soul. All he could do was watch and listen to the being who this hungry darkness had empowered to do its wishes.

The dark god looked toward the Pantheon with deep contempt. "This champion of yours won't be but a slight delay from the warm greeting I wish to give you all."

Cadrith then returned his gaze to Dugan. "No more tricks then Galgalli." He grinned. "Now we end this and I can go on to end your masters' lives."

Cadrith then unleashed two attacks simultaneously. His fist rushed into Dugan's cowled face with a loud cracking sound and more blood from the Galgalli's jaw and mouth. While the Galgalli was struggling and staggering from the punch, The Master's eyes glowed a brilliant purple which then burst into a thick beam shooting out of his sockets into the Galgalli's chest. Dugan fell backward as if he'd been kicked by a mule, breast plate bubbling and melting off his bronze flesh like butter on a hot skillet. His sword though stayed in the hand of The Master, who held onto it's flaming surface without any sign of discomfort as he watched the effect of his most recent attack. Dugan's suffering continued to the bronze skin under the armor which sizzled and boiled too as the destructive energy ate away at the tissue beneath his metallic flesh.

Dugan could do nothing but look up at Cadrith with tired eyes. His breathing was labored, and he ached all over. The wound on his chest was more caustic than the worst acid as it burned through muscle now, then bone and then his heart…Unless he could find a way to either squelch his injury or defeat Cadrith in one strike he wasn't going to be able to uphold his duty.

He was going to fail.

"Are you watching?" Cadrith again looked over to the Pantheon who hadn't wavered from their previous location.

"This," he motioned to the dying Dugan with the avenging angel's own sword, "is what awaits you all. So which of you will be foolish enough to face me first? Which of you will be the first to wet this blade – let it lick at the blood of so called gods."

"I don't believe it." Khuthon cursed. "That was a Galgalli! A *Galgalli*! It should have at least slowed him down."

"He is infused with the presence of our ancient enemy." Dradin was far from encouraging. "The time that was purchased was the best we could hope for."

"So what do we–" Panthor started to ask but was interrupted by Rheminas' scream as he ran out to challenge Cadrith.

"The time for talk is over." Aero stretched his back. "It's a time of action." The god of the elves then ran out after the Flame Lord. Khuthon followed him as did Drued, Endarien, Asorlok, then Ganatar.

"If we all stand against him now we stand a better chance of victory." Dradin encouraged those who remained, "but only if we all rise up to fight." All who remained turned to Saredhel, then at Dradin's words.

"I will join you," the seer said, and it was good enough for the rest of them to take up their arms and charge into the fray– all of the Pantheon fighting as one for its very survival and the continuance of a world.

Cadrith was ecstatic.

Whereas any other god would have been petrified with the potential onslaught of so many gods rushing toward them at once The Master simply grew more excited in the oncoming rush of concentrated presence. He'd enjoy crushing them all en masse or individually. It made little difference to him, save that they would all fall. The only thing he regretted was not having the scepter in hand, but he'd retrieve it soon enough after the battle. He'd need it if he'd want to put an end to The Darkness which thought it pulled the strings of this 'puppet'.

Rheminas arrived first, fiery sword and dagger hungry for bloodly retribution. The Master wasn't going to give it to him. He blocked the sword strike with Dugan's own flaming sword and the dagger by his black staff. Rheminas snarled and ground his teeth back and forth in his attempt to push through the blockade of blades but was held fast by The Master. Red fire appeared in the corner of Rheminas' eyes and then swiftly overcame his sockets.

"Die!" The Flame Lord growled as the fire shot forth from his eyes to blaze onto the lich turned dark god. Instantly The Master was covered in bloodstained flame which seemed alive as it wriggled and writhed over his frame.

Instead of being harmed, however, the dark god seemed unaffected and remained where he was, only lowering his weapons after Rheminas did so to watch the fiery spectacle before him. It was at this time that Aero had come beside Rheminas and swung twice into the pyre of a god with his sword. These attacks passed right through him though, much to the elven god's amazement.

"Have you finished?" The Master asked sarcastically.

The fire then went out as a dark countenance went over his face, highlighting a sinister smile. Before either could answer he was upon them – sword flashing before Aero and an orchid blast of energy from his staff at Rheminas. Both were barely able to prepare for the attack and were hard-pressed to keep from getting wounded or grievously maimed...even outright killed. Both could also sense the presence behind The Master, Rheminas especially, who was sent flying back by the force of the staff's blast. His place was quickly filled by Khuthon, who wasted no time in landing his meaty fist into The Master's chin. There was a strong crack, like thunder rolling across the expansive sky as Cadrith rolled with the strong punch, then rolled right back to glare at the Father of Giants unharmed; face dripping in hate.

"For that," Cadrith sneered. "You will suffer."

The Master brought his stolen blade down hard upon the god of war but had it blocked by Khuthon's own sword. "We shall see." The god of war's grim humor danced in his eyes as he parried The Master's sword to strike with his own.

Cadrith parried this attack even as Aero rushed forward again. The Elyelmic god was bleeding from the last attack but still able and willing to suffer more in hopes of destroying this threat before him. A swift punch to the head sent the elven god spinning unconscious to the ground. No matter, for the rest of the Pantheon closed in behind him, ready to strike en masse against Cadrith. He only had a few moments to enjoy the brief challenge before they were upon him.

A heated exchange of fury backed with steel proceeded as each unleashed the full force of their strength against the other. One the god of strength and the strongest of the gods of Tralodren, the other augmented to be his equal – and then some. Neither side could get another wound on the other, but Khuthon was weakened under the consistent onslaught. Each blow from Cadrith sapped more and more of his essence, his being, and he suffered for it. The god of war took a step back with one strike…then another.

"You're weak." Cadrith grunted his disapproval as he drove Khuthon further backwards with each new crashing sword swing. "Weak just like the rest." Cadrith eyed the other gods, who were now before him, and ready to make their move against him.

Khuthon said nothing, merely took another step back as he attempted to block each menacing jab of mystically instilled, flaming steel. Cadrith pushed him hard, calling for every reserve of Khuthon to come into play just to push the black blade back from his chest, neck, and face. Each strike sapped strength – sucking him dry. The Darkness did it of course, but he could do nothing against it but stand and fight against it's current pawn. The strain on his muscles was considerable and he knew he couldn't hold him back forever…which was seemingly more impossible with each passing moment.

"Just make it easier on yourself and submit to your weakness. Why torture yourself before the end?" Cadrith's snide words mocked at the tones of a consoling ally that he was trying to imitate.

"I surrender to no one." Khuthon stopped to look at the dark god dead in the eyes.

Cadrith was not impressed, merely blasted the god of war with his staff to cover him with a dark nimbus of serpentine energy which drove him to his knees amid muffled cries of agony.

"This conflict is over." Cadrith looked down at the wounded Khuthon in disgust. "I'd be rid of your wasted existence and attempts to stop the inevitable–"

Cadrith never got to finish his boastful speech because of Endarien flying into him hard from the line of gods rushing toward him. The dark god dropped his staff and stolen sword; the tackling blow was so strong he was knocked flat to his back and slid for a good many feet before he came to a stop; Endarien relented enough to get up before the dark god.

"So eager to die?" Cadrith glared back at his attacker.

"Are *you*?" Endarien replied smugly. "Why don't we end this once and for all then?"

"Agreed." Cadrith rose from the long trench he had created in the rock by being dragged over and then through it by the winged god's assault. He wasn't wounded and knew he wouldn't be with the protection of his patron. "I don't need a staff or sword to take care of you."

Before any more could be said or done, there was an explosion of purple light with such force as to shake the ground and all those present. The explosion had come from behind Cadrith, but he didn't turn to investigate its cause for The Darkness had already told him who it was and why it had come.

"Gurthghol." A thin smile outlined the dark god's lips. "So nice of you to finally join us."

Cadrith turned to face the god of chaos.

Chapter 39

Hoodwink waited in the stillness of the labyrinthian tunnels. Waited and thought. What would he do? What should he do? That was a big question, and he felt he knew the answer – well part of it anyway. He'd supposed he always knew that part of the answer since slightly after he'd found his way in the small room in the temple on Rexatious. The only challenge was getting the other part, and then following through on that decision. Following through was the crucial deal in all this.

He could feel a few more tremors about him. He watched a handful of dust and small pebbles fall from above, and dreaded being left alone in such a place. He could only hope that Gilban would come back.

He began to pace around the small section of tunnel he deemed safe enough to do so – not wishing to push into areas that seemed to intimidate him more than the shaking and faint roars he could hear.

The battle must be a sight.

He tried to think what it looked like when gods fought and couldn't even bring an image to mind. It was too fantastic for the former spinner of tales to piece together.

"You have a great destiny," Hoodwink mimicked Gilban's voice nearly perfectly. "Doesn't look too great to me," the goblin continued in his own voice as he continued to pace. He found it helpful to pace and talk out loud as he thought – it helped bring some clarity to the whole matter in his head by forcing him to reason it out as best he could.

"So I'm on Thangaria, gods are fighting above me and I'm supposed to do something great…" He stopped his pacing to kick a small stone down the facing corridor of rock, then sighed as he watched in skip away into the shadows.

"Should have just stayed back at the temple on Rexatious. At least there I was safe."

"But you were far from your destiny." Hoodwink turned to see the same dark clothed woman who had visited him in the temple of Saredhel – the one who had started him on this wild journey in the first place.

"You."

"Rest easy Hoodwink," the woman held up a warding comforting hand which stilled the goblin's unease. "I'm here to help."

"Then get me out of here." The goblin spouted as another tremor rumbled above. "You got me into this mess to begin with and now I–"

"Is that what you really want?" The woman took a step closer to him, drawing back the inky hood as she did so. Hoodwink watched her approach transfixed at the transformation occurring as the woman neared. Her black robes were lightening to a dingy gray and then finally white as the hood was totally pulled away to vanish into nothingness along with the former frame as Galba now stood before him.

"I-I," he stammered for a moment as he was taken aback once more by the brilliance and beauty of the supernatural female before him. "I'd like some answers."

"About what?" The majestic woman lovingly inquired.

"Everything." The goblin released the word in frustration. "This whole quest, the war going up over my head, the endless references to me having some great calling or purpose or destiny: *everything.*"

Galba nodded slowly as she listened.

Hoodwink waited for a response.

Silence instead filled the chamber.

Hoodwink grew restless with the silence; found awkwardness inside it and so began to pantomime: rolling his right hand along in a gesture to indicate that Galba should start talking now.

She didn't take the bait.

He finally blurted out his mind.

"Don't you have anything to say?"

"Why are you troubled to be alone with your thoughts?" Galba remained calm as ever. "Could it be you've already made up your mind and now you are afraid to follow through on that decision?"

It was Hoodwink's turn to be silent now as the words dug deep inside the core of his being, into his soul and past it into his spirit. There was much truth to those words…much truth.

Galba continued. "Gilban brought you here to make a choice… or follow through on one you already made."

"That's what he said." Hoodwink was tight lipped; mind racing over the thoughts and decisions in his head.

"Has it been made?" Galba leaned forward with another step as if she were drawing closer to hear a faint whisper.

"Almost." Hoodwink's answer was smaller than his stature.

"Time is not your ally, Hoodwink." There was some sadness now that tinged Galba's voice. Like the voice of a mother saying farewell to her adult children after a recent visit.

"I know I just–" he let out a sigh, then continued. "I don't know why anyone would pick me out for being a 'champion' as Gilban says I am. What can I do that's so great? What have I done to stop The Master? Nothing."

Galba listened to the goblin's inner dialogue as he spoke it aloud with the most caring of green eyes. Eyes that made one feel like they were the only ones in the whole universe worthy of giving their full attention.

"This Light must be pretty confused to have picked me with the others that were lumped together for this quest, or whatever it is. Dugan was tough, Rowan too, Gilban was…or is – or whatever he is now – he was good too. I'm just…"

"You're just *you*." Galba smiled with all the warmth of a proud mother beaming down on her child in whom she delighted.

"Exactly." Discouragement slouched the small goblin's shoulders.

"You're just you and that is why I chose you." Galba repeated with true joy in the figure before her.

Hoodwink looked with a sudden intake of breath into the eyes of Galba. "*You* chose me? *You're* The *Light*?"

"An aspect of it, yes." Galba's eyes twinkled.

"I don't get any of this." The goblin shook his head.

"I chose you because of who you are, what you represent. You have such wonderful qualities about you. Qualities that set you apart from all the others of your race. Haven't you often wondered why you were so different than your kin?"

Hoodwink nodded. He had done just that – almost daily dwelling on it in his time in Takta Lu Lama.

"You have made good choices, hold to good beliefs and have taken the step into a new world that few of your race, if any, will ever take. For these reasons you were chosen, for you have the skill needed to be my champion. I've watched you since you were born, and kept you safe until this time. You are the most important of my champions who I've called to this task." Galba moved to put a gentle hand upon the goblin's shoulder.

Hoodwink didn't object to what she was saying, as it was all making sense to him – to the deepest parts of him. "In fact," Galba added, "all of the others were called merely to *help* you get to this point."

Hoodwink looked over to the woman with wide eyes. "Right." He wasn't going to believe that. He couldn't in any good conscience.

"They all had a part to carry out and they did it. Now it is time for you to do the most important task which has been prepared for you by the others."

"What's that then?" Hoodwink still didn't know what he was being called to do…but he did have a hint, a strong hint that was growing in strength with each passing heartbeat to do it.

"My counterpart, the one who opposes me, has risen up its champion and so have I. It has used people, events and situations to mold and create The Master. I have used people, events and situations to propel you along to this point – the others helping you along your way. They found and helped free you from the ruins of Takta Lu Lama, took you to the first confrontation with The Master, and now you are at the second and last."

"Why though?" Hoodwink could see this all beginning to make some sense, at least he could begin to believe it was making sense, but what was he supposed to be doing in all this? "What's my purpose in all this?"

Suddenly there was a terrible commotion above him; rock and dust raining down and all about while a overpowering explosion shook everything. He couldn't see as he was blinded by the debris and couldn't hear from the deafening crash. When he could see again he noticed that Galba was gone and a silver scepter, the same one which Gilban had retrieved from Gorallis by the look of it, though much larger, was lodged into the ground a little ways from him. Having crashed though the chambers ceiling above it was awash with illumination as well – beaming with an eldritch glimmer that was at once enticing and repellent to the small creature.

Nevertheless, he dared to take a step closer to the scepter, looking up and around him to make sure no more falling rubble would land on top of him in the process. As he made it over to the scepter he heard the voice of Galba in his head.

This is part of your purpose. Wield it as my champion.

Then the voice was gone.

Hoodwink stopped before the large object, uncertain of what he was to do with it, how he was supposed to wield it…if he *wanted to* even. Course, he knew he wanted to do, always did, just was afraid to admit it – afraid to take the first step forward into grasping his dreams and making them a reality. Was it a dream of his to challenge The Master?

No, but it was a dream of his to do something great, to be someone great. Taking up the action currently presented him could very well help him achieve that dream…if he should survive. If he didn't though would that really be so bad either?

"It's time." Gilban's ghost shimmered before the goblin and behind the scepter so suddenly that Hoodwink jumped out of his thoughts and trembled in his flesh. "Decide quickly."

"Where did you go?" Hoodwink regained his composure.

"To places and matters that concern me, not you." Gilban's curtness amazed the goblin.

Hoodwink's hearing had returned enough to understand what the ghost had said over the slight ringing which still remained. If the sands were running low in the hourglass then, there weren't but a few faint grains left tossing about on their spiral descent. Now it was just a matter of following through on the choice he had already made but he was unwilling to follow through until now. He just wanted to make sure though, one last time, that he understood this all as best he could before he picked up the scepter and moved into the greater folds of destiny's robes.

"So Galba is an aspect of The Light?" Hoodwink was still trying to take this in.

"Yes." The ghostly priest dryly replied. Hoodwink could tell Gilban was growing more anxious for him to take action.

"And The Light is good then and can't lie?" Hoodwink's gaze meandered over to the shimmering silver scepter once again.

"It is good and can't lie." Gilban's answer was a bit hurried. Hoodwink could almost hear Gilban thinking: *Hurry up Hoodwink and make your move…*

"Then I've made my choice." Hoodwink placed his hand upon the scepter whereupon it shrank back down to its normal size to fit neatly into his grip.

"The scepter is activated already so you just need to take it and strike true." There was some measured pride in Gilban's tone as he advised the goblin.

"And *that* will destroy The Master?" Hoodwink stared at the magnificent object in his hand, observing and being enchanted by the soft steady hum and glamour about the scepter which reflected about his green hued face.

"It will destroy the enemy of the Pantheon and Tralodren, yes. Now go. Be quick and strike true." Gilban pointed out one of the tunnels to the goblin with a spectral hand.

Hoodwink looked toward the tunnel, then Gilban and then started to run down the corridor as the ghost directed.

The final move had been made.

Chapter 40

urthghol took a good hard look at The Master.
Neither one moved, only fixed their gaze at the other.

There were no words to speak, nothing that had to be said. Each knew the other through and through in the matters of this confrontation, and the end each desired. The only question was who was going to win their desire? All the other gods present stilled themselves, as those who had recently fallen rose to witness this confrontation; Endarien himself taking a few steps away from Cadrith as well.

"I was wondering when you might show up." Cadrith studied the throne of Vkar. It was unchanged since last he saw it at the circle of Galba. The lich knew, however, it was a power to be reckoned with and understood that he faced his even match now before him. "I didn't know you feared me so much that you'd steal the throne to fight me."

"I did what was necessary." Gurthghol's face became a scowl. "Sacrifices had to be made and I took them to keep you from getting out of your place."

"And where is my place?" Cadrith's sarcasm was suffocating.

Gurthghol boldly returned. "Where you should have stayed for the rest of time: the Abyss."

"If the Abyss can't hold me then what hope do you have in defeating me?" Cadrith took one step closer. "So what do we do now? Fight to the death? Is that what you want?"

"What *you* want." Gurthghol remained still on his seat. Already he was comfortable with it – the past centuries of use returning into his memory and body once more. This was once again, a very familiar situation.

"Then I won't disappoint," the dark god summoned his fallen staff to his hand with ease then raised it before Gurthghol, who simply remained still in his seat. All the other gods could do nothing – not now. The throne was greater than all of them and with Gurthghol in it's seat they couldn't even come close to matching it in divine strength. This revelation and the shock in knowing Gurthghol would have had to pull it up and out of Tralodren without their knowledge was all too much for them to currently process.

Gurthghol still didn't do anything as Cadrith's eyes twinkled with a black sheen and then let loose a spray of deadly, inky energy hungry for the god before it. What should have consumed the seated deity in terrible agony did nothing but pass into him as Gurthghol absorbed the attack into himself. Cadrith screamed in rage.

"Have you had your fill?" The god of chaos' words were even toned, his expression mild. "I'm not Vkar and I won't be as easy to kill as he was."

Cadrith howled as he let loose the same bolts of energy which had felled Dugan right into Gurthghol's face. To his dismay, this attack did nothing either save be sucked into the plum skinned god like water going down a drain. Undaunted, Cadrith resorted to a more primitive method and threw a punch but found his hand hitting hard upon Gurthghol's unrelenting jaw. The sound of bones cracking told him his hand was broken, if the blood oozing from its various punctures and abrasions didn't already.

"Finished yet?" Gurthghol mocked with a grin.

"You can't stand against The Darkness behind me. You're scared of it, you all are, I can feel it. You can't win." Cadrith focused on healing his hand as he spouted out this small tirade. He would win and if he was able to get his hands on the throne as well…with the scepter and the throne he'd be the most powerful being in the cosmos. Fate was certainly lavishing him with gifts of late and he'd be a fool to not take advantage of them as they arrived...

"Am I?" Mischief danced in the dark eyes of Gurthghol.

"I'll still bring this Pantheon to dust. With the power behind me I can't lose."

"No." Gurthghol mused, "I think you're right. With it you are a threat but without it..."

Cadrith had managed to heal his hand, and now watched Gurthghol hawkishly. What was he playing at? What sort of trick or attack was he getting ready to unleash? Why was he even listening to this when he should just slaughter him outright? He didn't know really, only that he should gauge the god of chaos and darkness just a little bit more. There was something about him that brought great unease to the lich turned dark god.

"Frightened?" It was now Gurthghol's turn to mock. "You should be, for in this throne I'm more powerful than you." The god of chaos and darkness pointed his finger toward the lich who instantly became enveloped in a globe of swimming pitch. "Without your patron behind you, you're nothing." Gurthghol's smile was frightening to behold as Cadrith screamed in bitter agony as this pitch globe about him faded away or rather was drained away from him and into Gurthghol who simply sat on his chair, observing and enjoying it all.

"Wha– what's happening?" The Master dropped to his knees and started to hack up blood as more fell from his chest, pooling and then swimming over to the throne where it then was absorbed. He tried to will himself well, to force himself into a frame of wholeness, but he found himself unable to do so, as if he was being drained of the divine abilities he once possessed. This shouldn't be this way at all.

He was a god.

A god!

Further, the augmentation The Darkness had instilled into him was fading away as well. Something wasn't right, and he had to figure out how to correct it in light of the fail-safe he had insured just in cause something might happen to him...but did he have enough time and power left?

"I'm taking back the dark mantle you'd been given as well as the godhood you stole with it's aid," said Gurthghol.

"I received my ascension on my *own* merit." Cadrith snarled through his pain like a wounded animal.

"No." Gurthghol shook his head. "You did all that you did only because your patron moved you along to its own ends. You weren't even half that great of a mage as you thought you where."

The Master's face fell into charred flesh, his hair singed away in an invisible fire which seemed to cover the rest of his body in rapid speed; eating away at what he once was to reveal instead how he appeared when he had last battled Endarien on top of the clouds before his divine ascendance. In the fleeting moments of his life The Master held up his hands with wonder.

"No..." he half whispered, half screamed, "...I'm a god..."

"You were a pawn who has outlived his usefulness." Gurthghol flatly corrected.

Everyone present looked on as the lich could do nothing more than lay flat on his back as his ruined, dying frame fell into death and was reduced back to his normal size.

"Go ahead and ask your patron if you dare." Gurthghol chided the decaying figure as the last of The Darkness was sucked from him into the god of darkness and chaos and the Throne of Vkar.

"You promised..." Cadrith's words were weaker than his frame.

I said what I wanted to say. The Darkness then came to the fallen god's mind. *I never grant life in favor of death. When I first intervened I simply reversed your body a bit into the past, but never healed you of your wounds. I needed you alive to do one last task and now, even in your death you served me well. So enjoy the gift I bring to all now: the gift of oblivion.*

The Master then faded away into dust which blew away into nothingness leaving not even a single strand of thread behind from his robe or even molecule of his staff, which had also been consumed. None who had seen the event, who had been captivated by it so as to be like statues around him, let loose a single breath.

All was still.

All waited in silence…until Gurthghol spoke.

"It is finished." It was said softly but carried far in that silent assembly. More so that their ears had been strained to hear what the god who sat on the throne of Vkar would say.

"Why?" Asora asked Gurthghol as she was joined with the other gods around his throne. "Why did you take up the throne again?"

"There was no other way," said the god of chaos. "It had to be done."

"We were willing to fight – we were already fighting." Khuthon grumbled.

"You would have failed." Gurthghol returned the god of war's frustrated gaze. "You all would have failed."

"So you had to break the agreements we laid down at the beginning by bringing the throne of Vkar back to us?" Olthon was upset as well. She had no love of Gurthghol claiming the ancestral seat.

"Taking this throne was the last thing I wanted to do, but Saredhel's prophecy made it necessary-"

"How?" Rheminas rather brazenly asked his uncle.

"She told us that a sacrifice had to be made in order to stop this threat," said Gurthghol.

"A sacrifice to be made to stop Cadrith from claiming godhood." Endarien spoke up. "We all made plans for that and voted on the matter. None of us would have voted for this." He jabbed an accusatory finger at Gurthghol.

"I know." Gurthghol nodded. "But that wasn't the real meaning of the prophecy and why what we all decided to do didn't work with that lich. I say the true meaning to what Saredhel had said after Endarien had left. It was right there in front of my face: I had to shackle myself to the throne again, to sacrifice my own freedom to save the Pantheon. This recent success should show everyone that I was right."

Gurthghol motioned to Saredhel who stood silent and still beside the gathered group. "Tell them I was right."

Thirty eyes found their way toward the enigmatic goddess.

Thirty eyes waited to hear her response.

"This is what I told you: If one of us is willing to make a great sacrifice we would gain an advantage over this new threat. Confrontation against the dark patron's agent that would take something dear from the confronter as payment for success" Saredhel repeated the prophecy. "If you are looking for confirmation of right action, I can only say that what was done with Endarien *and* with Gurthghol was answering what I have spoken."

"So we were *both* right?" Endarien wrinkled his brow. "How can that be?"

Dugan's groans then washed over the stillness that followed the question. As the others pondered that meaning, Asora was moved into action, running to Dugan's side. The Galgalli's flesh had been eaten away around his chest; muscles fading way to bone and pulsating, moist organs underneath. She wouldn't have the avenging angel suffer longer than he already had. "Rest easy and be made whole." Placing her hands over the wounds she gave the battered Galgalli the empathetic gaze of a mother. "You helped do a great service today."

Under the goddess' hand the Galgalli's ragged breathing eased and his sullen complexion filled with a healthy color once more.

New tissue grew over his bones and bronze flesh wrapped up the wound completely. When he could breath freely once more Dugan removed his hood and sat up to see what had happened around him.

"Is it over then?" He turned toward Asora who had now stood up to look over toward the scepter.

"It seems that way, yes." She answered with a tired sigh.

"So all that – all that fighting was for nothing?" Dugan stood up with only some minor challenges. He had been completely healed, but he still was a bit lightheaded from suddenly rising from the ground.

Asora didn't answer. She didn't have to. Everyone around them and even the gods themselves were just as uncertain as the Galgalli as to what had happened and why. Was the whole confrontation really over now? The entire build up to the event just left them with such a feeling of anticlimactic action that none knew just what to make of it, if anything. Had they really been hoping for more death and destruction than what had been unleashed? Had they really thought they would lose their life or expected to be seriously wounded in the fight?

The answer to those question seemed to be yes.

"Now." Gurthghol took hold of the stone armrests with a deathlike grip, ignoring the rising emotions from his family. "It's time I ended this once and for all." He then closed his eyes in concentration.

"What are you doing?" Endarien asked with slight concern, echoing the thoughts of all the other gathered deities as they turned toward the seated deity in wonder.

"What my father couldn't." The god of chaos didn't open his eyes to respond. Suddenly there came upon Thangaria a great heaviness, weighing down all who stood around the seated dark god.

Saredhel's voice carried over far from her lips to land into Gurthghol's lap. "Make sure this is the course you wish to take."

"I'm sure." He opened one eye then closed it again. There was then a terrible rumble and the sound of a million inaudible screams as the sky above was ripped in two; cleft down the center from horizon to horizon.

"Stop him!" Asora screamed as she rose from beside Dugan. She could feel the great rift being rent in the cosmos, to the very core of the substance of life itself. "Someone stop him! He's tearing apart the cosmos!"

Before she could get any closer to Gurthghol or any one of them could do anything, there was a powerful change in pressure about them, popping ears and bringing on headaches for a moment before it was swallowed whole by a raging wind storm that suddenly came over the whole chunk of realm. The storm picked up bits of fallen weaponry, the recently slain and other debris to churn and funnel about all above the hall and the god's who stood outside it.

"Gurthghol–" Ganatar started to raised his voice over the roar of the wind.

"It's too late to stop me, I know what I'm doing." The plum hued god held up his hand to hold back the questioning. It didn't matter anyway, for none could argue any further when the wind settled down and a very unsettling calm fell upon all present. Divinities, former mortal soldiers and other creatures alike all took to the recent sights with great dread for they could see the unease – even feel it from some of their Pantheon. If the wind hadn't taken them into this pit of worry then they would follow the example of their gods.

The formerly airborne bodies and debris fell away to the ground or in some cases, off into the scattered chunks of the former world, where they hovered away to form their own orbit. As the winds died down there appeared two beings before Gurthghol:

one robed in light, the other in pitch darkness. The one in light was Galba, the other though was something of a humanoid frame but lacking in the finer details of appearance due to a long hooded cloak which covered the figure from head to toe.

Together these two figures stood before Gurthghol in silence.

"What have you done?" Dradin's tone was fearfully reverent.

"He has made his choice," said Galba "And it is a very poor one at that."

"We shall see about that." Gurthghol smiled. "I'm going to get rid of this threat to our existence once and for all." He addressed his mortified family and their followers around them. "No longer will we have to cower before these two entities and be part of their games. I'm going to finish off Nuhl and Awntodgenee forever."

"Take heed in your actions," said Galba, the representative of The Light, who was also called Awntodgenee. "Are you sure you want to attempt this?"

Gurthghol nodded as his grin widened. "I was sure when I used the throne to call you both here and am more certain now that I will be rid of you both as well as doing the cosmos a great favor." He then closed his eyes in concentration and willed the two entities into the throne, into the very object which had been created to tap into their essence in the first place.

All were amazed at Gurthghol's success as he began to pull at first a thin trickle and then a wider beam of light and then darkness, snaking from Galba and the dark cloaked figure, into the throne right above his head. Neither of the representative figures said anything, only joined with the onlookers as this occurred. None of them heard the nearing footfalls of some tiny goblin feet, nor would they much care even if they did. Awntodgenee did though and it made the entity glad – a great destiny was being forged.

"Arrogant worm," laughed the representative of The Darkness (also called Nuhl), whose voice was callous and cold, "you'll feed my hunger before you come even close to fulfilling your fantasy." It was at once male and female but also cruel and hungry. "Just as your daughter did."

The words struck Gurthghol hard. His face grew even more rancorous then and darker of shade from the rage which burned beneath. Ever since his daughter had betrayed him, Gurthghol hated to be reminded that he even had once had any children.

Sidra, his only child, was enough of a disappointment and embarrassment to stop him from ever having any other children ever again. Moreover, Gurthghol viewed it as an insult to him as well because his own flesh and blood was not only used by the very force the whole Pantheon was fighting against again, but his child was corrupted and manipulated under his very watch. There was that issue of fear too which stopped him from having any more offspring. Fear that any child he should sire would be susceptible to the corruption of these two entities before him.

"You used her for your own ends – twisted her with your games and schemes." Gurthghol growled. "She would have made me proud, but you robbed me of that along with the lives of my parents and many of my family and allies."

Gurthghol's brow wrinkled as he pushed himself to the brink of his abilities, willing the chair to do even more and so increased the flow of Darkness and Light so that now it was a river of energy being absorbed by the throne. He would win out in this matter in the end. He would achieve what his father couldn't, and be free of these meddling entities – beings who had turned his daughter against him and her true family.

Gurthghol was so focused on the task at hand that he didn't hear the final approach of the goblin before he was more than a few feet from him. Even when he finally did, he paid it little mind…or would have had he not felt an energy source near by the goblin's hand, an energy source he recognized a hair too late to properly resist…

Hoodwink had taken the scepter and begun his run down the hallway pointed to him by Gilban. He thought the trek would have taken hours given the seemingly endless expanse of the tunnels, but he soon found himself rising upward in a very short matter of time and then up into what seemed to be a grand hallway decorated with all manner of finery found only in the grand corridors of the gods: riches beyond description.

Here he pushed himself as hard as he could, harder than what he thought he could do to bring himself to the end of of the breathtaking corridor and toward a great door which happened to be slightly ajar. Hoodwink was more than a little thankful for this for he knew if they were closed, his tiny frame wouldn't be able to even impact them in the slightest since they were so large and solid. Squeezing out from between these he made his way into the outside courtyard where the battle between The Master and another party was coming to an end.

He couldn't see this fight, but he could hear it and smell it – electrical heat and blood mingling with the small burning fires and the odor of dying soldiers already present from The Master's arrival. As he grew closer, Hoodwink could make out the form of a winged being lying prone on the ground and the dark god standing over him to gloat. There he was, the enemy to the Pantheon and Tralodren as Gilban had said.

Hoodwink began to move toward the lich when he just as suddenly stopped. The dark god was quickly surrounded by a handful of what the goblin came to understand were other gods of the Pantheon. He watched as they started to fight against him, warring with blades, fists and will. Maybe he didn't need to attack him in the first place. Maybe these other gods would finish him off. But then he wouldn't have a destiny to fulfill if that was the case.

Hoodwink didn't need to dwell much further on that thought as he witnessed all the divine challengers rush toward The Master and fall one by one to his attacks. He'd have to get closer to the fighting if he wanted to us the scepter on The Master, of that much he was certain. As certain of his understanding that he'd only get one good chance to make the most of this scepter and that was it.

He needed to time his attack and plan it out just right...

So he began to sneak his way closer, though he doubted that any one of these giant-sized divinities and strong warriors would notice him pass between them. If not for the height differential, then the fact that all attention was fastened on the battle at hand. As he got closer his stomach backed up into his throat; acidic bile creeping up the back of his tongue.

He watched The Master carefully now, studied him as best he could from between the tall pillars of people comprising the crowded throng he waded through.

Even as he plotted his next course of action Endarien collided with the dark god and sent him skidding down the rocky ground for a fair distance, which actually helped to bring the lich closer to the goblin's location. Here too he waited to make his move as Endarien and Cadrith were preparing to fight one another. Hoodwink had no desire to get into the middle of such an encounter. He'd wait for his moment to arrive, but be prepared when it did.

However, it was then that Gurthghol had arrived and destroyed The Master with what seemed to be simple ease. Hoodwink was breathless at this development, as were many around him. So what did this mean? The threat had been eliminated and without him. This made little sense.

For what seemed like a very long time the goblin could do nothing but keep a tight grip on the scepter and stare at the seated throne before him in fevered contemplation and speculation.

As the gods had their conversation and the Galgalli was healed, Hoodwink watched; heart pounding in his chest. What to do? What to do? He was truly beside himself until he watched in horror and surprise at what Gurthghol started to do next. Hoodwink had to weather the winds that followed by nestling between the strong legs of a divinity, barely keeping himself from being flung away into the sky with the other dead bodies and debris that were being sucked up and tossed heavenward.

When the storm ended he saw Galba standing before Gurthghol. Another figure was with her as well. One that Hoodwink couldn't quite figure out. It was heavily covered with a black cloak. He couldn't hear what was being exchanged before them but he did see Galba's eye turn toward him, could feel himself being sucked into them as she did so. Then he heard her words in his head.

This is the threat.

Hoodwink then understood that she was referring to Gurthghol.

Be ready to strike. You will know the appropriate time.

And shortly after she had spoken to his mind, Hoodwink found himself running forward with all his might focused on putting in a good swing against Gurthghol and completing his destiny…

Hoodwink finished his energized run with a boisterous yell and flying leap which brought him right into the lap of the seated god of chaos at the same time he brought down the scepter with the greatest degree of force he could muster down onto his chest, right over his heart. It happened so quickly that even the gods gathered were amazed at its occurrence. The weapon crafted by Jarl Knorrsen centuries before proved still potent, however, much to Gurthghol's displeasure.

The god of chaos and darkness screamed from the pain of having his very spirit torn away; draining away like an open artery spilling out it's precious cargo. This wrenching cry chilled the heart of the Pantheon who knew what had happened to their kindred deity and wouldn't wish it on any of their number…save The Master.

"Insolent wretch." Gurthghol snarled and snapped through the gnawing pain at Hoodwink who had managed to somersault, with mild success, a short distance from the throne. The goblin looked back into those purple hued black eyes with dread. He had no other options left to him now. The scepter had been used. He just hoped he'd made a wise decision.

"I was so close..." Gurthghol drew his attention back toward Galba and the dark cloaked figure. The beams of light and darkness being sucked into the throne had lessened. He could feel his hold over the throne slipping as more of his will and spirit were reduced. However, the more he tried to pull strength from the throne, the more it seemed he grew weaker. It was as if he was trying to just keep himself alive now from the throne which was trying to suck all of his existence from him.

Gurthghol struggled against the forces trying to devour him and pushed on with his plan, willing the leeching of the two entities to continue. And it did so...for a short burst of time, but then fizzled down to even a thinner trickle of a stream than it had been before.

The aspect of Nuhl laughed in delight. "I may win out yet – I can claim at least one of your number even if my champion failed."

Gurthghol opened his eyes; sweat streaming from his face now as he glared at Hoodwink who had managed to right himself from his recent acrobatic maneuver but remained transfixed, as all the rest were, at the spectacle of the deity in the throne before them. How could he not be so amazed for not only being in the presence of a god in their truest self but also having just been able to strike and even wound one of their number as well.

Gurthghol though was far from impressed with his would be assailant and opened his mouth to belch out a burst of orchid veined, black flame which enveloped the small goblin where he stood.

Hoodwink knew nothing after that moment.

An instant later, only the smoldering scepter remained; rattling on the ground from being rapidly dropped by the goblin who once had held it. While this might have given Gurthghol satisfaction, it didn't do anything for his situation in terms of improving it – he felt weaker still.

"You have made your choice. Gurthghol," said Galba. "You've stolen your father's throne and now have tried to follow in his footsteps at the risk of ripping asunder the whole of the cosmos."

"I've done nothing but attempt to *save* the cosmos from *you*." Gurthghol leaned back in the throne now. He was very weak now. "Tralodren and the Pantheon would have been safe…forever…" It was getting harder to keep consciousness – sheer force to keep his mind focused on the task at hand; to keep himself focused on the matter before him.

"You've made a poor choice." Came back Galba's authoritative words. "You've almost placed Tralodren and all of the Pantheon into the hand of Nuhl by your actions after victory had been achieved."

"Lies." Gurthghol spat. "You…can't hide the truth…my father…my father was on the verge of discovering…" The god of chaos was near the point of delirium as the trickle of light and darkness faded away like spider webs in a strong wind. "…he was going to liberate the cosmos from your tyranny and I was…I am going to bring his desire to pass."

"Shall I show you truth?" Nuhl's aspect mocked the ailing, enthroned god. From out of the folds of the thick, draping cloak a black, gelatinous, tentacle shot out to wrap itself around the throne and its occupant. The tentacle was covered in hundreds of tiny, white toothed maws which opened and closed hungrily to reveal rows of razor sharp teeth.

"Him only." Galba raised a hand of warding. "My champion won the day. Yours has lost."

"Agreed." Answered both the many mouths of the tentacle and the voice from under the hood of Nuhl's aspect in unison.

"I still have the throne." Gurthghol was weak still, but had at least stopped getting weaker. He was still struck by why the throne was failing him, why it didn't augment his abilities any more as he knew it should, even if he'd been struck by that accursed scepter. What was happening? It was harder for him to think clearly, harder to reason out what he could do let alone should do.

"You can't harm me–" Gurthghol began to say.

"We shall see." The aspect of Nuhl's voice was delighted.

Gurthghol roared in rage as the tentacle enlarged itself so as to envelope the whole of the throne, hiding both the throne and its occupant from sight by forming a coal hued globe about the object and occupant. This globe was then drawn toward the cloaked being like molasses or a puddle of ink being poured out onto the rocky earth. The mouths then started to twitch and chomp amid their swarthy drool as the globe grew smaller and smaller until it fit quite easily into and under the cloak of Nuhl's representative. The chattering of those teeth as this all took place was like a march of insects all over the flesh of those present causing everyone who heard it to shudder in disgust. When the opening of the cloak closed, the tentacle and what it had ensnared were no longer seen.

"Tralodren and your Pantheon is safe from harm once more." Galba raised her hand to the sky and there was a bright flash of light, then the two entities were gone. In their passing the sky was returned to normal and all was as it had been before their appearance, save the still smoldering silver scepter and the absence of both the throne and Gurthghol.

Chapter 41

The gods were silent now as they contemplated what had just happened before them. It had occurred so fast and yet had been so filled with activity that each had to process it in their own way. They had seen Gurthghol appear not only on the throne of Vkar, but also saw him use it to try and destroy the two primordial entities. These same beings had destroyed him...or taken him away (the majority of the unspoken conscious was thought that the plum skinned god wasn't coming back). But the strangest of all was the goblin and the silver scepter he'd wielded against Gurthghol to weaken him. The silver scepter which still smoked away near where the goblin had once stood.

"What just happened?" Endarien turned to Saredhel, which was quickly duplicated by all the rest of the Pantheon. The divinities and warriors of the gods simply focused on the spot where the throne had just been moments ago.

Saredhel words were but a few, and those tossed out like dead embers. "A sacrifice was made."

"*Two* sacrifices were made." Panthor corrected. "That goblin–"

"He did his task well." Saredhel nodded slightly in approval.

"What is going on here?" Perlosa's cold sneer was more twisted than usual in her frustration at feeling as if she were being left in the dark on some matter. "It sounds like plotting behind our backs."

"Since when is that new to you?" Rheminas glared at his sister who merely rebuffed his comment by turning up her nose. "I want to know why Gurthghol took the throne – that was *the* throne wasn't it? Not some trick of his."

"It was authentic." Dradin settled the doubt, but escalated the worried uncertainty in their number.

"Oh, what has he done?" Asora lowered her eyes and wrung her hands as she pondered aloud.

"Saved us it looks like." Drued's pragmatism was voiced.

"By trying to kill us all first." Aero griped.

"We wouldn't be in this mess if Saredhel had just told us what we needed to know." Perlosa's haughty lips fluttered over pearl-like teeth.

"I said what was needed to be heard." The white cowled goddess responded with a calm voice.

"Of course." Asorlok sneered. "But what now? What will become of the Pantheon in his absence?"

"*Absence?*" Khuthon was intrigued. "He's not dead then?"

"I haven't felt him cross over yet, no." Asorlok sheathed his weapon as he spoke. "But that doesn't mean he won't in time either."

"At any rate." Rheminas started into the conversation. "This has changed things."

"Yes," Khuthon stroked his tough patch of chin hair. "The balance of power has shifted."

"I don't believe it has." Olthon faced her brother's question.

"He's not here." Khuthon bristled under his sister's comment. He'd been one god who had always had his eye on leading the Pantheon, but he'd settle for being the head of the dark gods if he couldn't reach the former aspiration just yet. "He's probably dead or in the very least imprisoned somewhere so what can we do for him?"

"Nothing." The god of war answered himself.

"If he's not dead, then he's still on the throne." Olthon let her gaze fall over all the others gathered, "and is still more powerful than any of us."

"He didn't look that strong after that goblin, " Rheminas gestured to where the still hot, but no longer silver scepter rested for further emphasis, "attacked him with that scepter."

"This matter needs to be discussed." Dradin was staring rubbing his beard in thought, "That much I do know."

"Agreed." Ganatar nodded. "That doesn't mean, however, things have changed or that they will." Ganatar cautioned all present. "But we will need to discuss this matter and redefine the rules of the previous council now that Galba is gone and we have broken our own rules by making Thangaria a battlefield as well as having Vkar's throne recently lost from us."

"And then there is the matter of the scepter to discuss," Dradin added.

Drued sheathed his axe. "So we better get to that table then and discuss all this, for I've a realm to sort out and warriors to bury."

"We all have much to do but this has to come first. The order we have established between us and preserving it for the time to come must be our chief concern," said Ganatar.

"That's it then?" Panthor was confused and upset. "We're just going to leave Gurthghol–" she stopped herself when she realized the next phrase she was going to say.

"To his own fate?" Olthon finished Panthor's statement.

"But he's part of your family." Panthor lowered her head in a reflection of the loss that had transpired.

"He made a choice." Saredhel calmly replied to Panthor's troubled face.

"And he is stuck with the consequences of his actions until we can find some remedy." Ganatar put his hand to the pommel of his sheathed sword.

"So you're still going to help him then?" Panthor's eyes brightened.

"Some consequences are easier than others to endure." The flat words of the god of order dimmed those same eyes.

"So let's get started then." Endarien flapped his wings and then lifted off into the air on route to their meeting room inside the hall. In passing he found one of his servants who yet lived, a high priest of his worship when he was a mortal man, and ordered him by mental command to give aid to Cadrissa – the Storm Lord hated unfulfilled obligations.

"The sooner the better." Rheminas added and then turned to follow after his cousin. "By the time we're done this place should be cleaned up and the troops sent home."

The others of the Pantheon slowly followed suit, leaving the Galgalli alone for a moment to watch them go. "So what happens now?" Dugan asked Asora as he stood by feeling a bit out of place now after his task had been performed.

"That is for the council to talk about." The goddess of life had already started to make her way toward the hall along with the other gods. "For now you must return to Helii and take some rest, you're earned it." Like a silent funerary procession the rest of the gods made their way toward the hall for another council and more debate.

"And the scepter?" Dugan asked after her. "What do you think should be done with it?"

"We'll keep it well guarded." Dugan looked beside him to see two Guardians, one of them, the one who had spoken, holding the object already in hand. Dugan looked back to the departing gods to try and get their answer to this but found they had already left.

"The Pantheon would prefer us to keep it." The Guardian holding the scepter continued to speak. "We are the most trusted divinities in all the cosmos and have served them well for eons already. It is our calling, as I'm sure you are now fully aware of yours."

Dugan said nothing, merely nodded.

The two Guardians vanished in a flash of white light leaving Dugan alone with his thoughts, the still-smouldering rubble and the broken masses being collected to their own.

Chapter 42

Rowan was lost in a sleepy gaze at his shield. The images of the two dragon heads drew what little concentration he had left. He had removed it from his back and set it down not too far from where he had lain the body of Clara, sword next to the shield. He'd managed to find some shelter, a small, stone stable of some type where he had seen fit to lay the dead elf beside an elderly, empty trough.

It seemed like he had been sitting and staring at the shield for hours. He hadn't heard the clash of Dugan and Cadrith, nor the final demise of a dark god and Gurthghol's judgment. The whole world had been pushed away in favor of his internal landscape which was darker than even The Master could have wished upon his foes.

Cadrissa rested her hand upon Rowan's knee. The action woke him from his daydream and turned him toward the smiling mage's face. She had been the first to find the stable and rest inside after running to it when the fighting had grown more intense. She may have been curious but not even her curiosity could have urged her into the great hall. Instead she motioned the young knight inside as he passed by with Clara's body and allowed him to unload his burdens.

She *had* heard the crashing sounds of combat, the shaking explosions and dreaded them. Fearful for her life, she had little cause for exhalation when the sounds of combat ceased. Rather, she felt the uncertainty of the situation call to mind a dark reality to come. What had they gotten into and why? What was the meaning to all this madness? She thought she had known before, but it all seemed to melt away in comparison with this…

Then there was the guilt and fear she felt over what the medallion had done to her – what it had made her do as well as revealed to her about herself…

"Rowan?" Cadrissa quietly questioned the knight.

He didn't respond, only continued to stare at the shield as he had since he put it down. Cadrissa could do nothing but watch with some sorrow of her own. She had a hint of what Rowan was going through based upon what she had felt with Dugan's death, but didn't dare say she knew *exactly* what he felt because both he and Clara had been able to express their feelings to each other since they met. A relationship had developed in the mage's absence and blossomed far beyond the mere bud of infatuation as had been the case with her and Dugan. She didn't know how to comfort him either. Near the point of numbness on all fronts from being assaulted from possession to worse, she knew that she'd be little help to Rowan now, let alone a sturdy shoulder to rest upon at the moment. If anything, she might choke him with the dark clouds hanging about her head.

Rowan tried to drown out his thoughts – drive them all away like a wolf scattering a flock of sheep, but he wasn't that successful with the encounter with Clara. Having her tell him those things, about herself and about their budding relationship…it was the worst blow of all. To lose the one you loved and then hear them say that your love wasn't real after all was a terrible, terrible wound to be dealt. 'The strike of a friend wounds deepest of all' the skalds said. He supposed it was doubly true in matters of love.

But it wasn't just love was it? No, he was a man with a divided mind – divided opinions. He had left to the southern lands on a mission with the most organized and strongest of beliefs in himself, his race, his goddess, his order…all that had gone now. Now he was uncertain and fractured. Nothing made any sense anymore. Told by his own goddess that the order he served was a lie, shown by Nabu and Clara that he had been indoctrinated to hate the elven race, and now told that even the woman who he thought he loved and loved him wasn't even of the same mind after all…well, it was far from good.

"She was right." Rowan barely muttered beneath his breath.

Cadrissa was going to say something, but caught herself when she realized the knight had to speak to help himself through this whole mess. The young man had come to an epiphany of sorts, from somewhere deep inside himself he felt like some inner truth on some matter had come to light now. Whether it had been through his brooding musings or the past few months on his journey up to this point he wasn't sure…he just knew that it was true.

"*I* didn't love her either." The words came easier now and more audible too. "I never did love *her*, just what she *stood* for."

Cadrissa listened in wonder. Her hand was still on his leg, and she kept it there to let the youth have some form of compassion, meager though her offer might be. And she kept it there when the tears started to pour from the Nordicans's face; shoulders arching forward and body slouched into a near fetal position from where he sat on an empty stone block beside a row of spartan stone stalls.

Rowan let himself go then. He let out the pain and the fear, the confusion and hurt – let it flow from his eyes and find expression in his shaking sobs. He had lost all of whom he thought he was, all he thought he had been.

It was all a lie, all of it. From the faith of the Knighthood he'd come to embrace, the woman he thought he had loved…maybe even his faith in Panthor herself…

Where could he go now?

Where *would* he go?

Why go anywhere at all when he could just die right here? If he had a purpose, a great purpose like Panthor had said, he didn't see it now. He didn't see how any of this, let alone him could be pulled together for some higher calling of sorts when all he had to work was a bunch of half-truths and lies. She hadn't even tried to speak to him or come to his aid when he had prayed for her aid in healing Clara.

He didn't know how long he cried but he did know that Cadrissa never left his side. With her hand, which had moved on to his back, the knight knew that she had stayed with him until the tears ran dry and sobbing subsided – until he felt empty of all his doubts…and hopes.

"So this is the end?" His red rimmed eyes found the mage's own slick green pools.

"It is the end of something." She replied in half-hearted hope for she didn't know what had happened outside the stable walls. "But it isn't our end."

"Not yet." Rowan coated the room with some of his Nordic pessimism.

"If the gods had fallen, I think we would have know about it by now." She dared another simple smile.

It made Rowan grin weakly himself. "I suppose you're right."

The knight stood up then, stretching his back as he did so. He didn't realize how sore he was. He must have been sitting down hunched over for longer than he thought. Then he recalled the long run through the forest of Arid Land, the battle with The Master at Galba, the trek in Frigia and understood he'd waged a very tough campaign against himself in a very short span of time.

"What about you?" Cadrissa grew concerned.

Rowan's weak grin melted away into a stoic face. "I'll survive."

"That's not what I meant." Cadrissa pushed the matter.

Rowan looked away toward the entrance of the stable.

Cadrissa got the message.

"Do you think we should step out and see what happened?" The knight kept his gaze hard upon the door.

Cadrissa sighed, running a hand through her dark tresses. "We can't stay in here forever." She made her way outside the stone stable, the knight close behind her leaving his sword and shield behind with Clara.

Outside the stable was silence and stillness. Thangaria had returned to the dead chunk of rock it had been before. Here and there dotted with the thin spires of fading fire and a spattering of debris near the opening of the courtyard, Rowan and Cadrissa could clearly see the warriors who hadn't fallen tending to those who had; aiding those who were wounded.

Much of the shattered gate had been piled into two cairn-like mounds of stone, twisted, burnt metal and other bric-a-brac. Neither Cadrissa, nor Rowan saw the gods in their private circle around the spot where Gurthghol had recently resided, nor could they see them retreat back to the hall for another council. To their mortal eyes they could see only the assembled warriors milling about, the cooled pools of blood and those working on cleaning them up.

The battle was over.

"Did *we* win?" Rowan's words hovered in the air.

"Depends on who *we* is." The mage continued to survey the scene. "If you mean the *Pantheon* I would say yes, given the fact that this place still exists and these warriors are dealing with the dead."

"It's a pretty hollow feeling, *victory*," said the knight.

"But Tralodren has been saved. That's a prize worth fighting for." The mage tried to bring some higher spirits to the discussion.

"But we didn't really fight." Rowan's arms crossed now as he turned back around to face the hall where the gods had been gathered. "*They* did all the fighting as we were led around like trained dogs to perform their various errands or play in their unknowable games for some pointless sport. This whole road we've been forced to take has led us around to a dead end. After all this, what do we have to show for it?"

"We have our lives." Cadrissa was soft spoken in her answer.

"But nothing to live for anymore." Rowan's pessimism countered. "It's all been tarnished or torn – all of what we held dear."

"We've all lost something Rowan." Cadrissa turned the knight roughly around to face him. "We've all suffered. Now are you going to let the bad out weigh the good here because the Rowan I got to know and the Rowan I saw before we came here wanted to believe in something greater than himself, something good in himself, in others and in the cosmos."

"If you turn from that now, if you turn from who you are, then you've lost everything and you have no hope and might as well just crawl back in that stable and lay down beside Clara."

Rowan bristled with her analogy, but Cadrissa wouldn't let him speak. No, not yet. She had to have this said and she knew Rowan needed to hear it.

"Have we been used like pawns? Yes. Have we had to suffer much to bring about this end? Yes. It hasn't been easy, but don't destroy who you are Rowan. Not now, not after what you've been through. You did what you came to do: you stopped the information in Takta Lu Lama from falling into the hands of the Elyellium, and you rescued me from The Master."

"You've done what you came to do, now go back home and heal and grow up into the man you need to be. Don't throw away what Clara saw as the good in you, and what I and the rest of us respected about you. Just go home and heal and grow…" Cadrissa came back to herself then as if she didn't know the depths of her own words being spoken until just then and felt very amazed at having said them as well as the effect brought about on the already troubled Nordican.

Rowan let out a deep, body shuddering sigh then rested his troubled mind to return his face to the mage. "Where did that come from?"

"I don't know…but it's the truth." She blushed from her own force of words, but was happy to see they had done and were doing their work.

Rowan said nothing, only nodded slowly.

"I have to at least own up to my duty, my obligations." The knight responded. "I've always known that in my heart, but didn't know how I could after everything I've learned and gone through. I suppose it's best to at least put forth the effort and do my best at what needs to be done, regardless of how it turns out, and then move on with my life as best I can after that."

"Now that sounds like the Rowan I've come to know." Cadrissa's smile widened.

"What about you then?" Rowan asked. "What are you going to do now?"

Cadrissa absentmindedly began to reach for the now missing medallion around her neck and stopped herself in mid-action when she realized what she was doing, returning her hand to rest beside her…"I suppose go back to Elandor and retrieve my books I have stored there – if they're still there, that is, and then I guess decide what do to do after that. Probably rest for a while too. Now that the medallion is gone, I'm finally feeling how weak and worn out I am."

As they spoke a wind picked up and centered behind them in a whirlwind which revealed a new figure which took an immediate notice of their visitor. Both of them turned to see a middle aged Telborian man with the priestly robes of an Endari, a follower of Endarien, shuffling in the wind as he bowed in greeting to the pair. His long smoky white moustache curled at the end of his chin, framed his smiling in soft, regal splendor.

"Greetings." His voice was boisterous and welcoming.

"Hello." Cadrissa answered hesitantly. Rowan remained suspicious as well and wished he had his sword in hand as he felt naked before this new figure, no matter how peaceful he seemed to be.

"What can we do for you?" Rowan politely asked, though the politeness had to be forced.

The priest's greenish-gray eyes sparkled with blue sparks in amusement. "Peace, sir knight, I mean you no harm." He turned his head toward Cadrissa, letting the present light reveal the silver highlights in his gunmetal gray locks augment his overall appearance with a sense of fatherly maturity. "Nor her either."

Rowan kept his eyes on the quiver on the figure's pack filled with golden javelins and the silver war hammer dangling from his gray leather belt.

The priest followed Rowan's eyes and laughed a gusty wind of mirth. "Still have not won your trust I see. I am Bran," he bowed again in greeting, "high priest of Endarien."

"What do you want?" Rowan was unimpressed with the title or name but was a little more comfortable with the priest's disposition after this introduction; impoliteness faded away as well from his words.

"I've been sent by Endarien to help you get back to Tralodren." The priest grinned, then turned to Cadrissa. "It seems the Storm Lord owes you a favor that he has yet to repay."

The wizardress smirked. "I thought he wasn't going to honor his word."

"On the contrary, Endarien was severely distracted at that moment when you needed him and by the time he could come to your aid he was unable for you were in the clutches of another force greater than he."

"That dark pit…" Cadrissa said to herself then shuddered at the memory of the place.

"Indeed." Bran comfirmed the mage's memory.

"I have griffins standing at the ready to take you to wherever you wish to go. Compliments of my god for a debt repaid."

"*Griffins?*" Cadrissa's face lightened at the word. "I've never seen one before."

"Well, you can get to see two of them up close." Bran beamed in amusement at the mage's excited curiosity.

"I'll have to get my things first," said Rowan.

"Your mount will be here and waiting for you when you return." Bran cheerily replied.

"So then it *is* really over then?" Cadrissa asked Bran as Rowan made his way back to the stable. A seriousness returned to her face for a moment as she wanted to know this part of her life was over so she could move on to form a new existence in the days ahead. "Our quest or whatever it was we were called to do is done now?"

"Yes. The Master is defeated as is his patron." Bran said with a stoic face.

"So what happened to the scepter?" Cadrissa's heart skipped a beat when she mentioned the object; hopeful that she might get to at least take something back with her to make this whole ordeal worthwhile. She would love to study it more closely, learn from it and increase her insights so as to travel further along the Path of Knowledge. At least that was what she told herself. She didn't want to acknowledge the hidden hunger deep within crying for something else...

"That I don't know and it's not our place to know," said Bran. "I can say with some confidence though that it won't be found on Tralodren ever again that is for sure."

"Probably for the best." Cadrissa felt the butterflies flutter out of her stomach with the statement; a release of something addictive from her system by the priest's statement.

"Indeed, as is your getting back to where *you* belong. So are you ready to leave then?" The priest waved his hand behind him in invitation. "I have the griffins waiting."

"I want to wait to say good bye to Rowan." Cadrissa tried to contain the excitement welling up inside her from seeing such a fantastic beast as a griffin. She still wanted to make sure Rowan would be okay before she left. The mage couldn't be distracted too much before then as she knew she might be lost in her curiosity to even pay the knight any mind at all.

"But I'd love to have a peek while I'm waiting." Okay, maybe she could allow herself some degree of distraction...for the moment.

Bran smiled with a nod. "Sure. You'll find they're not as frightening as some tales would have your believe..." Bran lead the mage over to the beasts.

While Cadrissa spoke with the priest of Endarien, Rowan had made his way inside the stable. Immediately setting his sights on Clara's body, he made his way toward it and his shield and sword thoughtfully. Impressed and amazed by the words Cadrissa had spoken to him, he knew that what he had to do – what he should do, wouldn't be easy. Now was the time of hard choices and he had to make them or be under their heel for the rest of his life as they crushed all the life out of him. That was part of being a man – being mature in understanding his obligations and responsibilities.

He had two pictures of who he was: one of how he was and one of how he could be if he so chose. The choice though was where the strife would lie, the real maelstrom brewing that he had to face. Could he make the right choice though and do what he believed to be right, even if he would be standing in opposition to his very culture and Knighthood? Did he have the strength to make and stick with that decision?

Rowan picked up his items and returned them to his person then looked back down at the peaceful face of Clara. Though it was bloody and empty of life the once sparkling beauty she possessed still remained in faint echo about her frame. He would miss her, but not in the sense that he thought he once would – not after he'd discovered the source of his previous emotions…

He was startled by the low growl of a gray panther that had suddenly appeared to recline on the same stone block Rowan had rested on just a few moments ago. He looked at it with some apprehension, but the great cat was passive, greeting him with a tongue-stretching yawn.

You have done much.

Rowan looked above and around himself to find the source of Panthor's voice. He was unsuccessful as it continued in his head.

I am proud of you for your journey. You've come so far and learned so much and the trial is almost over.

"Almost over?" Rowan asked the roof of the stable.

When you have returned home and made your stand in the decision for whom you are going to be, what you're going to believe, then the final test will be over and you shall be able to enter in to what I have made ready for you.

You will then be ready to take hold of your destiny and the purpose I have called you to.

"But why did this all have to happen?" Rowan focused again at Clara.

"Why Clara?"

You were called away from your world to another to see the truth and be released from the false things which held you fast. You've been given a choice now to be able to see two realities and to embrace one over the other.

There was no other way to strip away these things from you and give you sight to see the truth of the matter to make a truly informed decision.

"The three tests of the dedication." Rowan turned to tell the panther on the stone slab who was now licking its paws.

The three tests will be completed upon your return to Valkoria.

"Why didn't you answer my prayer? You let Clara die."

I could do nothing more for her than the Lord of Life who had come to your aid. I heard your prayer Rowan, but her time had come.

Rowan took a moment to let that reality sink deeper into his person; traveling from his head to his heart. When it had finished that journey he could see things clearer and actually let more of the whole situation go, freeing himself up from what was really entangling him from moving forward.

"I still can't see the wisdom in not letting her live, even if we figured out we weren't for each other, but I suppose that was all part of the process to get me to see." The emotions were still raw on the matter, but the knight managed to hold his pain in check; his tears back from sore eyes.

I cannot take someone back from Asorlok's grip when their time has come. It would take a being mightier than I to do that. So take heart in the understanding that it was her appointed time and it was natural if not at least in how it was brought about but in the fact that it came to her. Then take the next step into your destiny.

"I don't know if I can do what I need to do." Rowan confessed to the panther who stopped to look up at him with its strangely intelligent yellow eyes. "I don't even know what to believe about anything anymore, even you."

Let me be your strength. The goddess' words caressed his troubled thoughts. *Let me guide you. Have faith that I will direct you to where you need to be and move you into the places where you will come into yourself and true potential.*

Don't take more than a few steps at a time and I will guide you if you let me. Panthor's words did much to calm the knight's thoughts, but some still lingered.

"But what about Clara's body?"

The panther looked toward the dead elf then with ponderous eyes.

She has passed on to her own end. Where you are headed though, should you so choose, you can't take her with you. You're going to have to leave a lot behind and let go of much if you wish to follow through in the harder, but more rewarding of the two choices.

One of the things you will have to let go of will be Clara. Though you have seen now the truth of your affection for her, you have to leave her body behind. It can't go with you.

"What will happen to it then?" The knight took one more deep gaze at the corpse.

It will be returned to her family and homeland, get the proper burial and her life honored as it should be. That is a journey outside of you though Rowan–

"I have to let it go." He finished Panthor's statement.

He took one more look at the corpse, sighed, then turned back to the panther. "What's waiting for me if I stand by the harder choice?" He asked the great gray cat. The feline did nothing but roll its eyes up at him letting its head stay to rest over its two crossed front paws.

More than you can possibly imagine. Came the goddess' reply.

What you saw at Galba is just a taste of what is in store for you if you would let me guide you into your future. I have a plan for the human race which has yet to be realized and the time to bring it about has finally come and you are the one who would be able to carry it out.

You will see much before you die if you follow the harder path. You'll witness many amazing things and see a land rebuilt and a world reforged but only if you make the choice to stand firm in your decision of your faith for and in me to bring this all about and keep you safe in it.

Rowan dropped to his knee beside the panther. "Forgive me Panthor."

There is nothing to forgive, Rowan. Your heart has been pure from the beginning and though your mind had become and still is a bit troubled, you still remained true to me throughout it all.

"But I questioned you," Rowan keep his head low, "I doubted you."

But you didn't leave me. Even your challenged faith in me was still able to help you in spite of it all…in spite of the prayer I didn't answer for Clara.

So what have you decided then Rowan?

Which are you going to chose?

What life are you going to lead?

Rowan remained on his knee as he thought. It really wasn't much of a tough matter to decide, however, and he found the choice quite naturally once he let himself choose with his heart.

"I can't go back to how I was after what I've seen and heard and now understand."

Then rise and return to Valkoria and claim your destiny which awaits you there.

Rowan arose. "Will I still be able to speak to you as we are now?"

I will be just as close to you as now, guiding you and helping you as you take on this purpose I have waiting for you.

Rowan than made his way out of the stable, stopping to turn back to look inside one last time before he left.

"Goodbye Clara." Rowan held back the lump in his throat. It still wasn't that easy to say goodbye, but it was getting easier as the minutes passed. "I pray you've found peace and happiness and love wherever you are." The knight then left the stable, and walked toward the griffins that waited for him to fly away into his future destiny.

Epilogue

"But all endings are also beginnings.
We just don't know it at the time."

Mitch Albom
The Five People You Meet In Heaven
pg. 1 line 3-4

1

It was toward nightfall when the lone dwarven male dared peer inside the lair of Cael. The cool, snippy air already had chilled much of the day's former warmth away and the young man shivered a bit from the declining temperature. His shiver was intensified as well by his location, though he didn't want to think too much upon that.

His white knuckles were clamped tight upon the handle of a strong mace. Better just to get in, do what he had to do and get out once more. Never mind that he was closer to the foul Troll's lair than he wanted to be. No, just look inside and see what he could see then return back to report to the clan.

The young dwarf was just old enough to grow a beard and had entered the first year of his adult life, and so it was a rite of passage in a way that called him to his present task. Once he got back to the council he wouldn't have to worry about the Troll...at least for a while. While many didn't think Vinder would survive his ordeal, there were a few who held out hope of him at least being able to make it out with most of his body still intact. These were his family of course, but many didn't know how well one dwarf could do in standing before the onslaught of the deadly and dangerous Cael.

This young dwarf though was about to find out...

He had made it around the opening of the cave and managed to slide his face inside to scope around the lair without any incident, though his chest heaved and heart rang truer than a forge's anvil now from his cheeks and neck. His eyes quickly adjusted to the dim, rocky interior and soon he could pick out the bones littering the floor.

At first he didn't know what to think of them. They could have been from anything – including the remains of Cael's last meal. The longer he gazed upon them though, the clearer they became to him in shape. Quite rapidly he was able to discern a familiar form. They were a Troll's bones! Astonished by the discovery, the young dwarf dared a step further inside.

Could this be some rival Troll Cael slew?

Hunched over with spring loaded legs, ready to dash up and away at the first sign of trouble, he inched deeper into the lair. Seeing nothing leap out at him, sparked up some courage, which soon kindled a tiny flame that moved him still deeper into the cave. When he reached the bones, he looked around the whole cave once more; scanning it in a panoramic sweep, then turned to the skeletal remains. If Cael should jump out now he would have little to defend himself with, save his mace and fright. Not the best of weapons, and so the young dwarf prayed for Drued to keep him safe a little while longer.

It wasn't until he got to the bones that he finally saw Vinder's corpse turned toward the skeleton – axe blade cleft into the vertebrae of the slain giant. The head of the Troll lay a little bit away from where the blow was dealt, but the image was clear enough. However this battle may have been fought, Vinder clearly managed to kill Cael, though he died in the process.

Though how Vinder had done this was beyond the youth. He had never known of a way to kill anything that left it devoid of its flesh and blood. Perhaps Trolls were different than other creatures, and upon death they shed all of their flesh save their bones. There wasn't anything which he knew of that spoke of this *not* being the case.

Be that as it may, Vinder, one lone dwarf, had stood up against Cael and regained not only his own honor, but elevated his family and safe guarded his clan from any further attacks the giant would have made against them. He would be remembered always as a hero – a man of superhuman abilities. The bards would surely tell tales about him for generations to come. This was a feat few lone dwarves could ever hope to achieve. Vinder may not have been able to enjoy his reclaimed honor, but certainly his family's honor had been restored for all time because of his deed.

The young dwarf dropped to his knee and maneuvered Vinder toward his back with a gentle push. Clearing the stray hairs from his cold face and beard, he smoothed them about to make him more presentable to those who would later come to pay him homage. Hefting up Vinder's axe, the dwarf placed it over Vinder's chest and then arranged his hands around it to hold it fast. A little more adjusting of his outfit and a few more gray strands of hair finally satisfied the younger dwarf.

He stopped for a moment when he noticed the small icon of Drued attached to a necklace Vinder wore about his neck. It seemed somehow fitting that he should wear it and so the young dwarf arranged the necklace neatly about Vinder's throat; the icon resting across the top of his hands as they gripped the hilt of the axe.

Stepping back, he looked over the figure. It seemed to be missing something…After a moment he knew what it was and picked up Cael's skull to place it beneath Vinder's feet. Satisfied, he smiled a stoic stretch of gray lips.

"Rest well honorable warrior."

With a nod he left the scene and made his way back to the clan where he would soon be followed again, he was sure, by a large portion of, if not all the clan itself to see the spectacle of Vinder's redemption. Behind him the battle scarred dwarf seemed to slumber in a fitful peace as the dark silence of night fell over the Diamant Mountains.

2

The sun was bleeding away in the wintry sky when Rowan reached the outskirts of the clearing that surrounded the Knighthood's keep. The griffin brought him to a remote enough location to keep his landing from any prying eyes of the watch or nearby folk. Having such a beast drop him off would have caused more of a stir than he would have wanted. Given that he figured the Frost Giant would have made it back before him and in the very least, told about his refusal to board. In the very worst, reported him back to his superiors as an elf lover. He had enough to report as it was and didn't need the added weight of explanations.

The trip had been very short though. He hadn't known just how far or fast they had flown, but it seemed only hours until he found his way from Thangaria to the shores of Valkoria. He supposed that was a good thing too since it wouldn't make him even more delayed for his report. At this point, he was a good ways out from when he was expected to report in and his time would have to be accounted for as best as he could. Rowan wouldn't – couldn't – lie, he just had to stand up for the life he had chosen for himself.

He had made up his mind on the journey over after the brief and awkward goodbye between him and Cadrissa. He didn't know what to say to her at all. He'd known her, but not as well as the others, and it showed when they parted. For her part, Cadrissa managed well. For all the knight supposed she'd been through she seemed able-bodied and healthy of mind, if not so much so in spirit. Though what she must have been going through inside after her ordeals Rowan was far from even waging a guess. He knew it wasn't anything good, he could be sure of that much at least.

The mage wished him well and then asked what he would do with Clara's body. After telling her it was taken care of, she let the matter die. He supposed he'd never see Cadrissa again. Their paths had finally unraveled the great ball of yarn that had bound them before. He was just glad he had been able to rescue her. He didn't want to think what could have occurred to her if she'd been left to her own devices. At least he had been faithful to the cause he'd sent out to maintain when he'd left Valkoria in the first place.

Coming home again revealed to him just how little had changed. The keep and the area around it was as he remembered it all those months ago before he set out to take on his mission – his first mission for his Knighthood. Perlosa, it seemed had come to quickly grab hold of the land with a tight grip, piling up dunes of snow here and there amid his path. The snow was a bit earlier than expected but not unusual from the cycle of years past where the Queen of Frost was known to visit a bit earlier at times than expected.

Rowan didn't dwell upon the early snows, his mind was elsewhere. He had changed and had decided to follow that change through to reach the destiny his goddess had for him. The young knight felt somehow *seasoned* – like his leather armor was broken in more than when he'd first left – more like something of his old self had passed away to be replaced with something different that was now at work defining his character.

Because of this he seemed out of place in the terrain. Not only because he wasn't dressed that well for the weather and most of his equipment he'd left with had been lost, but he somehow carried himself different than his peers. At least Rowan thought so, and felt so. He had seen more than most of his kinsman, even his fellow knights and he was still only a dedicate. He had gone through so much emotionally and spiritually as well. Was this the measure of manhood: how much one has endured? If so, then Rowan felt that he indeed had grown up considerably. But what would he report about all this though?

What could he?

He didn't want to tell more than he had to, that much was certain. He already had hidden the panther paw amulet under his armor to stymie any questions it might cause to arise. He wouldn't lie, that much was for certain, but did he really have to tell Journey Knight Fronel all that had transpired? His meeting of Clara? The battle with The Master? That hadn't been part of his mission. A sidetrek of it perhaps true, but not the true objective for why he had been sent back...After all how could he tell it all to his superior? How would he understand what had just happened to the youth? How would he react if Rowan told him Panthor herself had told him the real story of the Knighthood and that he now believed she had called him to some great destiny?

Was that right to withhold all this though? Was partial truth regarding these matters the best truth? None of the knights knew their age old moorings, he was sure of it. Had they known the nature by which the institution was founded he was sure many knights – and perhaps even priests might start to have some serious doubts. Should he allow those doubts to enter into the order? These were challenging matters with which to contend in thought – matters he wouldn't have been able to grapple with had he been the boy of his earlier departure still.

You're a man now Rowan, he heard his father's voice in his mind, *and a man's world looks much different from a child's.*

Rowan sighed from the heavy weights of his thoughts as he spied the thick walls of the keep, standing like some dominate giant over the flat plain area not far from the coast. Rowan used to listen to the sluggish, frigid waves, smelled the salty air and felt the cold moist air dig into his joints and flesh. Rowan looked up at the thick oaken doors shod with iron; latched in the finest steel. They covered an opening large enough for two mounted men to comfortably enter side by side. Latched and bolted from the inside, amid the granite walls the keep was impregnable.

The snow had been cleared away from the outside of these doors and nearby roads so the Knighthood could function and do their duties should they be needed in a moments notice. Rowan found himself recalling how he'd been put in charge of keeping the roadway clear one winter soon after his admittance into the Knighthood. Though it brought back a good reflection to him, the knight now found the thought flat and hallow. In fact the whole Knighthood seemed hollow to him, and he found himself wondering if this was really for him now – what he was doing here.

The final test.

It was the one thing to which he clung to and anchored his faith. This was the last test from his goddess. He wanted to – had to – pass the final of the three tests if he really wanted to come into what Panthor had for him, or so he believed. He just prayed it was worth it and sighed, resigning himself to the situation at hand.

A watchman on the wall overlooking the plain below looked down at Rowan as he approached. He had watched him advance in wonder since the knight wasn't dressed that wisely for the season. The watchmen also hadn't seen any vessels come to dock recently, though few would if any – even if this was the mildest part of the upcoming winter.

"Halt. Who goes there?" The watchman was a dedicate, and not much younger than Rowan if he could judge the voice and frame of the watchman from his elevated distance.

"Rowan Cortak, Knight of Valkoria. I've come to report back to Journey Knight Fronel in regards to the mission from which I've just returned."

The younger knight didn't respond, instead turning around behind himself and motioning to men below to open the door to the keep. In a moment a large clank was heard, then the doors opened into the keep, the knight on the wall welcoming him inside.

"Welcome back Sir Cortak. It is good to have you here safe and sound. I'll notify Journey Knight Fronel of your arrival."

"Thank you." Rowan entered into the keep, and the familiar life he had left behind when the world seemed smaller and not so confusing. Taking a calming breath Rowan walked inside the world he now knew to be a shadow. A shadowy world which he waded through in pursuit of the gleaming brilliance of truth which resided at the end of his path.

Rowan quietly walked through the warm halls of his order. Decorated in wool tapestries depicting famed battles of the Knighthood along with stone carved busts of past Grand Champions, heroes of the order and High Fathers. Where as he had nearly idolized these busts before; been fed on their tales while he was trained, he now found himself wondering which of them might have known the real history and purpose of the institution.

Panthers also made their appearances in the corridors and elsewhere throughout the keep. Whether they were sleek onyx statuary, stuffed panthers themselves or even stylized mosaics and paintings cluttering the walls, ceilings and even floors, the eyes of his tribes totem as well as his goddess' symbol watched him as he neared the office of Journey Knight Fronel.

He had decided to be truthful in his answers to Fronel. He wouldn't say anything more than what he was asked. That sounded fair, and in truth, honest enough. It wasn't breaking the Code, which he still honored, for it was tied to his faith more than his order he believed, but getting very close to bending it. He'd have to be careful of the fine line he was setting himself up to walk.

Part of the change that had overcome him from his travel experiences was a new sense of boldness which came from knowing a little better who he was. In a way he had to leave all that he knew to find all he was capable of being, and in turn, find himself. While it sounded like something a skald might say, it was true. Rowan had done more in this one adventurous trip down south than he knew any of his tribesman had done in their lives. For that he felt proud and worthy of the mantle of manhood he now felt himself growing into.

The knight thought back to a time not too long ago when he had walked this same corridor, not more than two hundred feet from the great hall where he had been inducted into the Knighthood, more than five months ago. Approaching from the opposite side, he still felt a sense of completion as he neared the office; a sense that he had come full circle in a way with his life and was now ready to move forward – to move on. His mind and heart would have to wait their turn though, as they had some more issues to hash out now that he was home again. He needed to obey duty first and fulfill what was required of him as a Knight of Valkoria. He reached the door of Journey Knight Fronel and stopped. Taking a deep breath he sighed, asked Panthor for guidance, then rapped on the hard oak.

"Enter." Fronel's voice came from behind the door.

Rowan pushed the door open.

Inside Journey Knight Fronel was just as Rowan remembered, though maybe a little older than he had first seen him. He seemed to carry a heavy weight on his shoulders. When he was first in his office Rowan had taken it to be the air of authority he wore. Now he sensed it was the responsibility of his command, a duty and responsibility that Rowan could presently understand in part and sympathized with the man from what he'd gleamed from his own past experiences.

Fronel's office was unchanged as well. It still held the same wooden desk, the shield with the crest of the order, a side profile of a silhouetted panther, behind him, and a shelf of ledger books, scrolls, and various other records of the missions and tasks the Knighthood was about and planning to do. A layer of parchment covered his desk as well as a few open, worn books in which the Journey Knight had been writing.

A simple oil lamp burned away on the top left corner of the desk. It allowed for some light to spill out and over the confines of the desk and shelf, where it was aided by a circular bronze candle stand awash with wax and light that did much to decorate the rest of the room with illumination.

Rowan did notice some differences to the office, however. Maps now decorated the western wall revealing all of the Valkorian Islands or Northlands as they were called by the people living further south. Each was rendered in such detail that Rowan thought they might have been works of art themselves. Further, dotted here and there amid the streams, rivers, towns and terrain where small silver pins affixed with heads that resembled the head of a roaring panther. Rowan looked at them for a moment, then affixed his attention to the Journey Knight.

"Journey Knight Fronel." Rowan bowed his head respectably to the elder and higher ranked knight.

"Please sit Sir Cortak." Fronel motioned to a simple pine chair before his desk.

Rowan did so.

"I see you noticed our new focus then?" Fronel turned his head to the maps."

"New focus sir?" Rowan joined his gaze.

"Yes. We've decided to increase our presence on the Valkorian Islands. The High Father has put forth a challenge to us that we should have a keep on each of the continents, even Troll Island, as to increase our influence and Panthor's influence in this part of the world and to turn the savage religions of the tribes into the civilized and proper worship of the goddess."

"I see." Rowan stated. He looked closer at the maps, seeing that silver pins were inside the territory of his own tribe along with several others tribes on other parts of the Northlands as well. He wondered for a moment what his parents were experiencing with such an encounter. Then he wondered when and if he'd get to see them or his tribe again. Working the thought into the corners of his mind he pulled himself back to the matter at hand and how he was going to deal with it.

Looking at the map to help him gather his thoughts and see just what this group of men were about. He knew that each pin represented more than just one knight, in fact it was a small handful of knights along with several priests he was sure – enough to begin to teach the people the true faith and the authority tied to it as well. The thought of expansion though, which once would have filled him with great delight, instead only made the hollowness of the institution seem that much more pronounced somehow.

"But that is getting ahead of ourselves." Fronel's words drew the youth to his desk. "You have returned from your mission alive and in once piece. Well done, Sir Cortak."

"Thank you sir." Rowan replied.

"We thought we lost you." Said Fronel. "When the boat we sent you on came back without you we feared the worst."

"I'm sorry to have raised such concern sir. My mission took longer and was more involved than I thought." Rowan again nodded to the older knight.

"When we inquired of the captain for your whereabouts he said you had an elven woman with you; tried to bring her on board. What was her part in all this then?" Fronel turned a new page in one of the larger volumes, dipped his goose feather quill and began to write.

The knot in Rowan's gut tightened as his mouth went dry and tongue froze to the roof of his mouth. A light, cold sweat had started to cover his forehead and hands, his own heart became a rapid gallop.

"He said you said she was vital to your mission." Fronel continued. "Naturally the captain refused due to common sense, but you remained behind, persistent that you both board together. I wonder why that was, Sir Cortak."

"She was an important part of the mission, sir, just as I said." Rowan felt his throat grow tighter as he contemplated what to say next. "She led a group that was on the same quest that I was."

"Really?" Fronel's quill drank deep from the ink well before fluttering into a flurry of text. "Elves on the same mission as the Knights of Valkoria? This should be a very interesting report indeed."

Rowan peered down at the quill between the Journey Knight's ink stained fingers. A simple silent prayer to Panthor was all he could do. Moving his eyes to the Journey Knight's own as they peered up at him, inviting him to proceed with this tale, he knew he was ready and just what to say.

"I left the Frost Giant on the dock of Elandor, a southern Telborian Kingdom, as you may well know. No sooner had I left the ship then I was robbed by a small street urchin..."

And so Rowan told his tale as he had rehearsed it in his heart. It was the truth, but unless asked he didn't share any revelations from Panthor, the battle with The Master at Galba or even his own going to Thangaria. No, he stuck to the facts, omitting things that were not important where he could, but was true to Panthor's Code. As to Clara he would speak nothing of their love for she had admitted she didn't really love him anyway and, in truth, Rowan had come to see the truth in Clara's declaration that he only loved her for being exotic and forbidden – for being an elf.

When he had finished his report he left to pray in the altar room. Unloading his mind and spirit he felt able to sleep with a clean conscious. When he did finally get to sleep he did so with the understanding deep inside him that he had taken the first step into a much larger and amazing destiny that would only grow more wondrous as the years were added to the young man's life and he became the image he saw in the portal at Galba.

3

It was a familiar scene which greeted the lich when he opened his eyes. Looking past the blurriness until his vision cleared, he noticed the darkened chamber as common to those he had seen before, but the smell brought it all back to him faster than anything else. Brimstone and blood laced with hot metal and other noxious gases filled The Master's lungs with searing claws. But it wasn't really smelling he was doing was it? No, he didn't need to breathe anymore and his heart wasn't beating in his chest either. Somehow he *felt* these acrid smells – absorbing them *through* his body rather than into his nose. The screams then fluttered by his ears and a chill went up his spine. Screams he'd heard and had grown accustomed to in the long years he'd been trapped in his former sanctuary turned prison. They were louder though now, and somehow more wrenching than he thought anything could be. It was as if he not only heard the physical agony of another, but could actually feel, through their sounds, their very spirit being shredded; their soul being endlessly tortured.

It was then that The Master realized he shouldn't be feeling any of this – shouldn't be hearing any of this. Just as he could feel the toxic fumes about him and he felt no heart beating inside him; he was alive but not in the same manner he had once known while on Tralodren. He could have existed with these discoveries without much challenge. After all, this was what much of his existence had been for hundreds of years as a lich. However, the deeper revelation he was without the added power he had once felt coursing through his veins gave him great alarm. That, and the sudden understanding he was naked, save for a loin cloth added to his growing concern. No longer a deity, no longer a wizard, he was nothing but a mortal in the heart of the Abyss.

"Ah, you're awake." The deep, familiar voice shook the room.

"I warn you Balon, don't try me." The Master turned around to face the horrific visage of the demon. This time he was whole. No longer a shadow, he had solid form again; strong substance that rippled with the rage contained behind the ocher skin. Small rivers of serpentine flame snaked around his body, lapping up the air in small gouts.

The Master took a step away from the rough wall which he'd been resting his back against, only to find four thick chains held him to the stone. Shackles on his ankles and wrists hindered him from moving. The heat generated from the frenetic fire ontop the demon's head was intense.

"Let me go and I'll let you live." The Master bluffed. He had nothing left in his arsenal now *but* bluffs.

Balon's laughter bellowed throughout the rectangular room just large enough to allow the eleven foot tall demon to comfortably stand and move about, even with his bull-like horns that stood another foot from his head. His laughter was more chilling than the screams had been earlier. The reality of his situation was sinking deeper and deeper in the dark mage and he was growing more panicked by the moment.

"You're nothing here. You have none of your power, none of your tricks left and no where to go." Balon's eyes flared for a moment with a ringlet of yellow flame about his eyes as he smiled. "Asorlok has brought you to me for all eternity."

The Master said nothing, only stared into the fiend's bright neon yellow eyes with all the hate and boldness he could muster. He wouldn't give him the pleasure of seeing his frustration or his growing fears.

"As you can see I've reclaimed my spot in the hierarchy again – even ruling over my own subjects once more." Balon spread his black, bat-like wings as far as the room would allow in pride. "And you helped me all the way. I was driven by my hatred at being betrayed by you in those ruins." The demon's wings folded behind him as he drew closer to the former mage. "I told myself it was only a matter of time before we'd meet again and when we did, I wanted to be ready."

"So here I am." The Master rattled his chains. He knew there was no way he could break them now. Here he was powerless and frail – just a man, a mortal man who had entered into his final dwelling place for all eternity and nothing more.

"I assume you want to take out your revenge on me then, eh? Well you forget that you weren't the only one I dealt with in this pit. I have allies still here as well."

"Allies that have little love of you and would stand with me against you." The Master boasted. It was a lie of course, but he felt better saying it to himself; felt better hearing the illusion of comfort they brought. He knew that no demon or devil for that matter could be truly trusted with anything. They were like a wild dog who only respected the most ferocious and strongest among them. Show them a sign of weakness and like dogs they would tear you to shreds.

"I discovered that after I returned here." Balon drew close and bent down toward the lich's human face, a thick smile revealing the deadly maw. His even closer presence made The Master break out in a sweat. It was like facing a raging inferno now, and he could do little to avoid it. "However, any agreement they once had is gone now. They all saw how you reward your allies when I returned and it was with their help I reclaimed my throne and full strength. Now that you have been made low once again I don't think even you would be so foolish as to try and call upon their aid now."

"You have no one left, mage." The demon's words were rich in the suffering they caused. "It's just you and me now and it will be that way until the end of time."

Balon pulled out a steel sword, forged to look like a tongue of flame: wavy and tipped with a deadly point. His cruel face twisted into a sadistic delight to match his previously spoken words as he brought it close to The Master's chest.

"One thing you will learn here, Cadrith, is that you are immortal. Your body may be gone, but your soul and spirit and I will live on for quite a long while indeed." Balon drew the blade down The Master's ribcage stopping when he got to his thigh. The Master only gritted his teeth and tried his best to contain his painful bodily convulsions in protest, stifling his pain with his iron will as the 'flesh' of the former Wizard King was filleted; loin cloth growing rich in spilt blood.

"You'll find though that in the Abyss, as with all other realms and planes, you'll soon get a new nature tied to your spiritual body. In the Abyss that nature is a great increase in the ability to feel and experience pain – even as if you were still alive in a physical body."

"Good for me," Balon thrust his large claw into the cut he just made, digging deep into The Master's internal anatomy. The Master let out a low, controlled growl mixed with some more spastic jerkings as sweat began to pour from his forehead and mingled with the river of tears from his eyes. "But bad for you."

The demon chuckled.

Balon moved his claw lower to slosh about the dark mage's innards some more and then pulled his hand out, taking a clump of intestines with him. The Master let out a barely contained low cry of agony. He wouldn't give Balon the satisfaction of a full scream if he could help it. He was still The Master and no one would get the better of him – no one!

He would still get out of this if he just bided his time and–

"The best thing is that because you never die, you can be made to suffer some wonderful agonies that would have killed you before when you had a body of flesh and blood. " Balon began to fish out more of the intestines with his fingers. Like a bloated string of sausages they continued to spill out in a wet, ripping sound reminiscent of a child mixing mud pies; soiled loin cloth becoming more the gruesome apron of some demented butcher.

"This just gives me some time to really have fun and be more *creative* in my entertainment." One of the demon's claws which gripped the intestines began to light up with a reddish flame which quickly leapt onto the spilling intestines, worming its way inside the former dark mage. At this The Master let out a horrendous scream.

He couldn't hold it back and hated himself for it.

"Ah, I think I've finally gotten through to you." Balon dropped the intestines to the floor with a moist thud and brought his sword toward the former dark god once more.

"Welcome to the Abyss Cadrith." Balon plunged his sword into the former lich's chest. Cadrith howled as he could feel what he thought to be his heart but understood in his head to be the very binding elements of his soul and spirit – the threads that wove the two together being undone. It was beyond any pain the lich could imagine or inflict upon anyone.

"I'm looking forward to enjoying your company for a long, long time."

4

Cadrissa looked out at The Master's tower which had now been turned to smoldering ruins. The sky was overcast, but clearing as if a heavy storm had just passed and thinking back to the first storm she had experienced in the tower and who caused it, the mage shuddered. The smell of ozone was still heavy in the air and she found it hard to breathe, as if a heavy weight hovered over her lungs. Turning in a full circle, she took stock of the scenery around her. She saw the two craters and the evidence of magical battle: scorched ground and the fallen tower, the faint vapors of mystical energy that still clung about the air like a stubborn invisible fog.

Cadrissa dared a few steps closer to the ruins, picked up a piece of fallen rock then let it fall from her hand. She almost felt she could hear faint voices whispering something to her – telling her some secret she knew she wanted to hear…

Cadrissa hung her head under a sudden onslaught of pictures and words. They seemed to overflow into any open area of mental lucidity and threatened to overwhelm her if she didn't get control of them and soon. With great effort, Cadrissa, opened her eyes and again looked to the smoky ruins. However, she now noticed her hands had become skeletal. All the flesh had fled from them to leave only bone, which still managed to cling together to form a hand – even without sinew keeping it in shape. She didn't know what to think or do. Pushing her sleeve up with her left hand, the mage discovered her whole arm was bone.

No flesh remained on it whatsoever!

Fear gripped her as she moved her hand up her arm to her shoulder, then chest and back. All of it under her robe was bone!

What was happening to her?

She heard laughter then – cold, familiar laughter, and spun around to see The Master looking at her just as she had first appeared upon his arrival on Tralodren through the portal in the ruins of Takta Lu Lama.

"You'll make a fine apprentice." The Master's hauntingly familiar voice mocked her.

Cadrissa shot up in bed. Sweat was pouring down her face. Her heart was pounding away like a horse's gallop; she felt as if she had almost died. Seeing that face/skull again just filled her with the worse sense of dread she had yet known. She immediately got out of bed and moved toward a plain wooden chair in the sparse room in an Elandorian inn she had recently come to rent and sat down. Near the foot of her bed was a large chest housing the books she had placed in storage before they had traveled in the Marshes of Gondad and beyond. Amazingly, after all this time, they were still there and not in the least bit disturbed. It was a small comfort to her as she tried to calm herself by staring out her window. She watched a gray and wet collection of snow gather about the cobblestone streets and walkways until she could feel herself regaining control over her senses.

The dream was something she didn't want to delve into that much, but knew most of its meaning…and dreaded that even more. She thought of what she'd been through and learned since last she had been in Elandor. She had come a long way indeed. Cadrissa sighed and sunk lower in the chair. She was still weak and tired from her recent adventures and it felt good to sit down somewhere civilized for a change, safe. The mage had tried for a quick nap but it seemed her conscience wouldn't let her rest yet.

The whole ride back had been a wonder, however. The griffin was a very majestic beast and a rapid transport to Tralodren. She scarcely found herself getting back to Talatheal before she had started to wonder how long the trip might take. Having the griffin land in a nearby wooded area she made her way to Elandor on foot so as not to arose any onlookers or suspicions. She had the desire to be an average person and blend in harmlessly for a while. The mage had her share of confrontation and conflict that would last for quite some time. If she could just be left alone for a while and blend in with the rest of the swell of mortalkind, then that suited her just fine for the time being.

Things had at least reached some form of closure for Cadrissa. It was good to have a feeling that at least the bulk of what she had been put through since Gilban and Clara recruited her in Haven was now over. She'd said goodbye to Rowan before she left, but somehow she felt like he wasn't that much into the idea of farewells though he did his best to oblige. She could tell his mind was elsewhere, and his heart was for his homeland.

As to Clara, Cadrissa had little idea as to her bodily whereabouts. Upon asking the knight for answer, he brushed it aside. Cadrissa supposed she didn't expect Rowan to take it home with him and so he'd probably left Clara's body in the stable. It could have been in far worse places. The mage surmised it would find its way where it should be anyway given it had been left in the very place of meeting chosen by the gods.

She was sure Rowan would be okay too. Shaken from his journeys obviously, but he would survive. The mage assumed the same of herself and had a feeling she would feel even better after she took a bath. She needed some new clothes as well. Not only were they soiled but also carried too many memories that she didn't want to be reflecting on so soon after the events occurred. Shedding her clothes would also help her shed the sense of the lich's presence, something she couldn't help feeling still clung to her after all her ordeals and his demise.

Cadrissa had planned to do this after her nap, but for now was content to recover from her dream; letting her mind drift out of the plate glass window before her. The snow was too slushy to take and melted before it even rested on the ground for a few moments, but it would be piling up soon enough as winter had come to the land of Talatheal and would be growing in intensity with each passing day. So if she wanted to travel back to Haven it had better be soon.

She'd toyed with the idea of going back to the academy to continue her training, but wasn't quite sure if that was what she wanted. Not only was the tuition going to be due for another year, but the idea seemed somehow…less exciting to her now that she had experienced so much already. And of course there was the dream. The dream which spoke to her of her own inner conflict over the truth that she'd taken a step onto the Path of Power and had enjoyed it.

She didn't want to admit to herself that wearing the medallion had awakened something in her – something that made her think it was a sleeping dragon waiting to be unleashed. It was so tempting – and then there was the guilty pleasure with her exhilaration of being dominated by the medallion in the tower. It wasn't so much for the feeling of being dominated, but the rush of power, the well from within that seemed unending at her command. It was so wonderful to have that feeling at her fingertips–

Cadrissa stopped herself in mid-thought.

That wasn't her path and she knew it.

She was against it.

She followed the Path of Knowledge, which abhorred the Path of Power. The two were opposites of the other…weren't they? But wasn't knowledge in itself a form of power and couldn't power be used to secure knowledge? Hadn't both of these points been validated in her recent adventures?

No.

She had made a choice when she started her mystical studies and chose the Path of Knowledge. It had become who she was – defined her and her magic. Even as Cadrissa thought these things she was reminded of that horrid face of The Master in her dream; the fleshless appendages and later body…

Perhaps it would be best to get those new clothes and bath now before the weather turned any worse and while she still had some coin to do so. Though her mind agreed this was best, her body was slow to react and she found herself looking out the window; daydreaming of her life to come in the days ahead…and the truth about knowledge and power.

5

The soft temperate breezes washed over the bald head of Hoodwink resting beside the rock in an open, quiet glade. The blue skies overhead were thick with fat, white clouds the same color of his silk robe. He was barefoot and relaxed, eyes closed to the wonderful beauty as he rested in the still, comforting nature of the surrounding area.

The whole set of recent affairs that had lead him here were now seemingly less than a gauzy mist in his mind. In time even that mist would be gone, and nothing but the pleasant thoughts and memories of this new place he had found would dominate his thinking. For the moment though, he could still recall Gurthghol's black flame spinning toward him, and how it felt to be seared over his entire body until it just suddenly stopped. It was then that the goblin found himself immersed in a world of light. He hovered in a great sea of it under a pure white sky – all around him being pure illumination.

He wasn't quite sure what had happened then. That much was already fading away from his recollection, but he seemed to still be able to recall a reflection of what took place: a soft voice speaking something of encouragement into his ear and then...and then... what had happened? It seemed so faint now; so distant from his current plane of existence that he didn't even know for sure that it had happened at all, though he knew that it had to.

All that made sense to him was he'd been told he had done well and then left the place of surrounding light for where he now resided. Hoodwink then discovered he was dressed in the white robe which he now wore, his feet were bare and his heart and mind were no longer troubled. He was at total peace and comfort. Further, there was nothing here to disturb him, for all was at peace in this plane called Paradise. From the top of the drifting clouds sailing above the first level of Paradise, called The First Heaven, to The Second Heaven and The Third Heaven above that, to the bottom of the rock on which Hoodwink rested, all was at peace and filled with an overpowering sense of goodness.

Hoodwink let out a dreamy sigh and wiggled his toes in the lush grass.

Though many had come to call this place home for eternity over the centuries, the goblin wasn't crowded. Indeed, the place seemed an unfolding infinity in all directions; beauty flowing into still more beauty. As to the decree of the Pantheon, only those who had met the requirements of entrance and had passed the scrutiny of Asorlok at the twelfth gate (though Hoodwink had no memory of even meeting Asorlok at all) found their way to the place that even the gods were said to retire to when they die.

Here the goblin would be governed by no god, but by the Lords of Good, the rulers of the Third Heaven and all of Paradise beneath them. Administering angels would carry out their decrees and help to ensure that all who called this plane home would have an untroubled and peaceful stay for eternity. It wasn't what the small goblin had expected for his afterlife, but he could get used to it.

Yup.

He could get used to it.

6

"**W**ell played." Nuhl's compliment was genuine.
"You as well." Awntodgenee hovered in the vast empty plane like rolling fog on the top of a lake of darkness.

"I don't feel so badly about losing my pawn now since you lost something of equal value." Nuhl bubbled up through the clinging mist like a seething pitch stew.

"In truth it was time for it to go anyway." Awntodgenee confessed. "It was getting to be too much of a temptation for some and an annoyance for me. We have a far more interesting set of events now that the throne is in the hands of Gurthghol once more."

"Agreed," said Nuhl. "Though I don't think he will be using it to his advantage anytime soon. There might be some way of using this to our advantage when next we return for another culling of this world."

"Perhaps," Awntodgenee was coalescing now into a thicker radiant mass. "Time will tell. I have a suspicion that when we return to this place it will be vastly different than it is now. We have seen much shaken by this visitation."

"I know." Nuhl delighted.

"We will still have to watch Gurthghol though," said Awntodgenee. "He's nothing like his father, but he could learn to be if given enough time."

Nuhl laughed. "I'll keep a close eye on him as I let him suffer for his foolishness. I'll have my sport from him yet before I tire of him and extinguish his existence. It's a small consolation to my loss, but I will welcome it."

Awntodgenee had now formed itself into a solid ball of white illumination. "So you're not worried about giving him too long a leash in your keeping then?"

"No," came Nuhl's reply as it transformed itself into a collection of thousands of sharp toothed mouths. "It will be many a year until he can ever hope to become the threat his father had become. Before he gets that far though, the chair will either have destroyed him or he'll be rid of it since he has such a loathing for the device."

"So then you're ready to move on to the next world?" asked Awntodgenee.

"Yes." Nuhl's eagerness was nearly overwhelming. "And I plan on winning this time. You don't have any of the champions you used to defeat me on Tralodren there."

"That I don't, but let us see how it will turn out." Awntodgenee seemed eager to prove Nuhl wrong yet again.

"In my favor you will see." Nuhl delighted again.

"We will see," Awntodgenee gently countered.

7

𝕴n a vast sea of endless, starless space there is a throne. It hovers amid the nothingness, floating amid the coal colored landscape like a tombstone. In this throne sits a frail, plum skinned figure whose odd colored eyes search out the ebony sea about him in vain hope of release. Black iron chains bind him fast keeping him hindered and hampered.

There is only the throne and its chained occupant.

No sound.

No light.

No strength of will to free himself – barely enough essence of true self to sustain his meager form.

No thoughts but his own. The figure is forever alone, bound, and trapped in the empty expanse and yet can't help but look for a way out; hoping for escape…for rescue.

But no one will come, the sacrifice has been made.

And so he searches throughout the ebony sea with his odd-colored eyes, but he searches in vain; hoping against hope.

So he has sat, sits now and will sit in the endless years upon years to come for he is a god and time has no meaning to him save when used now as the lash to strike him further with agony in his imprisonment.

Thus is the fate of Gurthghol, first son of Vkar.

A Minnesota native since his birth in 1977, Chad Corrie has long had a love affair with his creative side. Dabbling in art, film, music and acting, it wasn't until he found writing that he began to excel at something with which he'd found a healthy outlet and addiction.

Since that time he has written a wide array of material from such varied genres as horror, sci-fi and contemporary fiction amid comic scripting, poetry, screen plays, stage plays and more. It wasn't until recently that he discovered fantasy and began to work more in this interesting and very broad genre.

Read the whole Divine Gambit Trilogy!

The Divine Gambit Trilogy
Seer's Quest
Path of Power
Gambit's End

Other Books by Chad Corrie
Tales of Tralodren: The Beginning (Graphic Novel)
The Adventures of Corwyn

Visit Chad on the web at **www.chadcorrie.com** for all the latest updates and insights into **The World of Tralodren™** and other projects and events.

You can also visit the websites of the two artists who have contributed to this book.

More of Carrie Hall's (cover artist) artwork can be seen at **www.nexisofworlds.net.**

Ed Waysek's (interior artist) work can be viewed at **www.edwaysek.com.**

Appendices

Appendix A: Pronunciation Guide
Appendix B: A Genealogy of the Tralodroen Pantheon

Appendix A: Basic Pronunciation Guide

Nations/Lands

Altorbia	Al-TOR-be-ah
Baltan	BALL-tan
Belda-thal	BELL-DAH-thall
Colloni	Co-LOAN-ee
Diam	DIME
Elandor	EE-LAND-oar
Frigia	FRIDGE-ee-ah
Gondad	GONE-dad
Gondadian	GONE-DAD-ee-un
Ino	I-KNOW
Rexatious	REX-AH- toy- US
Romain	ROW-main
Takta Lu Lama	TALK-tah loo LAH-ma
Talatheal	TALA-theal
Tralodren	TRAH-low-DRIN
Tralodroen	TRAH-low-DROW-in
Valkoria	Val-CORE-re-AH
Vanhyrm	Van-HEARum
Yoan Ocean	Yown

Races

Ajuba	Ah-JEW-bah
Celetor	SELL-ah-TOR
Celetoric	SELL-ah-TOR-ick
Elonum	EE-LONE-um
Elyellium	EL-YELL-e-um
Elyelmic	EL-YELL-mick
Napowese	NAH-POW-ease
Nordican	NOR-DUH-kin
Pacoloes	Pak-COAL-lees
Patrious	PAY-TREE-US

Syvanese	SIH-vah-KNEES
Syvani	Sih-VON-ee
Telborian	Tell-BOAR-e-UN
Telborous	TELL-BOAR-ohs

Tralodroen™ Pantheon

Aerotription	Arrow-TRIP-tee-ON
Asora	Ah-SOAR-ah
Asorlins	Ah-SORE-lynns
Asorlok	AS-oar-LOCK
Causilla	CAW-SILL-ah
Dradin	DRAY-din
Drued	DRUID
Endarien	EN-DAR-en
Gurthghol	GIRTH-gaul
Ganatar	GAN-AH-TAR
Khuthon	KOO-THONE
Olthon	OLE-THONE
Panian	PAN-ee-un
Panthor	PAN-THOR
Panthorian	PAN-THOR-e-un
Perlosa	Per-LOWES-ah
Remani	Rah-MAN-ee
Rheminas	REM-MIN-noss
Saredhel	SAIR-RAH-dell
Sarellianite	Saw-WRELL-LEE-en-ITE
Shiril	SHAH-RIL
Sidra	SID-rah
Vkar	Vah-CAR
Xora	ZOAR-ah

Supporting Characters

Awntodgenee	ON-TODGE-EH-knee
Cadrith	CAD-rith
Charbis	CHARR-biss

Cracius Evans	CRASS-SEA-us Evans
Galba	GAUL-BAH
Nuhl	NULL
Tebow Narlsmith	TEA-BOW GNARL-smith

Main Characters

Cadrissa	CAH-DRISS-sah
Clara Airdes	CLAIR-rah AIR-DEES
Dugan	Do-GAN
Gilban Polcrates	GILL-ben Pole-CRAY-tay
Hoodwink	HOOD-WINK
Rowan Cortak	ROW-in CORE-tack
Vinder	VIN-DER

Planes/Realms

Boda	BO-dah
Civis	SIH-VISS
Helii	HE-lee
Mortis	MORE-tiss
Sheol	SHE-ole
Thangaria	Than-GAR-REE-ah

Appendix B: A Genealogy of the Tralodroen Pantheon

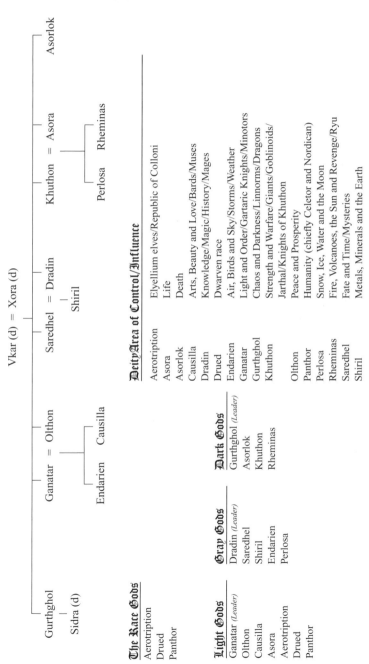

The Tralodroen Pantheon

Vkar (d) = Xora (d)

- Gurthghol
  - Sidra (d)
- Ganatar = Olthon
  - Endarien, Causilla
- Saredhel = Dradin
  - Shiril
- Khuthon = Asora
  - Perlosa, Rheminas
- Asorlok

Deity	Area of Control/Influence
Aerotription	Elyellium elves/Republic of Colloni
Asora	Life
Asorlok	Death
Causilla	Arts, Beauty and Love/Bards/Muses
Dradin	Knowledge/Magic/History/Mages
Drued	Dwarven race
Endarien	Air, Birds and Sky/Storms/Weather
Ganatar	Light and Order/Gartaric Knights/Minotaurs
Gurthghol	Chaos and Darkness/Linnorms/Dragons
Khuthon	Strength and Warfare/Giants/Goblinoids/Jarthal/Knights of Khuthon
Olthon	Peace and Prosperity
Panthor	Humanity (chiefly Celetor and Nordican)
Perlosa	Snow, Ice, Water and the Moon
Rheminas	Fire, Volcanoes, the Sun and Revenge/Ryu
Saredhel	Fate and Time/Mysteries
Shiril	Metals, Minerals and the Earth

The Race Gods
Aerotription
Drued
Panthor

Light Gods
Ganatar (*Leader*)
Olthon
Causilla
Asora
Aerotription
Drued
Panthor

Gray Gods
Dradin (*Leader*)
Saredhel
Shiril
Endarien
Perlosa

Dark Gods
Gurthghol (*Leader*)
Asorlok
Khuthon
Rheminas

We hope you enjoyed the third and final installment of the exciting *Divine Gambit Trilogy*. Be sure to check out other upcoming works from Chad Corrie in the near future. Your comments and thoughts concerning this book or AMI are welcome.

www.aspirationsmediainc.com

If you're a writer or know of one who has a work that they'd love to see in print – then send it our way. We're always looking for great manuscripts that meet our guidelines. Aspirations Media is looking forward to hearing from you and/or any others you may refer to us.

Thank you for purchasing this Aspirations Media publication.